HIGH SEAS
CTHULHU

FIRST EDITION
10 9 8 7 6 5 4 3 2
Published in 2007

ISBN: 1-934501-02-6

Printed in the U.S.A.

Published by Elder Signs Press
P.O. Box 389
Lake Orion, MI 48361-0389
www.eldersignspress.com

HIGH SEAS
CTHULHU

EDITED BY WILLIAM JONES

2007

CONTENTS

We live on a placid island of ignorance in the midst of black seas of infinity, and it was not meant that we should voyage far.
—H.P. Lovecraft, "The Call of Cthulhu"

'God save thee, ancient Mariner!
From the fiends, that plague thee thus!—
Why look'st thou so?'—With my cross-bow
I shot the ALBATROSS.
—Samuel Taylor Coleridge,
"The Rime of the Ancient Mariner"

THE IDOL
IN HIS HAND

BY DARRELL SCHWEITZER

I FOUND BLACKLEG BILL BURTON in a haunt of sailors that was disreputable even by the standards of such establishments, and I was there not so much out of the courage of youth but because of the stupidity of youth. After all, this was for a *class*. We novice journalists had been sent out like a flock of suddenly released pigeons throughout the city of New York to interview somebody, anybody, who would give us a taste of *life in the raw*, of genuine *adventure*, and I, who had probably read way too much of Edgar Rice Burroughs, Jack London, Rider Haggard, and Robert Louis Stevenson was all too eager to leap in, feet first and brain to the hindmost. So I sought my real-life adventurer not merely in a dump or a dive, but in an absolute *pest-hole*, which took several references, some bribes, a secret password, a fist in the face, and the likelihood of getting my throat slit or at least my wallet lifted for the sheer privilege of being conducted to such a location. But once I was there, despite my incongruous appearance—I, who was clearly an upper-class city boy and not at all adept at "slumming"—I seemed to fit right in, and it was fate or luck or more likely brazen stupidity that directed me forthwith to a booth in the back, where slouched the disreputable gentleman I was obviously looking for, who would tell me his story for the price of liquor.

As my wallet had *not* actually been lifted, I was quick to oblige. When I said, "Grog," the waiter just shrugged and came back with two beers.

The begrimed, bedraggled, gristled, and heavily scarred gentleman opposite me, *who really wore an earring,* poured his into a glass, and said, *"Arrrrghhh!"*

"I beg your pardon?"

"Arrrrgh! That's what ye were expectin', warn't it, laddie, when ye came a-lookin' for old Blackleg Bill Burton? Pirate talk. Tales o' bloodshed on the high seas, the black spot, maroonin', buried treasure, all that. . . ."

I had the unsettling feeling that he knew everything I was going to say or even think before I did.

"Well, I–"

"Well, you—Well *I* really was a pirate once, you know. Blackbeard himself thought well of me."

I smiled. I couldn't help but blurt out, "Uh, excuse me sir, but Blackbeard was killed in 1718, so that would make you–"

He reached out, faster than my eye could follow, and hooked a not-so-clean finger under my jaw, till he had me like a fish on a line, and said, "I been sailin' the seven seas for more years than you got hairs on yer dainty chin. I'm older than I look."

Even I had enough sense not to try to explain that most of my ancestors came from Sweden or the north of England, so I'm just naturally fair and smooth-skinned and was likewise older than the child he apparently took me for. The first rule of journalism is not to intrude into the story. This wasn't supposed to be about me, but about him. My job was not to argue, but to get him talking and try to remember what he said.

He stared me right in the eye with that petrifying gaze of his—I felt more like a mouse hypnotized by a rattlesnake that intends to eat it; I lack an aquatic metaphor; I don't think sharks do anything of the kind—and shook my chin again and said, "Know ye, there've been pirates on this earth since the time of Cain, him that killed his brother Abel and was marked by the curse of God just like somebody seems to have walloped you on the forehead and given you that nasty bruise—"

It wasn't my place to tell him what exactly had happened in the previous establishment before I'd found my way to this one.

"—and I tell you that because of his mark, Cain was cursed and feared by all, but he *could not die,* and so, as soon as men took to seafaring, Cain was there to rob 'em. He pulled right up alongside Noah's ark and would've given 'im a broadside then and there, except that cannons hadn't been invented yet–"

He let go of me and sat there, just daring me to laugh or call him a liar, and his no doubt carefully-practiced prologue had its intended effect, that I was no position to express doubt about *anything* further that he said. I noticed that his "piratical" manner of speaking began to slip away, and he had merely an indefinable accent, which was almost Scottish but not quite like any I had ever heard before.

He had finished his beer and noticed I had not touched mine, so without asking permission, he poured mine into his glass, took a sip, and began his tale.

I *was* a pirate [said Blackleg Bill Burton], and I *did* know Blackbeard, and also Blackbottom Bailey, and Bucketbrains Beauford and several more. It wasn't the letter "b" we was fixated on, just that alliteration made the names easy to remember—I also knew a Cutthroat Calvin—he didn't get to be famous, though, because he got his own throat cut much too early in his career—but there are times, I tell you in all seriousness, that a seafaring man encounters such things as makes it hard enough to come away sane, and so it's a help to be able to remember your own name.

So, I sailed for the first time with *Drake,* Sir Francis Drake he later became, but just Captain Drake in what must have been . . . *Fifteen* Seventy-something, and don't you be askin' no questions about years and ages, at least not yet.

I was young then, almost as young and stupid as you, but I had the sense to say "Yes Sir" and "Aye-aye, Sir" to Drake himself and let my betters do the arguing; because there was some arguing to be done as we set out across the Atlantic, and, pillaging our way through the Spanish colonies, and around the tip of South America—we was the first Englishmen ever to sail those waters—and up the *Pacific side* where the Dons—which is what we called the Spaniards—thought they had the world all to themselves.

Well you can read about that in the history books. There was pillagin' and lootin' aplenty, and lots of killing too, but not much raping, because Captain Drake he was all on about duty and gentlemanly honor and our service to the Virgin Queen and the Glory of England, whereas most of us crewmen were less than gentlemen or patriots when it came to piratin'. There was a quarrel. You can read in the books how one of Drake's ships got separated from him and lost. Well that's not entirely true. It was a matter that we was more interested in greed than in Albion's glory, and some of us wanted to not just loot the Spanish, but rob the whole world, and at least a couple of us had already sold our souls to the Devil for good measure.

Drake would have none of that, but he was too smart and too wary for anybody to jump him or knife him in the back, and we didn't have any objections to what he did to the Spanish—he sacked Valparaiso a little while after—and so those of the company who were more exceedingly wicked than the rest got onto one ship and Drake and his crew was on the *Golden Hind*. When we lost track of each other in a cold, wet fog one night off the coast of Chile, well, it wasn't entirely an accident.

I sailed on that sinful ship, then, because I was already wicked, or at least I aspired to be. Every boy must have his ambitions.

Prophet Pike was our captain. Actually his name was Hieronymus Pike, but who could remember that? And he was prophetical, so that was how he was named. He convinced every man-jack among us that he was *magic*, that he was the servant of dark forces older and more powerful than Satan, and so, whereas, as soon as we parted from Drake, most of the men wanted to rechristen our ship *The Devil's Own*—if you can call that a christening—but Captain Pike he changed the ship's name to *Ftagn*, for all that nobody knew what that meant.

It was because Prophet stood on the deck at night talking to the darkness, and the darkness *answered back*; and sometimes he would climb to the top of the mast on moonless nights and all of us *knew* there was something up there with him, darker than the blackness of the night, impossible to make out except when it blotted out the stars with what might have been great wings.

He never slept, did Prophet Pike. At night he conversed with the darkness. By day he stood at the wheel, steering us on a course no other man knew. We were all afraid to ask, but our wickedness led us on, and Prophet Pike knew where there was prey such as would satisfy the likes of us. We took Spanish ships, and some towns, and there was plenty of killing and looting and we wasn't gentlemen at all.

But that was never his main purpose. It was a distraction. We would lie around in the fo'csle at night whispering amongst ourselves, but mostly just silent, wondering. Nobody sang any sailor songs on this voyage, not even the bloody ones pirates sing. No, this was like a dream, drifting into some unknowable darkness, but all of us too committed to wickedness to even think of turning back; and when the bo'sun finally spoke for all of us and demanded to know what we were up to and what was in it for all of us, Captain Pike merely took him up the mast with him one night, and the two of them was up there for hours, and when they came back down, the bo'sun wouldn't say a word further.

From the look in his eye, you could tell there was nothing to be said, and so it was torture for us, our greed and wickedness pulling against our fear.

We sailed west, due west, into utterly uncharted waters. After many days we came to an island, right where Prophet Pike said it would be, a place of windswept, grassy hillsides where the huge heads of heathen idols stood all in rows. We went ashore, and killed some of the heathens there, and took water and fresh fruit and had our way with their women, but there wasn't any gold, so when Captain Pike said we was finished with our "pleasure stop," we all got back into the ship and sailed on.

The first time we actually saw some gold, it was sticking through the bo'sun's neck as he died.

It happened like this. For days and nights we sailed, the Captain, ever unsleeping at the helm, and they were strange days and nights too, with *things* passing by in the water, seaweed almost like fleshy ropes, and schools of something that might have been dolphins but didn't move like dolphins and certainly didn't need to come up for air. The nights were filled with voices, and sometimes, from far away, there was something crying out, and the captain on top of the mast answering back in a language we didn't know, and the sounds he made didn't sound like anything that should come from a human throat, ever.

But I was talking about how the bo'sun died. It was like this. One day Prophet Pike gathered us all together on the deck and said that very soon we'd find very great treasure indeed, and there would be fighting, and sure enough there was, that very night, in a strange combination of fog low on the sea and a bright, full moon high overhead, so we seemed to be drifting through glowing, golden smoke. Then suddenly the lookout gave a shout, and there loomed before us an enormous, golden vessel, like no ship I had ever seen before, oared, with a high, curving stern, and a bow carved in the likeness of *nothing that ever lived on Earth,* some Hell-creature half like a squid, half like a man, not at all like either. The vessel had only one mast, and a black sail marked with strange signs all in streaks of gold.

This ship bore upon us so fast I thought we was going to crash, but at the last moment Captain Pike gave the wheel a turn, so we slid right alongside the other ship, and our keel cut through a bank of oars, smashing them like trees blown over in a hurricane; and you could hear the shouts and screams of the men on the other end of those oars. Then the bo'sun gave the order and we let loose with our cannons and our muskets and raked the quarry's deck.

The men on that other ship shot back at us with *golden* arrows, and one of them went right down the bo'sun's mouth and out the back of his neck, and he died choking on it.

But the rest swarmed onto the quarry's deck with swords flashing and muskets blasting, in finest piratical style, and we slaughtered the men we found there, white men, paler than even ourselves, but savages of some sort, naked but for a skirt and sandals and beehive-shaped helmets made *all of gold.* Their weapons was gold too, but of no use against such a lot as us, so the battle was over quickly, for all those who hadn't been busted by the oars we'd rammed into came swarming up from below decks, and we was outnumbered ten to one.

It was easy enough to slaughter them. We did it all in a frenzy, as if somehow the way they looked or the way they moved made us *loathe* them in a manner I can't put into words, and at one point amid the red fury of it all I couldn't see straight or think straight and it almost seemed to me as if we were killing, not men, but gigantic, fishbelly-pale *frogs,* or something like that, misshapen, just human enough to *insult* the human form and the human race and make us instinctively want to kill them all.

Kill them we did, and Captain Pike the Prophet waded across their decks knee-deep in gore, but it happened that I, not he, was the first to confront the enemy ship's captain, who did not look at all human, but stood eight feet tall and had webbed hands and feet, like a fish with arms and legs. As I cut my way toward the stern, and climbed over the last few corpses, and came toward him with my sword upraised, he did not resist me, or even shield himself, but instead he bowed his head—and he looked all the taller because he wore a golden crown of some sort, like a bishop's mitre—and he held out his hand to me, in a fist, and he said, *in English,* "Take this, William Burton of *England.* This is your destiny. The Great Ones we serve have called you unto them."

He pressed something into my left hand—I still held my sword in my right—and I obediently took it, as if he had bewitched me with the sound of his voice.

But then Captain Pike lopped the fish-man's head clean off with one swipe of his cutlass. The golden crown went rolling across the deck, but the head landed with a splash of blood, and *still alive,* it spoke to Pike *in English,* saying, "You think to betray us, you who are the greatest fool of all, you who are as a tiny vermin crawling upon the flesh of the Master, who can pick you off and crush you as you would a louse–"

Then the conversation continued in that *other* language which we had heard in the night, until, suddenly Captain Pike grabbed me by the left wrist and forced whatever I had been given out of my hand.

He held it up admiringly. "Ah yes," he said to himself. "Yes, yes. It *is*–"

He held a small statue of some kind, pale, carven of ivory or bone.

The head on the deck sputtered something in its strange language. I didn't have to know the words to understand it was a threat or a curse or both.

But Captain Pike merely said, in English, "I fear you not," and chopped the head in two as one might a melon. I think the two halves were *still* alive, but they just bubbled and steamed, and didn't say anything more.

By now all the slaughtering was done, and the crew stood watching the Captain. He turned to them, and held aloft the thing he had taken as if it were a great prize. But he didn't explain what it was. He merely told the men to get on with the serious pirating work, like butchering the wounded, and gathering up the loot, all *lively,*

lively, get on with it ye dogs, and such things as pirate captains are expected to say at such moments.

But he told us, too, that we would soon have more treasures of these *Lemurians,* as he called them, and we would soon rob the stronghold of the *Master* that the *Lemurians* served, dreadful and fearful monstrosity that he, Prophet Pike, did not fear, because he had captured the secret of *Lemurian* magic.

By which he meant the statuette or whatever it was. I still had not seen it clearly. Young as I was and stupid as I might have been, I still had enough sense not to object, *Hey, that's mine! He gave it to me!* But I did *think* it. My destiny and all. I felt its grip on me, even as the captain's fingers clutched the ivory thing tightly.

We burned the *Lemurian* ship. The wind blew the smoke toward us and the smell was strange and terrible, and seemed to linger even days later, when we sailed into waters no man had ever charted, and it seemed there was something wrong with the sky itself, as if the sun could not rise, but just hovered at the edge of the world, while the sky filled with fog and mist; and the mist glowed at night whether there was any moon overhead or not.

I tell you, though we were loaded with strange gold—carvings and ornaments and weapons like none we had ever seen before, stranger even than the heathen stuff the Spanish get from America—many a man crossed himself in the dark of the fo'csle and prayed to Jesu or the Devil for deliverance. But we feared Prophet Pike our captain as much as we admired him, and he seemed a *god* to us, and I do not lie when I tell you that some of us prayed to *him.* He remained perpetually at the wheel now, speaking into the darkness and distance and holding converse with the things that dwelt and loomed there. We passed other islands with golden cities upon them, and saw other ships of the *Lemurians,* but did not molest them; for now our captain was intent on some greater quest, and we, like lice upon his body, could only go where he went and move as he moved.

I cannot say that we saw the last island actually *rise* from the sea, but it did not seem that we approached it as a ship normally approaches land. That day the mists drew back a little ways, and for a time there was nothing seen in any direction, and we seemed utterly becalmed, and then the island was merely *there,* and water still ran down the flanks of its mountains and cliffs as if it had newly risen from the ocean's bottom.

I call them mountains and cliffs because there is no other word. There actually are no words for what we saw then, because the *island* seemed no ordinary mass of earth, nothing the eye could quite take in or the mind could encompass. It was like looking into a mirror of a mirror of a mirror, only the *angles* were all wrong, all twisted; and there was a *city* there, of strange angles and stranger carvings, which we feared to look upon.

Yet the captain bade us go ashore and we went ashore, all of us, in two longboats. The ship was left at anchor, but no one remained aboard to guard her. In these waters, what danger could there be from other *men?*

As we pulled the boats up onto the beach, even the sand felt *wrong,* its texture beneath our boots not what honest earthly sand should have.

We ascended what was sometimes a slope and sometimes a stairway into the city, or temple, or whatever it was. I tell you that *Hell* would have been a more comfortable place to take a stroll through. All of us, I am sure, except maybe the Captain, who was mad, or beyond human feelings and weaknesses altogether, felt an overwhelming sense of *wrongness,* that we or nothing of this world should have come to such a place. I think we even forgot about *greed,* about treasure; but still we followed, like lice upon the body.

I think one of the men disappeared into an angle in a building. One moment he was there, by a straight way. The next, there was a corner, and he was gone. The eye could not follow it.

Yet still we climbed.

At last we all stood before a great door, which, again, the eye could not encompass. It seemed both horizontal and sloping upward at the same time. Another man, who tried to climb along its edge, disappeared, but we heeded him not, for by then the Captain had begun chanting, almost singing, in that *other* language which was not a speech of human beings at all, I was certain by now, not even a speech known to Satan or his devils or even—I blasphemed at the thought—even by God. It seemed that the ground beneath us, the green, dripping stones of the city, and most especially the *door* began to vibrate with the rhythm of it.

And with a great grinding of ancient stone, the door began to slide open, vanishing, impossibly into its own angles. The darkness beneath us or before us was infinite, and after a time we saw *stars* within it, as if the Captain had torn a hole through the Earth and revealed the night sky seen from the other side. But these stars, too, were *wrong,* and there was an indescribable foulness of the air that blew in great gusts out of the abyss.

And from that abyss there came, again, the voice we had heard in the night, in the speech which was not of mankind.

And the Captain answered.

And a great *thing,* moving in the darkness below, drew nearer.

The Captain said to me, "Come here, boy," though I was not really a boy, but this was no time to argue that I was older than I looked. He put his hand on my shoulder, as a father might, and he held up the thing he had stolen from me. I saw that it was indeed a statue, carved out of a whitish or greenish stone, very deceitful to the eye, as if its shape were not quite part of the natural world. It looked, at first, like a cylinder carven exquisitely into a bust mounted on a pedestal, a Grecian thing; but it changed even as I gazed upon it. Now it was a degenerate parody of all that was beautiful, the face upon it contorted in terror and in deformity; and then, somehow, it wasn't human at all, but a crouching monstrosity of claws and wings and a face covered with tendrils that seemed alive.

"I have the key," said Captain Pike. "I shall command the forces I have unleashed. I shall rule the world. I shall not serve but *be* served. I shall be greater than God."

That was when I truly understood that the Captain was more than merely mad. If a louse upon the body of a giant thinks to control the giant and to seize its treasures, then it is, to say the very least, sadly deluded, but its madness is far beyond such usual insanities as may afflict lice.

We had opened the door to the ultimate chaos, which, I learned much later, is called in certain ancient and forbidden books, *Azathoth,* and through this doorway would come, to the utter destruction of mankind, the servants of *Azathoth,* who have many shapes and many names.

I understood, too, that Prophet Pike our Captain had long since been a servant of the servants of *Azathoth,* but, as any pirate would, he sought to betray them, and seize the power of *Azathoth* for himself, madly deluded vermin that he was.

He explained this to me, not because he had any fatherly affection for me, or because he felt any remorse for having filched the magic talisman, which was *my* destiny, out of my hand—for he was beyond *all* human feelings now, and he had never known remorse. I think he did it for his own satisfaction, for one *last bit* of human gloating before he was transformed and passed beyond all humanity, beyond all considerations of good and evil, as he actually aspired to take *Azathoth* into himself, to *become* the God of Ultimate Nothingness.

It was also his intention to toss me into the abyss, as an offering to the gods or servants of gods that dwell within the infinite darkness. I don't think he needed any of the crew to be *witnesses.* Only morsels. Only dumb things standing around waiting to be slaughtered, like chickens in a barnyard.

That was where he was mistaken. He was in such awe of the vista before us that he forgot that *I* could still harbor such a spiteful, vengeful thought as *Mine, you thieving bastard!*

He was taken completely by surprise as I snatched the carving out of his hand, shoved my dagger into his gut and then heaved him with all my strength over the edge.

He vanished with a howling wail, while I crouched there, clutching the carving, the talisman, whatever you will call it, thinking only *Mine, I have it. Mine. Precious thing. Mine.* Its hold over my mind was so great I could think of nothing else.

But then I came to my senses, just a little. The stars vanished in the abyss, and darkness poured forth like a tangible thing. There was a wet, slopping sound, as if something huge were moving down there, drawing ever nearer.

I looked up at the terrified crew, and there was no need to say anything. We all ran as one, down toward the beach. But we could not find the beach, amid the weirdly-angled stones, and those who went *down* found themselves *high up,* and those who turned to the *right* found themselves rejoining their shipmates from the *left.* Several more vanished into angles.

Only five of us made it to one of the boats, shoved off, and clambered in. We rowed for our lives, but to no use, for the mountainous, ever-changing shape of a living mountain was upon us. More liquid than solid, it *poured* beneath us, blackening the water, and we looked ahead in horror and hopelessness to see its great arms rising out of the sea like the Kraken to tear our ship to pieces and drag it under.

But, perhaps because I held the precious carven thing, we were spared, at least, from immediate death; though in the days that followed that seemed no particular mercy. The blackness and foulness continued to pour from the opening, and we five sailors in our little boat were carried far upon a black current of something viscous and alive, until at last we were abandoned far out at sea, in the cold and the fog, without any provisions. I looked down into the dark waters and saw, always and constantly, dead *Lemurians* drifting alongside our boat, their eyes open, but blank, each *Lemurian* floating on his back, his long pale hair streaming, each of them holding in his hands, crossed upon his breast, a carven statuette like the one I clutched so tightly in my pocket.

I don't know if the other men saw any of this. Before long, they started to go mad. One drank seawater and died, but the rest of us, in our extremity—I too partook of this sin—*ate him* and drank his blood, and prolonged our agony a little while longer.

All the while, I was sure, the *Lemurians* were not dead at all, but laughing at us, even as I imagined, in my terrible dreams when I lapsed into delirium that I had heard from the deepest abyss, when Captain Pike tumbled to his doom, the laughter of *Azathoth*.

We ate another crew member, and another. In the end, when the last surviving man stood over me, a bloody human thighbone in his hands as he made ready to bash out my brains, I looked up at him sadly and said, "What devils have we sold our souls to, my friend?"

That made him hesitate for just a second, long enough for me to clutch the carven statuette to my breast and fall backward over the side, into the water.

And Blackleg Bill Burton the pirate was *laughing* and *laughing*, as he reached across the table and grabbed me again, by the front of my coat this time, and he shook me as he said, "Arrgh, matey, now that be a true tale of piratin' adventure like ye war lookin' for."

I could say nothing. He had me in his spell, like a hypnotized mouse.

"And you be wantin' to know the ending, which is that I didn't even try to swim, but sank down, down into the deep water, while the cold arms of the *Lemurians* closed around me, and I drifted with them for a very long time, until we came to a city at the bottom of the sea, where enormous marble buildings lay half-buried in the mud. Like Grecian temples they were, with beautiful carvings on the outside. But when we went into the biggest of them, where the pulsing light was, where the music and chanting came from, I saw that the statues and the carvings became steadily more horrible, less human, until they were not human at all. Inside was another door, which opened unto *Azathoth,* which we all worshipped.

"And you are wondering why I did not drown. Because of the statuette. It has such powers that I cannot even begin to describe.

"And why, you ask, did the *Lemurian* then give up his, to me, before the Captain stole it? Because after a passage of years, you're *changed,* and you don't need it no more. So you pass it on to somebody else, to *recruit* them into the brotherhood.

"You want to know if I'm reading your mind, answerin' your questions before you can ask them. You want to know how come I am called Blackleg Bill. Well, that's another story for another time, and it's a dreadful one. You are still green behind the gills, and I have been around long enough now that anything you *can* think or ask I have *already* thought or asked. I've changed a bit, aged very slowly, gotten quite a bit uglier, but I have *grown wiser,* and you, as far as I can tell, are not very bright."

Then he was laughing again, and he pushed the empty glasses and the beer bottles over to my side of the table. He'd somehow acquired and emptied five more bottles without my noticing, while he was telling his story.

"Don't forget to pay for these," he said. "Ye wouldn't want to be thought a *thievin' pirate,* now, would ye?"

And I decided that I did not *like* the way he laughed. There was something I can't describe about it, something utterly inhuman and repulsive. I liked even less the way he *moved,* not quite like a man with all his bones, as he *oozed* and *slithered* out of his seat and shambled across the floor toward the exit like a half-empty sack come alive.

It was only then that I realized that he'd pressed something into my right hand, a small statuette carven of greenish white stone.

Yes, I know, it *is* a preposterous story. I had, admittedly, suffered a nasty blow to the head and might have hallucinated the whole thing.

But I have my reasons for being certain that this is not so.

I have learned much since the experience of that encounter. I know, as is anciently written, *that One Ones' servants never die, for all they might eternal lie.*

I am older than I look. You take me for, what? Twenty-five? Almost thirty? But this is 2007. I first sat down with Blackleg Bill Burton in a speakeasy on the New York waterfront in *Nineteen Twenty-Three.*

I have conversed with him many times since, not necessarily on dry land, or even upon the Earth, and he has told me much.

Here. Give me your hand. Take this. It's a *present.*

THE TIP OF THE ICEBERG

BY *JOHN SHIRE*

I T MAY SURPRISE YOU to learn that I am now perfectly content to die on this ice at the bottom of the world. My indifference would certainly have surprised my previous companions. William, I am sure, would have been the first to express a wish to survive and tell our tale in person. But he was not allowed the chance, while I am to pass away cold and alone. I shall not grow old bones.

I believed I was the first to sign up for our momentous journey and thus, in some small way, stood at the forefront of what my father insisted on calling "a voyage in the grand tradition of the ship of fools." I was also the youngest, and by far the least famous and the least qualified, to join a scientific expedition into the Southern Oceans. But I was ambitious; more, I was a strutting intellectual, as confident of my own genius as I was of the rightness of our course.

"I have no idea what you are talking about," William said to me, within a week of the *Caliban* leaving port. "You are, sir, extravagantly well read in the most fashionable theories I have ever had the pleasure to encounter. But you are not, my lad, on a par with my friends and I. It matters not, however, as we are all glad to have your company and your contribution to our efforts. I have no doubt that the Royal Society will welcome you back with open arms when we are successful." He paused, and smiled. "But I get ahead of myself. I shall introduce you to the others and we shall let you in on our little secret because, as you can see only too well by now, we are sufficiently trapped by the elements to ensure our project and our findings remain within these bulkheads."

He was right of course. We were heading south from the Cape into unknown waters. Captain Cook had passed this way and Weddell had mapped some airy possibilities but, truth be told, soon enough there would be no one else within a thousand miles, except such whalers as braved the eternal cold. We too were on a whaling ship, such as it was, named appropriately for the wizard's pet monster. It had been recast, at considerable expense, as an exploratory vessel, and was now capable of pandering to needs of a more scientific nature. Our Captain, Adam Seaborn (an unlikely name, perhaps concealing an unsavory past, I felt), told us that he was enormously fond of his ship and that, monstrous though she was in both looks and title, she had the strength of a beast and would survive the most brutal travails.

So it was that, fortified with port and brandy, I was officially introduced to Robert Amos Bennett, geologist, evangelist and teetotaller, and to Willis George Emerson, gentleman, experimenter, atheist and drunkard. Somewhere between the two, in both consumption and conception, was William Bradshaw. He had been a friend of my father's until some trifling falling out had separated them for some years. I, for my part, had always enjoyed Bradshaw's company and kept in touch, especially when my education began to lead me toward his peers. William, with his secure family income and influential friends, had helped me through Oxford and suggested my name to the panel that had put together this private expedition. So, in a way, he is the one I have to thank for my present state. Damn his eyes.

"You want to be a botanist, I hear," boomed Emerson, not deigning to avert his eyes from the brandy in his glass in order to look at me.

"Yes, sir. I have studied Lamarck in detail and I have had the pleasure of a personal interview with a certain Mr Darwin on his return from a most fascinating voyage. I believe I can see great things emerging in this field and would like to make my mark there."

"I don't hold with it," remarked Bennett. "I consider it a trespass upon the dominion of religion." He sat upright at the table, swaddled in a greatcoat and furs and apparently unaffected by any movement of the ship. This, before it had even turned cold. He suffered well and gladly and I found him a very strange man. I was not, however, cowed by his objection.

"You are a geologist, are you not? Why does one discipline serve the Lord and another displease him? Are we not all God's work?"

"His work is done. It is there for us to see and explore. These theories of life are not the same as a history of the rock we live on. Nature, His will, does not continually tinker with His living creations. Processes, developments, are an illusion. The Great Chain of Being is thoroughly in place and is precisely that: a chain with which we are bound. We shall prove it. There are ways."

I had thought to take the argument further but William stepped between us.

"Our little secret, remember? Don't you want to know what we are all doing here, youngster?"

"I had thought we were on a voyage of discovery," I replied, looking pointedly at Bennett, "Was I incorrect?"

"Oh, not at all, lad," said Emerson, "We are on the greatest journey of all time, mark my words. We shall toast the heavens, or possibly the depths, if we are right."

"If Symmes is right," corrected William. "Do you know him, lad? John Cleeve Symmes of Ohio, North America?"

"I fear I have not had the pleasure."

"A great man," William continued. "A visionary." To add drama to this suddenly grand tone, he took a step back and gave a short speech which, as I soon grasped, all three men already knew well.

" 'I declare the earth is hollow and habitable within; containing a number of solid concentric spheres, one within the other, and that it is open at the poles twelve or sixteen degrees. I pledge my life in support of this truth, and am ready to explore the hollow, if the world will support and aid me in the undertaking.'"

He declaimed this in such reverent tones that the others looked up at him as if he might have been quoting scripture. I felt a distinct sinking feeling in my stomach, separate from the rise and fall of the ship. Emerson, enlivened now that our project was at last out in the open, stood with his brandy to complete the picture.

"Yes, that was his proclamation in 1818 to the world. Of course he was ignored. He sent his letter to all and sundry, claiming Sir

Humphrey Davy and Von Humboldt as protectors. He wanted to pursue an expedition to the North Pole there and then. Again, it came to nothing. But we and our backers, of whom you may have heard but I cannot name names, looked into this with interest. And, finally, we have set upon this course of action. The *Caliban* shall sail to the edge of the world, the hole in the pole, to prove his theories and to make our names as legends . . ."

I drank no more that night. I had discovered much that disagreed with me and would not have added to my sickness.

The next morning I stood alone on deck. The gray sea and rolling cloud could not distract me from my dismay. I confess that my reputation was the uppermost thought in my mind. The reputation I had not even the chance to gain before it would be dashed by their nonsense. I feared that my father was right. I sailed on a ship of fools, amongst them, his old friend.

Captain Seaborn shouted orders over the winds, keeping his sailors in good order and preparing for inevitable storms. They worked tirelessly, it would seem, knowing their trade inside out. Seeing me slumped over the railings, the Captain tipped his hat in my direction. I acknowledged him with a wave of the hand, feeling better, suddenly, for his attention. Perhaps I should still be able to make something of this. Of course I should. I had my work to do, just as every man here did. I was still in a unique and enviable position, regardless of my companion's theories. If I had a reputation to make, then I would make it in opposition to such ridiculous notions, if need be. I felt a blast of cold wind take the ship in a new direction and, newly fortified by such minor omens, resolved not to allow the others to distract me from my researches.

This is not to say that, after that first strengthening morning, all conflict was at an end. On the contrary, I spent many hours in futile argument with Emerson and Bennett while William attempted in vain to keep us on an even keel. I pointed to any number of perfectly adequate theories that would have proved my points to the most ignorant savage but it was to no avail. Emerson opposed me with every technical detail at his disposal and, as a scientist, he could not be faulted in his handling of rhetoric, tying me up in knots whenever I took him to task on the nature, age and construction of the planet. I found I had no issue with him on many subjects. It was only the conjectures of a hollow earth that sustained a rift between us.

Bennett, on the other hand, was consistently and coldly angry during our frequent debates. He accused me of having limitations in both learning and imagination. I took offense that a man so bound by religious dogma could accuse a fellow scientist of having a limited imagination. William was duty bound to step in at this juncture. He managed to silence Bennett's riposte. I feel sure the man was about tell me that I was not considered a "fellow" anything.

I did talk to William about my predicament. I told him that I was disappointed that he had kept such an extraordinary interest from me until after our departure. To his credit, he immediately recognized my position and apologised as best he could.

"But all the same, don't you feel it? This is the opportunity of a lifetime. To change our view of the world forever. To travel beyond limits. In all honesty, my young friend, deep down I have my own doubts about our hypotheses but it will not keep me from trying. There is something here, I swear it."

He was right of course. At the time I could not deny it as it appealed to my new and personal sense of purpose. Now I know he was right and it leaves me cold. Very cold indeed.

We saw our first iceberg on a fine day. A line of white on the horizon became a block, then an island, then a vast blue-white monument. It silenced us all. No matter what our beliefs, all four of us stared at the thing as it slid past. The whalers and the Captain, intent on not hitting the huge block, carried on their essential tasks as ever. They had seen them before.

As it receded, we all began to talk at once. I marvelled at the colors, looking forward to mobile colonies of penguins and seals. Bennett wondered aloud how we could obtain samples. Emerson described the layering of the ice, the colors, the possibility of sediments, the origins. William simply said, innocently, "I wonder how old it is?"

I cannot dwell on the following weeks. Excitement gave way to numbing, eternal cold. Soon enough the sea began to freeze. Captain Seaborn had urgent and private meetings with William. I was told we had gone further south than any previous explorer. Moving through a never-ending daylight, we pushed on. Icebergs now became our constant companions and, instead of working, the crew took to grumbling and worrying. Arguments broke out, more significant and heated than our precious academic rivalries. The *Caliban*, that big and ugly monster, pressed on, cracking the sea before it like an axe. As I hung down over the bow, to watch the then thin ice break up before us, I slowly became aware that the landscape was taking us over. The heavy weight of the ship, so solid and imponderable out there on the calm ocean, was being overwhelmed by the cold and its physical avatar, the unending ice.

In the Southern Ocean we had endured but one single storm, though it had lasted a good three days. A miracle, Captain Seaborn had declared. An omen, said Bennett, with a challenge to me in his eyes. Quite enough, was all I could manage to contribute. Since then, a very reasonable wind had kept us on course.

Then it was gone.

We drifted this way and that, the ice pushing us hither and thither. After our evening meal, or what passed for an evening and a meal at that latitude, I found I had drunk a little too much.

"Where is it then?"

"I beg your pardon?"

"Where is it? The hole? Six thousand miles across, you told me only last week. Yes, Emerson, I understand, before you jump in. We may not notice the change. The edges will be vast. Soon enough we will be sailing upside down! Inside the earth! Without a care in the world presumably. Where it is warm. With an internal sun. Or even two. Sirs, I do not care for this new definition of heat."

Whatever the truth behind my outburst, I had gone too far. Bennett rose without a word and left the room to retire to his cabin. The cold as he left also announced the arrival of the Captain. He had the look of single-minded intent about him. I wished more than ever that I had not drunk so much.

"Mr Bradshaw," he always addressed William in the first instance, considering him, rightly or wrongly, the leader of our merry band, "we must turn back if and when we can. In all honesty, the crew and I fear for the safety of the ship and our lives. We have seen no land and no change in the weather. We cannot go forward like this. In fact we cannot go forward at all. We must push off with staves, crack the ice and find open water, in readiness for a wind, which, God willing, will soon come. I'm sorry, sir, but I see no other course of action."

It was the first time that the full content of William's conversations with the Captain had been placed openly before us, though we could all have guessed had we wished to do so.

"Damn it," shouted Emerson, slamming his glass down, "I put all my money into this. I'll not be turned around by the cold."

"Robert, you do not feel it with brandies to insulate you. What will you do when they run out? And you cannot deny, that will be very soon." It appeared that William had had enough of playing the arbiter. Emerson drained his glass. William turned to the Captain. "Do as you see fit, Captain Seaborn. We have achieved a great many things on this voyage. We already have a wealth of information to impart, both scientifically and geographically. It would be a shame if that was lost as a result of . . . an excess of zeal on our parts." The Captain barely had time to express his thanks before he was up the stairs, shouting at the crew to break out the something or others and get us out of this damned ice.

Draining the last port from the ship's decanter, Emerson rose unsteadily from his chair and addressed his parting remarks to me. "I hope you're satisfied now, lad. Tell 'em what you like. Waste of time and money. Fools. Damn them all." In my equally befuddled and somewhat embarrassed state, I could not establish precisely to whom he was referring and so let him leave without comment. The cold as the door opened once again did at least serve to sober me somewhat.

"I'm sorry, William."

"Don't concern yourself. He will be over it in the morning."

"No, I mean about the expedition, about the . . . venture. About the new land in the earth."

"Ah, that," he sighed quietly, looking deep into the last glass of port. "Yes, it would be good to feel the heat of another sun, to sail under an alien sky. Just the once."

I felt, but did not mention, that we were doing just that.

Outside, the crew set to work with a ferocity born of fear. I have to admit that our tiny band of intellectuals, cocooned in abstract work and even more abstract beliefs, realized little of the fatal potential in our situation. All of us, myself included, simply left the sailing to the sailors, retreating to our notebooks and categorizing, our greatest irritation, the frozen ink. I tried to comfort myself with the mass of observations I had made. Naturally I had a certain advantage over the others. As yet, my hopes and dreams of success and recognition remained not entirely fanciful. As such, I was pleased when I felt the ship move once more.

As I made my way on to the deck, bundled up as best I could be against a light wind that, I hoped, heralded our retreat from the ice, I saw, for the first time, the iceberg. The weak, low sun shone behind it, darkening some areas, glinting off others. It seemed unusual in shape, though I doubt I was an expert on these things. It listed in the water, and the surface, relatively flat but with a thick spire pulling one side down and exposing new blue ice at its side, appeared to be a confused mass of broken snow. At the railing, I saw the crew hastening back on board. Around us the cracked ice slid over itself, creaking and splashing. The iceberg was drawing nearer all the time. I could see flashes of black open water in its path.

"I fear we may have got ourselves a travelling companion. This wind's blowing it in our direction but we can't move out," muttered Captain Seaborn, appearing beside me.

"How big would you say?"

"Bigger than it looks. They always are, up close."

Amidst the increasingly shrill shouts and orders, the iceberg approached the side of the ship. In a few hours, both wind and temperature dropped. We became stuck fast again with the berg a few dozen feet away. The spire loomed above us, so close the sailors took to throwing ice at it until the Captain gave them better things to do. I walked the length of the ship to get a look at the blue ice near the base. William joined me, shivering with cold.

"I fear Emerson is coming down with some degree of frostbite. I have no idea what Bennett may be suffering. How are you, lad?"

"I am fine for the moment. Rather overwhelmed by this mountain. William, can you see that, down there by the ice line?"

In the transparency, shapes emerged. Dark colors hid in the ice. We looked closely. Clarity eluded us, but there was something.

"Should we look further?" I wondered. William went to talk to the Captain. I considered informing the others but decided to let William make the decisions. I did not wish to make myself more unpopular than I had already become. Eventually William returned with worrying news.

"We can do as we wish, he says. I am afraid he is not in the best of moods, with us, his employers, in particular. His crew will be out on the ice using ice saws to cut us free, he hopes. That thing will only hinder our escape. This has become altogether too dangerous a venture for him."

"But we should go regardless," I pressed. "Bennett will want to study this thing at close quarters at least."

The three of us stood on the ice before a clear blue wall. Emerson, refusing to join us, was finishing what he claimed was his last and best bottle of wine. I believe he never saw our Pandora's Box.

"What is that?" William said. Three men of science, at the bottom of the world, rendered almost speechless.

"I cannot see," said Bennett, stepping closer, and brushing damp and ice from the berg's side. We gazed through his makeshift portal at another world.

"Titans," I suggested, my imaginings spoken aloud.

Nearest the surface, some form of huge plant leaned at an impossible angle toward us. Tendrils from it passed though the ice, further confusing any solid outline. A five-lobed head emerged from a barrel-shaped body. Similar figures, two, perhaps three, were behind it, twisted and rent in a way that brought to mind some fearsome struggle. For behind them all, and the source of the darker color I had spied from the boat, was a vast mass of shapeless matter, seeping between the pieces, like tentacles, hands ripping the bodies asunder. This mass descended far into the berg, beyond our limited, confused vision. Some ancient avalanche had caught these creatures in the midst of their titanic battle. Centuries of gradual movement had twisted their bodies into these ghastly shapes. Surely that must be the explanation.

But they were like nothing I had ever seen. The closest approximations to their general structure were the creatures seen through a microscope but here they were, larger than life. And this possibility went no way toward explaining the preposterous nature of the dark mass behind them. As I peered still further, I thought I could make out other organs erupting from the darkness. Pseudopods, mouths, even teeth, vestigial eyes glared back at me. I stepped away. None of this was clear. The ice was too deep for any certainty. I remembered William's simple question: how old?

Before I could formulate any useful enquiry, Bennett stomped quickly back to the ship, passing through the men sawing at the ice with singular purpose.

William repeated himself, quietly, as if he asked the question of God.

"What is that?"

I returned to the ship, stepping more carefully than Bennett on that thin ice, unnerved, but keen to get my sketch and note books. Emerson snored fitfully in the cabin. In my haste I could not find sufficient paper and went to ask Bennett for assistance. Excitement overcame my dislike of the man. I found him crouched over a huge volume that I had never seen before. All in all, there were many things I had never seen before, the most surprising of which were his tears.

"Proof, you wanted," he said to me before I could open my mouth. "Proof of other worlds. Well, I am sorry to say that I have had it here all the time." There was an edge of hysteria in his voice which kept me silent. "I was led here by this, this passage; I felt, I believed in my innocence, that the South Pole was 'where the Spheres meet.' I took this as a . . . a literal metaphor so to speak, a ray of light in this otherwise repulsive work of a damnably insane foreigner. A precursor of Symmes, the origin of legends. But now, oh now, there are other things that come out of the pages. Abominable tales of creatures like those remains out there. What can this tell us now, eh? What does this prove? If this blasphemous compilation of hoary myths can lead me here and show me this, of what else is the Lord capable? Look for yourself, damn you! See where science can lead!"

I saw little of science in my swift perusal of the ancient tome. I saw alien sorcery, fantastic names, Kadath, Yog-Sothoth and ritualistic cadences in apocalyptic Biblical style: "Their hand is at your throat, yet ye see them not." How anyone could lend credence to such nonsense was beyond me. But it had affected Bennett so strongly. And even I could see, perhaps, some familiarity in singular descriptions of certain ancient demons. And here we were, in an undeniable "ice desert of the South" as the book mentioned. My first thoughts, though, and I said as much to the staring Bennett, were of Lamarck and his theories of the development of organs in living creatures. I said this to calm his nerves but instead he laughed at me, causing frozen tears to fall to the floor.

I suppose it was this encounter that saved me, if that is an apt description of my current state. Recovering my books and writing utensils, I set out in a daze, over the side of our poor frozen ship, past the increasingly frantic crew and out onto the endless plain of ice. Too many thoughts crowded my mind. The limitless glowing horizon was not sufficient distraction from the enormity of my thoughts. I stumbled and fell before finally turning to survey the activity behind me. Automatically I took up a pencil and sketched the scene.

The possibility that we were the agents of our own destruction is the cause of much absorbing debate between myself and the seals hereabouts. I could see William, still intent on the side of the berg. He was approached, warned presumably, to step away, by the Captain. The crew, with their sawing and hacking, appeared to be making little impact on the ice plain that encased the ship and, from this small distance, I could hear an ominous increase in the creak and strain of our natural prison.

A resounding crack echoed over the ice. Dark water appeared between the berg and the ship. With awful clarity I saw both William and Captain Seaborn drawn under the ice, hands slipping on the blue wall. The ice pinnacle rose above the ship. It seemed for all the world that the thing was intent on attacking the vessel. The crew scattered, jumping for their lives over disintegrating masses of unstable ice. Few were successful in maintaining themselves for more than a minute. I believe I saw Bennett emerge onto the deck. He was looking upward at the aggressor, holding his arms aloft as if he welcomed the end.

The iceberg turned over in the water. The pinnacle, now some giant spike of an ice-axe, smashed through the decking. Spars and timbers splintered beneath its weight. Debris was flung out by the impact, scattered beyond even my position. I barely noticed the black lightning forks of water approaching me. The tall, ice-encrusted masts fell together, showering the scene in glinting ice crystals. I thought of Emerson, drunk and drowned.

A pattern emerged. This was not the worst of it. Black silhouettes of the crew, either scrambling on ice rafts or bobbing about in that lethal water, began to scream. Why not, I thought, numbly.

Why not? Then I saw the underside of the iceberg, newly exposed to the pale sun.

There was more of the dark creature there. As water ran away over the smooth curves, it became apparent that the berg's underside was far larger than we had imagined. Whether this inversion is a common occurrence, or even, I hesitate to add, a natural phenomenon, I will never be in a position to know. The organic mass took up fully two thirds of the exposed ice which nestled firmly against the listing, drowning *Caliban*. In some places chunks had been broken away by the violent upheaval, exposing what I can only think of as naked flesh.

My encounter with Bennett and his outrageous tome had already left me irreparably confused. My indistinct vision of the prodigious creature in the ice and its ridiculous organs, the unavoidable questions of age and provenance, all combined to overwhelm any semblance of scientific detachment. How old? How can such things come into being? How can such a protean mass develop such recognisable and yet arbitrary limbs? Over how many epochs? And yet, in one organism? Retaining all functions over that time? What of the smaller, plant creatures, torn apart so long ago? By the ice? By their pursuer? What manner of life had existed here? Any theories I ever knew, any foundation I had ever believed in, was inexorably crushed, drowned and frozen.

It was still alive.

The exposed flesh seeped like a viscous fluid over the surface of the berg then reared up in anomalous shapes, as if searching for the correct form, adapting before my very eyes to an environment so hostile to the screaming men left alive. When I saw this I took an involuntary step forward. It was not the last vestiges of scientific wonder that drew me. Instead, it was more some primeval urge to throw myself into the thing's questing embrace, to make the questions cease once and for all. I felt it call inside my head. More debris clattered and splashed around me as the thing twisted about. It remained trapped in the ice while the wreckage of the *Caliban*, appearing to grow stronger in her death throes, bore down on it, masts and sails snapped and unravelled. It touched men and they fell beneath its embrace. Others chose death by water. As I said, I could hear screaming but by the end there was only mine and that of the creature, indistinguishable in my head.

The iceberg, the creature and the wreck of the *Caliban* formed an unstable alliance. First one and then another righted itself, all, to my view, showing a distinct will to survive. Soon enough though, they all lost the fight and sank, bubbling, beneath the cold sea. As they disappeared the ice floes moved to cover the exposed wound and I felt a shudder when the patch of ice on which I stood became detached. I fell, scattering paper. Not daring to move as I drifted, I saw bodies, ice-rimed, floating in the water, surrounded by splinters of wood. There was no more noise, except the odd bump of ice against ice. I stared at the white sky and white ground as the sea froze around me once again. Only one thing attracted my attention, a tiny object, ejected toward me during the battle and lying only a few feet away. When I felt sufficiently safe to move, I crawled toward it.

My fingers are blackened beneath these gloves. My feet are no longer my own. Why, in this world of whiteness, does flesh turn to the reverse? The seals have joined me, remaining at a distance and laughing at my end. The world is not as I believed it to be, and I am no longer sure we can hope for a better one to come. The last thing I found, washed up from the archaic depths, was an ornament. A fashioned, deliberate, metallic decoration, a small model of one of the plant creatures, wrenched from the unthinkable past for a few moments only to be lost again as surely as before. Why was this my final revelation? Perhaps it was merely to prove to me, before I died, that advanced civilizations of monstrosities, not animals, not plants, had lived and flourished long before Man, that the universe is upside down, and that my world is, as predicted, hollow.

PASSAGE TO OBLIVION

BY LEE CLARK ZUMPE

i.

"To this state of general peace with which we have been blessed, one only exception exists. Tripoli, the least considerable of the Barbary States, had come forward with demands unfounded either in right or in compact, and had permitted itself to denounce war on our failure to comply before a given day. The style of the demand admitted but one answer. I sent a small squadron of frigates into the Mediterranean, with assurances to that power of our sincere desire to remain in peace, but with orders to protect our commerce against the threatened attack."
—President Thomas Jefferson, first annual message,
Dec. 8, 1801.

"THEY TORTURED YOU?" ELIJAH Greenheath studied the bloodied and bruised victim in flickering lantern light. Deep inside the guarded and fortified walls of a makeshift fort appropriated by General William Eaton, he questioned the traumatized Arkham scholar. Hours earlier, the man had been liberated from a squalid dungeon along with a dozen other hostages of various nationalities. Though his wounds were numerous and terrible, many other prisoners had suffered far more grievous injuries than he. "Judging by your condition, they had a difficult time obtaining the information they desired."

"They learned nothing from me," Silas Trimble said. For such a slight, scrawny man, Trimble spoke with an air of confidence and defiance bordering on impudence. A noted academician affiliated with several institutions of higher learning, he had earned a reputation amongst his peers for being as overbearing as he was astute. "My silence matters little, though. The Piri Reis map and the accompanying documents are in their hands now. This theft represents an incomparable tragedy for the school."

Outside the American fortification, fighting raged on as Eaton's troops battled for control of the pirate fortress of Derna. Set between the weathered peaks of the craggy Jebel Akhdar Mountains and the intense blue of Mediterranean waters, the stronghold had become a haven for privateers preying on American interests along the Barbary coast. Greenheath had accompanied the ragtag militia on their march out of Alexandria across hundreds of miles of desert. The general hoped the capture of Derna and subsequent installation of a ruler sympathetic to American trade would bring an end to the dominance of Barbary pirates.

While Greenheath's loyalties lay firmly with the fledgling American forces intent on protecting commercial interests, his clandestine pursuit provided him with an alternate agenda that kept him from actively participating in the daring assault. He had come for Trimble—or, more accurately, he had come for the map Trimble had been carrying.

"It does exist, then?" Greenheath's tone revealed an underlying astonishment. An agent of the secretive Sodalitas Invictus, he had been charged with locating and securing an obscure nautical chart allegedly reproduced from sources dating back to the days of Carthage. Ottoman sultans had long denied its existence. European collectors of antiquities had spent more than a century trying to locate it without success. Even his counselors doubted the validity of the artifact. "So many have failed in attempts to retrieve it . . . how exactly did you come to possess it?"

"I may not look like a particularly brave man, Mr Greenheath," Trimble said, elbows resting on his knees as he sat on a crudely constructed bench. "I contracted with disreputable dealers and traders and engaged in acts which if disclosed would serve to discredit my research and disgrace my good name." He spoke of his deeds with conspicuous displeasure. His obsession had undoubtedly exposed him to the darkest depravities the world endured. The prize, though, could not be more precious. The map purportedly depicted a phantom island believed by certain scholars to be the only surviving site of an unknown civilization. Over the centuries, many names had been ascribed to the enigmatic atoll: Plato's lost Atlantis, City of the Golden Gates, Bal-Sagoth and—more recently—Lindeman's Saxemberg. To most, it was no more than archaic lore or the folly of weary sailors. To Trimble, it would be the discovery of a lifetime. "What does al-Qaramanli plan to do with the map?"

"The pasha knows nothing of the Piri Reis map. Even if he did, he would not pursue it. He has no interest in graves and forgotten gods." Yusuf ibn Ali al-Qaramanli, usurper of the throne of Tripolitania, had more pressing matters of state to occupy his time. A few years earlier, he had declared war on the United States by chopping down the flagpole in front of the American consulate in Tripoli. "Your map is now the property of the cutthroat Mustapha al-Muqaffa."

Greenheath offered Trimble a moistened cloth to wash his wounds, a tankard of warm ale to lift his spirits. Born a Sentinel, Greenheath's youthful features gave no hint of his actual age. He had reached his seventieth year without a single gray hair or wrinkle. Aside from unconventional longevity, his birthright assured him extraordinary mental capacity, amplified insightfulness and imposing physical strength and dexterity. With the advantageous concessions, though, came the endless custodianship of civilization.

Though the passing years had not dulled his senses, taxed his vitality or diminished his youthfulness, the passage of time had affected him in other ways. Greenheath had watched his family and friends grow old, stood by solemnly as they took to their graves. He had witnessed the birth of a nation and the subjugation and slaughter of America's indigenous peoples. Moreover, because of his lot in life, he had faced the nightmares that yet roamed the earth.

"The pirate al-Muqaffa?" Trimble raised a trembling hand and rubbed his sore jaw. His face had taken more than a few fists during his long incarceration.

"None other." Among the Turkish corsairs that had been plundering ships in the western Mediterranean, none rivaled the abject cruelty regularly displayed by al-Muqaffa. A degenerate privateer as well as a ruthless slave trader, he intimidated even the House of

Osman in Istanbul. "Your sponsors at Miskatonic Liberal College will be most disheartened by this turn of events."

"As will your benefactors, whomever they may be," Trimble said, the incongruent assertiveness returning to his voice. "While I appreciate my freedom, I have no doubt that you were sent to recover the map. My life, by comparison, is of little concern to you or those who fund you." Professor Trimble—perhaps the leading intellectual in the field of Near Eastern Languages and Civilizations—had promptly and correctly deduced Greenheath's intentions. To Trimble, Greenheath was no better than al-Muqaffa—a prospective thief who arrived too late to filch a document that belonged in the province of scholars. Prepared for the *Kitab-i Bahriye* but omitted from the edition presented to Suleiman the Magnificent by Piri Reis, the map was more than 200 years old. "It would be best left to those who will work to unearth its mysteries, to study it and to preserve it for future generations. Instead, the map will most likely disappear once more, a relic purchased by some private collector who sees it as a possession instead of an instrument of illumination."

"You think al-Muqaffa will sell it?"

"Yes, assuredly, to the highest bidder."

"If only it were that simple." Sodalitas Invictus had gathered sufficient information to consider al-Muqaffa a significant threat. The corsair had not just blundered into the situation. He had orchestrated the capture of the 36-gun sailing frigate USS *Philadelphia* in the Tripoli harbor. He had arranged to have the vessel's solitary civilian passenger transferred to his custody while the ship's officers and men were enslaved. "I assure you, al-Muqaffa will not easily part with the map."

"What then? He is a brigand and a rogue. Surely he will seek to prosper from it."

"The man is an opportunist," Greenheath agreed. Though his familiarity with the Piri Reis map was unparalleled, Trimble's understanding of it apparently extended no farther than his scholarly appreciation of the potential wisdom that might be gleaned from it after prolonged scrutiny. For a utilitarian, pragmatic individual like al-Muqaffa, the map held the promise of unimagined wealth and power, and of alliances with those malevolent entities said to reside on the island. Sodalitas Invictus, unsurpassed in its acquaintance with Things Which in Dark Quarters Dwell, could not even begin to catalogue the ominous legends affixed to that place. "I believe he intends to find his fortune pillaging the ruins. Should he make landfall, what he uncovers on that accursed island may bring ruin to us all."

"Then it falls upon us to pursue him, to prevent him from achieving his goals." Trimble's sudden re-evaluation of the situation took Greenheath by surprise. His unanticipated interest in taking an active part in the recovery of the map seemed uncharacteristic, considering his patrician background.

"That will be difficult, if not impossible, without the map . . ."

"Mr Greenheath," Trimble said, standing. "I spent several weeks studying that map before I even boarded the USS *Philadelphia*." As he emptied his tankard, a flash of recognition sparkled in his eyes. "Russian Imperial Stout," he said, "from Thrale's Brewery, London." He identified it by its pungent aroma. It smelled like leather and licorice, tasted like bitter chocolate. "My mental faculties exceed those of the common man. Anything I have ever tasted, smelled, heard or read remains fresh in my memory."

"You memorized the map?"

"If you can provide a ship, Mr Greenheath," Trimble said, "I will provide the course. Understand, though," he continued, his self-assurance more than slightly exasperating, "Should we recover the map, it will become property of Miskatonic."

"My overseers will frown upon it," Greenheath said, considering his limited options. "It seems you have left me little choice. I have a ship waiting."

"Then let us not waste another minute."

ii.

"From the geographical notes prefixed to Perouse's voyage I learn that this island was discovered by John Lindestz Lindeman, a Hollander, in 1670 . . . It does not appear that this island has ever been seen since, although many ships have sought for it."
—Matthew Flinders, journal of the HMS Investigator, Oct. 2, 1801.

"Lindeman justifiably sought to hide its actual location in his oth-

erwise meticulous notes, though the seafarer's vanity precluded any thought of wholly concealing its existence. I have lost four good men trying to put ashore on that awful isle, and though it is behind us now, the stars overhead are no longer familiar and inexplicable shadows swarm beneath restless waters. The sea shelters aberrations no man was meant to witness.

—Fletcher Edwards, journal of the HMS *Pandora*,
Jan. 17, 1804.

Dawn foundered in a gossamer mist drifting above the Atlantic, stretching from horizon to horizon. The smothering white miasma had hidden the heavens throughout the previous night and had left the crew of the sturdy sloop-of-war unsettled and anxious. Since their hasty departure from embattled Derna, Elijah Greenheath had consulted frequently with the master and commander of the *Vigilant*, a man he both respected and trusted.

Through his family's trade and export business based in Smithville, North Carolina, Greenheath had associated with Langdon Cuthbert for years and had retained his services on more than one occasion. On undertakings assigned by Sodalitas Invictus, the seaman's prudence and discretion had proved invaluable. A man who kept few close acquaintants, the Sentinel considered Cuthbert an indispensable friend. He had never known him to convey bare-faced uneasiness—particularly in the company of his crew and passengers.

"Is it the perturbation of the sea or some incongruous apprehension that disconcerts you?" Greenheath asked, hoping to rally Cuthbert from his melancholy mood. The two men stood on the quarterdeck as the square-rigged sails of the three-masted *Vigilant* blossomed before a light, fair wind. The Sentinel could sense his friend had slept little over the course of a long night. "What troubles you, old sea dog?"

"The sea," Cuthbert answered, his gaze examining the surf. He scratched his iron gray beard. "The skies. The air itself." The master and commander paused, callused fingers rubbing his bloodshot eyes so violently they seemed to recede into their sockets. "Everything is amiss, Elijah. In all my years abaft the mast, I've never experienced so many ill omens on what should be an ordinary voyage."

"There is nothing ordinary about our destination, Langdon."

"If the destination you refer to is the Dutchman's phantom island, I'll reserve judgment about the validity of its reputation until land has been sighted. Even if we manage to keep to our track-line and stay true to the course that smug highbrow Trimble described," Cuthbert said, digging through his pocket, "I doubt we'll find the shores described by Lindeman and Edwards." Cuthbert retrieved a fine English compass from his pocket. Housed in a square mahogany case with polished bronze hinges, the instrument's needle spun frenziedly, refusing to settle on a bearing. "We have been sailing blindly for days. Overcast skies and unreliable compass readings make celestial navigation useless."

"Your concern is certainly justified, but I know of no other man I would rather have at my side." Both merchant and mercenary, Cuthbert had ample experience in overcoming adversities. He had trafficked with notorious traders in seedy ports, dealing for exotic and often banned goods such as the famed incense of Irem, elixirs derived from the black lotus of Sung and crystal shards smuggled out of Leng. As a sword-for-hire, he had patrolled Mediterranean waters sinking pirate ships along the Barbary Coast and had seen a dozen freebooters to Davy Jones' grip. "I have faith in your aptitude as well as your valor."

"As a veteran of these waters, I have faith in the sea's ability to deceive an old hand and swallow a ship and her crew without so much as a hint of impending peril." Cuthbert applied a flask to his lips and downed a nip of bumbo before offering it to Greenheath. "Of all people, you should know what prowls the depths far beneath the water's surface."

"I also know Mustapha al-Muqaffa and his ilk," Greenheath said. For all the whispered horrors secreted by the sea, the hardhearted Turkish corsair had caused more grief, suffering and fear in his two decades of piratical violence than all the haunters of the murky fathoms. "I would not have involved you in a mission of vengeance or recklessness. Wherever the map leads us, something awaits us there that must not be left to a band of degenerate scalawags. Whatever vestiges of antiquity remain, al-Muqaffa must not be granted access to them."

"Some day, Elijah, your righteousness and stubbornness will likely conspire to doom you."

"Let us hope that today is not that day," Silas Trimble said, approaching the men from amidships. He had finally managed to rouse himself from slumber and take leave of his berth. "If you will excuse us for a moment, Captain . . ."

Cuthbert nodded courteously, though he skinned a wicked eye as he made his way to the forecastle to convene with his quartermaster.

"I hope your memory is as impeccable as you believe it to be, Mr Trimble." Greenheath had spoken with the Arkham academician only intermittently since boarding the *Vigilant*. His intentional evasion of the man stemmed from both conventional caution and persistent, unsubstantiated reservations he had experienced since liberating Trimble from the dismal dungeon in Derna. Something about Trimble left him with an impression of incongruity and anachronism. "Neither the master and commander nor the ship's navigator have been able to fix our position. Only by dead reckoning can they approximate our course."

"I suppose that will have to suffice." Trimble ravenously devoured slingers as his morning meal. The coffee looked as thick and black as tar. The hardtack, at least, had not yet been infested with maggots. Nevertheless, Trimble knocked the biscuit against the gunwale to be certain. "She's not a particularly well-armed vessel, is she? Will we stand a chance against al-Muqaffa?"

"The *Vigilant* boasts fourteen four-pound cannon on her gun deck and a clever crew always prepared to defend her. What she lacks in firepower, she more than makes up for in speed and maneuverability." Cuthbert had ably demonstrated the competence of his vessel and her crew in countless skirmishes with Barbary corsairs, pirates of the Caribbean as well as Cheng I Sao's notorious Red Fleet commanded by Chang Pao. "If any man can hope to best al-Muqaffa on the high seas, it is Cuthbert."

"If you are willing to place your confidence in him, then that is reason enough for me to do the same." Trimble's unexpected acquiescence startled Greenheath. "I see by your surprise that you expected an argument. Let me explain, Mr Greenheath: I know who—or rather what you are." Trimble brushed the crumbs of his breakfast from his chinstrap. "Though the study of esoteric societies is not my specialty, my colleagues at Miskatonic have often spoken of Sodalitas Invictus and its agents of mischief and surveillance. I admit I thought the likelihood of such an order somewhat dubious. It is the nineteenth century, after all, and such superstitions as those your fraternity purportedly protects are, by modern standards, passé."

"I have no idea . . ."

"Don't be elusive, Mr Greenheath. The birthmark on your forearm leaves little doubt." Greenheath reflexively glanced at the long sleeve of his japanned-leather blue jacket. The star-shaped blemish that signified his providence remained hidden beneath it. "Odd that those ordained to a cryptic existence should be branded in such a perceptible manner."

"Very well," Greenheath said, acknowledging Trimble's discovery. "What about you, Mr Trimble? Something suggests that you are similarly out of place here."

Before Trimble could address the Sentinel's accusation, a call rang out from the crow's nest atop the mainmast.

"Ahoy!" The lookout, spyglass extended, directed the crew's attention to the starboard. No more than a quarter league away, a ship drifted through the murky fog. Its sails tattered, its timbers shattered, the vessel appeared to be at the mercy of the ocean's currents.

"About ship," Cuthbert commanded, preparing for the worst. "All hands, make ready for battle." On the gun deck, the master gunner gave the order to clear for quarters, and his teams stowed their hammocks and readied the gunpowder and cannonballs. Above board, the boatswain rationed out weaponry including sangrenels, caltrops, swivel guns, cutlasses and muskets. Greenheath retrieved his Kaintuck rifle and offered the unarmed Trimble a flintlock pistol for defense.

However, over the span of the next few nervous moments, it became clear that combat would be unnecessary. As the *Vigilant* sailed alongside the ghost ship, grappling irons flew threw the air and gripped the corsair's flagship to facilitate a boarding.

"It's al-Muqaffa's shebec, the *Hayreddin Barbarossa*. She's adrift and appears to be taking on water." Cuthbert permitted only a handful of crewman aboard to investigate the ship's demise. He cautiously scanned the deck as he stepped through a scupper. The shebec's lateen-rigged masts had been splintered, her surviving oars swayed back and forth above the water's surface. "I see no evidence of conflict. The damage may have resulted from a severe squall or rogue wave."

"Unlikely, that," Trimble said, leaning close to Greenheath. He pointed to the binnacle. A bloody mound of threadbare and charred flesh tapered into blackened bones near the ship's wheel. A brain-soaked tricorne rested atop the carcass. "If I am not mistaken, that is what remains of the coxswain."

More mutilated corpses littered the main deck, their bodies disfigured, dismembered and debased. Below, victims lay frozen in unsettling shadows, faces maligned by fear, eyes portraying the torment of their final, beleaguered moments.

"No anomaly of nature could cause this degree of carnage," Greenheath said, his voice no more than a whisper. "And though my wits may delude me, I feel that the author of this massacre has not abandoned the ship."

Despite a mounting sense of danger, they probed further, inspecting the officer's quarters judiciously. Sea charts lay scattered across a table along with navigational instruments including a compass, an astrolabe and a sexton. Among the documents strewn about, Trimble identified and collected the appropriated Piri Reis map.

"Could it be an affliction that doomed them?" Cuthbert knelt close to a rotting casualty, examined its blackened flesh, its pus-encrusted lacerations, its innards which had been disgorged through every observable orifice. "Is it some plague that now will hasten our own calamity?"

"A plague, yes," Trimble agreed, as he fixated over the map with an alarming fascination. "A plague of darkness, to be precise. This world has long been tainted by a scourge straight out of oblivion."

"We must turn back," the master and commander of the *Vigilant* said abruptly, spinning on the heels of his boots as he sought to leave the butchery behind him. "I'll not endanger my crew by counting on this highbrow's wild delusions. I'll not risk everything on a fool's errand, not even for you, Elijah."

"Langdon," Greenheath called after his old friend. "Langdon, we must be close now. Letting this opportunity slip away would be a disservice to all mankind."

When Greenheath and Trimble caught up with Cuthbert on deck, they found themselves silenced along with all those aboard the *Vigilant*. The mist had subsided, banished to the far horizons, revealing that which Lindeman and Edwards and a handful of other seafarers had recorded as an unexplored island in the middle of the

Atlantic—a fabled remnant of some forgotten civilization.

"Atlantis," said one deckhand, the menacing sight leaving him otherwise speechless.

"Bal-Sagoth," said the quartermaster, clutching his spyglass in one hand and a dusägge in the other.

"Septe Cidades," said the Portuguese cooper, pangs of greed eclipsed by numbing fear.

"That is no island . . ." Greenheath strained his neck as his gaze swept the gleaming black colossus towering before him. An immense wall extended from the depths stretching skyward and extending several leagues in either direction. Its sleek raven surface defied comprehension. No model of architectural ingenuity could compare to its construction. No enterprise in the history of mankind could measure up to such an extraordinary exhibition of design and execution. Greenheath knew that this spectacle mimicking a landmass could be rivaled only by the machinations of nature, yet, no natural phenomenon had created this magnum opus. "Nor is this the residue of some forgotten, antediluvian society."

iii.

" . . . and in a single day and night of misfortune all your warlike men in a body sank into the earth, and the island of Atlantis in like manner disappeared in the depths of the sea. For which reason the sea in those parts is impassable and impenetrable, because there is a shoal of mud in the way; and this was caused by the subsidence of the island."
—Plato, *Timaeus*, circa 360 BCE.

Darkness descended with the presumptuousness of vicious pestilence.

"Unlike you, Elijah, I have little interest in serving humanity's best interests." Langdon Cuthbert put flame to a lantern in his quarters as evening's shadows congregated. Though the fog had receded, the familiar stars of night failed to ignite as the sun, with customary negligence, discourteously disappeared. An ebon dusk bereft of consolatory twilight thrived above those unfortunate few relegated to tend the dogwatch. The balance of the crew cowered below decks where Cuthbert had confined them after anchoring abreast of the muddy shoals surrounding the massive fortification. "I have lingered this long only at your behest. Articulate your line of reasoning promptly before my crew transforms into mutineers—and forget neither the *Hayreddin Barbarossa* nor the countless other vessels in the graveyard of ships which now surrounds us."

Cuthbert did not exaggerate in his description of the scene the crew had witnessed that afternoon. They had sailed along the massive barrier searching for what Silas Trimble described as the Passage to Oblivion—the single point of access to a supposed citadel within the walls. In the shallows skirting the walls, vessels of every imaginable design and from every conceivable age lay abandoned, disintegrating in the unforgiving surf. While some of the crew mistook the swarming shadows on those fusty shipwrecks for ghosts of long-dead sailors, Elijah Greenheath inferred a less spiritual, more disconcerting derivation in their configuration.

"Afford me a longboat and sufficient time to explore this place." Greenheath could offer no rationale that would warrant the approval of the master and commander. Cuthbert could hardly begin to comprehend the possibility that an ancient civilization had mastered construction techniques surpassing anything nineteenth century architects could imagine. Should the Sentinel reveal what he believed to be the true origin of the phantom island, Cuthbert would think him a madman. "If I have not returned by dawn, weigh anchor and leave this land never to return."

"And what if dawn does not find us in this Godforsaken place?"

"Have you ever known me to mislead you, Langdon?" Greenheath managed a dry smile, one not as convincing as he had hoped to conjure. Still, he knew his old friend would not disappoint him.

"Go. Do what you must." Cuthbert cupped his face in his hands. "Do not make me maroon you here, Elijah."

Greenheath and Trimble ascended a narrow set of stone steps carved into the vast wall. Each man carried an oil lantern but the profuse darkness enveloping them pitched its weight against the feeble light. Far below, heaving swells crashed against the walls agitating the fleet of stranded ships. With nightfall, the chatter of uncanny entities arose from the battered hulks and now echoed along the constricted passage. Their fervent prattle no doubt perturbed those aboard the *Vigilant*.

"You have heard those voices before, have you not, Sentinel?" For such a meager looking man, Trimble displayed extraordinary courage. His uncharacteristic bravado reminded Greenheath of his suspicions. "As an agent of Sodalitas Invictus, you have perhaps beheld analogous monstrosities throughout the world. Have you ever questioned the source of these things?"

"Most of them have abided here longer than mankind. Their beginnings have been lost to time." Greenheath shed his discretion, realizing Trimble knew as much about the hidden world as he. "You seem equally comfortable in the presence of the unexplained," Greenheath said. "Perhaps you might enlighten me as to your own origin. You are no more my contemporary than this island is an innovation of a prehistoric civilization."

"Your powers of observation exceed their reputation." Each man minded every footfall as the titan steps grew increasingly more slick and slippery as if saturated with sea-slime or some relentless form of fungi. The scanty glow of their lanterns now exposed along the flanking walls an endless expanse of text in diverse manners including cuneiform, hieroglyphs and other unrecognizable icons and symbols. "I have lived many lives in many places across the span of time. Though I come from another time, I do now consider Arkham my home."

"Are there others like you?"

"A few," Trimble admitted. "Most are scattered throughout the ages. We are the final survivors, the culmination of many millennia of evolution, technological progress and genetic endurance. And this," Trimble said, his face full of pride as he gestured to the surrounding walls, "this is the last vestige of our future civilization, projected back through time to the dawn of life on earth." Moments after Trimble's revelation, the men reached the summit. Spread before them, luminous monoliths towered, their apexes scratching at the starless night skies. Gargantuan statues—too abstract to be identifiable in nineteenth century terms—invoked idols of un-dreamt religions, while altars festooned with incandescent crystals surged with curious power. "I must apologize. This all must seem like magic to you."

"Magic is nothing more than science beyond the comprehension of modern intellect." Still, Greenheath staggered at the sight of the deviant, non-Euclidian geometry that served as a foundation for the layout of the metropolis. Its perimeter distended unnaturally toward an insidious void as all remaining attributes evocative of earth faded from view. Lines skewed, angles fluctuated and mass and measurement became subjective. At the center of the tumult, swirling chaos manifested itself in the form of an unbridled vortex at variance with its surroundings. Greenheath felt its intimidating influence, discerned the distortion it affected on all adjacent matter. "You have constructed a portal through time . . ."

"A means of escape," Trimble said. "We are refugees, Mr Greenheath. Thousands of years from now, the world will be conquered and humanity enslaved. Our most learned scholars utilized this device to seed civilization, dispersing bits of knowledge throughout history. I was the last to traverse the corridor and I believed I successfully programmed the vortex to seal itself behind me." Trimble accessed a nearby console divided into dozens of dimly lit squares. His fingers danced across its surface, tapping at various characters in sequential order. "Somehow, those who besieged our world managed to reactivate it, to exploit it to advance their subjugation of mankind."

"Those creatures haunting the shipwrecks below—is that what ultimately will inherit the earth?"

"Those are only shadowmen—pathetic minions of the overlords, the foot soldiers in an infinite army of godlike warriors." Trimble completed his task and scanned the dark horizon. Writhing shadows shambled along the periphery, crimson eyes shimmering. "They are all around us, stranded here, too ineffectual to convey themselves across the Atlantic, too lethargic to trouble themselves confronting two uninvited guests. It surprises me that they took such an active interest in al-Muqaffa's shebec. The real threat to the earth comes from the more powerful entities—things you and your brethren have been battling for centuries. You are the advanced guard defending earth against a coming invasion, Elijah."

"What of the *Vigilant*?" Greenheath recalled the wanton and unnecessary bloodshed aboard the Turkish corsair's vessel and feared he had doomed his friend Cuthbert to a similar fate. "What about Langdon?"

"We will find both the ship and crew intact thanks to a protective implement I left in my cabin. Should I not return for any reason, I leave it in your capable hands." Trimble led Greenheath back to the passage. "We have little time now. I have set the vortex to collapse. Without its energy, the city will recede beneath the waves."

Before they could begin their descent, a high-pitched noise alerted Trimble to another setback.

"Go on," he said, urging Greenheath toward the steps. "Something is trying to traverse the portal. I will have to stay here, to keep it at bay."

"Mankind cannot afford to lose your knowledge of the future, Trimble."

"If I fail to contain this entity, neither one of us will see home again." Trimble faced the bulging vortex, its borders reaching beyond the established parameters. The monoliths and statues curved inward, teetering on the brink of the black abyss. The crystal-powered altars pulsed with radiance. "Go, Elijah. Get back to the ship. Sodalitas Invictus has need of your skills. There is much work to be done."

Greenheath nodded, his appreciation evident in his expression. Even as he turned toward the passageway, thousands of pallid tentacles slithered over the lip of the portal and slid across the floor spreading out in all directions. Trimble stood firm, his hands grasping the console as he fought to accelerate the degeneration of the temporal distortion.

Greenheath stumbled down the steps barely maintaining his balance. The Atlantic raced up toward him as the island began its gradual descent into oblivion. The Sentinel felt space and time warp around him, felt the weight of centuries subsiding into the swirling abyss. He heard the desperate screams of dying shadowmen and caught a glimpse of the horror that might have slipped through the portal had it not been for the vigilance of Trimble. Though trapped at the threshold of the doorway, the nightmare manifested itself in one appalling instant, imprinting its degeneracy and malevolence and repugnance upon every living thing in the vicinity.

Darkness descended once more, but this time Greenheath welcomed it as a reprieve from utter desolation and anguish.

Greenheath awoke and felt the sun on his face. Wind filled the sails of the *Vigilant* as she made for familiar ports along the Bulge of Africa. Bruised and battered, the Sentinel did not bother to look abaft, knowing no sign of the island would be found.

"I had the surgeon bring you up on deck. I thought the fresh air might stir you." Cuthbert offered Greenheath a bonded jacky. "You've been out for three days. You were lucky we found you at all after what happened back there."

"Trimble?"

"No," Cuthbert said, glancing over the gunwale. Though he never cared for the man, the master and commander took any casualty under his watch personally. "No trace of him. We searched as long as we dared before setting sail. Even with the island beneath the sea where it belongs, I could not spend another night listening to those wailing shades howl into the darkness."

"Your crew . . . how did they fare in all this?"

"Well enough, all things considered. The men complain of dark dreams even now." Cuthbert admitted to no such nightmares, but his sullen look betrayed his trepidation. "The sea holds many mysteries, Elijah . . . its depths conceal as many secrets as the black gulfs between the distant stars. Maybe men are not meant to unlock every enigma, to explore every shadowed recess on earth."

"We cannot move forward without exploration, Langdon." Greenheath stood and placed a firm hand on his friend's shoulder. From the quarterdeck, beneath affable skies, the sea regained much of its allure. "If but one stone is left unturned, could our ultimate doom not flourish unchecked in that refuge?"

"What will you do with it, Elijah? What will you do with the Piri Reis map?"

"I made a vow I intend to keep," Greenheath said. "Besides, I have always wanted to visit Arkham."

DARK BLUE

BY *ALAN DEAN FOSTER*

T HE SEA BELOW THE keel of the ocean-going ketch *Repera* was the bluest blue Chase Rontgern had ever seen. It was bluer than blue. Bluer than the clearest sky, bluer than all the lapis-lazuli in Afghanistan, bluer than sapphire or azurite or a studio track by Coltrane. Rontgern had spent considerable time on a number of boats on two oceans but he had never seen blue like this. He asked Captain Santos about it.

"There are no fish here, in this deep, deep water. No fish because no zooplankton. No zooplankton because no phytoplankton." Standing on the flying bridge with his long hair tucked under his cap and dark wrap-around shades shielding his eyes from the sun and wind, Santos nodded to port. "With no microscopic life in the water, no life of any kind, there nothing to scatter the sunshine. Everything get absorbed except the blue. The sun pours down unobstructed and just keep going, going, until it fade away to indigo-black."

Rontgern nodded his understanding as he raised the expensive binoculars that were hanging from the padded strap around his neck. They hadn't seen a thing since leaving Pitcairn behind. Only a few patrolling seabirds searching diligently for the fish Santos insisted were not there.

They had tried but had been unable to land at Pitcairn. The island's famous swells were too high for their single rigid inflatable to chance a dash for the concrete and rock breakwater that protected the tiny artificial harbor at Bounty Bay, and given the rough conditions the islanders were not inclined to risk one of their vital Moss aluminum longboats just to venture out and say hello to those on board a tramp ketch like the *Repera*.

As it had sailed on eastward out of sight of Pitcairn's towering green-clad peaks, Rontgern had reflected in passing that the original Bounty mutineers had indeed succeeded in isolating themselves on one of the least accessible islands in the entire South Pacific. Now the *Repera* was headed for a speck of land that was even more inaccessible than Pitcairn, and devoid even of the resilient descendents of rowdy mutineers and their dedicated vahines.

A more or less oval chunk of solid coralline limestone rising straight up out of the ocean from a depth of three and a half kilometers, Henderson Island lay another two hundred kilometers northeast of Pitcairn, which in turn was more than twice that distance from where he had met up with the *Repera* in the Gambier islands of southern French Polynesia. The nearest airstrip to Henderson was on Mangareva, more than six hundred kilometers away in the Gambiers. No aircraft could land on Pitcairn and it was too far to reach by chopper. The closest outpost of civilization to Henderson in the other direction was Easter Island, which lay so far over the dead-flat horizon that the inhabitants of Mangareva were next-door neighbors by comparison.

"Why on Earth would you want to go to a god-forsaken place like this Henderson?" his wealthy friends had asked him once he'd explained what and where it was. "Why not go to Maui, or the Bahamas? You say there's nothing on Henderson but birds, and you're not a birder."

That much was true. Chase Rontgern did not collect bird sightings. Nor was he an especially avid scuba diver. What he did collect was money, and at that he was very good.

For more than two years he had been researching the history of ships that had gone missing in Henderson's vicinity. Ships that had been blown off course, or had become lost due to navigational error, or had simply foundered in storms. Vessels that disappeared in this part of the Pacific well and truly vanished. No ship that encountered trouble in the azure wasteland could expect help.

Since leaving Mangareva they had seen exactly one other vessel; a big container ship heading for Cape Horn. Most commercial traffic bound from the South Pacific for the Atlantic took the easier, much faster route north to the Panama Canal. As for fishing boats, there were no long-liners here, no purse seiners, because as Captain Santos had pointed out, there were no fish. There were no fish because there was nothing for them to eat. Concerning bottom trawlers—the bottom was three or four kilometers down and unknown. Too deep to trawl safely for too little potential reward for a big dragliner to take the risk.

When Henderson itself finally hove into view days later its appearance was something of an anticlimax. Rontgern was not disillusioned. The reality matched the few pictures he had been able to find of the place. Unlike Bora Bora or Rarotonga, Pacific islands that boasted dramatic central peaks and gleaming turquoise lagoons, Henderson was a makatea island. Several others were scattered around the Pacific; huge blocks of limestone and coral that had been uplifted and exposed to the air when the sea levels had fallen during the last ice age. Not only were they usually devoid of beaches, a visitor could not even walk very easily on a makatea. Rain eroded the limestone into razor-sharp, boot-slicing, flesh-shearing blades and pinnacles of solid rock.

As opposed to animals and humans, certain well-adapted birds and vegetation thrived in the otherwise hostile makatea environment. Shearwaters and noddys, petrels and four species of endemics made their home on Henderson. Its only regular human visitors were Pitcairners who came once or twice a year to collect valuable hardwood like miro for the carvings that constituted a substantial part of their income. Other than that, Henderson had been left to the birds, the crabs, a few lizards, and the ubiquitous Polynesian rat. Except for one rumored spring visible only on the single narrow beach at low tide there was not even any fresh water to be had. Not a good place, Rontgern reflected, on which to be marooned.

But then, he was not interested in spending time on Henderson, however wildly attractive the place might be to the rare visiting scientist.

It was a photograph that had finally brought him to this, one of the most isolated tropical islands on Earth. It was the same photograph that had led him to charter the *Repera* and its somewhat taciturn but efficient crew. His cultivated friends in New York had been right about one thing: no one anywhere much wanted to go to Henderson. It had taken him months, a lot of searching on the net, and an extensive exchange of querulous emails before he found a captain with a ship willing to travel so far from the bounds of civilization, to waters where no help could be expected in the event of trouble, no passing ship could be hailed for assistance, and there was nothing to see and no one to visit. Happily, in the course of their exchange of emails Salvatore Santos had not pressed his prospective employer for a trip rationale. All that had been necessary was to agree on a price.

Henderson slid past astern, its stark white thirty-meter high cliffs gleaming like chalk in the sun, its population of seabirds forming a flat, hazy gray cloud above the trees as they cherished the one bit of dry land for hundreds of kilometers in every direction. The island was still in view astern when Rontgern checked his GPS one more time, turned to the Captain, and declared with confidence, "This is the place."

Looking up from the wheel and his bridge instruments, the unshaven Portuguese-Tahitian squinted at his employer. "Here?" He waved a sun-cured hand at the surrounding sea, which obligingly had subsided almost to a flat calm. "You want to drop anchor *here*?"

Rontgern smirked. He knew something the Captain didn't know. If his two years of painstaking research was right, he knew something *nobody* else knew. With the possible exception of the bored astronaut on board the space shuttle who had taken the photograph that the energetic Rontgern had scanned in more detail than anyone at NOAA or NASA.

"Check your depth finder."

Santos had not bothered to look at that particular readout since leaving Pitcairn. The ocean out here was benthonic, and even this close to Henderson it dropped off sharply into the abyss. Under the circumstances, the Captain showed remarkable aplomb as he checked the relevant monitor and reported.

"What do you know? There is an uneven but largely flat surface thirty meters directly below us. I am assuming it is a seamount. It is very small and at a depth that renders it harmless to passing ships, of which there are not any around here anyway. So it not surprising it is absent from the charts."

"It's not all that small." Having looked forward for so long to springing this knowledge on someone else, Rontgern found that he was enjoying himself immensely. "Not just a seamount."

Santos eyed him uncertainly. Out of the corner of an eye Rontgern could see several members of the half-dozen strong crew watching the two men from the deck. The Captain finally smiled.

"Ah, I understand now. You are a crazy man. I knew that when you hired me and my boat to bring you all this way. But that didn't bother me. A man can be as crazy as he like, so long as his money is sane."

Kneeling, Rontgern opened the small watertight Pelican case that occupied a compartment on the bridge near his feet. It contained none of the expensive camera gear it was designed to coddle and protect. Instead, it was full of envelopes, flash drives, and a laptop computer. Selecting and unsealing one of the envelopes, he removed several glossy 8x10 prints and handed the top one to Santos.

"Have a look at this."

The Captain examined the photo with fresh interest. "Henderson," he observed immediately. "Taken from space. View slightly from the south. Even with the clouds, you can't mistake the shape."

"Very good." Rontgern handed him the next picture.

Studying it, Santos frowned. "Henderson again, much closer view." He tapped the picture with a forefinger. "Here; the water is so clear, you can see a suggestion of the seamount we are over right now."

Rontgern repressed a knowing smirk as he passed over the third and last picture. "That last one was a blowup, multiple magnification. Here's a much better one, with the resolution computer and radar-enhanced and corrected for depth, shadow, atmospheric distortion, and other obscuring factors I needn't go into in detail."

Santos studied the picture. Looked at it for a long time. Then he handed it back to its owner. "I still think it is nothing but a seamount."

"Seamounts have broken crowns. Or they're conical in shape. Or capped with solidified lava, or they sport a sunken lagoon." He gestured with the photo. "This one is as flat on top as a Los Angeles parking lot. Except for the bumps. Bumps with very distinctive shapes."

A corner of the Captain's mouth twitched slightly upward. "You think it is a parking lot?"

Rontgern had to laugh. "I'm not crazy, Salvatore, despite what you might think. Those 'bumps' are ships that have gone down here. At least four, maybe as many as ten. Maybe more than that, once we get down there. Two of the four are definitely pre-nineteenth century. You know what that means? Maybe treasure galleons that were sailing back to Spain from the Philippines. Trying to sneak around the Horn instead of sailing to Peru or Panama along routes that were haunted by English privateers like Drake. Before they could reach the Horn they got lost, or slammed into Henderson's rocks. Most went down to the depths. But a few," and again he tapped the photo, "a few fetched up here. At a depth reachable with nothing more elaborate than conventional sport diving equipment." He stared hard as he slipped the pictures back into the envelope. "Put down the anchor."

Santos hesitated a moment longer. Then he shrugged. "It your money, Mr Rontgern. You may be right. There may be a ship or two down there. But I no think there any treasure. And even if there is, anything we might find belongs to the British government. Henderson is part of the Pitcairn British Overseas Territory."

"That's absolutely correct." With slow deliberation, Rontgern returned the envelope to the watertight case. "And you can see for yourself how well this part of that territory is policed. Should we find anything we'll declare it immediately when we return to Mangareva. I'm sure you will be the first to go out of your way to inform the British consul in Papeete about any discoveries we may make."

The Captain pursed his lips. To Rontgern they almost seemed to be moving slowly in and out, in and out, in concert with the Captain's thoughts. Finally Santos smiled; a broad, wide smile.

Rontgern nodded curtly. He had gambled on just such a reaction. As soon as he had met Santos, he knew it was not much of a gamble. "We understand each other, I think."

"Perfectly, Mr Rontgern. I will tell Bartolomeo to start readying the scuba gear."

The water was not just clear: in the absence of microscopic pelagic life and located thousands of kilometers from the nearest source of pollutants, it was virtually transparent. As soon as he hit the water and started down, Rontgern felt as if he were diving in air. The only sound following his entry was the regularity of his respiration and the sporadic mutter of bubbles from the regulator.

As for the questions that had brought him to this isolated corner of the planet, they were answered as soon as he entered the water.

Just by looking down and without the aid of any special equipment he could see the outlines of sunken ships resting atop the seamount thirty meters below. Not only could he see the ships, the water was so clear that he could identify each vessel's type, condition, approximate age, and a host of other informative factors. Twisting as he slowly descended fins first, he located Santos and gave him the thumbs-up sign. His hair drifting lazily behind him like black seaweed, the Captain nodded and responded in kind.

Inclining his head and body downward, an excited Rontgern accelerated his descent.

Inner exploration of the various shipwrecks and the actual search for treasure and other valuables would take place on future dives, with additional equipment. A thirty-meter descent would require a proper surface interval before the next dive. No matter. Now that his research had been confirmed, he found that he was not impatient. After all, it was not as if they were likely to be interrupted by other divers in the course of their salvage work during the next couple of weeks.

They would remove the most valuable items first, hide them in the *Repera's* ballast lockers and elsewhere on the ketch, unload the prizes at night onto the private plane he would charter at Mangareva, and then return here for more. He was not worried about parceling out shares. There should be sufficient booty for all, and he would see to it that enough went to the crew of the ketch so that any notion of, say, tossing him overboard and keeping it all for themselves did not have any reason to get a grip on their thoughts. Besides, he knew more about this place than did any of them. He might know more than they could see. Unless they were utterly stupid, they would want to keep him alive in order to make use of that knowledge.

He was elated to see that there were not two but three galleons—and one ship that despite its state of advanced decrepitude looked decidedly Chinese. A load of Ming porcelain—now that would be a treasure indeed! As for the other, more recent shipwrecks, they could hold all manner of lucrative cargo. But it was the prospect of finding older vessels that had drawn him here, and it was those antique craft that understandably now captured the greater part of his interest.

One galleon in particular seemed to be in much better shape than the others. Unfortunately, it teetered on the steep-sided edge of the seamount. Even at this depth there was the danger that a particularly strong storm surge might send it toppling over into unreachable depths. He reassured himself that since it had laid thus for hundreds of years he was probably worrying unnecessarily. Signaling to Santos and to the other diver who was accompanying them, he finned off in the direction of the precariously balanced vessel.

It would be all right, he saw as he began to circle it. Its position was more stable than he had first surmised. Though lying at a sharp angle on its port side, the keel was jammed firmly against a long, narrow ridge of rock that protruded from the top of the seamount. Swimming parallel to the bottom, he swam from the bow toward the stern. Off to his right the ocean dropped away to cold, dark depths unknown.

Strange rock formation, he decided. It almost looked as if it could have been carved. That was impossible, of course. It was simply a natural limestone or lava ridge that had eroded away to form an unusually straight bulwark atop the rest of the underlying rock. He remained convinced of that until he reached the stern of the galleon. Hovering there, he was able to read the name below the great cabin: *Santa Isabella de Castillo*. Researching that name once he was back on dry land would likely tell him the ship's history and the cargo she had been carrying on her last, ill-fated voyage.

Something else at the stern caught his eye. More rock, mounded up to form a V-shaped fissure. The stern of the galleon had been wedged directly into this crevice.

How could that have happened, he wondered? It seemed too perfect, too unnaturally precise a fit to be a consequence of the unruly action of wind and wave and current. Still, it was not an impossible coincidence. Storm-driven sub-surface currents could certainly have slammed the ship hard into such a pocket of waiting rock.

It was when he saw the second galleon, and soon afterward the first steamship, jammed stern-first into exactly identical crevices that his thoughts began wandering to places that had nothing to do with treasure salvage, archeology, or the conventional history of South Pacific exploration.

Spinning around in the water, he saw that Santos had come up very close behind him. Gesturing at the third wedged ship, Rontgern formed a vee-shape with his hands, gestured at the vessel, and pushed his chin toward the vee. Santos nodded to show that he immediately grasped what the other man was striving to convey. By way of further response he gestured downward, over the side of the seamount, and indicated that Rontgern should follow. Thoughts churning, the bemused entrepreneur started to comply, but a check of his air dissuaded him. They had been exploring at depth for a substantial period of time. He had just enough air left in his tank to manage a proper slow, safe ascent coupled with a conservative safety stop at five meters.

Hovering over the side of the seamount, however, Santos kept gesturing for Rontgern to follow him downward. Rontgern shook his head. No doubt a better, more experienced diver than the Manhattan-bound entrepreneur, the Captain would naturally have used less air and would have more remaining, as would the deckhand who accompanied them. A cautious Rontgern saw that the other man was excited. Reluctantly, he kicked away from the stern of the sunken steamship and followed the Portuguese to the edge, wondering what was so important that the Captain felt the need to emphasize it so close to the end of the first of what would be many dives.

Instead of pausing to wait for him, Captain and crewman promptly lowered their heads—and started to swim straight down.

Rontgern immediately held back. What was wrong with them? Were they suffering from a combination of exhilaration and nitrogen narcosis? Had they lost their bearings, control of their senses? He hovered in open water at the edge of the seamount as the two divers continued their rapid and inexplicable descent. If they went much deeper they would find themselves in real danger no matter how much air they had left.

That was when Rontgern saw that something was coming *up* out of the abyss.

At first he thought his eyes were playing tricks on him. It was no stretch of the imagination to envision something like that occurring at this depth, even in absolutely clear water. Weaving and working its way downward, unobstructed sunlight wove lazily intertwining patterns in the open water column. As Rontgern stared, wide-eyed, some of the patterns began to darken. Each rising shape slowly became something solid. Each was individually as big as the sunken steamship. Independent of the light that illuminated them, they writhed and twisted and coiled expectantly in the transparent, pellucid liquid. Splotches and dark streaks grew visible on the side of each . . .

Tentacle.

Expelling bubbles in a violent, explosive stream, Rontgern started kicking for the surface. Santos and his companion were forgotten. If luck held, their presence might be enough to divert the ascending monster away from Rontgern. *Architeuthis*, he thought wildly as he swam for the surface. Giant squid. Or perhaps the fabled Colossal squid, slithered up from the Antarctic to graze on passing whales. Rontgern kicked as he had never kicked in his life.

He had no choice but to pause at five meters and decompress. If he did not outgas the nitrogen bubbles that had accumulated in his bloodstream, the bends would kill him as surely and as painfully as any sea monster. He forced himself not to look down, not to seek for what even now might be reaching up for him. If it came for him, better that his last conscious view was not one of hooked, flesh-ripping suckers and sharp slicing beak. Taken by the kraken, he thought wildly. What an end for a wily double-dealer from New York.

He did, however, have to periodically check his dive computer. Three minutes left on the safety stop—then two. Was it possible for a man to sweat underwater? He fought back the urge to cut short the decompress time and shoot for the surface early.

Only seconds left to go now . . . .

He did not so much pop out of the water as breach. Flailing and kicking, he made it to the side of the ketch in minutes. Hands were waiting to take his weighted buoyancy compensator and tank and haul him out after them. Gasping for air, he collapsed on the warm, worn teak deck. Then it occurred to him: what if the monster came up after the boat itself? Though he had not seen its body, judging from the length of those monstrous tentacles alone it was more than big enough to drag the ketch down to its doom, like some lost, forlorn ship in an ancient Spanish woodcut.

Rushing to the side, he peered hesitantly over the gunwale just in time to see emerging from the water right where he had come up—the Captain, and his deckhand. Of the monster there was no sign.

He was there when the crew helped Santos onto the deck. Sucking in fresh, uncompressed air, the Captain looked perfectly unfazed. A bewildered Rontgern found himself wondering if they really had encountered anything more substantial down there other than a trick of light and water.

"Did you see it?" he stammered. "Did either of you *see* it?"

"Of course we saw it." With the help of a crewman Santos started to peel himself out of his wetsuit. "What do you think I was pointing out to you?"

So perfunctory was this response that Rontgern found himself momentarily at a loss for words. "You mean, you saw that monster and you deliberately swam *toward* it? And beckoned for me to join you?"

Santos was stepping out of the suit now and left standing in his Speedos. When a crewmember offered a towel, the Captain waved it off. The sun would dry him.

"Beautiful, wasn't He?"

"*Beautiful?*" A stunned Rontgern could only gape. "I don't know, I didn't see more than the arms, and I didn't hang around long enough to . . . .." He paused in mid-sentence. His brow creased. "What do you mean, 'he'?"

"The Great Old One. He who waits dreaming. Only when rarely disturbed does He rise, and then usually only for a few precious moments." The Captain's eyes glittered. "You should have followed. You would have been privy to a sight accorded so very few. I have to thank you, Mr Rontgern. It is expensive to bring my people here to pay homage. We would have come another time anyway, but you have paid for that and more, and for that I thank you."

"Visit? Your 'people'? What the hell are you blithering on about?"

"We come here sometimes," Santos told him. "To pray. Others have come before us, and others will come after us." He gestured over the side. "They are down there, believers and unbelievers together. Sacrifices to Him who is Lord of the sunken city. No one else comes here. Few ships pass over this part of the southern ocean. There is no oil. There is no tuna. He is safe there in His House, dreaming the dead, until the time comes when He shall rise again."

The Captain ceased the drivel. But though no more words emerged from his mouth, his lips continued to move in and out, in and out, as they had on one or two previous occasions. The curious habit reminded a suddenly startled Rontgern of a breathing fish. He started to back away. But there was nowhere to back away to, there on the deck of the sunstruck ketch in the middle of the great empty southern ocean.

"If you were coming anyway," he stammered, "then why did you want to risk bringing me along? I'm not part of your stupid cult, whatever it is. Not that I care. I'm only interested in the ships that are down there and their contents. You can worship your big squid god or whatever it is all you want. I'll even contribute an appropriate offering, if that will make you feel better about working on this site."

"A further offering on your part is not necessary," Santos burbled softly. "That is for His disciples to provide, at a later and appropriate time. But we are glad you are with us nonetheless."

The rest of the crew was closing in now, Rontgern saw. So quietly that he hadn't noticed. Like a shoal of sharks. Their lips began to pulse in and out, in and out, in a whispered, concerted, croaking chant, forming words in a language he did not recognize. For the first time in his adult life he was suddenly very, very scared. If only he had not been so confident in his own abilities to dominate others, if only he had taken more time to check out the credentials of the ship and its crew.

If only someone had bothered to tell him that *repera* means "leper" in the Tahitian language.

"If you don't want me to make an offering and you're not going to make one yourselves, then why do you care that I'm here with you?" he mumbled.

One of the crew, streaked and sweaty, was very close to him now. It struck Rontgern forcefully that the man smelled strongly of fish. No, that wasn't quite right. He corrected himself. The man smelled fishy.

Santos was smiling at him again. A wide smile. Too wide, in fact, for a face that Rontgern could now see was not entirely human.

"As you know, it a long way here from Mangareva, and a long way back, and we all of us get so very, very tired of whole trip eat nothing but seafood."

THE ISLE OF DREAMS

BY *CHARLES P. ZAGLANIS*

August 8th, 1799. Somewhere near 47° 9' S, 126° 42' W in the southern Pacific Ocean.

FIRST LIEUTENANT THOMAS SOLOMON woke from an uneasy slumber. Unable to recall what had frightened him, but too nervous to return to sleep, Thomas dressed and strode onto the deck of the 44 gun privateer *HMS Relentless*. As he emerged, a warm salty gale—the same that urged the ship forward at top speeds—threatened to strip the hat from his crown and expose long brown hair to the elements. Thomas tucked the tri-corned hat in the crook of his arm and surged forward with the gust. Ahead, the ruddy-faced fourteen year old Second Lieutenant stood next to the helmsman, barking orders like a seasoned master.

"I wish this little breeze were at our backs when we'd left home, Mr Samualson."

"I agree," Harry replied. "We could've cut our travel short by six months at least, sir." The lad did a marvelous job of hiding the full-bodied grin a boy his age should possess; only a shadow of it played at his lips. Otherwise, his delivery was as stolid as any old salt's.

Thomas cast about the vessel, taking in the barefoot sailors scurrying about the deck and rigging. Ants on a cadaver. He did a quick head count and noticed a discrepancy. "I see you roused some of the dogs from their kennel."

"That I did, sir. T'was too much wind for my skeletal crew to handle on our own. I trust ye'll notice I chose the worst of the layabouts and bellyachers for this chore?"

"Yes, Mr Samualson, I did. It's for the best, I'm sure; they were starting to get fat and sassy."

Thomas couldn't help but smile. There was no such thing as a lazy sailor on a proper English vessel, nor was rumor mongering tolerated; the tender mercies of nautical discipline saw to that. There were men, however, mostly those brought aboard by the indelicate invitation of a "press gang" who needed a bit more stick than carrot to be motivated. Normally a bit of pressure from the crew, perhaps a kiss or two from the lash, and such folk performed as well as they could get away with. For the others—well, the sea and those who sailed her were not known as the coddling sort.

A blustery wind grabbed the frigate with an angry hand, shaking it until the seamen grasped the rigging. Taken by surprise, two men dangled from the ropes, gripped by fellow crewmen.

"Ye'll mind your footing if ye plan ta see yer wives and whores, ye dogs," shouted Harry, waving his hat for attention.

"I don't like these seas, sir," Harry said to his superior in a conspiratorial tone. "I've never heard a good word—though many a bad one—about them. There'll be a cracked brain before we're clear o' this gust, mark me."

Thomas looked toward the sky, trying to think of words to comfort the younger officer and perhaps find some to quiet his own misgivings about their voyage. He had heard the stories of ships gone missing or found adrift and filled with spoils without a crewman aboard. They were far from the normal haunts of their typical prey, the French navy, on a mission whose importance only the Captain knew.

Captain Rogers' successes, his generosity with French spoils, were near legendary; the man's reputation was what drove Thomas to seek out the Captain when word spread he was putting to sea again. When he told his crew they'd be gone for two years or more, but they'd all return rich men, they kissed their lady loves goodbye and signed on. The Captain neglected to tell them they would be sailing uncharted waters where rumors whispered that Death itself kept hearth and home.

A sliver of the moon peered from the firmament as though fearing to peek on the benighted souls below. Not a star pierced the sky's black raiment, nor a cloud offered hope of sweet summer rain to refill the empty barrels now rolling about the deck. Two days ago the grog had taken on a poisonous taste, what was left of the water was under strict rationing. Thomas swore at least once a day that this would be his only voyage with this ill-fated vessel.

"Squalls such as this have a way of dying as suddenly as they begin. These are good men, most of them anyway; I'm confident you'll get them through until morning."

Harry's thin fingers began drumming a staccato beat on his hat as he spoke. "I appreciate ye'r confidence, sir. To be quite honest, 's not just the tales nor the wind that be botherin' me really," the young officer's voice became so low it barely carried on the wind to Thomas's ears, "*it's the boy.*"

Startled, Thomas snapped at the red haired young man. "Second Lieutenant Samualson, I hope for your sake you are not putting any truck in the superstitious fancies of a few ignorant sailors."

Harry's eyes bulged and his body went rigid as if he'd already been dealt the first stripe from the Captain's knotted lash.

"N-n-oo, sir! Not at all, sir!"

Having garnered the young man's attention, Thomas directed him to a more isolated part of the deck with a nod before walking there himself and softening his tone.

"Now then, Mr Samualson, please enlighten me. What could a nine year old boy, the Captain's only son I might add, possibly do to foster alarm in the youngest officer I've been privileged to serve with? Especially within earshot of men who might wish to see blood shed on the decks just to relieve their boredom." Thomas let his gaze trail to the helmsman fighting with the wheel.

"Sorry, sir, I forgot m'self for a moment." The young man took in a large breath and expelled it in a huff. "Jonas scampered out here, about ten o'clock if that moon's t'be trusted, an' plopped himself down on those steps, muttering the whole time in that queer way o' his." Harry pointed toward the starboard stairs leading up to the stern of the ship.

"It's not unusual for him to give his father the slip and come watch the stars. Was he rattling off numbers again?"

"Yes, sir, he was, but . . . he fascinates me, sir, I'll not lie about it. I got as close as I could and I heard him say, 'How do they dream if they've never lived? Seven thirteen. Deep down deep, deep down deep. The servants of the dead, they never sleep, but they do eat. The servants of the dead priest learned hunger from their masters. Where did I hide that wind? We'll never escape if I can't find my wind.' And as quick as ye please, this gale started. I had the lads unfurl all the masts to catch every bit of it. The boy has me scared Scratch hi'self is after us."

"I doubt that, lad. Some say the Lord blessed young Jonas with a powerful mind for maths and navigation, but He saw fit to addle the boy as well. If so, then truly He works in mysterious ways." Thomas let out a snort at such fancies; he'd long ago lost faith in his Creator.

"Jonas may not show it, but he takes in everything around him. I've heard him repeat whole conversations from two weeks prior verbatim. Some say he knows where the French ships will be because he's blessed with 'The Sight,' others that he's driven by demons. I think he just listens to reports of ship movements and forms intuitive deductions. I also think he's more than a little lucky."

Thomas straightened his topcoat and laid a reassuring hand on Harry's shoulder as he said, "Well then, I'd best steer Jonas back to his cabin, idle hands and all."

He proceeded up the steps to the deck above the officer's quarters and passed by the skylight leading to Captain Rogers' bedroom. Gibbous flame produced by the Captain's whale oil lamp barely threw a glow against the glass. Beyond, Jonas' wan body leaned halfway over the gunwale. Thomas wondered whether the child watched the wake of the ship or contemplated throwing himself to the sharks that invariably followed any vessel that produced garbage.

Determining how close or for how long one could be around Jonas was a daily exercise, since he had bad days and somewhat better ones. Thomas had learned to read the boy's involuntary quirks like it was another language in his repertoire. Ever since that bloody bit of business with Malone, the boy stomached the lieutenant more than anyone save his father. For that reason perhaps Thomas was able to get close enough to the boy to hear his hushed words.

"Eighty feet . . . seventy feet . . . sixty feet . . ."

It's obvious the boy is counting off distances, but to what? The officer wondered, *there's nothing that close behind us—perhaps below?* Looking down, he saw a faint glowing ring become gradually brighter as the water aft of the vessel grew increasingly agitated. Thomas reached out reflexively toward Jonas just as a huge whale burst from the water like a shot from a cannon. Thomas and the boy screamed as the giant made a horrendous sound. The beast's dinner plate eye, close enough that it could have been hit with a lead ball from a musket, was open wide and bulging grotesquely outward.

As the mighty leviathan tried to swim into the sky, several lightly luminescent-black tentacles, ridged with fanged maws where suckers should be, lashed out from the water, wrapping themselves around the whale. Whatever hell-birthed thing lay below the ocean, its strength was such that it effortlessly held the whale in the air as the flukes of the giant's tail thrashed the water. All the while, chattering mouths tore noisily at blubber and meat. A slick of blood and flesh pooled on the ocean's dark surface before the still living whale was dragged below the waves to its final fate mere seconds after its breach.

Water, blood, and offal surged over the railing in a wave, covering Thomas and Jonas. Behind them, an alarm bell signaled all hands to the deck while sailors scrambled from their roosts screaming and praying. Thomas cooed nonsensically at Jonas in an attempt to soothe the lad while he tried to think of what he'd tell the men. He was sure of only one thing—there'd be no sleep this night.

Bedlam reigned aboard the deck of the *Relentless*. Men who sailed valiantly into the face of Napoleonic cannon fire now alternately prayed to and cursed their Creator in the face of something He never made. Thomas saw lantern light flare to life through the mottled glass of the skylight. He was sure that young Harry was commanding the men to get back to their posts but his voice was carried to some faraway land by the fierce, salty gust at their backs. As he gingerly guided Jonas to the steps leading down to the main deck, Thomas only slipped once on a piece of wayward blubber to the tittering amusement of the boy.

Once on deck, Thomas added his voice to the commands of the younger officer, "Mind the rigging men, or fear will put us at the bottom of the sea! Nigel, trim the mizzen! Quit your crying, the lot of you, you sound like old widows!" The men, chastened by the officers' remarks and faced with the more immediate threat posed by the wind, began to ease back into their normal duties.

Suddenly, the door to the officers' quarters flew open with a bang and everyone on deck froze and stared as Captain Rogers, the scourge of the Napoleonic navy, strode out of the darkness with his knotted leather knittle in hand and a storm in his eyes. The roaring wind hushed as it died down to a more manageable gust, as if it feared that which stomped out onto the main deck. Rogers had taken on a hungry, feral look as the voyage progressed; his uniform hung on his emaciated frame like a loose sail on a mainmast; his hair was a wild thing that knew no comb or wig. Always before, it was the French navy who feared his coming. He'd garnered a reputation of always appearing when a ship was least capable of defending itself; but of late it was his own crew whose stomachs grew sour when his grim visage stalked the decks.

The Captain was about to bellow out a command when he stopped short and picked up a chunk of blubber instead. Looking back, he took note of the water-soaked stairs leading down from the upper deck to the helm, a little boy standing between shadowy patches darker than seawater. Wonder visibly shifted back to anger; with a clawed gesture Captain Rogers summoned his youngest officer to his side.

"Come here Lieutenant Samualson, I would have a word."

Harry blanched and looked quickly to Thomas, who thought for a moment that the boy was going to bolt over the side and take his chances with the strange fish in this cursed speck of ocean. But instead, he shuffled forward, eyes averted and head down, to give a report as best he could. He looked to be composing his thoughts when Captain Rogers clouted him on the side of the head with the handle of his knittle, driving Harry to the deck.

Warm blood mixed with cold near the helm as the Captain straddled the lad, repeatedly screaming "What have you done to my ship?"

A knot sprang up next to Harry's left eye—his hand slowly reached up to touch it and came away bloody. His teeth clicked together and he shivered as though cold. He seemed to concentrate on the Captain standing over him. Then, a nervous giggle escaped Harry's lips, a tittering laugh that evinced no grasp of his circumstances.

"Laugh at me, will you? Spit in my face after I took a chance and promoted you? Well, It's a hard lesson I'll teach you, you ungrateful bastard!" Spittle flew and teeth gnashed as Rogers unfurled the knittle in his right hand; the lash whose knots had tasted the blood of French and English alike.

Thomas had seen that look on the Captain's face before, enraged, pitiless and without remorse, when he had whipped Malone to death. The First Lieutenant ran forward waving his arms, trying desperately to get the Captain's attention as he yelled, "No Captain, he's just a boy!"

The knittle sang out, stopping a fly's wing short of Thomas's eye with a sharp *crack*, an image of fanged mouths gnashing along its length occupied Thomas for a moment as he heard the Captain speak.

"I'll suffer no mutiny aboard my ship Mr Solomon, so stay your ground. The day this 'boy' was made an officer aboard the *Relentless*, he became a man. If he can't comport himself well for a dressing down, then there's no place for him here."

Thomas took two steps back—he could see that the diversion had worked, the killing rage was suppressed . . . for now.

To everyone's surprise, including his own, Harrison Smith, the ship's surgeon, stepped up next to Thomas and said, "Sir, judging by the chatter of his teeth and his pallor, I'd say you've addled the young man right proper. With your permission, I'd like to take him below and tend to that cut. Some of the men told me that Lieutenant Solomon was there when this ruckus started. Perhaps he can provide answers to your satisfaction."

Perhaps noticing the throng of anxious faces staring at him for the first time, Rogers began rewinding his knittle. He gazed upon the bleeding young man at his feet, whose eyes roamed in their sockets without hint of purpose. Thomas saw a new expression slither painfully across the Captain's face. He wondered if Rogers felt the first sick pangs of remorse he'd allowed himself in quite some time. "You two men, quit your gawking and help Mr Smith with Samualson. I suggest the rest of you seek your rest, I promise it will be a busy day tomorrow."

Two men broke ranks with the mob and lifted Harry by his shoulders and knees. As they made their way to the stairs followed by Harrison, another man detached himself and spoke up, "Pardon, sir, but what shall we do about the kraken?"

"Kraken?" Rogers asked.

"Yes, sir. Me an' George," the sailor pointed to a man on his left, who looked uncomfortable at being singled out, "was up on the main yard checking for chafing when we spies this monster of a whale come leapin' out of the sea. I was about to tell George about a whaling vessel I'd worked once, when snaky arms wraps about the dumb beast and pulls it under."

Captain Rogers looked to Thomas, who returned a slight nod, then said, "Fascinating. Since we are not encircled by tentacles, it would appear that a whale is enough to stave off the beast's hunger. Mr Solomon, David here, as well as George and three men of your choosing, have volunteered to break out the holystones and clean this filth off my ship. When the Sun crests the yardarm, I want all the lines inspected for chafing. Tell the cook I want the last cock and hen, as well as any eggs, cooked for breakfast, at which I'll expect both you and Mr Samualson to join me."

Turning on his heel, the Captain strode over to Jonas, knelt down to his level, and lightly cupped a hand against the boy's cheek.

"Come to bed now my son, you've had enough adventure for one evening."

The boy started to lean into his father's hand, and then stopped short as a tremble rippled through him. Staring through the sailors, past the bowsprit, and beyond the horizon, Jonas murmured, "There'll be rain tomorrow . . . and a terrible storm."

Rogers kissed his son on the head and steered him toward the waiting dark.

"Lash those barrels back to the gunwales Mr Solomon; we'll be needing them to collect water tomorrow."

"Aye, aye, sir," Thomas said, trying to absorb all that he had witnessed this night. He felt his mind sailing through uncharted waters, or at least seas to which he'd burned the maps long ago. Pondering his lack of faith, he wondered if perhaps there were some higher power after all, and if so, what terrible designs it had for all of them.

Thomas dreams.

In his waking hours he dreads thinking about Malone, but in the night he has no control where his conscience sails. He knows he is dreaming because it starts the way this particular nightmare always does. Thomas stands next to the helmsman as young Harry flys out of the hold, tripping on the coaming to land at Thomas's feet.

The First Lieutenant lets out a guffaw welling up from his toes. Thomas's perspective swings from observer to participant without rhyme or reason, yet it feels as natural as walking and whistling. He stoops to help the midshipman to his feet; the boy will make a fine officer in a few years. He's about to offer a gentle reprimand about appearances and dignity, but the look on the boy's face chokes the words in the officer's throat.

"Jonas was wandering about below decks, sir, an' he woke up Lieutenant Malone, sir. I think Mr Malone's going to hurt him, sir!"

Thomas curses and leaps onto the steps, skipping every two until he hits the deck running. He hears Malone's bombastic voice carry back from the bow.

Malone is known as a devout man, though he tends to quote the bloodier bits of the *Old Testament* more than the "Love thy brother" passages. There is no love lost between the officers, not once the zealot figured out his superior's religious predilections. Malone has made it plain that atheists and Catholics are equally damned in the eyes of the Lord and little boys who act queerly, who seem able to "see things," are marked by Lucifer himself.

"Where is your cursed father taking us, you little witch? Are you sailing us to Hell?"

Thomas can barely make out a knot of men just aft of Harrison's quarters. He calls out, but no one turns to look. He surges through shadows broken only by sickly lanterns turned low to conserve oil. The hammocks swinging to and fro with the movement of the ship turn to gallows ropes slapping against him, foretelling doom.

The shadows pull at Thomas; they hunger for life and warm blood. The boy lets out a squawk—Thomas knows that Malone has him by the neck now—has him by the neck and he's starting to squeeze. The First Lieutenant roars and the shadows scuttle away. The men turn and part for his passage. Malone glowers at him, a belaying pin in one hand and a choking child in the other.

"So the Devil calls and his servant comes to save him," Malone sneers as the shadows add their hiss.

"Put the boy down or I swear I'll knot the rope from which you'll hang."

"Not bloody likely, heathen," Malone spits as he lets go of the sputtering child. He starts swinging his improvised club at Thomas's head. The crewmen push back against the hull to give the officers room. Silently, the shadows point out to Thomas that his opponent is the larger, hardier man.

The way is clear if Thomas chooses to run, but he stands his ground and feints with his adversary. They duck and weave in the dance of the mongoose and the cobra. Thomas gets caught up in a hammock as the ship lolls to starboard, throwing him to the ground.

Malone readies for a crushing blow to his enemy's skull as he and the shadows let out a laugh brimming with victory and hate. Thomas cannot tell who sounds the more ghoulish.

Thunder sounds in the hull and lightning flashes in the form of a lead ball, striking Malone's knee and bursting it. The leg bends in a way it shouldn't and Malone joins Thomas on the floor.

The shadows give way to darkness greater then themselves. Captain Rogers strides into view, smoking pistol in one hand, knotted knittle in the other. A respectful distance behind and to the left of the Captain lurks the helmsman, eyes slit in pleasure, wearing the manic smile of a hatter too long in the trade.

Rogers looks his son over, ordering, "Help Mr Solomon to his feet." A many armed thing lifts Thomas off the deck, holding him until he gets his footing.

Shark eyes, cold as the endless deep, bore into Thomas as the knittle is thrust into his hands.

"Ten lashes, Mr Solomon." A murmur goes up from the many-armed thing as Harrison finally manages to break free from his quarters.

"That's a death sentence, Captain," the surgeon cries out.

"Yes. Tie him to the capstan and call 'all hands.' Come Jonas."

Jonas wanders within a hair's breadth of touching Thomas as he walks by, and Thomas knows that something has changed between them. Rough hands drag the praying Malone into the light. Smeared blood marks his passage.

The bell tolls and men spring from every cranny to answer its call. The Captain begins an oratory about murder and discipline but Thomas is having trouble concentrating on it. He does not recognize his crewmates. Their faces run like wax and become jackals. The

Captain—composed entirely of darkness, save for eyes the color of a hunter's moon—orders Thomas to do his duty.

Thomas takes his place behind a praying Malone. The man, tied to a vertical wheel, doesn't ask for succor, but demands vengeance from his Lord instead. The lash sets to and a bloody welt appears on Malone's bare shoulders. The knittle urges Thomas to dig deeper into the man but he reins it back. Five lashes and the knotted whip tries harder to tear its victim apart with each blow. As the lash swings backward for another go, a steely claw snatches it away.

"He didn't spill soup on you, Mr Solomon; he tried to kill two of my crew." In the hands of the darkness, the knittle sings of pain and degradation and Malone adds his voice to the choir. Knots catch flesh and strip it from the bone. Malone stops breathing before the Captain gets to the tenth lash but it does its butcher's work anyway.

"Bring me the midshipman."

Harry is pushed to the fore. He turns fish belly white when he sees what's left of Malone.

"What's your name boy?" the Captain asks.

"Harold Samualson, sir."

"Well, it's Second Lieutenant Samualson now. I want this carcass heaved over the side without ceremony and I want this ship cleaned up. Do you understand?"

"Aye aye, sir."

The jackals voice their dissent, though none steps forth as their spokesman. The darkness that is Captain Rogers fixes his gaze upon them, saying, "Some of you may wish to entertain the idea of mutiny. If you have the stones, you're welcome to try, but you'll wish you'd suffered Malone's fate when I'm done with you. And, if you should somehow succeed, let me remind the lot of you that there'll be no one to navigate your way home. Grow rich as I promised and retire in the land of your fathers, or die on some foreign shore if you're lucky."

The darkness turns and strides away, son in tow, perhaps seeking solace within his cabin. What is left of Malone is pitched over the side, to the delight of the gray-finned vultures that swim behind, and no one says a word to mark his passing.

"Sir? We'll be expected at breakfast soon," Harry called out from the hallway as he knocked on Thomas' door.

"Come in, Harry. I'm decent."

Thomas swung out of his hammock in a practiced motion, fully dressed save for his coat and boots. He splashed some water on his face to freshen up as Harry shuffled in. Thomas gawked at the younger officer before catching himself. Young Samualson's temple played host to a massive goose egg stitched with cat gut. The skin around his eye was predominately purplish-black; however, other rainbow hues danced there as well. The orb itself was red as a wound, nearly as red as the eyes of Captain Rogers in Thomas' dream.

"Ach, no one can claim that Harrison is a seamstress, there'll be a scar there for sure. Perhaps it'll lend your face some much needed character."

"One can only hope, sir." Harry grinned, mostly using one side of his face, and said, "I wish I'd made a wager with ye about someone gettin' their brain cracked, though I'd no idea I'd be the lucky git."

"It's a hard way to earn a few shillings. How's the weather?" Thomas asked as he slipped into his boots and coat.

"Looks like rain. Looks like a lot of rain if ye be askin' me, sir."

"Really?" Thomas strolled out onto the deck, Harry in tow. He let fly a low whistle as he beheld the storm front they'd sailed into. Purplish black clouds hung low and pregnant, ready to break their water at any moment. Men scrambled to secure the rigging against the coming tempest; sails were only as strong as the weakest line holding them in place. The welcome smell of roast chicken wafted up from the hold below as Thomas heard Harry's stomach grumble.

"A spot of rain will do us just fine lad; perhaps some salted beef might fall from the sky and save us from starvation as well."

"It's not loaves and fishes, but it'd be sore welcome indeed, sir."

The officers turned back and meandered their way to Captain Rogers' cabin at the stern of the ship. They glanced at each other significantly, as if to say "Are you ready for this?" Then Thomas rapped upon the door.

Jonas let the officers in, his eyes cast toward the floor.

"That's a good lad Jonas; now close the door behind them, please," Rogers said.

The room was sumptuously decorated, or would have been if someone who cared were still there to see to things. Once rich tapestries hung from the walls accompanied by a large portrait of Captain Rogers, younger, more robust, and smiling. Seated next to him was a lovely woman with raven black locks and blue eyes. In her lap was a toddler who shared her delicate bone structure, but, oddly, possessed one sky blue eye and one as dark as fresh turned grave dirt. Thomas remembered hearing that the Captain's wife was named Elizabeth, that she'd passed away during the last voyage of this vessel. Large windows took up much of the stern; through them, the officers watched as storm clouds chased away the sun.

Captain Rogers sat at the end of a long table set to receive a meal. As often a host to charts, books, and letters, this morning the table was covered with a clean sheet, some wooden plates, silverware, mugs, a wine bottle, and a silver dome covered trestle.

Rogers motioned his officers over to the table. "Come, sit, you almost missed the first course."

Thomas took a seat on the Captain's left, while Harry sat next to Jonas on his right, looking thankful to have the boy between them. A strange, gamey smell hovered about the table, its origin the silver clad trestle. The Captain lifted the lid and revealed its inhabitant, a brownish-gray loaf of meat the length and width of a strong man's forearm. It lay smothered in a gelatinous glaze, surrounded by equally coated potatoes and onions. Harry covered his mouth as the sight and smell of the thing assailed him. Thomas swallowed his bile and asked, "What . . . is . . . it, sir?"

Arching an eyebrow as he answered, Captain Rogers replied, "Why, this is the whale you and Jonas met last night. Cook gathered up the meatier bits, rendered down the blubber and boiled the thing in the creature's own fat. He assured me it's an old family recipe from his mother's side; I believe they were Scandinavian." The Captain uncorked the wine and filled the four mugs, after which he cut off four thick grey slices of whale and set one on each plate, accompanied by potatoes and onions.

"Lord," Rogers intoned solemnly as all lowered heads, "we give thanks for this meal we are about to receive and humbly ask that you bless our voyage and all the men aboard this ship. Amen."

"If I may be so bold, sir; I wasn't aware that you were a man of deep faith," Thomas said, somewhat taken aback by the conviction in the Captain's voice; it seemed at odds with the living nightmare Thomas had come to be familiar with.

"There's much about me you don't know, Mr Solomon. It's my own fault, of course; I've held to my own counsel for the entire voyage. Unfortunately, it took the events of last night to make me see what a monster I've become." Rogers looked pointedly at Harry's stitches, causing the boy to blush. "To answer your question, Elizabeth had us lead each meal with prayer; I try to honor her memory by continuing to do so. Now let us sample this hearty repast Cook has labored to provide us."

While Thomas endeavored to saw through the tough meat, he noted that Harry merely moved his meal about the plate. The Captain stabbed at each piece like a carrion bird going for the eyes of some dead thing. Jonas, Thomas noticed, cut all his food into circles. Captain Rogers, seeing Thomas watch his son's plate, said, "You'll have to excuse Jonas his eccentricities, he doesn't like sharp angles; fears a dog might find its way through one or some such nonsense."

"They prowl through time, fallen and hungry," Jonas said to his meal somberly, making Harry visibly shudder

"I suppose that I too shall prowl hungrily if this filth is the best that Cook can do today and Mr Samualson even more so, seeing as how he won't even try his meat. At least Mr Solomon had the good grace to swallow a bite, though he looks a bit green from the effort."

"At least the wine's good, sir," Harry said weakly.

"That it is. One of the better reasons for killing Frenchmen. They are sure to have fine wine and food with them."

Thomas raised his mug and pushed his plate away, saying, "Then let's hope we never go to war with the Scandinavians."

Harry laughed as he and Captain Rogers repeated the first officer's toast. A knock sounded at the door. Cook entered with two men bearing the main course, roast chickens and hard boiled eggs; whereupon he was threatened with keelhauling if he tried to poison the officers again. Shaken, the cook and his helpers cleared away the first course and left as the remaining four tore shark-like into the more palatable meal before them. For some time, the only sound heard coming from the table was the occasional hum or moan of bliss.

After the food was cleared and the cook heartily congratulated, a fresh bottle was poured and talk sailed into more serious waters. Thomas noticed that the midnight clouds had finally overrun the sun. The horizon was naught but darkness, above and below. "Sir," he began, "can you tell us anything about where we are going?"

"We go to seek our fortune on the Island of Dreams."

Thomas looked at Harry who shrugged his ignorance in return. "We aren't familiar with this island you speak of, sir."

"I'd expect you wouldn't be, Mr Solomon, no civilized man alive is, except Jonas and I." Captain Rogers settled himself into his chair more comfortably, taking a long pull on his wine. The lambent glow from the lamps made queer shadow plays in the dark of the room. Rain began to tap on the windows with a steady insistence. In the distance, they could hear thunder roll across the face of the deep.

"I don't understand," said Thomas.

"No, I suppose not," said the Captain. He smiled grimly to himself, then leaned forward, pressing together the tips of his fingers. "Let me tell you what happened. It's not a long story, but . . .

"It was raining much like this, the night we caught the *Diligente*. She'd been at sea searching for pirates and privateers and made a good accounting for herself according to her log. Unfortunately for her, I had Jonas to tell me the when and where to strike her best. I'm no seventh son, nor is he, but he was born with a caul and he has the eyes of a seer. It was about midnight, darker than Lucifer's arsehole it was, when we spotted her lights and gave her our cannon. Our chain shot flew true, shredding her back stays. More than one unlucky crewman fell to our grapeshot. We dropped anchor, club hauled around, firing off a second salvo to good effect. I think it was that round that killed their captain. The slow-witted fools finally figured out what was happening and fired back, catching the rear of the *Relentless* . . . killing my sweet Elizabeth, though I didn't know it at the time."

"The *Diligente* was a much bigger ship, one hundred guns in all, but I'd cut off her head and wore her down under cover of darkness and storm. It was fortunate that no one aboard thought to douse her lights, but I guess they weren't thinking clearly with all the pandemonium. Personally, I believed the crew a bit quick to raise their white flag, but they were Frenchies after all and I suppose they realized I had them caught between the Devil and the deep blue sea and no pitch hot."

Rain rapped angrily on the window panes. Thunder, sounding like cannon fire, boomed close and the sky lit up with lightning strikes as the heavens made war with the sea. Captain Rogers picked up a sleeping Jonas, carrying him to his berth; then procured a golden pineapple from a chest. He set the statue on the table, and then took his seat, staring out the windows as he continued his tale.

"We freed the prisoners, finding Bloody Jack Watson among them. We'd served together in younger years and he'd made a name for himself as a captain. He sailed the *Diligente* home. I took on a quarter of the French prisoners and my choice of the spoils, among them a solid gold pineapple, the captain's log, and a battered book filled with strange writing."

"Once I found out what had happened to Elizabeth. Well . . ."

The Captain broke off here, his hand running over the pineapple. Thomas remembered the stories about how the ship had been brought in and the shape of the prisoners. Many had to be carried off and all evinced signs of torture and neglect. Rogers had been brought up on charges, but the Admiralty had been unwilling to act.

The Captain produced a pipe, packing it with strong tobacco. He lit it, a reddish hue coloring the man's face, giving it a devilish cast. Thomas looked out the windows behind him, seeing a sky that was a dark mirror of the ocean below. Bemused, he wondered if they weren't sailing along cloudstuff, in defiance of the laws of Nature. The room spun until he closed his eyes and focused on the Captain's voice.

"I interred Elizabeth in the family mausoleum and spent much of my time there. Jonas was fascinated by that gold pineapple. I'd come home and he would be sitting there, playing with that damned thing, turning it . . . turning it. He read the log and then set to the other book. As near as I can tell, Jonas sees everything in terms of math. He breaks down codes and ciphers like I read the King's English. The journal was written in coded Dutch, the nationality of the traders whose vessel the French came across. Bored and mostly sober, I listened as Jonas translated the book aloud, and coupled with the log from the French ship, discovered an interesting tale.

"These Dutch did a brisk trade with villages along the Western side of South America for coca leaves and such. After they left their last port o' call, their navigator took ill, then several crewmen joined him below decks. The men, still hale, did their best but they went hopelessly off course. A bit of foul weather was had and they found themselves a stone's throw from the island. Some of the lads went ashore looking for fruit and maybe a native girl to rut with. They came across fresh hoof prints that led them to a cascading waterfall pouring into a large pool. Drinking from the water was a milk white stallion with a spiraling antennae jutting from its crown and a beard fit to shame a billy goat."

Harry, feeling the effects of his wine, sputtered into his mug, "They saw a unicorn?"

"That's what they claim. The horse flicked its ears in their direction and ran off as the men stared after it. The sound of laughter, feminine laughter, washed over them from the other end of the pool. Several native girls lolled there, watching the sailors with frank bemusement. They say the women were not the squat, moon-faced savages they'd expected; indeed, the shortest amongst them was taller than the tallest of the Dutchmen. The women were long of limb and features, though not unpleasantly so, and they looked much like a Greek or Spanish lass, if she'd been stretched a bit. The islanders bore a fascination with the sailors' clothes, of which the women apparently wore none, and the men found the lasses quite accommodating to their needs.

"When the love-play was done, the women led the Dutchmen to their village. Instead of huts, they lived in columned homes like the old ruins in Athens, but more ornate. The men and women of the village greeted the sailors as long lost brothers might. There were feasts and revels. There was singing, and not a sailor's eye was left dry for the beauty of the song. The village's men folk were proportionate in size to their women as we are to ours and shared their strange, yet handsome, features. They too were fascinated by the sailors' clothing, which it had never occurred to them to make. Apparently, the savages regarded both men and women as equals, each performing tasks to which he or she was most suited.

"The captain was fetched, as well as some samples of trade goods. After enjoying the tribe's hospitality, the Dutchman made clear to them his remorse that they had nothing of tangible value to trade with him. A girl of no more than seven years brought the captain a lush pineapple, but he sadly shook his head. Then the child laid hands upon the fruit and her eyes fluttered as the thing turned to solid gold. The villagers were able to express that they used their dreams to change reality and they would teach this skill to their little brothers from across the sea if they would bring them back clothes that fit them. The captain readily agreed and set course for home, laying out the path back as near as he could figure it and coding it into his journal. The French found the ship derelict and took the cargo that was still salvageable. The book and pineapple were an oddity to be examined by the captain at his leisure."

"Preposterous!" Thomas cried out, his tongue loosened by drink. "That's nothing but sea serpent and sirine tales."

"Perhaps, but last night we were nearly beset by a kraken, and there is the matter of this," Captain Rogers flicked the gold pineapple, which produced a dull thud. "It bears no seam or sign of flash. You can see every pore, every vein, and every natural imperfection. I am satisfied that this was once a living fruit."

"Be that as it may, sir," Thomas pressed, "you're already a rich man. Why risk it all on a missing Dutchman's tale of alchemy?"

"I'm not doing this for gold, though it'll be a well deserved reward to never have to kill a man for my pay. I wouldn't have poisoned the grog when I smelled mutiny if it was just for gold. The savages know how to shape dreams into reality, and I have but two dreams: to see my son grow to be a normal man of character and to have my Elizabeth by my side once more."

It was late afternoon when the island was spotted, though the ship nearly ran aground before the beach was seen due to the weather. The sky sobbed widow's tears, hard and fast, as Captain Rogers addressed the men below decks. Flanking him were his two officers while Jonas sat upon one of two barrels labeled "pitch" brought up from the hold at the Captain's insistence.

"You lot have been on a hell of a journey with me to this island and earned your keep the whole way." The crowd murmured its agreement. "And I intend to do right by you as well. I'll be leaving shortly; while I'm gone, I've decided to give you lads a much deserved reward. Mr Solomon, spike the mainbrace if you will."

"Aye, sir," Thomas said, producing a hammer and chisel and proceeding to remove the top from one of the barrels. Cheers erupted as those closest to the containers saw what sloshed within.

"Now, this isn't grog, lads; it's good Jamaican rum. There'll be plenty of hard work tomorrow, and comely lasses to kiss I'll warrant, so don't make me regret this come the morning, or I'll be certain to make *you* regret it. Mr Solomon has already spoken to a few of you about carrying trade goods to the village. I need this cask that Jonas is sitting on and one of the crates from the aft hold put in the starboard dingy. I'll be expecting you in ten minutes. I've put Mr Samualson in charge of the keg, No more than five cups to a man. If all goes according to plan, we'll wind up as rich as we've ever dreamed." Men raised their voices in impromptu song while others scrambled for tin cups. Thomas knew Harry would be fighting a losing battle.

Once topside, Thomas was soon soaked to the marrow with warm rain water. He leaned close to Captain Rogers and asked, "Do you think it wise to take Jonas with you?"

Rogers nodded, checked that his sword and pistol were in place. "The natives sounded friendly enough, more importantly, he demands to go, and if I don't take him then our navigator won't help us if we need to leave. He can be frustratingly stubborn that way." Rogers scurried down the rope ladder into the loaded boat and signaled the men to begin rowing to shore.

Despite the warmth, Thomas felt a momentary chill, and wondered if the Captain was making a terrible mistake

An hour inched by when Harry joined Thomas on the main deck. "I tried stopping 'em, sir, but they're too deep in their cups. I threatened ta seal the barrel an' they started asking about if there be a cabin boy aboard."

"Pay them no mind Harry. They shan't remember in the morning and they'll have the Devil's due to pay."

"Speakin' of the Captain, there be no sign of 'em?"

Thomas looked at the nearly empty hourglass resting on the steps. "No, but I don't know how deep into the jungle he has to travel to reach the village. I'll give it another two turns before I start feeling concerned."

"Do ye think there be any truth to what the Captain said, sir?"

Thomas saw birds scatter from the top of the canopy, no common occurrence in this foul weather, and he thought he detected movement in the brush closest to shore as he absently replied, "I believe the Captain believes it. To be honest, I almost hope he's wrong. If he's right, I'll have to change my whole outlook on things. Worse yet, so will the world."

Thomas pointed toward the beach, saying, "Do you see something moving there Harry?"

A man stumbled out of the jungle, staggering toward the water. He fell onto the sand as lightning smote a nearby tree, illuminating the figure in a background of flaming debris. The blaze allowed Thomas to identify him as the Captain.

Thomas ran to a rowboat and leapt in. "Lower me, then rouse what men you can, Harry. Back the ship off a fair distance. If I don't come back in an hour, form a proper search party and come looking for me at first light . . . and come ready to kill, Harry. If you see me wave my hat over the Captain, send some men to get him; otherwise, it's too late."

The trip through ebon waters went quicker than Thomas expected thanks to a swift current pushing him toward shore. Once there, it was obvious that Captain Rogers was beyond saving; many parts of him were shredded to the bone.

"What happened, sir? What did this to you? Where's your son?" Thomas asked.

Blood pooled and oozed out of Roger's mouth. Thomas could hear the Captain's lungs fight for air through a gash in the man's chest.

"Everyone . . . dead. Find . . . my boy . . . find . . . Jonas." Captain Rogers shuddered and wheezed through his pierced lung, then finally lay still.

Thomas took the man's sword and pistol, then padded into the jungle swearing an oath to recover his Captain's child. Woe to anything that interfered. A trail leading inland from the beach was found, as was a strange man-like skeleton. It lay roughly five feet long, adorned with small horns jutting from its skull as well as cloven goat hooves instead of feet. Near its hand lay a set of pan pipes lashed together with twine. The rest of the trek to the village was uneventful, though Thomas felt as if a malignant gaze watched and judged him at every turn.

Once reaching the village, Thomas found it was as the Dutchman had described it, though changed for the worse since his departure. Skeletons, long of limb and clothes-less, littered the ground like discarded fruit cores in London's open-air market. Nestled amongst this ghoulish fertilizer were red, raw strawberry patches of human flesh. Thomas called out Jonas' name as loud as he dared. On the third try, an answering cry came from an ornately chiseled cave mouth in a hill overlooking a short avenue.

Thomas ran up the hill, stopping at the cave mouth, shocked at the sight he beheld. Jonas sat stoking the embers of a small fire; while beside him lay the body of an elderly tribesman. Strange sigils were painted on the walls, floor, and ceiling in what Thomas hoped was red dye. "Come, Jonas, time to leave now." Thomas said as calmly as possible.

Jonas' gaze met Thomas' as he said in a robust voice, "Wonderful, Thomas, I'm quite ready to go."

The boy sprang to his feet and strolled forward smiling too widely for Thomas' taste. Leveling the pistol at the child's head, Thomas asked, "What have you done to Jonas?"

The smile slipped away as the child said, "I'll explain along the way, but we must leave now. The Messenger is here to fetch me back." A sound like all the cats in all the world fighting at once echoed out of the tree line. "He comes! We must run!"

Jonas ran sure-footed and strong; he neither panted nor wiped the rainwater from his eyes. In fact, Thomas began to suspect that the boy was holding back so that he could keep pace with the older man.

"I am one of the beings who dwell in Kaddath in the frozen wastes of the Dreamlands," The thing within Jonas said. "Throughout time your kind has worshipped us as gods, but we are kept and protected by terrible Outer Gods, of which our pursuer is the soul and messenger."

Trees broke and snapped behind them as something monstrously large crashed its way through the foliage. Thomas stumbled over roots and vines while his breath came in gasps and his heart felt like it twisted in his chest. Jonas slipped his hand into Thomas' and immediately the older man felt lighter and more vibrant.

"I grew tired of dancing at the behest of others. I attached myself to a powerful dreamer and awoke in the world of men. I grew to care for the people of this world. I taught them art and reason and beget children with them who grew up tall, strong, and fair as I did with the people of this island. The last time I escaped, the Messenger had me accused of crimes against the State and nailed to a tree. It amused him that the ones I'd come to help destroyed me."

The pair broke from the path and made directly for the beach. Behind them, trees snapped and rocks shattered beneath the bulk of the Cyclopean menace pursuing them. Thankfully, the trees kept them free from the worst of the storm.

"I don't understand, why jump ship from the old man to the boy? What do you want from us?" Thomas asked, his mind teetering on the edge of insanity due to the implications of what he'd heard.

"I'd preserved my host well beyond his allotted span, it was time to seek another. I have seen your world through Jonas's eyes; you need me as much as I need you. Take me to London with you. With enough dreamers I won't need a mortal body. I give you my word that I'll fix the boy and bring about a golden age for him to grow up in."

A chunk of tree shot past, smashing into a palm tree. The creature's breath was heavy with the stench of rot. Any moment now, Thomas knew they would be dismembered by a horror beyond comprehension.

"I agree to your terms," Thomas said. "Now let's hope we can get off this damned island."

As they reached the beach, the cacophony behind them became silent, and a black man—black of skin, hair, eyes, teeth, tongue, and anywhere else Thomas cared to look on the nude figure—stood between them and the boat, idly scratching a tiger behind the ear while it purred in pleasure.

"There can be no hope once I've set my gaze upon you, Thomas Michael Solomon," the Black Man said in a honeyed voice.

"The Messenger!" the thing in Jonas' body cried.

Thomas stared in wonderment, saying "But you were behind us and huge."

"I am chaos, worm. My form is mutable and unimportant; my intent is all that matters. I intend to bring the godling home." The tiger growled low in its throat.

"You killed my men and the villagers."

"Oh, I killed your men all right, and they were *delicious*; but I cannot take full responsibility for the villagers. It was mostly the Dutch traders' fault; they brought disease to the island. I just made sure they were exposed to it. I evened things for the villagers though; I made sure no Dutchmen lived to tell the tale."

"But you don't need me there. I'm just a source of trouble," the godling said.

"Actually, you're a source of amusement. If you were trouble, I'd strip your mind and set you to dancing in the Court of Azathoth. You and your brethren do a great service to reality when you dance." The Black Man spread his arms wide. "All of this, everything, including me, are the dreams of an idiot god. Should the flautists and the dancers ever fail to lull him into slumber he will waken fully and all will be wiped away."

"You cannot directly harm me, the rules of the covenant state . . ."

"You're right; I choose to follow the covenant. Do you see that man on the forecastle trying to make out what's going on through all this rain?" The Black Man asked without turning to look.

"No," Thomas replied.

Instantly the rain stopped. "Now?"

Richard saw Harry look up in wonder. Then a black and red bolt of lightning blasted from the sky, cooking the young man to the bone, then blasting his remains across the deck.

"Goddamn you! No!" Sick to his stomach and enraged beyond reason, Thomas pulled the Captain's pistol from his belt and fired it into the dark god's chest. The slug, report, even the recoil, were drawn into the creature. It was like Thomas had tried to shoot an empty gun.

"You would have been better served shooting the tiger. I am as far removed from the godling as he is from you, you never stood a chance."

Thomas sank to his knees and cried without shame. He couldn't believe such a fine life was cut down for no reason whatsoever. None of this made any sense to him.

"I'll go," the godling said.

"Oh, I don't know. I'm growing rather fond of this mudball. Perhaps I'll throw a massive tidal wave across an ocean or launch a plague." The Black Man laughed, obviously warming to the idea.

"Please, take me back home," the godling grated through

clenched teeth. "I want to dance to appease your master."

The Black Man nodded as a hole like an infected wound ripped open in the sky. Thomas felt glacial winds and looked up to see majestic Kaddath, home of the gods of Earth, its giant walls, minarets, and buttresses squatting upon a snow covered peak.

The godling laid a child's hand upon Thomas' crown and said, "I'm sorry about Harry and the others, Thomas, it was never my intent for anyone to get hurt. You need to screw up your courage and help Jonas find his way in life. He's my last gift to the world, take good care of him and yourself."

Jonas threw back his head and howled. Light in all its glory followed sound as it regurgitated out of the boy and fled back to its mountain home in the polar wastes of the land of dreams. When Jonas was finally spent, he wrapped his arms around the only human left alive on the island and sobbed like a normal child who'd lost everything, and perhaps gained more than anyone should.

And the Black Man left as he arrived, without a word, to sow chaos and reap despair in realities without number; and stave off, for a time at least, the end of all things.

ENSNARED

BY *PAUL MELNICZEK*

I STOOD ON THE REAR of our ship, the *Sea Queen,* my face stinging from the bite of an angry westerly wind as we churned on, making a last sweep with our huge fishing nets before embarking on the journey back to our home ports at *Redinburry Dock.* As long as I lived, I would always be in awe of the vastness of the seas and the mystery of their great secret deeps, a frontier that would never be conquered by men.

The past two days had been dreadfully barren of anything resembling a decent catch—it was as if the thriving vitality of the sea had been swallowed whole by some unknown blight, the normal schools of teeming fish eradicated or chased away. Captain Fleming stalked the wooden decks muttering epitaphs against every element known to mankind, blowing huge smoke rings from his West Indian long-pipe, his craggy face molded into a perpetual scowl.

The mates did everything they could to avoid him in his black mood, keeping busy with routine and creating additional labors just to maintain the facade of diligence. My duty was to oversee the trawling itself, and I was unable to separate my duties from the Captain's unceasing notice. On that last evening before our scheduled departure, I stared out at the vastness before me, mystified as to our unsuccess.

The breeze had picked up considerably, and it was clear that a sizable storm was brewing, as enormous dark thunderheads loomed in the distance, rolling across the heavens toward us with eager vaporish hands.

The first mate Riley was arguing with the Captain, the only man on the ship with the fortitude to do such, I might add. Their voices rose in disagreement a scant few yards behind me, and they were discussing the approaching weather, with Riley urging an immediate modification to our course, and the Captain pressing for one final swing with the nets.

"Damn it, man. You'll be looking for work in a cleaning house with this load. It has got to improve—I've never been witness to such a region of depravity as this."

I glanced backward at the Captain's bearded face, intensely scanning the oceans, the younger man at his side. Riley's face was almost boyish, with pepper-black hair and a normally infectious smile, now subdued and shadowed by his pale demeanor.

"I wish it were otherwise, Captain, but an ill wind blows our way—and I do not like the taste of these waters." Riley gripped the side railing, leaning over and gazing into the depths below.

"So, you feel it too?" Captain Fleming nodded, puffing from the cumbersome pipe. "In truth, it makes me uneasy as well. There are tales of such areas, where waters are but a cloak over ageless secrets hidden deep below the surface—things that are best left beyond the reach of men."

I wondered as to their musings, feeling disturbed at such talk, blaming it on superstitious sailor prattle, which all of us on the seas were guilty of to some degree. It is impossible to venture upon the unpredictable immensity of the earth's waters and not feel the awe, and give appropriate respect to that which is not fully understood. Tenuous is the life of seamen, granted the privilege of crossing the waves which can rise up in unrestrainable fury without notice.

Listening further to their discourse, I almost jumped my skin when a call bellowed forth from the men working the pulleys. I bounded down toward them, wondering if our fortune had finally pivoted, allowing us a worthy catch after all.

The nets were hauled back, and I then discovered the source of their excitement. It appeared that a significant resistance was being exerted against the levers, as if something of tremendous weight was caught in our nets. Shouting for help, I reached the foremost winches and signaled for more cautious action, unwilling to damage our equipment and make the precarious situation even worse.

Captain Fleming was already at my side, breathing heavily, with one large hand on my shoulder. "What is it, Harvis? Our long-awaited prize?"

"I don't know, Captain," I returned. "It seems we have snagged onto something, but a care must be made not to rip the netting."

The depth was unusually long, at the Captain's request, and I was curious as to what could have been resting at such distance to restrict our trawling. I was convinced it was not a large catch of fish, or even a whale. The nets were incredibly strong, and would haul in such creatures with little trouble.

"Perhaps we have latched onto some type of structure," I offered.

Captain Fleming gazed onward with a strange look in his eye, and for a moment I saw concern etched into the emerald-green orbs, but then it was gone. Riley joined us, speaking to some additional crewmen who now appeared to lend support.

"Again," I yelled. "Bring it in slowly—we'll see if it gives, and let's hope that we're not entangled on something that will fray the nets."

The sky above us grew preternaturally dark, and a few drops of rain smacked onto our heads. The air was cool, a brisk autumn chill, and I shivered beneath my hooded jacket. Riley stared upward with concern, but Fleming ignored the strengthening wind, his attention solely on the movement below. The levers moaned in protest, and I thought they would surely snap. After several tense moments, the nets again moved, although it was obvious that something of monumental weight was now ensnared in their trappings. Minutes crawled by agonizingly and we all waited to see the revelation of our catch.

Captain Fleming was silent, lost in the workings of his keen mind, and I pranced around making sure the supports were not cracking. Tension surrounded me at every angle, and we held our collective breath as the pulleys creaked in rotation.

Riley whispered in Fleming's ear, and with reluctance the Captain nodded and his first mate disappeared, calling a change of course at last. He questioned me several times on how much longer until the unknown catch would surface, and I informed him that it would be a while yet. All that time, the Captain stood unmoving—he could have been a carving himself, molded from the living wood of the ship.

I lost track of the minutes, concentrating on keeping our equipment from wearing down, but at last we came to the end of the net. The process had been deliberate and guarded, and now the last lengths were being drawn. Someone shouted an exclamation and the waters broke, revealing the top of the mysterious object at last.

At first, I believed that we had captured a huge piece of rock from the fathoms below, so vast was the structure that emerged before us, but my expression quickly changed to one of disbelieving awe. It was a statue, the hue a murky brown, as if from centuries of burial in muck, staining it permanently, coated with green slime and leeching crustaceans the like which dwelt at the lightless bottom of the ocean floor. Shouts of amazement uttered forth from the lips of the astonished crewmen, straining with every vestige of their might as I ordered ropes to be flung outward for greater leverage, if it were even possible to wrest the humungous bulk onto our vessel.

Captain Fleming's jaw gaped wide as he was lost for words, instead clutching at his chest, and I wondered if he suffered from a seizure of some sort.

The figurine now cleared the water, and I was stricken by the sight of the fantastic artifact being hoisted toward us. It was sculpted in the likeness of a monstrous creature, the head rounded and lacking eye sockets, attached only with a pair of granite stalks, which I took to represent feelers. The creature's chest was covered with plated scales, each section oval-shaped like a warrior's shield, two clawed appendages reaching outward as if to rend asunder the very world. Countless tentacles protruded from its ghastly trunk, like the arms of a nightmarish octopus, and folded wings rested on the capacious back.

I nearly swooned as the statue came nearer, for an abominable stench issued forth as if the thing had been uncovered from a pit filled with a thousand decaying carcasses, so foul was the odor. Several of the men stepped backward, gagging over the railing and falling to their knees, nauseous and sweating.

"What is this horrific creation?" I gasped. "From what diabolical nether region have we dredged such a monument? Surely, there is no culture known to man which gave rise to this abomination?"

The Captain seemed dazed and indecisive, and the wind blew

increasingly harsh, accompanied by heavier rainfall. A stocky form came into view, and I recognized the man to be Rolfus, a grizzled but unquestionably reliable seaman respected by all, notwithstanding even the Captain. His scarred face was marrow-white, and he looked sickly in the dim light.

"Cut it loose, Captain," he rasped, his voice coarse and low. "Drop it back down to the black depths from whence it came."

Fleming was about to answer when Riley returned, pounding his hands together. "Are you mad, Rolfus? Look at that specimen, it's incredible. Something this old is worth a fortune, man. Captain, we must secure the statue and return to port. This will fetch enough money for a dozen voyages. They can't deny you this."

The Captain licked his parched lips, and I sensed the inner struggle being waged within his mind. He actually feared the sculpture to some degree, but weighed the possibility of reward against this hesitation.

Rolfus stood directly before the other men, pleading with them to unfasten the netting. "Look at this monstrosity, can't you feel the evil in its creation, the intent of the makers? Whatever nameless city it came from was never meant to be touched by the hand of man. I beseech you, Captain, set it loose, before you bring misfortune down upon our heads."

I thought Fleming would concede, but his vision grew dark, and he finally spoke, looking sideways first at Riley, then at myself, as if daring us to contradict his unspoken decision.

"Tie it fast to the ship, and let us make haste. This storm rises up swiftly and we must depart the region. Rolfus, if you don't wish to gaze upon the statue then go beneath deck and find some other errand. Now leave me."

With that, he pivoted on his heel, stomping toward the midsection of the vessel and barking orders to the scattered crew. I turned my attention to the matter at hand, and watched as the statue was strewn with dozens of sturdy coils to maintain its balance so as not to plunge under the waters and become forever lost.

My own thoughts were shaken as I wondered as to the origin of the ancient figurine. I shuddered at the grotesque magnificence of the sculpture, a stone creation of colossal proportion and mass. Large as it was, I failed to comprehend the type of rock which gave it this weight, and I shook my head at such a feat. Worse yet, what fractured imagination lent sustenance to the making of the most hideous of caricatures, what tormented madness had enabled the creators to carve the creature? Was it a forbidden relic, as Rolfus had said, lifted from the Stygian depths far below the ocean surface, impossibly dredged from a resting slumber in a freakish stroke of luck from our fishing nets?

Images swam in my head then, of a cold, lifeless city, laying in ruins on the ocean floor, filled with vast towers of monolithic structures and crumbling buildings, shrine-havens to the frightful and enormous idols like the one we managed to tow upward and bring to the surface after incalculable eons of abandonment. Men look to the infinite stars, gazing in wonder, but in the same breath understand nothing of what lurks beneath the fastnesses of our own world, and the ageless vaults of our untold histories.

Satisfied with the handiwork of my men, I looked again upon the ugliness of the statue, shuddering with loathing and wondering whether such a detestable, fantastical brute had ever walked within our universe.

The vessel headed for calmer seas, and I retired to my quarters for a quick nap. I was a bit nervous about the weather, but held confidence in the Captain's maneuverings—he was experienced and not one to take foolish risks, but it made me recall the words of Rolfus. The man had been deadly serious about the statue, and it was almost as if Fleming partly believed him, at last deciding that money in the hand was a sounder prospect than superstitious ramblings.

I slumped onto my bed, which I shared with Chanders, the second mate, who was now on deck manning the wheel with Riley. Lulled to slumber by the ceaseless rocking of the ship, my eyelids fluttered as weariness took hold of my body.

Restlessly I dreamed of an ancient city, where monstrous beings slept in pillared halls filled with fearful servants, unwavering in their blindly fanatical loyalty. In the midst of all was the grisly statue, and to my utter dream-horror it peered hatefully at me with its hideous, eyeless face, but I could not run away as it approached me with dreadful steps. I suddenly awakened, a scream lodged within my constricted throat. I was sweating like a feverish man, and I grabbed the blankets covering my quivering form as the horrific yell greeted my nudged consciousness. Had I carried the nightmare with my waking mind? I thought.

It was then I realized that a very real scream echoed through the ship, coming from the upper deck. Several screams, for that matter. Fearing the worst, I sprang from the room, hoping that the storm had not damaged the hull, but my heart raced with the notion of a sinking vessel on an open sea.

As I burst up the steps leading to the deck, I heard the shouts of men, but I was unable to make out intelligible words—it sounded like cries of pure, unrelenting horror. I broke the surface and was thrown mercilessly against one of the wooden masts, narrowly missing a blow to my head. The boat listed heavily to the side, and men were yelling like banshees in the blaring wind, the rain pelting downward and soaking everything with its cold grip.

Chaos rained upon the hapless sailors, and I saw two men swept from the back of the vessel by a bulging mass of gray, like the trunk of an enormous tree come to life. To my horror, I glimpsed several more of these writhing appendages, and knew that some vast denizen of the deep oceans was responsible for the assault, perhaps a monstrous octopus or squid, emerging as a waking legend angered by the intrusion of our ship into its domain.

Had the storm disturbed the beast from its subterranean lair, causing it to surface, thus finding us in its path? I hadn't the time to seek answers to such questions, and I looked about for a suitable weapon, eyeing a jagged harpoon of the type used for whaling.

I caught a glimpse of Fleming near the center of the fiercest activity, urging men to his aid and the defense of the ship. The battle must have been going on for several minutes before I became aware, for most of the crewmen were aft. Huge appendages flayed through the air, sending men overboard and crushing others. Harpoons and knives were flung at the creature's body, but from where I stood it was obscured, and I could only guess at the unseen girth of the behemoth.

I worked my way closer, frightened past reason at this point, numb and shivering. Above the fray I heard the voice of Rolfus, yelling to "cut it loose," but that was all. Riley crouched next to Fleming, and he heaved his shaft at the monster, tumbling forward with the exertion. I was about two dozen yards from the fight, and began to make out more clearly what the adversary looked like.

No word, expression, or gesture of exclamation can adequately describe the strangled terror which seized my body, squeezing out my courage and rationality like a crushing vice of iron, as I recognized the creature to be a living duplicate of that most wretched statue which had been skewered by our nets from the abysmal ocean depths.

The monster raged against the crew, towering over the vessel with bulbous claws grabbing at anything within its dreadful reach. Tentacles thrashed with incredible fury, battering the proud planking of the *Sea Queen,* and I knew that our attempts were pathetically frail and hopeless against such power.

Men were already fleeing to the boats in fear for their lives, scrambling like rats to leave the vessel. A huge blast of wind thundered across the seas, propelling the ship forward, and without warning the beast disappeared beneath the waves with a tremendous splash, spraying geysers of foam over the beleaguered sailors. This happened so swiftly that we all stared in shock at the rising surf, wondering if it had been but a terrible dream. Rolfus sprang toward the net, holding a two-handed ax, hacking away at the thick lines.

"Help me, you fools! Can't you see what evil this idol has brought down upon us?" No one moved, they looked at him in stunned silence—even Fleming was lost for words, leaning heavily against the inner mast and gasping for breath.

"Captain!" shouted Riley. "Some of the men are untying the rafts."

"Who can blame them?" spat Rolfus. "We are only sailors and fishermen, not warriors or madmen to fight such a demon."

The Captain snapped out of his inaction, waving his fist at the first mate. "Stop those men, the creature is gone. They'll be lost in this storm." Riley started off, then hesitated, staring at Rolfus. "What about the statue, Captain? How do we know it's not a charm, maybe even warding off the monster? Perhaps the beast defends these very waters, attacking us as we wandered here, thus explaining the lack of fish."

I was shocked that he could conceive such a notion. The monster was a primeval terror from another age, awakened from sleep because of our extraordinary dredging of the statue. Improbabilities swarmed throughout all of our scattered minds, but Riley's opinion was outrageous, yet Fleming clearly was indecisive.

"Captain, this is utter madness. We've lost a dozen men already, if we fail to act now you'll condemn the entire vessel to its grave."

Fleming spoke to Riley, sending him to restrain the sailors who were unhooking the boats. "We must not act too rashly, Rolfus. The ship has a strong wind pressing us onward, and I think the creature cannot hope to stay with us at this speed. I command you to hold your weapon."

I was as surprised as Rolfus by the statement, and he stood motionless, the ax dropping to his side. "You have sealed the fate of the *Sea Queen,* Captain. The crew's blood is on your hands."

Fleming scowled at the older man and hurried toward the middle of the ship, ordering me to secure the statue and keep an eye out for the creature—and Rolfus. I nodded, wondering if he had indeed made a terrible mistake in allowing the statue to remain snared in the net.

He left us then, and I examined the lines, wrapped tightly around the idol and to the back of the ship. Rolfus whispered to me, and I was in turmoil at the choices before us, torn by my loyalty to the Captain, but at the same time my senses telling me that the statue was indeed to blame, and should be severed immediately to tumble back down to the lightless ocean floor forever.

I was unsure as to what my ultimate decision would have been, disobedience or allegiance, and the matter was quickly taken from my hands as a severe rumbling shook the vessel, knocking us all to the deck in confusion and renewed terror. There was little doubt as to the source of the disturbance—the monster had resurfaced. I caught a glimpse of whipping tentacles in the direction of the boats, and watched as wood erupted into splinters as the monster deliberately destroyed our small craft.

It lunged against the side of the *Sea Queen,* dangerously rocking the vessel and it was all I could do to hold onto a rail and avoid being tossed into the ocean. Rolfus was not so fortunate.

The battered man tumbled headlong into the nets and out to the deep waters, shouting in horror, then I lost sight of him. A series of vibrations rippled through the deck, and I knew the monster was breaking the ship through the middle. In desperation, I hurled myself toward the ax which Rolfus had used, hoisting it and chopping away at the numerous strands which held the horrendous statue. I was now alone at the back of the ship, and our momentum ceased as water poured into the bottom chambers. It was already too late to save the vessel, but my only thought was to set loose the statue and dispel the ancient monstrosity.

I never had the chance to finish the task as a huge section of the ship broke off behind me and I was thrown into the ocean, submerging until my lungs screamed for air, as I frantically grabbed for something to hold on to. I gained the surface, latching my arms about a long panel of wood which barely supported my weight.

The storm seemed to lessen, and I looked back at the *Sea Queen* sinking swiftly to a watery death. There was no sign of the creature, and I was beyond weariness and fear at this point, uncaring as to my own fate.

My other crew mates were lost, and I drifted off in the night, a solitary and forlorn man with no possibility of hope or comfort.

It is said that the mind washes away many bad memories, leaving fine details locked firmly beneath one's immediate recollection. Such it was with myself, for the next thing I recalled was being hauled up to a fishing vessel and placed upon a warm bed covered with flannel blankets, and I slept like the pharaohs of ancient Egypt in their golden tombs.

I was physically and mentally exhausted, unconscious for an interminable amount of time. Sleep came and went, accompanied by the hellish nightmares. It may indeed have been days until I regained any semblance of coherence, and that is when my awareness most likely became active again.

A tall, dark man stood before my bed, with a hawkish face and bristling beard, and I caught snatches of conversation between him and an older man, concerning myself and the circumstances which had brought me to them.

The words were clear, but my mind was shrouded in a haze. Several times I attempted to speak, but realized with horror that I was unable. Whether my vocal abilities were damaged, or even worse yet, my mental state, resulting in a lack of speech, I knew not, and I lay there, frightened and weak.

"Will he become well again, Frederick?"

"I don't know, only time will answer that question, I'm afraid, Captain. To go through what this man did, shipwrecked and set adrift, is incomprehensible to most of our blackest imaginations."

"No doubt—he is fortunate that we spotted the debris of his vessel."

I listened to their talk, hearing little to ease my pain or sorrow. I knew that I was awake, but frustrated at my limitations to communicate. The simple act of moving my hand several inches was a tremendous task.

"See, he is coming around, although his pupils are still dilated. Maybe after another day or two of rest he will be able to tell us something."

"Perhaps."

I heard a knock on the door, and someone greeted the other men, most likely another mate.

"Captain, you are needed on the rear deck," spoke the newcomer.

"Oh, for what reason, Collins? Another survivor?"

My heart leapt at the notion . . . Had one of my crew been found whole and well?

"No, sir. We have become tangled with the netting of the other ship, I believe. There is a great resistance, as if we are mired against an unyielding object, or some extremely heavy weight."

My mouth opened, but no words issued forth. A silent scream of horror echoed throughout the walls of my mind, but only within the depths of my eyes could they have read the truth, and the terror which awaited us all.

A KIND OF FEAR

BY *C.J. HENDERSON*

"Greed, like the love of comfort, is a kind of fear."

—Cyril Connolly

"**G**ENTLEMEN, REALLY, I MUST admit, I had my doubts earlier on during our negotiations, but I say, this is top notch work. Top notch—oh yes. Really much better than I expected."

The speaker was a tall man, annoyingly thin, pompously straight, with hair that stayed precisely in place despite the unnatural, bone-melting heat and humidity being generated that August in Mahone Bay. Newfoundland did not experience such summers often, and the men in the employ of Chester Brimford were not at all happy to be there.

A normal, happy-go-lucky crew, they did not enjoy the abnormal heat. They did not care for the cloying, sticky humidity. They did not like much about the massive clouds of mosquitoes to be found in the Bay that summer, either, and especially, they did not have much use for their employer.

"You fellows have just about got this finished, finally, don't you ..."

He was a terribly arrogant man, the type who spoke to those he considered beneath him in a tone of false friendship and government-approved brotherhood. Oddly enough, it was not a matter of race or property, religion or even eye-color as far as the men of Bently Carnahan's construction team could tell. Really, it seemed as if Chester Brimford considered the entire human race beneath his notice. They were, of course, happy to take his money, but that was all they were happy about as far as he was concerned.

"I'd say we were done, *sir*," Carnahan answered, the sting of sweat in his eyes charging his words with perhaps a bit too much of a snarl. Above it all, as he usually was, Brimford did not seem to notice the crew boss's implied insult as he inspected the work he had commissioned.

"Do you have any idea why I've had you men build all of this?" he asked as he continued to run his hands across the freshly-constructed brickwork. "Or even, what it might be?"

There was no answer from any of them, until the youngest, a boy newly turned-out from high school—one with no chance of college looking forward to a future of only back-breaking labor and then the grave—suggested, "I was thinkin' it might have something to do with some thing they call, the Money Pit?"

"Indeed, indeed," answered Brimford absently, "Go to the head of the class, young man. My word, now who would have thought any of you would have possessed even that much knowledge?"

Carnahan and his men had grown used to Brimford's inadvertently cruel remarks, had learned to put up with them as well, for the summer had been tight and he had offered a great deal more than his bizarre job was worth if they could accomplish it by a certain time. Days early, knowing there was a bonus in it for them, the men held their temper as their rail of an employer crawled about in his, his . . . his whatever it was, checking each row of bricks and droning on in his typically insulting way.

"Do any of you know the story of this island, have any idea what this Money Pit was?" The same young man ventured a guess that he remembered something about pirate treasure. Brimford sneered at the words, lecturing as he crawled about;

"Isn't that what they all say? And of course, in the simplest way of looking at things, that's almost the way of it. But only almost. There's no way of telling now, of course, but hundreds of years ago, this was just another tree-covered island here in the bay. Nothing special about it. Just a place for boys to go exploring, as was the case with young Daniel McGinnis back in the summer of 1795. It was on this spot, right here mind you, where he came across a ship's tackle block hanging from one of the lower branches of one of the island's many oaks."

Despite their distaste for the speaker, the subject of riches was one about which any of the desperately hot men there under the rays of the August sun could always bear to hear. And, since Brimford seemed content to tell the story and not comment on their workmanship, all were content to simply mop at their sweating brows and bodies as he told them McGinnis' tale.

"Having noted a depression under the branch, indicating to the youth's keen mind that at some time someone had dug a hole then filled it in, he marked the spot then went home, only to return the next day with two of his friends. They dug to a depth of four feet through the hard blue clay where they then encountered a layer of flagstones. This thrilled them, for the lads knew such stone didn't come from any of the islands—that the nearest place to secure such was over two miles away."

At this point, most of Carnahan's men began to grow somewhat curious. They did not believe what they had built would have much to do with the recovery of pirate gold. It was just a great bricked circle, precisely ten feet deep—much like some kind of primitive swimming pool, except for the odd towers arranged around the rim, and obviously the large stone slab there in the center.

"The story of McGinnis and his friends is long, and it's only the first of several, but suffice it to say, the three lads did not find the buccaneer booty they felt certain they would. At ten feet they found a layer of logs. Again at twenty feet, and again at thirty. The boys gave up eventually, but in the early 1800s a doctor raised the money to attempt a full-bore excavation."

Interest in the story grew at this point. On the one hand, the listeners realized no treasure could ever have been found, or why would Brimford be there. That lead one to to wonder how a pit not even a dozen feet deep was going to aid in recovering anything when a pit thirty feet did not. As the story continued, it answered neither question.

"The new group reached a depth of eighty feet, where they were certain they would find the treasure. But, like all common men, they were fools. A new barrier awaited them every ten feet further that they continued on."

Carnahan and his men baked while Brimford rambled. As his story spanned the centuries, their fascination with the continuing treasure search was equal to their distaste for the story's teller. Brimford knew his facts, and he told them in an interesting, even exciting manner. But his contempt for the poor fools who lost their fortunes, and even their lives, hunting for the elusive reward of Oak Island made them cringe—and growl. How could they not, considering it was men such as themselves at which he sneered with every breath.

"There was, after a while, no doubt of the involvement of pirates," he told them. "The type of putty used on ships was found as a building material throughout, as well as coconut fibers. Of course, they found all manner of things. For instance, at one point they found a massive stone slab, one covered with words carved in an unknown language." Brimford let the steaming afternoon drag on a moment, then added;

"Indeed, all the materials discovered used were mostly primitive, but they were masterfully applied. No ordinary lout, no typical lump you find walking the streets designed this safe. This was the work of genius."

Brimford took Carnahan and his men on a journey which lasted from the 1700s to the present day. He told them of each and every attempt to uncover the secrets of the Money Pit, and how all of them had ended in tragedy and failure. He related how the treasure's protectors had dug great flood gates and drains, had constructed massive, man-made sponges to hold tide water ready to fill any chamber created by those who did not know where to dig.

"The last serious attempt to uncover anything here was made in 1965, by a Robert Dunfield, a petroleum geologist. Low brute that he was, he brought in a seventy-foot clam digger. In a month and a half he created a hole some eighty feet wide and one hundred and thirty feet deep. One can give him an A for effort, I suppose, but the fool completely obliterated every last trace of all the work that went before him. And obviously, he found nothing as well, save for the humiliation and loss any gutter tramp deserves for forgetting his place."

"Mr Brimford," Carnahan barked with annoyance, "not that we aren't all fascinated, but truth to tell, it's hot and it's sticky and I'm just askin' what's on every man's mind here. Are we done? I mean, don't forget, until you dismiss us, we're still on the clock. I'd hate to have you think we're just tryin' to run out your tab on you."

"No, no," answered Brimford over his shoulder. Racing his hands along the top of the large flat stone work, the almost altar-like piece in the center of the pit, he continued, "although I appreciate your candor, mere money is of no concern. If I had another day and night's worth of inspections to make, I would retain you until I was absolutely certain I no longer had need for your strong backs and weak minds."

Carnahan waved his cap through the center of a small horde of mosquitoes heading for his head and neck. His irritation with Brimford had just about reached its zenith. If it were only cooler, if it weren't so sticky, if there weren't so many bugs, if Brimford wasn't such a complete horse's ass . . .

As his mind reeled off all the pressures challenging him to lose it, the back of the contract boss's mind whispered to him;

"C'mon now, Carnahan, be smarter than most of the guys in your graduating class. Wait until you get paid to kill him."

The bitter joke brought a smile to Carnahan's lips. Feeling at least some of the pressure releasing within him, he managed to ask without cursing;

"Are you sayin' we're finished with this job?"

And then, Brimford almost redeemed himself in the eyes of those he had insulted and degraded for so long by answering in the affirmative. He even complimented the men on their work, commenting that he was amazed at how perfect every detail was. Indeed, his compliment soon degenerated into another attack as he made it clear how incredible was his surprise that he could find nothing wrong with their endeavors.

Still, even that gibe passed as he pulled forth a wad of envelopes from his inner jacket pocket. More than one of the men marveled at his ability to wear a suit and tie in such miserable weather, and if they had not disliked him so, they might have told him. But they knew to a man, however, that doing so would simply give him the excuse to make some comment about proper, civilized behavior, and to remind them he realized that as members of the lower classes they simply could not relate to the ways of a man of proper breeding. One of the crew, however, the youngest, was able to bring himself to say something.

"Mr Brimford, I was wonderin," he asked, "if it's not some kind of secret, exactly what is it we built for you? I mean, does it even have anything to do with the treasure, or what?"

With a smile so wide it bordered on relief, Brimford turned to the young man and assured him that their efforts had everything to do with the treasure of the Money Pit. Leaning down on the flat stone before him, he rested his weight on his palms as he said;

"You see, the treasure cannot be recovered by conventional means. But that is because it was never meant to be recovered at all."

The eyes of the construction workers clouded over. Confused to a man, they simply stared. All wanted to know the answer, but none wanted to be the one subjected to Brimford's sarcasm to hear it. Such trepidation was hardly necessary, however, for Brimford seemed positively eager to reveal all. It turned out that their employer was an occultist, one who made his living telling fortunes, writing star charts, making stock predictions based on the movement of the planets, et cetera. His studies into such matters had brought him several items which though they seemed unrelated at first, soon proved to be intimately interconnected.

"I won't scorch your little minds with the trouble there is in putting it all together—no, suffice it to say that there was at one time a pirate who came across an extraordinary treasure. Piracy in his day was a thing confined to the Atlantic and the Mediterranean. Being too bold and too successful, he found himself hunted by the French, Spanish, British, and even the Portuguese, a situation which caused him to retreat down around the Cape of Good Hope and into the Pacific. And that was where he discovered a vicious race known as the Tcho Tcho."

Feeling as if they could bear a bit more of Brimford's arrogance, if it meant getting an interesting story to tell, two of Carnahan's men started passing around the last of their beer from the cooler they had taken to the job site every day. As the hungry men knocked back one can after another, Brimford said;

"A tribe of pygmy wizards he found on a remote island, the Tcho Tcho taught the good captain much of magic, blessing him and his men against harm in their raids. They knew where the wealth of the Pacific was hidden, and these wizards directed the pirate crew to mountains of gold and heaps of ivory, to silver and pearls and gem stones by the trunkful. At first the pirates were wildly enthusiastic, but eventually they began to wonder if they might not be endangering their souls by trafficking in magicks."

With a great flair for the dramatic, Brimford told the crew how the pirates, insane in their fear of the Tcho Tcho's possible effect on their eternal reward, put the village to the torch and murdered the natives. So frightened were they, that they rejected the booty they had collected, leaving it behind as too tainted to carry aboard ship. They did take away a treasure, however, one which they brought to Newfoundland to hide away from the sight of man.

"What they brought here was a fabulous treasure in gold and jewels, one they meant to keep from the sight of man for all time. They were the pieces the Tcho Tcho had used in their cursed rituals, and the very sight of these charmed trinkets made most of the crew uneasy to say the least. They created the Money Pit here in this remote area, building what they hoped would be a safe holding cell where these objects, charged with evil as they were, would never again be able to plague mankind. And, for nearly four hundred years, their plan has worked."

"You mean you're going to recover the treasure?"

"Precisely."

"But how?" Carnahan wiped at the sweat on his brows as it tried to crowd his eyes, adding, "It don't make sense."

"Not to you, of course. But what you don't realize is, our pirates had learned the ways of magick. Even though their actions in hiding this treasure were supposed to save their souls, they still used magicks to do the heavy lifting. In other words, Mr Carnahan, they did not hide their booty in the ground. The Money Pit was just a dodge to confound those who would follow. They hid the artifacts of the Tcho Tcho in *space*."

Several of the workers, happy to have their pay, and feeling slightly the effects of their liquid lunches, guffawed and hooted at Brimford. As the thin man rankled, one of the crew laughed;

"Well, 'at's just nuts. I mean, why dig the pit at all? Why not just dump the stuff in the ocean? Digging the pit just marked where the stuff was—right? If they don't want no one to get a'hold of it, then why leave any kind of tell-tale sign? Like that block and tackle no less?"

"Because, my slack-jawed disbeliever, there are those who can follow such objects anywhere. For certain wizards, finding this spot is no trouble. But once here, if they were left clues that showed the chest obviously buried, then perhaps they could be fooled to simply dig endlessly like so many others."

"Man, you just crazy."

"Oh, do you think so?" answered Brimford drily. "Would you care to see the treasure then . . . any of you?"

Carnahan's crew immediately responded, all of them eager to see their employer fetch a pirate horde out of thin air. Brimford said he would be happy to do so, even making a wager with the crew.

He bet them that if no treasure appeared, he would pay them all an extra hundred dollars. But, if it did appear, they would have to cart it to his vehicle for him for free.

Eager to win their bonus, the crew set to helping Brimford fetch the paraphernalia he needed to cast his spell. Within minutes the large slab in the center of his pit was covered with a dark cloth and numerous small bottles, carved boxes, and the such. Telling the men surrounding him to get ready for a little exercise, Brimford set right to work performing his magicks.

For the first few minutes, everyone's extra hundred dollar bill seemed a sure thing. Then suddenly, the air darkened, became harder to breathe, and the colors to be found within the pit began to merge and flicker. Before much longer, a thick mist belched from nowhere and poured upward out of the stonework, followed by four discernable shapes which began to take form atop the stone table. And, finally, as Brimford collapsed in a trembling pile against the wall of the pit, the fruit of his efforts was revealed. There, crammed up against each other on the altar top were four massive chests filled far beyond over-flowing with treasure.

As the wizard gasped for breath, the crew stood or sat slack-jawed, first amazed that anything had happened at all, and then overwhelmed at what had happened. After a moment, however, one of them jumped down into the pit, thrusting his hands into the staggering wealth of golden trinkets spilling out of one of the chests, screaming;

"We're rich, boys—*rich!*"

Others followed him, grabbing up the unusually carved artifacts and throwing them into the air or at each other. The men cavorted, shrieking wildly, until finally Brimford managed to catch his breath.

Pulling himself to his full height, he shouted;

"Gentlemen, and I of course know exactly how loosely I am using the term, what is it you think you are doing? This is *my* treasure. Mine and mine alone. It is not for spending on whores and Lotto tickets, on meatloaf and fried potatoes and video games; it is not for filling stomachs with cheap spirits that can be vomited back to the light of day later—it is for ruling the world!" As the panting wizard dragged himself back to the altar, he pushed his way through the contractors, screeching;

"You fools haven't the faintest idea what this moment means for me. Once I've bonded with these artifacts, all the galaxy will finally be under proper control! You wretched, disgusting bags of snot will be as nothing to the master of everything. Dust motes to be wiped from beneath his booted heel and nothing more—that's all you are! Nothing–"

Brimford seemed to want to say more, but was stopped rather firmly by the force of a shovel connecting with the back of his head. So violent was the blow in fact, that the back of his skull was opened instantly, blood and gray matter scattering everywhere.

"Shut up," screamed Carnahan as he bashed his employer with further blows. Raining shovel strikes down on Brimford, he simply punctuated each crash with a further;

"Shut up! Shut up! Shut up! Shut *up!*"

His crewmen stood about, more surprised at their leader's actions than at the bit of magic they had just seen performed. Dumbstruck, they waited in silence as Carnahan finally stopped, content to simply watch as the wizard's blood and bile dribbled from his body, down onto the treasure which only a moment earlier he had claimed would make him ruler of the world.

"I don't know about anyone else," one of the crew finally said, "but I'm glad you did it." Others joined in with the sentiment, but Carnahan countered them all, saying;

"It don't matter how much he deserved it, I've still killed a man in cold blood."

"A man . . ." suggested another, "from out of town. Who I doubt had any more friends elsewhere than he made here."

"He didn't have a contract with us, right," asked another. "He paid in cash, shook our hands instead of having us sign anything. There's no paper trail to us."

"I say we shove him in his car and slide it into Fergeson's Bog. You all know how many other unwanted items that bit of real estate has gobbled up."

"Yeah," added another. "We do that, then we only have to fill in this stupid hole, and divide his treasure up amongst ourselves and call it a day."

"Most all of it's solid gold. We melt it down, then recast it as dead weights. We've got the smeltin' rig over at Roy's from the Gleason job."

Carnahan thought about it for a moment. After all, it was not as if he had killed the President, or a nun. He had put a stop to a hateful wizard, who claimed he was about to take over the world. Why not be done with him? Why shed a tear or suffer even a single second over him?

"Let's do it," agreed Carnahan. "Billy, drag his ass up out of there and stuff him in his car. Everyone else, let's get that gold out of there and into Kelly's van. After that, let's fill in this damn hole and go make ourselves rich."

As the men cheered and set merrily to their work, the essence of Brimford smiled. He had sacrificed himself for great Cthulhu, bloodied the offering and become one with it. Soon would follow the heat, and his spirit would fuse with the gold, making him completely one with it.

And, after that, would come the greed of men, that would reach up through the blood and wealth and murderous rage and chew the juice of time until finally the moment would arrive when salt water would boil, and the earth would shake, and eyelids the size of elephants would flutter, and the master of the universe would take up his scepter once more.

LA ARMADA INVENCIBLE

BY *MICHAEL McBRIDE*

M Y VOYAGE INTO MADNESS began on 19 July 1588, precisely two days following the sighting of *la Armada Invencible* off the coast of Cornwall. Beneath the cover of night, we launched aboard *The Revenge* under the command of Sir Francis Drake, a scoundrel of significant notoriety who earned his reputation as well as his fortune staging raids of piracy on Spanish ports and seafaring vessels in the Caribbean. To a man, we fear for our lives should we engage The Great Armada, but worse are the shadowy deaths that stalk a sailor under the flag of lunacy and the protective stare of the moon. Typhoid and dysentery are two snapping heads of the silent and murderous hydra lurking beneath every hull; the third and most fearsome the slavering head of wild-eyed insanity. One cannot sail to ports-of-call unknown without encountering that vile trinity en route to the watery grave that awaits us all.

My own journey followed the circuitous cobblestone path from Leicester through University and finally into Her Majesty Queen Elizabeth's Royal Navy. I hesitate to declare myself an educated man as I know nothing of the world beyond English shores, where I hear tell of spotted girafa with necks that reach the clouds and entire continents rich with veins of gold and precious treasures worth ten times the amassed fortune of the Royal Treasury. As nephew to Robert Dudley, Earl of Leicester, I care little for the financial pursuits that drive the other men of service, for such baser necessities are not of concern to the entitled, once removed though the case may be. My quest—should God deem me worthy—leads me into the great and vast unknown in search of knowledge some might call arcane. Such terminology to me seems absurd as was once all fact not considered so? As a boy I was fascinated by the fantastic stories the fisherman and merchants dragged in from the wharves, regaling me with tales beyond even what my imagination could conjure. So enthralled did I become that I reveled in the speculative sciences of mathematics and physics, if only to find the loopholes that might allow for the existence of the windows into fantasy within our castles of logic. But no such tale held me enrapt to the degree of the yarn that spooled from the lips of that terror-stricken Spaniard on the night of 31 July, when his teeth parted and opened the gates to unimaginable horrors beyond even my learned comprehension, inspiring in me a fear the likes of which I have never known.

At midnight on 28 July, with all one hundred and thirty ships of *la Armada Invencible* moored off the coast of Calais in their defensive half-moon formation, eight English merchant vessels were filled with gunpowder, set ablaze, and floated downwind into their midst. While the ruse caused only minimal damage, many of the Spanish warhorses cut their cables and separated from the others in the ensuing chaos. Sir Drake's strategy was to instigate this confusion so that the smaller and faster British craft would be able to harass the much larger and clumsier Spanish Hulks, a ploy that played to perfection.

It was widely rumored that Captain Drake had sold his soul to the devil in exchange for mastery of the sea and military genius. While the idea of the second ranking officer in the entire royal fleet entering into any such dark transaction is laughable, I can attest to his naval prowess. What should have been a Spanish rout in our own English Channel ended with the Spaniards on the run and the surprised Royal Navy in pursuit.

In the midst of the bedlam of retreat, an unnaturally ferocious storm settled upon the Straits of Dover, causing the *Santa Catalina* to collide with her sister ship the *Nuestra Señora del Rosario*, the Andalusian section flag vessel under the command of Don Pedro de Valdés. By the time *The Revenge* came upon the remains, the wreckage of the *Santa Catalina* was settling onto the ocean floor and the *Nuestra Señora del Rosario* was taking on water in an attempt to do the same. The survivors were taken prisoner and shackled in the brig, babbling incoherently in shock and terror. As my societal standing allows me the luxury of not engaging in the hand-to-hand combat befitting the enlisted men and my education grants me other privileges, my duty is to merely supervise the interrogation of the six higher ranking Spanish officers stolen from the awaiting jaws of the denizens of the deep. My mediocre Spanish is matched only by their paraphernalia-laden English, but it isn't their stance on King Phillip the Second's Catholic Church and its battle with Her Royal Majesty and her Protestant leanings that intrigues me. It is the wildly imaginative stories of the sudden storm and the circumstances of their sinking that piques my curiosity.

Tales of monsters and nautical myth abound in seafaring folk with only one consistency amongst the tales: the lack of congruous detail and evidence. While one day may bring a drunken scallywag, stumbling into a tavern spewing farfetched recounts of maidens with the lower halves of fish, the following quite often brings the blubbery meat of the sea cow in various carnations of edibles and fuel. Thus, you can imagine my surprise at the fact that all six of the Spaniards recounted the same fantastical story independent of one another. Each sailor was isolated from the others and testified to the events of the disaster that led to the sinking of their monolithic ship, their stories unwavering even as the thumbscrews tried to instill a modicum of doubt. The most convincing testimony came from a bearded brigand by the name of Juan Soto de Valdés, second cousin to the commander of the sunken *Nuestra Señora del Rosario*. His situation mirrored mine in the sense that his entitlement guaranteed him special standing amidst the ruffian lot of Andalusians, his dainty hands bereft of the scars and calluses of the other ragamuffins. While his ambitions were more political than my own, I did feel a certain kinship to this fellow whose words appeared to startle him even as they came out of his mouth.

His vessel had been moored off the coast of Calais while waiting for Alessandro Farnese, Duke of Parma, to assemble his invading force in Dunkirk. Their instructions were to provide safe transport for the barges filled with Parma's troops across the English Channel to the estuaries of the River Thames where my own uncle, Earl of Leicester, had amassed a defensive front to prevent a siege upon

London. Had their plan been successful, the sixteen-thousand Spaniards would have easily overwhelmed my uncle's army of only four thousand and Alonzo de Guzman el Bueno, Seventh Duke of Medina Sidonia and commander of the Great Armada, would have claimed Queen Elizabeth's head as fair trade for the beheading of Mary Stuart, whom the Catholic Spanish supported as heir to the throne. Sir Drake's preemptive maneuver of launching the burning ships into their formation had proven his unquestionable brilliance, the timing so precise that it was uncanny. Soto's ship had been one of the first to see the flaming frigates on the horizon and cut away from the others as the *Nuestra Señora del Rosario* was among the most heavily fortified with nearly fifty cannons lining her formidable bow. While their scheme had been conceived in a moment of panic, it had nonetheless been strategically sound. They would race the wind to the northwest through the Straits of Dover to the seaport of Gravelines on the Flanders Coast, where they would turn and meet the English face-to-face, showcasing their awesome firepower as they simultaneously decimated the Royal Fleet and provided cover for Parma's ground forces. Before they reached Gravelines, however, with the White Cliffs of Dover towering over them, they met with what they all agreed to be the worst storm they had ever encountered and undoubtedly of supernatural origin.

"*La tempestad de Diablo,*" Soto had called it, crossing himself after speaking the name. The Devil's Storm.

According to Soto, the three-hundred and fifty foot cliffs had arisen to the north like the crest of a gargantuan bony fish breaking the surface of the choppy waters. As they had grown near, the chalky cliffs had taken form, capped with an emerald crown of grass, its venerable face marred by myriad ambitious clumps. They were flat and rose jaggedly to the heavens as though God Himself had taken a chisel and broken away the sloping bank, leaving only the perilous and insurmountable faces of crumbling stone. Soto claims to remember thinking that this coast would be the perfect place for an ambush as even were they able to swim to shore from a sinking vessel, there would be no way of climbing onto land. Presumably sensing the same thing, Don Pedro de Valdés had taken to the bow himself with his eyeglass to scan the horizon. Soto had been at his right and recounted watching the elongated monocle begin to shake in his cousin's grasp. Never in his life had he witnessed such a display of weakness from the stoic Captain, whose face had gone as chalky white as the very cliffs he stared upon. The Captain had turned to Soto and opened his mouth as if to speak, but had emitted no sound, instead offering the eyeglass to Soto, who turned its magnified gaze upon the English coast.

What this man claims to have seen and purveyed to me defies everything I know of the land of my birth and her children. While our heritage is rich in the heretical foundations of the Celts and other Pagan sects, mother England as a nation has embraced Christianity and its holy tenets. Furthermore, the Queen has decreed that her people become Protestant and forsake all other beliefs, a royal commandment that demands complete compliance. This Spaniard claims to have seen rites perverse on many levels; illegal in defiance to the Queen's proclamation and sacrilegious in the eyes of Our Lord and Savior. While I initially found his recount absurd, a flight of lunatic fancy, an affront to my masterful knowledge of my own nation and the history of her people, the truth resonated in his words and quivered in his frightened eyes. Whether I believed what this enemy of the Crown was telling me or not, this man sitting across the wooden barrel from me, the contraption about his thumbs draining blood from the turned screws burrowing into his bones and eliciting screams of pure agony, the Spaniard's story never faltered once. Even staring grim death in the eye, he swore to the truth of every word.

Soto had sat across from me, his manacled hands in his lap, and detailed to me what he claimed to have seen atop those white cliffs of legend, his skittish eyes skirting mine as they danced about the dark quarters. When they finally locked upon mine, I saw behind them a man not scared for his life or in fear of captivity, but the unimpassioned acquiescence of a living corpse who has already witnessed far worse than his own demise.

According to this haunted man, what he had witnessed atop those cliffs had been a vision of heresy straight out of the writings of learned scholars. There had been three cloaked bodies atop each of the two highest crests of land, joined at the hands and spinning in circles. It was obviously not a dance of any kind, but immediately purveyed a sinister aura of the macabre. In their ebon robes they had twirled, their exertions becoming feverish and deliberate. A cone of light the consistency of smoke had arisen from between them and reached up into the sky, expanding into massive thunderheads from where the pinnacle met with the azure atmosphere. These clouds grew in height and width until they appeared to be mountains forming above, their black hearts darkening until day turned to night, spreading across the entire horizon, which came to life with strobes of electricity slashing through the fabric of reality. Their insidious rite complete, those who had summoned the wrath of nature from the tops of those steep white cliffs released hands and watched as the remainder of their conical spire dissipated into the grumbling thunderheads, finally turning to align themselves with the edge of the land to bear witness to their devilish deeds. Soto had glimpsed one of their faces, partially obscured by shadow beneath that velvet cowl. There had been a crown of some kind ringing the forehead, carved into obscene designs of what appeared to be stone. Beneath, the brows were thin and thready, as though constructed of random lengths of black twine like the wiry whiskers of a catfish. It was the eyes, however, that had chilled the Spaniard to his eternal soul. They had been inordinately wide, as though poised to spill right out of those shadowed sockets.

"Not once did they blink," he had said. Instead they had leered straight through the eyeglass as though able to capture his stare, even from such phenomenal distance. Soto had wrested his gaze away, sighting a wide-lipped, horizontal mouth rimmed with bristles and a weak chin that terminated in lateral folds of flesh trailing down the neck and into the gown. Those lips had moved around unrecognizable words, their croaking voices echoing within his head as though it was the source of the sound. *Cthulhu fhtagn. Iä! Iä! Ph'nglui mglw'nafh Cthulhu R'lyeh wgah'nagl fhtagn*, those voices intoned, rising and falling as they intertwined into a cacophony of subhuman sound.

That had been the moment where it felt as though the earth itself had been pulled out from beneath them.

The wind had arisen with such a scream that when the men on deck had finally noticed the figures atop the cliffs, they had instinctively feared them witches and the origin of the wailing. The formerly choppy waters had become tempestuous. Waves taller than the bow tossed the Spanish Hulk around, raising her thirty feet before dropping her sixty. Men were thrown over the sides and enveloped by the sea, dragged into the briny depths before they could open their mouths to scream. The *Rosario* canted from side to side so violently that she nearly rolled over. Soto had grabbed onto a rail and clung to it for dear life, watching in shock as an enormous white-capped wave swelled over the opposite side, the crest high enough to rip at the sails. It pounded down upon them, hurling Don Pedro into the air with a handful of others before swallowing them whole. The next wave to rise and tower over them brought with it the *Santa Catalina*, the smaller vessel hovering above them like the fist of the Almighty preparing to smite them.

All Soto could remember afterward was taking a deep inhalation of seawater. The crashing of breaking wood all around him. Sharp splinters tearing through his clothing and lancing into his flesh. The sting of salt in his wounds had driven him into the stranglehold of unconsciousness, his last fleeting thought to lock his hands onto his elbows and pray their union held.

When he had finally awakened, the sea had calmed to a greater degree, though still the *Rosario* rose and fell dramatically, teetering at the mercy of the waves. Soto had coughed out a flume of brine and collapsed to the deck, now riddled with gaping black maws through which he could see down into the quarters beneath. Survivors moaned from where they were either struggling to regain consciousness or pinned beneath debris. Wreckage was strewn all about them; random lengths of splintered wood and barrels full of supplies rose and fell throughout the clogged channel. Bodies floated facedown, arched backs like uniformed icebergs. Appendages protruded from the decimation, hiding the remainder of the body from sight. He spoke of sickly gray flesh the color of a dead mackerel's gills and loops of entrails floating atop the ocean, having been either beaten free from their hosts in the collision or freed by the sharp jaws of some eager scavenger.

Soto had wandered the deck, peering over the broken rails for any sign of his cousin, but even had he seen Don Pedro he doubted he would have been able to recognize his bloated corpse as schools of fish had begun nibbling strips away from the sloughing flesh. The sky had still been dreary and black, the clouds roiling like a burbling cauldron of tar. While formerly a deep blue, the water had absorbed the hue of the sky, save for the foaming caps of ivory. What followed, according to this man Soto, sounds as though it was stolen from a fever dream. None of the others aboard my ship believe him, for had I not seen the terror in his eyes when he recounted that horror on the sea, I can imagine I would have dismissed the story as ludicrous as well. These Spaniards had endured hell after all, only to be snatched from the jaws of death and enslaved by their mortal enemies. Had he snapped and absolved himself of his wit, it would have been completely understandable. As but a novice student of the human condition, I may not be able to decipher the various degrees of truth solicited by the methods of pain we use to make men talk, but no man can hide the kind of fear that emanated from his pores and caused his very soul to shudder. This is the sole caveat I hold forth as a witness to these events, for to hear what that man Soto claims happened next is to question his honor, to call him a fraud or liar, but I firmly believe that he is either unable to distinguish fancy from truth or events transpired precisely as he detailed.

The white caps he had mentioned upon the cresting waves had not dissipated as one would expect, but had gathered together, forming large aggregates that floated atop the water more like a layer of grease than foam. What he had at first mistaken for bubbles were something else entirely. They weren't clear, but rather milky and opaque, though it was not until he saw one of those faux bubbles blink that he knew exactly what he was looking at.

"Eyes," Soto had said, his words forever emblazoned into my mind. "A hundred eyes that took life. They taste me with sight."

His words had confused me at first, but as he struggled with his broken English, this is what I extrapolated. A calm sentience had awakened within those eyes that he could feel staring straight through him, prickling his flesh. They had all blinked as though independent of one another; raindrops pattering the ocean. They had swelled up together, rising like a wave, only this wave did not crest and fall, instead growing taller and taller until it stood as high as a man. Only there was not just one. There were countless others standing atop the water as Christ must have, gelatinous apparitions the color of the cataracts on the eyes of a dying man. Their outlines, he said, flapped like the frilled sides of a flukeworm, fluttering not on the air, but rather against it. They had floated like buoys, rising and falling rhythmically, one with the ocean.

A cloud of seagulls had descended from nowhere, cackling as they speared meaty morsels from the bodies.

These creatures of eyes had swelled upward until what appeared to be tortured heads manifested atop those chimerical forms, paused to inspect them, and then splashed down onto the surface, bubbling like oil as they expanded until they were a dozen feet wide. The orbs no longer blinked, but rather narrowed, their bodies becoming artificial waves, a pus-colored skein atop the sea, eyes moving throughout as though rocks in an avalanche. Cephalopod-like appendages had reached out from the masses, so many striking vipers, snatching those birds from their meals before they could even take to alarmed flight.

Soto said the sound of crunching bones had been deafening.

The feathers had not even settled yet by the time those hideous monstrosities moved on to the dead sailors, slurping sickeningly. A sheet of blood had spread out from the corpses only to be absorbed again by those gelatinous sponges.

Several of the other survivors had found their way to the railing beside Soto, watching in abject terror. None so much as spoke, as though doing so would incur the wrath of those beings that feasted upon their brethren.

"Shoggoth," one of the sailors, a haggard old sea dog had said, rupturing the awed silence. As though the speaking of that name had provoked them, those pools of vile pudding and eyes rose, momentarily mocking their human shapes with such perversion that God must have turned away in revulsion. Tentacles grew from them as they closed in upon the ship, pounding through the hull. Water thundered through the holes, demolishing the infrastructure of the vessel.

Several of the men had tried to run, only to have wrists and ankles snared by those awful things and ripped in startlingly opposite directions to the tune of fracturing bone and tearing skin. Serpentine arms wrapped around necks, grinding the vertebrae to powder and wrenching the swelling purple heads right off.

Soto said that what came next was too horrible to repeat. As did the other men, causing me to wonder what could possibly be so fantastic as to force these men to hold their tongues after everything they had already told me thus far. What could possibly be more frightening than these monsters of eyes they claim had torn their shipmates apart? Unfortunately for my curiosity, the thumbscrews could only be turned so far . . .

The Spaniard claims to have thrown himself to the deck and

scurried in the opposite direction, ending beneath a staircase with a group of other sobbing men, all praying for their lives. None could attest to how long they had cowered there, for the pathetic screams of the dying had surrounded them in stilled eternity until the point that *The Revenge* had sailed into sight.

I had been below deck when our men had salvaged those mongrels from the sinking remains, but those who brought them to the brig claimed the Spaniards had acted like beaten hounds. They had welcomed their impending imprisonment in a way our soldiers had never witnessed. It was almost as though once these nearly drowned rats had recognized their saviors as English soldiers, they had thrown themselves upon the mercies of the Crown.

Now, having thoroughly prepared and rehearsed my report for Captain Drake, I find myself with one lingering question gnawing at my mind, which is why I am again in this small dark chamber with my Spanish doppelgänger Soto.

"What do the words mean?" I ask, sitting on the floor across from this twitchy man. Blood flows from his fingertips as he repeatedly scratches them into the wooden planks. His long hair hangs over his face, wet with sweat, clinging to his beard, his eyes only leaving the wretched mess left behind his painful fingers to match my stare in random jerks.

"Speak not those words," he whispers.

"The other prisoners repeated that same incantation. Verbatim." I riffle through my crumpled notes, barely able to read my own hand. "Cthulhu fhtagn. I–"

"Shh!" he hisses, reaching for me as if to clap a bloody hand over my mouth to silence me, but the chains of the manacles restrain him.

"Why are you so afraid of those words? What do they mean?"

The man's wide eyes rise and meet mine, the irises shivering.

"He no sleep, but he dream."

"I don't understand."

Soto nods. "Good. Pray you not."

I crawl forward, inspecting the wooden floor. At first I assumed his repetitive scratching to be nerves or maybe some strange ritual. Now I see that it is a pattern, a design carved into the wood.

"You said the old man called the creatures 'shoggoth.'"

He trembled, unable to meet my gaze.

"I have never heard of such things."

"So he can see in dream."

"So who can see?"

Soto shakes his head, faster and faster still. With a shriek he scurries away and presses himself into the corner of the room, unconsciously dragging his hands along the splintery wall.

"Guard!" I call, lowering my gaze to inspect what this Spaniard has created.

"Sir?" the guard says from behind me.

"Your candle please."

I accept it from him and place it on the floor beside me. The blood shimmers under the diminutive flame, highlighting the fresh grooves in the grain. I smear it away to better inspect the design, only to learn that I have been wasting my time. I regret having allowed these Spaniards, these enemies of the Queen, to pique my curiosity, for what I stare upon now is sheer madness. It is an animal, or so I imagine. The head is the body of a squid with tentacles where the mouth should be. It is a crude design, almost making it appear as though this prisoner's hallucination has wings and the body of a beast.

"I have no further use for this one," I say, rising. "Do with him as you will."

I scoff at my own idiocy as I exit the cell and walk along the dark corridor toward the Captain's quarters. So willing to believe such flights of fancy was I that I hung on every word those lying hooligans spoke. Creatures made of eyes. Figures cloaked in shadows and summoning storms. Hah. A fool I am. I can only imagine how Captain Drake would have reacted had I foolishly stormed into his chamber spouting such nonsense.

I knock on the door.

"Enter," Captain Drake says from the other side.

"Thank you, Sir," I say, entering and clasping my hands behind my back.

"I was beginning to wonder what might have happened to you, Mister Dudley. It would have been unfortunate had I been cursed with the burden of regaling your uncle with tales of your incompetence."

"My apologies, Sir."

Captain Drake is an imposing man, sitting at his desk in full uniform. I try not to think about how many men have died at his hand and how many others must have wished they had been so fortunate. A predatory smile revealed his teeth.

"What have you learned from our captives?" he asks, reaching beneath his constrictive collar to scratch an odd fold of skin.

"Nothing of consequence to the Queen, Sir."

"Is it true then? Have these warriors of the Great Armada, these most ferocious conquistadors, proffered outlandish stories as my men have said?"

"I fear they have, Sir."

Captain Drake's smile reached his eyes, though instead of lighting them, they narrowed to slits.

"Do tell."

"Would that the good Captain had such time to waste on madness, Sir."

"Tell me, Dudley, for I have nothing if not time."

And so I unfurled my notes and weaved tapestries of monsters and unfathomable horrors that appeared from beneath the sudden storm, all the while watching his eyes, unable to determine if his amusement was at my expense. When I finished my exhausting recount, I again crumpled the pages into my pocket and turned to excuse myself.

"Well done, lad."

"Excuse me, Sir?" I ask, turning to face him.

"A mere day of interrogations and you bring me such fabulous stories."

Already disappointed with myself, I turn again for the door favoring a cowardly retreat to humiliation, even behind closed doors.

"Magical storms," he chuckles. "Cloaked heretics. Shoggoth. Were there no merfolk, Dudley?"

I pause with the doorknob in my hand, replaying my testimony in my head.

"I never said shoggoth," I whisper.

"Did you say something, Dudley?"

"No, Sir," I say, my stare rising to the back of the door. There was a golden plate mounted to the wood depicting a creature with an octopus for a head and the body of an unholy mating of a monstrous beast to what could only have been a dragon of lore.

I pause, my heart thrumming in my chest.

"You are excused," the Captain says, his voice so dry from the laughter of mocking me that it sounds like a croak.

"Thank you, Sir," I whisper, ducking out into the hallway and closing the door behind me.

I ponder the rumor that the Captain had sold his soul to the devil for mastery of the sea, but I realize now that those accounts had been wrong. Captain Drake had entered into an arrangement with a deity far more sinister.

And even now he dreams.

THE OTHERS

BY *STEWART STERNBERG*

L T. AVERY TRESSLER STEPPED up to the taffrail where Captain Culver, hands locked behind his back, gave full attention to the horizon. The mate followed the Captain's gaze, expecting to see the masts of a ship hull down. Rumor had it that *The Dolphin* was leading a patrol, but he doubted the frigate presented a serious threat. He stared at the choppy sea, chilled as a breeze from the northeast buffeted him. Turning, he met the Captain's worried gray eyes.

"Is something wrong, Captain?"

Instead of the expected shrug and stoic silence, the Captain said: "I had a bad night. Dreams. Nonsense."

The answer surprised Tressler, making the younger man feel uncomfortable. He almost asked the nature of the dreams but stopped himself from posing so personal a question. The Captain slid strong hands along the taffrail, grunting to himself as though settling something.

"Tell the lookout to keep a sharp eye," said Culver. "I don't want to be surprised."

"I don't think there's much danger of that," said Tressler, forgetting himself.

Culver waited.

"I only meant that Parliament is playing at politics. They don't really care about the slave trade. The embargo is a way to harass the French. Besides, what kind of prize is a little cargo ship like *The Delight*?"

"You would know more about matters of Parliament," said Culver. The reference to Tressler's family was unmistakable. Turning a broad back to the first mate, the Captain once again studied the horizon. Tressler knew he had been dismissed.

Culver didn't like him. The Captain was like a small, mean dog that barked to compensate for its size. He resented Tressler's self-confidence and social standing, a thought that amused the first mate when he imagined how Lord Tressler might respond to his son serving on a slave ship running illegal cargo to the West Indies.

"Lieutenant?" A dusky man with long greasy black hair approached them. A scar ran down the man's face, pulling with it the side of the mouth to leave its owner in perpetual sneer.

"Mr Quince?"

"There's been some unpleasantness below."

The Captain turned, waiting expectantly.

"A couple of the cargo have been killed," he said in a muddy Yorkshire brogue. "The slaves are needing an extra firm hand because of it."

"Be direct," said Culver. The Captain stepped forward, square jaw thrust outward in impatience.

Quince glanced about with uncertainty, as though suddenly fearing blame. "Looks like last night, someone took a knife to a couple of the boys," he said. "Cuts 'em up sweetly. Never seen such a mess. Thought you might care to see it for yourself 'fore things get cleaned up."

"Why would I want to do that?" asked the Captain.

Quince laughed uneasily. "Well, sir . . . it seems clear to me that it had been one of the crew what done it. I mean, the slaves being chained and all. I thought you might want to come down and inspect it."

The Captain snorted, directing a finger at Tressler. "You go down, Mr Tressler. When you've seen what there is to see, report back and we'll get to the bottom of this."

"Aye, aye, Captain."

The slave master turned, leading the way aft. Hearing voices above, Tressler stared up to see two men working together to trim the sail. The sky behind them was cloudy, but the diffused light still made him squint. Looking back down, he saw Quince waiting patiently by the large cauldrons which were used to mix gruel for the four hundred and twelve Africans that were their cargo.

Some of the Africans had been picked up in Ghana, while some had been received from boats farther down the coast. Tressler oversaw their stowage, pleased at how easily it seemed to go; he detached himself as much as possible from the operation, instead trusting the handling of the slaves to Quince. The Africans feared the thickly muscled overseer. Although Quince knew several African dialects, Tressler felt the slaves seemed to understand him better when the man spoke through the lash of a whip.

Quince paused at the hatch, holding it open for Tressler, who steeled himself as he peered into the darkness below. The smell of death hit him, along with the reek of feces and fear. This felt different than the usual offending odor of unwashed bodies and waste; it gave him an image of prey unsuspectingly entering the lair of a beast.

"Take this lantern, then," said Quince, handing one down.

The converted cargo ship possessed two slave areas. Unlike some ships which divided these areas with scaffolding to stack the slaves horizontally, side by side, *The Delight* kept them close to the floor and chained together. It was more humane, after all. At least the Africans could shift position a bit. Also, with stacking, one usually lost more than half the cargo and it was time-consuming moving the slaves for feeding and exercise.

Reaching the bottom of the ladder, Tressler turned, holding aloft the lantern. A group of faces looked up at him. Slaves huddling together, pulling at their chains, leaned away from something. Tressler thought some of them almost looked relieved to see him. He made eye contact with a lean man whose round eyes plaintively sought his own.

Quince brushed past and shook a scourge in the face of a young girl. Several of the slaves flinched.

"See?" said Quince. "I've been looking for that respect. I've got too many of these darkies on a hunger strike. The Captain's been asking me what I intend to do about it. Given a chance, I think they would kill themselves."

"Even a canary will fly fast to seek freedom."

"You give these savages too much credit," said Quince. Turning quickly on the ball of his foot, the slave master deftly flicked a wrist to make the whip sing out. A woman cried.

"I'm not here to oversee discipline right now," said Tressler, voice thick with disapproval. "Just show me."

Usually when Tressler was forced to make his way into the hold, something he did as little as possible, he grew accustomed to the smell. No, not accustomed to it, but at least was able to tolerate it. This time it was different.

Quince stepped around the slaves. Chains rattled. The lantern light exposed a corner of the hold where the wood ran red. Tressler's stomach rolled at the sight of splintered bits of bone sticking out from a pile of raw meat. Staring in growing horror, he could pick out an eyeless face in the gore before him. As the ship rose with a wave, the hideous mess oozed forward. Steadying himself by resting a hand on Quince's shoulder, Tressler swallowed several times to keep from vomiting. The other man chuckled rudely.

"Aye, it's something isn't it?" asked Quince.

The wall and floor of the hold was sprayed with blood and bits of matter. Both victims' throats were sliced open and both were disemboweled. The violence of the scene was the work of a powerful, brutal man who had not been satisfied with murder. Instead, the killer had set about to dismember and mutilate the torsos until the dead were barely recognizable as having ever been human.

"Lower the lantern" said Tressler. "This is horrible."

Quince tugged at a fat earlobe, looking away from the scene.

"Can you communicate with any of them?" asked Tressler. "Are any of them able to give you any idea of what happened?"

Quince laughed. "Well, I talked to a couple. There aren't many in this group I understand too well. I asked them what done this and their answers weren't no use. They're a superstitious lot, they are. Simple. They don't think like us."

Tressler stopped himself from responding sarcastically to the last comment. Quince's skin and features showed him to be less like the men on deck than he was to the miserable creatures chained to the flooring.

"What did they say?" asked Tressler. "The ones you could talk to."

"They said they woke up to screaming and didn't see no one about. It was dark. They said the thing that did this was a demon. But what else would they say?"

Tressler considered this. He braced himself and squatted by the corpses, looking for clues as to what weapon might have been used. Surely a cutlass and perhaps a cargo hook. If the slaves did this, then the weapon must still be down here. A shiver passed through him. Feeling vulnerable, he rose, calling for Quince to step closer with the lantern.

Nodding toward the slaves, Tressler said: "If they had a weapon, why would they waste an opportunity by slaughtering one of their own?"

"They don't all get along, sir. There's some would murder one another if given a chance."

Tressler studied the slaves without looking any of them directly in the eye. He gestured toward the bloody scene at their feet.

"Have the men come down and clean this up," said Tressler.

Turning, Tressler climbed quickly up the ladder, grateful to once again return to the light. Inhaling fresh air, he gripped a line running from the foremast to steady himself against a swell. Stopping at the fife rail, Tressler turned his attention to the whitecaps speckling the blue-gray sea.

He had seen horrible things on the battlefield. The images still churned through his dreams, pounding Tressler with shame, but what lay below decks was more disturbing to him than anything he had seen in Spain during the Peninsular War with France. Maybe it was because the battlefield had rules. The slaughter below made no sense other than as an act to slake a hunger for violence.

Culver was fastidious when it came to cleanliness. He washed several times a day and Tressler noticed that when the man shook hands, that he did so with reluctance. Now the Captain stood over a water basin, lathering with a thick bar of soap, ruthlessly scrubbing his palms.

The Captain's cabin was small and necessarily sparse in its furnishing. The only thing that wasn't functional hung on the wall above a small mirror. It was scrimshaw, etched with the image of a British ship of the line. Rumor among the crew was that Culver once had command as a post captain, the etching showing his former commission. The Captain did nothing to dispel the rumor, but Tressler knew the story to be untrue.

"You think the crew innocent of this deed?" asked Culver. The Captain's lips curled with derision. He held Tressler's gaze until the first mate looked away.

"I don't see how it could have been one of the men," said Tressler. "There would have been evidence. Whoever did it would have been covered in blood, leaving signs of red on the ladder or on the deck."

"Then it was one of the slaves," said the Captain.

"I can't confidently express that."

Turning, eyes searching Tressler's face, the Captain appeared amused. Thin lips formed a disdainful smile. His voice became scornful. "It's not the men. It's not the slaves. Then what else is on my ship?"

A blush came to Tressler's face while Culver studied him. The Captain's grin broadened, the silence between them growing uncomfortable, broken only by the sound of men working above. Lifting in the water, the ship listed slightly, forcing Tressler to put a hand against the wall of the cabin to steady himself. The Captain maintained balance without effort.

"The guilty party is one of the crew, Tressler. Quit mothering them. This isn't polite society," said Culver. "You have to show these dogs you mean business. We'll give the guilty party a chance to step forward, but . . ."

"But you don't believe that will happen," said Tressler, knowing his words were out of line.

"No, I don't. I'll tell you what *will* happen. We'll post an extra watch, cut back on their rum, and work them to exhaustion. The men will grumble but they'll put up with it. Because they have to. Then they'll either deliver the guilty party or at least make sure it won't happen again."

The Captain faced Tressler, a smug smile playing on his lips as he awaited further challenge from the first mate. When none was forthcoming, the Captain nodded with satisfaction.

"Two wogs are dead," said Culver. "Maybe someone did them a favor. What concerns me more is the lack of respect shown by tampering with my cargo. You're partly responsible, Mr Tressler. You're too soft and don't back me enough."

"I wasn't aware I had been shirking my duty."

"I'm not talking about your damned duties. I'm talking about your attitude. I'm talking about what's on your face."

Tressler didn't trust himself to respond.

"You've been in the military," continued Culver. "Do you believe the king or Old Boney has any real regard for their foot soldiers? They'd be useless heads of state if they did. The more power one has, the less one can allow emotion to figure into it. You have to rule with an iron hand. But then, you know this. You were an officer, weren't you?"

"I was given a commission."

"That's the problem. You've been given a sight too much. Do you know how old I was when I first came before the mast? Sixteen. Press gang took me. Didn't have no more to say about it than one of those wogs below. I was apprenticed to a smithy at the time. Thought I had my life figured out. Then suddenly I'm taken and for the next three years they reshape and mold me until the old Culver is gone and forgotten. But I had mettle. Had to. Else I'd still be running the rigging with the likes of this sad crew."

The Captain buttoned his jacket. Without further comment, he left the cabin. Tressler followed, resentment simmering ineffectually.

On deck they found the crew had already been assembled. Tressler nodded at the bosun's mate, a short man with a perpetually red face and bulbous veined nose.

"Mr Simpson," said Tressler, giving the man a smile which was enthusiastically returned.

Tressler raised his arms to silence the assembled. The Captain stepped forward, taking his time, slowly scrutinizing the faces of the crew as though being able to read minds. The wind tousled his red hair, giving him a wild look. He tried smoothing it back into place without success.

"You all know what happened last night," he called out. Men watched one another from out of the corners of their eyes. The wind picked up, causing creaks from the rigging. Culver examined the sails critically, eventually returning a gaze to the crew.

"I'm not a strict master," said Culver. "I give you all easy rein. I'm fair. Even the lubbers will agree with that. It may have been rough at first, but then that's the way things are."

The Captain stepped forward, his mouth tightening with anger.

"That being said, someone has taken a knife to two valuable pieces of property. I understand things happen. It was probably a bit of fun went too far. So, I'm asking that the man responsible step forward and take responsibility. I'm not talking about the whip. I'm talking settling accounts. I'm talking money. We'll lose a fair share of the darkies before the journey is through, but who's to say those two wouldn't have made it to the end?"

The men stood mute, studying Culver. He waited and turned to Tressler, an accusing expression darkening his eyes. Tressler met the gaze and felt the Captain expected him to say something. The Captain nodded to himself when Tressler didn't respond.

"No one?" asked the Captain, speaking to the crew but looking at his first mate. "No one willing to be a man about this? I'm not talking about paying full value, but some arrangement can be made."

Again he waited for someone to respond and again the men remained mute.

"Very well," said Culver. "Mr Tressler will increase the watches and make sure these dogs are too sleepy at day's end to get into too much trouble. Also make sure the grog ration is cut. Mr Tressler?"

"Aye, aye, Captain."

"And there had better be no more tampering with my cargo. Your shares are getting small enough and I'm done being patient."

The wind shook the rigging as Tressler peered aft, studying the dark water and the clouds that gathered in an impenetrable curtain on the horizon. By night they would be in it. The sea had become choppy and the man at the wheel worked to keep the course. Stepping toward the forecastle, Tressler's voice sang out instruction for the main-staysail and topmast-staysail to be unfurled in preparation for rough weather. The men worked diligently, motivated not just by loyalty to rank but also by self-preservation. Plenty of time before the weather turned, but Tressler chose caution.

Quince came into view, pushing twenty or so slaves to the larboard side. Waving his scourge at them and shouting with gusto, he indicated that they should dance for exercise. He clapped his hands and they unenthusiastically moved their feet. After their exercise, they would be fed from the large cauldrons, then taken below so the next group could be brought up. The Captain believed that spending time on deck helped ward off pestilence. Although this was Tressler's first stint on a slave ship, he agreed with the Captain, having seen many ships coming into port from the middle passage, the surviving slaves emerging from the holds, shuffling, eyes dead, mouths slack.

Three slaves stood apart from the others, rocking back and forth on their feet to avoid being disciplined. These men all had shaved heads and the same inky complexion. They also shared a hideous scarification that ran across their foreheads, down either side of the nose, along the jaw line, and down the neck to the shoulders.

Watching them, Tressler recalled the Captain's words about the necessary indifference of power. The world functioned regardless of human misery. Slaves, soldiers, sailors . . . in the end nothing mattered, and knowing this gave absolution to the overseer.

Quince noticed Tressler sauntering over. "Looks like we're in for it tonight, sir." The master grinned and scratched the blemished side of his face.

"I'm afraid so," said Tressler.

"Any word on who snicked the two darkies? Anyone come forward yet and own up to it?"

Tressler shook his head.

"There are some who will get mighty thirsty."

"Then they will be thirsty," said Tressler.

"Sorry sir, I wasn't meaning nothing by it," said Quince. He quickly changed the subject: "The mates who cleaned up the mess below have taken it badly. They've been spreading rumor that there's some beastie down there."

"What rubbish."

"The men get ideas. The lubbers are the worst."

"How so?"

"They never signed up for this duty, did they? They don't have the stomach for it. Not like us, sir. Some would just as soon dump the cargo and sail back home."

Tressler became aware of a sudden silence among the slaves. One tall man with a high forehead and strong jaw stood in a challenging posture before one of the three men with the scarified faces.

"Who are those three?" asked Tressler.

"The Others. That's what the slaves calls them. A dirty lot they are. The slaves don't cotton to them. Neither do any of the crew.

They're thieves. Wanderers. They steal babies. Can you imagine that?"

"Babies? Are they cannibals?" asked Tressler.

"I don't know."

The large man confronting the *Others* raised his voice and although Tressler couldn't understand the words, the tone was clearly insulting. Quince's lips curled into a smile as he shoved off from the barrel against which he had been leaning.

"Excuse me, sir."

Stepping toward the confrontation, gesturing to his men to intercede, Quince stopped as the larger slave launched, striking one of The Others first in the stomach, then the jaw. The man stumbled under the attack, struggling to raise his arms in defense.

Sailors cheered. The Africans on deck looked excitedly toward the violence, then nervously toward the captors.

Two of Quince's men turned to him for guidance. Fingering the bluish scar that ran down the side of his face, the slave master barked out a laugh.

"Give them a minute," he called out.

The men cheered again. The warrior who first struck, seeing that the fight was being allowed to continue, sprang like a cat that had been waiting for its prey. The prey had other ideas and with surprising speed, blocked the attack and countered with a stunning punch. The man who struck first flailed at the air before landing hard on the deck. The action brought a round of applause from the crew.

"We should stop this," said Tressler.

"It's letting off steam for everyone," argued Quince.

The Other, eyes orgiastic, jumped down, mouth open to reveal sharply filed teeth. Screaming shrilly, he jerked forward to bite the downed man's neck. His opponent used an arm to block the intended bite. Teeth tore through the muscular forearm and blood flowed quickly.

"Stop it, Quince!" Tressler rushed forward, angry at himself for having allowed this to continue.

"Awright," said Quince, stepping in to knock the scarified man with the blunt end of the cat-o-nine.

"Go on," shouted, Quince. "Go on."

The men immediately separated, bowing to avoid the flogging, but Quince laid into them, winking at his men as he did so. The business end of the leather whip produced pained expressions, but to their credit, neither of the slaves called out.

"Sabitini, see to this bite. Granger and Stoddard, take the savages below deck. Let's get the next group up here for feeding and watering."

Quince came back to Tressler. "Sorry about that, sir."

Tressler wanted to upbraid the man but stopped himself. He watched the slaves being herded into the hold, noting how most shied away from the three pariahs identified as The Others.

"I don't like those pointed teeth. I've heard of such things, but I've never seen it until now," remarked Tressler.

Quince nodded, leaning back against the rail. He shrugged.

"Some of them can be savages," he commented.

"They're godless creatures."

"Begging your pardon, sir, but they've got themselves a god. Only it's one that we wouldn't want no part of. The Others say it feeds off dreams. Nightmares. They calls it the Night Eater."

"A god who feeds off nightmares, what pagan rubbish." Tressler, who never considered himself a religious man found himself surprisingly offended at the concept.

Quince studied Tressler, leaning close to him to speak in quieter tones. "When I was growing up," he said, "my gran would teach the young ones a little rhyme: 'There's ghoulies and ghosties, and long-legged beasties, and things what go bump in the night.'"

"May the good Lord deliver us," said Tressler, his voice edged with impatience. "It's a prayer. You don't have it quite right."

"That may be the version you knew, but that's not how my gran closed it."

"What were her lines?"

"'They'll feed on your fear and bathe in your tears, but eat you, if you rise in the night.'"

Tressler snorted. "A rhyme used to scare children so that they wouldn't go wandering about the house in the dark."

"Maybe, but when I was little I took it to mean that once those things got to feeding, that sometimes they couldn't stop, that sometimes they wouldn't stop. Then, they would break out of the Dreamlands. My gran used to say the Dreamlands was where we went sometimes when we dreamed. And sometimes if you was to die in your sleep, you'd be trapped there, never to go to Heaven."

"The Dreamlands is it? You've been among the darkies too long, Quince. You're letting them affect you."

"They're not all animals," said Quince. "I know you know that."

"That's not for me to sort out."

A grimace showed the comment smarted the slave master. He pointed at the scar running down his face. "Know how I got this?" he asked. "I was having a nightmare. Woke up swimming in my own blood. God's truth."

Tressler scowled at the idea. "Something you dreamed tried to kill you?"

He turned his back to Quince, distracted by a shout from above. One of the lubbers had fouled the rigging and now the bossun was impotently shouting instructions to him. Tressler added his own feedback, then returned to Quince, but the man, perhaps sensing he had been dismissed, now stood with his crew, half-heartedly scourging the next group of slaves as they passed him.

Tressler watched the slave master, mulling over the man's words, reappraising and upgrading his estimation of the fellow's depth.

He should listen to Quince; although crude, the slave master probably knew more about the Africans than anyone. Tressler could learn from him. The Captain would have frowned on their exchange, considering the exchange to have become too familiar.

Being aware that he was dreaming didn't keep the terror from building. If anything, knowing that the warmth of the Spanish sun on his shoulders and the sweat trickling uncomfortably down the side of his face wasn't real made the sensations disturbing to him. Knowing what was about to happen and that he could stop it by rising from slumber heightened the frustration and anxiety.

The first volley of French cannon sounded and Tressler, fear drying his mouth and weakening his limbs, watched as the men faltered. Some turned toward him, their eyes seeking reassurance or further instruction. He kept his thin lips snapped shut while musket fire boomed around him. Death prowled the ranks, mindlessly downing first one soldier, then another.

His father would be pleased to see him in the middle of battle. This was the experience Lord Tressler wanted for him. When war broke out, his sister wrote that it was the first time she could remember hearing her father mentioning his son with pride. His mother had tried blocking him from going abroad, arguing weakly against Lord Tressler that his son's lack of direction was normal for someone youthful.

"It's normal for someone pampered," Lord Tressler responded. "It's normal for someone without appreciation or gratitude."

Knowing she couldn't persuade her husband against this course, she purchased a commission for Avery so at least he could enter the military as a major and lead with distinction.

"Keep formation," shouted Tressler, sword held high, voice tinny, uninspiring. Smoke from the battlefield half-blinded him.

The French drove forward. He tried urging the men to hold their ground, but the terror covered him like a cold skin. Shame gutting him, he backed down the hill, but resisted the urge to bolt for the safety of the copse of trees at the bottom. Men fired back, men stood their ground, men backed down the hill with their commander, some firing, others not.

Moving through the haze, rising above the blue and white uniforms of the French, the horror appeared. Black, insectoid, its bulbous body looked hard to the touch, an exoskeleton dripping slime. The thing sucked in the light and returned darkness.

Its head lifted and Tressler's mind reeled at the sight of a scarified human face on that monstrous body. Opening and shutting its mouth, it revealed pointed, red-dripping teeth. Round eyes made contact with him. Innocent eyes. Not the innocence of virginity, but the innocence of apathy. The thing fed as it moved among the dead, sucking at the fear in the air, like a hungry kitten nursing but never sating its hunger.

The men turned, looking for guidance. Even the older among the ranks, whom he knew talked about him behind his back, searched his face for direction.

Another cannon volley. A man danced back, looking like an acrobat in somersault, an enormous hole torn through his chest. Rolling to a stop on the brown soil, the soldier ended on his face, blood pooling beneath him. The man pushed himself up, standing slowly on uncertain legs, to look at Tressler with bleeding pig eyes. The man's mouth yawned open, black lips pulling back to reveal pointed teeth.

Men dropped their weapons and fled, their voices shrill with horror.

Tressler drove the steed down the hill, away from the violence and gore. Away from the thing with the soft, vulnerable eyes. Crying as he fled, tears streaming down his cheeks, stomach roiling with self-loathing. Abandoning his men to the sounds and smell of battle, he thought only of his own safety.

"Sir."

Tressler looked to his side, eyes wide with horror, face bathed in sweat. The cabin boy, small for his age, with a grim face, stood beside him. Tressler used his palms to wipe the tears away. The boy waited respectfully until he had a moment to collect himself.

"The Captain wants you on deck, sir."

Still disoriented by the hideous dream, Tressler swung from his hammock, almost losing his balance as the ship plunged downward. He hadn't expected the coming storm to be such a fury. How had he slept through this pounding? The Captain would be furious with him, and rightly so. Pulling on a coat, he guiltily wondered how long the boy had been standing over him and if he had perhaps said something in his sleep. No one knew about his display of cowardice, although some of his fellow officers at the time had made testing inferences. Tressler patted the side of the boy's face and nodded.

"Is the Captain angry then?"

"Furious," said the boy.

"Were you standing over me long?" asked Tressler casually.

"I don't catch your meaning, sir."

Tressler pushed past the boy. He braced himself against the cold spray, having to reach for a line to keep his balance. Eyes checking stern, he could barely make out the helmsman fighting to keep the course against the wind. He turned and struggled aft, grabbing hold of the halyard to stand next to the bosun's mate.

"It's turned into quite a blow," the bosun yelled.

"It has. Where's the old man?"

"Aft. Watch yourself. There's been trouble."

Before Tressler could ask for clarification, the mate had a trumpet to his lips and obviously following the Captain's instruction, was shouting to the crew to reef the sail.

Tressler left him, struggling forward, the rain coming down so hard that he had to turn his face from it. The crashing of the waves, the steady downpour, the groaning of the rigging, all combined to become nearly deafening. He kept aft until he found the Captain. Culver stood with four armed men, his face twisted with the effort of shouting to be heard over the storm.

Captain Culver's eyes became harsh as he saw Tressler. He waved him close, putting a crushing grip on the younger man's shoulder.

"You took your time about it," shouted the Captain.

"Sorry, sir."

Another swell. The way the ship responded made Tressler wonder if they were taking in water. The Captain gestured toward the men at his side.

"Someone went missing," shouted Culver. "Someone went missing so Quince took his men down to see what was stirring with the darkies. They haven't returned. Take these fellows with you and see what's what."

Tressler leaned to compensate for the roll of the ship. He nodded, taking a cutlass offered him by one of the men. Another man offered him a pistol. The Captain grabbed his wrist, giving his arm a twist.

"Show some guts," said Culver. "Show some guts, but don't you take no chances. Don't hesitate to kill someone if someone needs killing."

"I'll do my duty," Tressler shot back at him.

The Captain studied him but didn't let go. The older man's eyes were accusing, burning with intensity. "Don't hesitate to kill them. I won't tolerate a rebellion. I'd rather lose the entire cargo than suffer a rebellion. No wogs are going to take this ship from me. I won't have it. I'll set fire to the thing myself before I'll let that happen."

Tressler wanted to punch the man in the face. He continued to hold his ground against the Captain's glare. Culver released him. "Go on. Get down there. Make yourself useful."

"Aye sir," said Tressler.

With a curt nod to the four sailors assigned to him, he started back toward the hatch. The hatred he felt for Culver was replaced by growing trepidation as he considered what he was being asked to do. A rebellion. If that was the case, then wouldn't they be better off waiting for the storm to abate so all hands could attend to the matter? No. There was no telling what the slaves might get into if given time. They weren't seafarers. The storm would work to Tressler's advantage.

"Get a lantern!" Tressler yelled.

A light was handed to him. He exchanged reassuring looks with the men, then stood back while one of them slipped back the iron hasp securing the hatch. The ship brightened, an arc of lightning overhead illuminating everything too crisply. Thunder cracked, the sound of cannon.

"This is it then," called Tressler, working up courage. He had considered sending the men ahead of him, no one would blame him for that, but remembering the accusation in the Captain's voice, he started down first. Carefully making his way into the hold he thought about what he had seen the last time he was down there. He steeled himself for something equally horrible.

As always the smell was the first thing to hit him. He swallowed quickly to keep from retching. The sensation passed. Working into the hatch, the pistol stuck into his belt along with the cutlass, he started down. With his back exposed to the darkness, the vulnerability of his situation stiffened the muscles in his arms and legs and made the hairs along the back of his neck stand on end. The carrion smell grew stronger and so did the roiling within his stomach.

Holding the lantern up, Tressler finished the descent. He had tried preparing himself for the blood, but the sight of Quince staggered him. The overseer lay with his head turned backward and a fist-sized hole punched in his chest. The lower part of the overseer was separate from the torso. Beside him were the other two missing crewmembers, both horribly mangled. One slave lay among the gore. Tressler noted it was the corpse of the African who had earlier struck one of The Others.

Looking toward the scaffolding where the slaves were bolted into place, he noted that without exception they all slumbered. He had expected to find them crouched and ready for him, but here they were, at least those he could see, still shackled and sleeping like small children. And all of them appeared to be dreaming, eyes moving rapidly beneath eyelids.

Tressler felt the movement before he saw the thing in the yellowish light of the lantern. Rising from the still forms of the slaves, creeping among them as though it emerged from the opening of an invisible lair, something horrible took shape, becoming the thing from his nightmare. The human head, grotesquely mounted on a bloated body, turned to face him, opening a mouth with razor sharp teeth. The eyes studied him, widening so that the black irises were totally surrounded by white.

Night Eater.

One of the sailors who came down the hatch with him made a whimpering sound. Another stepped forward, holding his pistol out before him. The gun fired.

"What is it?" shouted one of the men. Shaking his head, Tressler realized with shame that tears ran down his cheeks. He used his sleeve to brush them away.

Another man shouted something, but Tressler couldn't move. The thing paused, two underdeveloped forelegs with scythe-like appendages dripped red. Another pistol fired.

The ship moved with the storm outside, sending them sliding first one way, then the other.

Tressler's eyes ran over the slaves nearest him, looking for the scarification that marked The Others, but couldn't see any of the outcasts. Remembering Quince's words, he kicked at the closest sleeping form.

"Wake them up!" he shouted. "Get them all awake."

Thinking of his dream and of Quince's superstitious ramblings, he now knew where the thing had come from: the Dreamlands. Summoned for revenge, it had broken through and now thrilled to the nightmares and miseries of those in bondage and of the crew above.

"Wake them," Tressler repeated, leaning forward to shake a small man with delicate features. The movement under the eyelids stopped. Tressler moved to another of the slaves, shaking him as well, watching the face for any change of expression.

"Come on, sir," a sailor urged.

"Wake them."

"If they can sleep through this, then they can't be wakened. Not by us."

Coming forward now, trailing oily threads of blackness, the creature stepped on the sleeping bodies, seeming to draw strength from contact.

"Go tell the Captain," cried Tressler, pushing one of the men toward the ladder. Turning, he faced the advancing threat, firing a shot at the monster. The pistol ball struck the thing below the right eye, sending out tendrils of blackness to meld with the dark.

"The face," called Tressler. "Aim for the face."

Two more pistols discharged.

Tressler charged, cutlass held before him. Short forearms parried his blade, countering with brutal stabbing motions that almost knocked the weapon from his hands.

The three sailors under his command took advantage of Tressler's charge to come in from the side, weapons striking the creature's chitin shell. Blades chopped, cracking off bits of tough matter and exposing something softer underneath. A groan ran through the slaves.

Seeing the damage they inflicted heartened Tressler. He called for them to strike again. The sailors moved as one, pulling the thing's attention away from their commander. Black talons sliced in their direction but found no target. Watching the head turn to get a better look, Tressler saw an opportunity, hacking at its neck. Steel sliced through skin, nearly severing the head. The monster opened its mouth to scream but the wail came from the sleeping slaves, their lips bursting open to let the cry of the Dreamlands fill the hold. The misery in their collective voice made Tressler feel small and lost. Hopeless.

Blackness poured from the neck of the beast, a foul expanding cloud. Watching, Tressler knew the thing was pulling nourishment from the slaves, healing itself.

"It won't die," whispered one of the men.

"It's tied to the slaves," said another. "Kill them."

"No," Tressler called. He held the lantern aloft, trying to decide on a course of action.

"We've got to get out of here," said another man, touching Tressler's shoulder in an attempt to gently guide him back.

They stepped to the ladder. The sailors tried getting Tressler to go first, but he shook his head. "You men start up. I'll go last."

The sailors scrambled toward the hatch. Tressler gave a last look at the hold, then started up after them. Their progress was abruptly halted. Fists pounded against wood and iron.

The man at the top of the ladder wept in frustration. "The hatch is closed. We're trapped."

"Culver's written us off."

Tressler dropped back down, the three sailors landing next to him, faces reflecting mounting desperation. Summoning courage, they turned, spreading feet slightly apart to compensate for the listing of the ship. With dread they peered through the gloom to see that the thing had almost reformed, it's bright eyes once again radiating intelligence.

"We can't kill it," said one sailor. "Hack it up, it just comes back."

Tressler spotted movement behind the monster. Crouching in a predatory manner, barely visible in the shadows, were the three men the slaves called The Others. Seeing them there, gesturing, looking as though they held open some rift through which the thing had entered, their presence disgusted and outraged him.

"Give me your pistol," he said to the man behind him.

"I need to reload," the sailor responded in a quivering voice.

"Do it. Quickly."

Scraping sounds drew his attention and Tressler instinctively jumped to a defensive stance. An ebony talon lashed toward him to be deflected by tempered metal. Another slash, another deflection. Again. Again. The flurry continued, with each strike potentially a killing blow.

A second blade joined his. The sailor stepping in, grim-faced, jaw clenched in determination, attacked with careless abandon, forcing the creature to back away. Pressing the attack, he slightly dropped his guard. A talon skewered him, another opened a red wound across the belly.

"The pistol."

The first sailor slapped the gun into Tressler's hand, then moved forward to take the place of his fallen comrade.

Tressler raised the pistol, narrowing one eye to sight the target. The ship listed sharply, the opportunity passed. Swearing, Tressler again tried finding his shot. The creature fended off the attacks of the two sailors, stepping back, head dipping low as forearms spasmed in readiness. The sailors raised their voices, charging forward to meet the challenge. Resisting the urge to fire at the creature, Tressler instead found his target again, this time pulling the trigger.

The Other took the shot in the chest, arms flailing as he fell backward. As the ball penetrated, the creature screamed, tufts of blackness lifting in tendrils from its chitin hide.

Running past the beast, almost tripping over the sleeping forms,

Tressler cast aside the pistol in favor of his cutlass. The wounded man crawled backward, leaving a trail of blood as he tried escaping harm's way. Mouth opening, a horrible hissing coming through filed teeth, the man focused at a spot over Tressler's shoulder. Without turning, the first mate could hear the beast turning, leaving off its attack to come to the villain's rescue.

"Mr Tressler!"

He knew the monster was at his back. Any second a talon would pierce him, or drive through his spine, severing bone and muscle. Without pause, Tressler swung the cutlass down, hacking at the African. The man writhed in pain. Another blow, this time the blade broke the man's sternum, slicing into the chest cavity. With the detachment of a butcher, ignoring the screams that rose from the sleeping slaves, Tressler kept at him until the man lay still.

A blast of cold, loathsome air passed over Tressler. Filmy black mist covered him as the creature returned to its place in the Dreamlands. Angry. Frustrated. It left with a final roar, trying to pull Tressler with it, but it the first mate stood his ground.

The slaves woke, shouting to one another in their strange languages. Tressler saw their faces through the dimly lit hold, felt the fear that gripped them and the hungry but insatiable hopelessness. Mustering a tone of authority, he shouted for them to stop their piteous wailing. One man reached out to him in supplication. Tressler kicked at him.

"Quiet them down," shouted Tressler.

The men looked at one another, unsure what to do.

Tressler strode across the hold, the slaves leaning to get out of his way. Gripping one sailor by the shoulders, he spoke to him in a low, angry tone: "Show them discipline. Teach them who we are and make sure they know their place."

"Aye, sir."

"Also, you'll find two more like that fellow. Scarred faces. Filed teeth. Kill them. Do it now. Make sure of it."

Tressler walked to the ladder, leaning against it while his men hurried back and forth among the cargo, checking the chains and administering punishment where they felt it warranted. A scream told him they had found another of The Others. A third scream. The third one struck down.

Tressler heard the men above, moving into place as the Captain shouted instruction to them. The storm having passed, the crew now prepared to handle the slaves below. The hasp groaned as it was pulled aside. Tressler shoved the hatch open, pausing as the fresh air hit him. He savored it, then climbed onto the deck.

Covered in dried blood and grime, the first mate slowly studied the faces of the crew, noting how several backed away, some dropping their eyes, others whispering to their neighbors. He wanted to smile at that, but kept his face free of emotion. Reaching down, he helped the other survivors to the deck.

"The three of you?" asked Culver.

"Five crewmen, five slaves. The situation below is under control."

Culver's lips curled at the corners. "So it all balances out."

Tressler considered that statement. He stood straighter, heels together, arms at his side. "Permission to go get cleaned up, Captain."

"Permission granted."

Tressler glanced upward. The sky was still cloudy. The sea air still had a cold bite to it. The sails, dirty gray, looking almost ragged, filled with wind, snapping smartly.

"Mr Tressler," the Captain called after him.

"Aye, Captain?"

"Was there a monster?" asked Culver, a tone of amusement in his voice.

Tressler looked at the men who had been in the hold with him. He gave both a warning glance. "Only those that we brought with us," he said.

"Just so," said Culver. Nodding to the bosun, the Captain instructed him to collect a few men and go below to retrieve the bodies of the fallen.

SIGNALS

BY *STEPHEN MARK RAINEY*

T HE JENKS 25-FOOT CABIN cruiser had been closing in on the strange lights for a good five minutes, and Dan Caefer had called several times for Rutherford to join him on the fly bridge, but he gathered his partner must be passed out drunk. Caefer had thrown back a few shots of rum himself in the past hour, but there was nothing wrong with his perceptions.

He knew one thing: the cameras wouldn't lie to him.

He checked the GPS coordinates he had recorded eight years ago. He was exactly on target. Through his binoculars, he could see dozens of brilliant, colorful spheres above the clouds, dancing and whirling around each other, emitting showers of violet sparks, leaving trails that looked like gold and crimson feathers.

Thrilled was how he felt. Jubilant. Ecstatic. It was like rediscovering a treasure he had once possessed but lost in a moment of carelessness. No, he had never "possessed" even the most elementary understanding of the phenomenon in the sky, but he had witnessed it so closely, experienced it so profoundly, that its effect had been to change his life.

"Ruth!" he called again, noting that the frequency of the prismatic ripples through the atmosphere was increasing. If history repeated itself, the lights would remain active for a scant few minutes, then they would fade, the twilight sky would darken, and as night settled over the northern Atlantic, no hint would remain that something magnificent had happened.

Except for the evidence that his cameras would have recorded.

"What is it?" The groggy voice came from behind him.

"Ruth! Look out there!"

Rutherford, a hefty, balding bear of forty-some years, ambled up to the fly bridge, rubbing his sleep-swollen eyes, and gave the sky above the horizon a quick scan. When his eyes fell on the congeries of multihued globes shifting and undulating above the purple clouds, his jaw nearly hit the rail.

"Good God, that's it."

"I told you. I told you this was the place."

"Somebody else has got to be watching," Rutherford said, lifting his own pair of binoculars to his eyes. "Airplanes up there. Satellites taking pictures. Other people *have* to know about this."

Caefer nodded vacantly. They were ninety miles out to sea, east-southeast of Barrington, Nova Scotia. Whatever was happening up there, it did not register on radar, and to the best of his knowledge, no satellite imagery of the phenomenon existed. But for its magnitude, it must have been visible at least thirty miles away.

Indeed, when he had seen the lights for the first time, almost fifty years earlier, he had been in an airplane, on his way with his parents to London.

Yet of the nearly two-hundred people on the airliner, he had been the only one fortunate enough to glimpse the event.

This spectacle, he thought, was *his*. It had always been *his*.

"Hey," Rutherford said, pointing to the gunmetal ocean beneath the luminous globes. "There's something out there."

Caefer's gaze followed Ruth's pointing finger. *My God, the man was right.* At a point directly beneath the lights—perhaps two miles distant—the sea was churning violently, and amid the white froth, he could see a long, dark shape, almost like a submarine that had just breached the surface. He focused his binoculars on that area, but he could make out no details; just a vague, black mass that might have been floating amid the ocean lather. But as he watched, a violet-tinted spray erupted from one end of the object, climbing steadily higher and higher, until it became a narrow stream of luminous mist that grappled its way toward the roiling mass of light above it. He knew immediately that this was no column of water vapor, but something else—something not propelled from below. No, it was more as if some sentient power were *drawing* it upward.

Rutherford, at least, had the presence of mind to aim one of the three cameras trained on the sky at the shape amid the waves.

"Are we getting this, Ruth?"

"Yeah," his partner said, smiling so broadly his teeth gleamed in the supernal light. "Looks good."

As the weird color beam approached its destination, the orbs' dance became more feverish and the individual nuclei intensified into dozens of miniature suns, all in utter silence, the only sound the rhythmic rumble of waves against the cruiser's hull. Then, as the leading edge of the misty column penetrated the first layer of rainbow-like haze that surrounded the mass, the world went abruptly white. Caefer threw a hand over his eyes, but only after glimpsing a monstrous bolt of lightning that arced into the heavens, *away* from the earth, as if the entity, as he had come to think of it, had fired a massive burst of energy into deep space.

As the bolt departed and his vision gradually returned, he saw, beyond the dark, lingering afterimage, the aerial spectacle in its dying glory: the bright spheres dimming, the surrounding, prismatic ripples slowing and fading to dull gray, the sparks spiraling away into streamers of black smoke that gradually thinned to nothingness. At last, only a huge, ghostly shadow remained, which soon mingled with the bronze-tinged cumulus clouds that glowered like sullen leviathans over the sea.

"My God," Caefer said, staring at the last remnants of the unbelievable—no, unimaginable!—spectacle. "We discovered gold, Ruth. That, sir, was gold."

Rutherford was not listening to him. Instead, he was pointing out to sea again, in the direction they had seen the drifting mass. "Oh, Jesus. Will you look at that!"

Caefer's eyes turned, and then his stomach lurched as if he had been sucker-punched.

The dark thing remained on the surface, still ringed by white froth. From its midst, a huge, spherical object had risen and was slowly rotating to reveal an icy violet hemisphere with a black disc in its center, which expanded within its shimmering field even as it came to rest, facing them.

"An eye," Rutherford whispered. "It's a God-damned eye."

"Get the cameras on it," was all Caefer could breathe, even as he began snapping shots with his personal Minolta digital. "Get pictures."

Rutherford moved like an automaton, his gaze never leaving the Cyclopean sphere, which appeared to be studying them as intently as they were it. The alien stare sent frozen daggers across the space between them, the impression of malevolence so palpable that, for the first time, Caefer felt a tremor of fear at what he might have gotten into.

"Let's pack it in," Rutherford said, echoing Caefer's unspoken sentiments. "I think we've seen enough, don't you?"

Caefer nodded, willpower alone restraining the cold terror that was now struggling to conquer his body. "Let's secure everything. We don't want to lose what we've gotten."

Rutherford needed no goading. Within a minute, he had stowed the cameras, and Caefer had turned the cruiser 180 degrees and firewalled the throttle.

When he turned back to view aft, the monstrous eye was gone, as was the dark mass and surrounding foam. The sea and sky had reverted to their rightful, timeless selves, and to God above, he thought, the speeding boat, with its two miniscule and fragile human occupants, would have been the only things that appeared out of place in the vast, twilight tableau.

"Can you fucking believe it?" Rutherford's eyes burned into Caefer's, almost as if to accuse him. "Gone. Every bit of it."

"Everything was set up correctly," Caefer said in a soft voice, afraid that if he spoke in a normal tone his voice would crack. "The digital and the 35-millimeter." He stared at the pile of useless photo paper, the murky gray and brown fields that should have displayed images of the colorful spheres dancing in the sky. When they had attempted to view the digital photographs and videos, his monitors revealed only meaningless mosaics of dull color, as if the pixels had been broken down and scattered randomly.

Rutherford turned to peer out the picture window of Caefer's seaside villa at the foaming waves breaking on the beach a hundred yards away. "We saw it on the monitors. Everything was working fine. The damned thing must give off some kind of energy field. Or something."

"But it didn't affect the GPS or the compass or any other instruments, at least that I know of."

"Damn near like it was willful."

"Willful," Caefer repeated. "You suppose that's possible?"

"Who knows? A thing like that…"

"It leaves us with no evidence."

"Still, we did see it. *We* know it's out there."

"If we report this, there's not a living soul who'll believe it. No sane one, anyway."

"We'll just have to brainstorm."

Caefer nodded, his blood seething with ecstasy, frustration, and sheer horror. Yes, they had seen something that, as far as he knew, no other human being had ever seen up close; but his painstaking efforts, his years of planning to compile incontrovertible evidence, all had gone up in smoke. He sat on his barstool, tossed back another slug of Porfidio rum, and wondered what he could do over the next eight years to ensure that he would bring home the proof he *had* to have before he could share such a monumental discovery.

"Well, I've got to get back," Rutherford said. "It's a long drive home."

"So soon?"

"I can't afford to miss any more work," he said. "This costs me more time than I can spare."

"Well. I'm glad you came. We'll figure out something. There's got to be a way."

Rutherford shrugged. "I suppose."

"I'll count on you for next time."

"Of course."

Caefer helped his friend gather his belongings in mostly sullen silence. This was not what either of them had expected—disappointment that overshadowed the exhilaration, the *awe* they should have felt after sharing such an experience. They had made the discovery of a lifetime, seen firsthand the evidence of something sentient and purpose-driven beyond human imagination, and to think that it could mean so little without the proof they needed to protect their reputations. It was wrong, and Caefer *knew* it was wrong, but no rationalization could lighten the heaviness of his heart.

"We'll talk," Rutherford said as he headed out the door toward his waiting Toyota Camry. He turned and gave Caefer a thoughtful stare. "We'll do it next time. We'll figure something out."

"Yes."

"See you in eight years."

Caefer's wife, Sarah, had no use for mysterious phenomena and only grudging patience for her husband's age-old obsession. She did enjoy living on the Nova Scotia coast, particularly since he had been able to retire at age fifty, with some measure of wealth, from his brokerage firm in New York City. She knew he had insisted on moving here because it placed him closer to the object of his mania, but indulging it seemed a small price to pay for the time it gave them together in a comfortable, picturesque setting.

Caefer had attempted to share his excitement about the subject with his wife for years, to no avail, but she was perceptive enough to understand that the deep turmoil he suffered in the wake of this outing was unlike any he had experienced before. He gave her a simple, accurate explanation of the events and showed her the useless mountain of evidence he had brought home. Quite to his surprise, this revelation appeared to spark her interest; for the first time in their nearly twenty-five years of marriage, she showed a hint of understanding the depth of his passion, his desire not only to learn the ultimate truth but to be credited with the discovery of a potentially earth-changing event.

"It's almost impossible to believe that there could be something like this without lots of other people knowing about it," she said to him as they nestled on the couch their modest living room. "Scientists. The government. I mean, you first saw it from a plane. Planes must pass over that part of the ocean all the time. Ships too."

"People *have* seen it. But it only lasts a for a few minutes, at eight-year intervals. You have to be at exactly the right place, at exactly the right time. There's just never been enough credible evidence to spark an official investigation." *Only mine,* he thought. *Only mine.*

His first encounter, when he was in the airplane, had been at age seven. When he was going on sixteen, he happened to read a news report of sailors having seen something like the Northern Lights in that particular area, even though atmospheric conditions virtually precluded any chance of such an event. However, that story had been sufficient to spark his memory, and that was when he first began investigating stellar and atmospheric phenomena. At age 24, when the approach of the comet Wolf occupied the pages of scientific journals, he discovered new reports of strange lights in the Atlantic by a few passengers of a cruise liner. The stories gained no official credence, yet he knew now that he was on to something.

At the next cycle of the comet, there came a few scattered accounts from travelers on ships and planes about "unusual lights," and by now, Caefer had begun an intense personal quest to gather relevant information. Something about the memory of those lights—how bright, how *alive* they had seemed—inspired his imagination like nothing else in his life. By day, he devoted all his energies to a lucrative, enjoyable vocation, but in his free moments, he became what he liked to term a "driven detective." It was during this time that Bob Rutherford, from Arkham, Massachusetts, answered one of his solicitations for people who "might have witnessed unusual phenomena" in a particular region of the Atlantic. Rutherford had also been on an airplane when he saw the lights in the sky.

At age 40, Caefer left his wife at home for a week, rented a cottage on the Nova Scotia coast, and chartered a boat to explore the ocean as Comet Wolf made its regular, predicted approach. While he was out at sea, he had glimpsed in the far distance a few brief flashes of colorful lightning and what appeared to be a luminous haze on the horizon. The event passed quickly, so that he had no chance to attempt to photograph it, but he made thorough notes of his boat's position and course.

By the next year of the cycle, GPS technology was available, and now Bob Rutherford joined him on his quest. This time, they got in relatively close, but an approaching storm prevented a clear view, and his photographs revealed only murky patches of light, which he assumed to be a result of the thick clouds and sporadic lightning.

Now he understood. The thing refused to *allow* itself to be photographed.

"Whatever this is," he said to Sarah, "there's no telling how long it's been here, or what it's actually doing. No one's ever put together the pieces before. I'm going to be the one to do it."

"Isn't having the knowledge enough?" she asked.

He shook his head. "What's the point if you can't share it? But it has to be done scientifically. Otherwise, I'm just another kook."

"You're not a kook."

"You know that," he said with a little chuckle.

The telephone on the end table rang, and he reached over to lift the receiver. "Hello?"

"Dan. It's Ruth."

His friend's voice sounded odd. "Ruth? What's going on?"

There was a long silence. "The eye we saw on the ocean. Remember?"

"Of course."

"I've seen it again."

Caefer's blood froze. "What?"

"Or something like it. Outside. Coming up from the river."

Caefer could barely speak. "Is it there now?"

"I don't see it. But I did, not five minutes ago. It was moving this way."

"You're certain that's what it was?"

"You don't think I'd mistake something like that, do you? You know my backyard faces the river, right? I was outside and noticed something moving in the water. That eye came up. Plain as day, I saw it."

"Good God. What are you going to do? Is Jean with you?"

"No, she and Darlene are out tonight. I'm alone."

"Maybe you should leave."

Another silence. "No," Rutherford said at last. "I'm going to hold out here and see what happens. If I've somehow made a connection with this thing, I have to follow through."

Caefer's heart pounded like a jackhammer. "Stay on the line with me, then."

"I will. I'm heading back outside now. I don't see anything. It's very quiet. Dog barking somewhere down the way. Nothing moving. Wait. There, I see something."

Caefer waited for Rutherford to speak again, but for several seconds, no further sound came through the earpiece. He finally asked, "Ruth? What's happening?"

A faint whisper drifted across the miles. Then the line went dead.

Two days later, he received word that Bob Rutherford had vanished without a trace, leaving behind a disabled wife and a young daughter.

This time, not only had Sarah agreed to come with him, she had insisted on it. When she could not dissuade him from going, she refused to remain behind.

The comet was on its timeless approach, though not currently visible. The rim of the sun had just touched the western horizon, and the darkening eastern sky seemed to be anticipating the event that would unfold at any moment. The GPS indicated they were precisely on target. Though the effort would likely prove futile, he had again armed himself with cameras, this time including a Raytheon thermal imaging model for photographing infrared, a Geiger counter, and—as almost an afterthought—a kit for collecting water samples. Sarah had become adept at running all the equipment, and she stood ready on the fly bridge with him, a look of excitement on her face—perhaps more for his sake than her own.

The only thing Caefer had learned in the last eight years was that the mystery of the Atlantic lights was deeper, more sinister, than he could have previously imagined. He remembered having sensed malevolence when facing the thing out on the ocean all those years ago, but until Rutherford's disappearance, he had interpreted it as a matter of his own ignorance rather than the darker alternative.

Federal investigators had eventually showed up at his door, having traced Rutherford's final call to him. Though it was perhaps the hardest thing he had ever done, he told them essentially nothing—that he and Rutherford had talked about their recent boat trip and made tentative plans to do it again. Telling the truth would have gained nothing for anyone, and the last thing he could afford to risk was his credibility.

After all these years, he knew only one thing: Bob Rutherford had ultimately learned the secrets that, so far, the Atlantic entity had withheld from him.

All the more reason, he thought, *not to give in to fear and abandon his quest, as Sarah had for so long begged him to do.*

A golden glow began to warm the violet clouds to the east, and a few seconds later, they materialized from nothingness: numerous clusters of huge, fiery globes, which immediately commenced their dance, emitting showers of multicolored sparks and sending prismatic ripples across the sky. Waves of light crept across the space to wash over the cruiser and sparkle in Sarah's eyes, which widened in awe at the sight. For a time, Caefer watched her rather than the display above, because now, at last, he was able to share the most important *thing* in his life with the most important person.

Whatever else he learned, whether he ever ended up revealing his discovery with the world, he realized now that it was unimportant. Sharing it with her would be enough.

It was against his better judgment that he kept the cruiser motoring slowly toward the entity, but something seemed to draw him onward. Even when Sarah touched his hand and shook her head, he could not bring himself to stop the boat and watch from a distance. He found himself looking straight up to view the heavenly ballet, and now he could feel warmth washing down over him—a smooth, velvet caress that was almost erotic in its softness. Sarah felt it too, for he saw her close her eyes and lean her head back, the corners of her mouth turned up in obvious pleasure.

His attention otherwise occupied, he failed to notice the water beginning to boil around the cruiser, the froth that gathered like cream on the churning waves. Only when something huge and black broke the surface a short distance ahead did their peril begin to register, and then he cried out in shock when he saw a huge, dark-colored sphere rising from the deep only a few yards to starboard. It rotated slowly until it revealed a shimmering violet face with an expanding black pupil in its center, and as its malevolent gaze focused on him, he realized that Sarah was gone.

"No."

He lurched to the side and peered into the water. No sign of her. Then he rushed from the fly bridge to search below. Not in the cabin or in the head.

"Sarah!"

The eye in the ocean leered at him, and if he could possibly attribute any human quality to the thing, it would have been wicked mirth.

Then the beam of pure color began to climb toward the congeries of light above, and when its leading edge reached the dancing shapes and the monstrous entity released its blinding signal into the heavens, he thought, for a perhaps a half a second, he heard his wife screaming.

He knew he screamed. He screamed until the alien eye returned to the depths and the horror in the sky had dissolved into an insubstantial black shadow.

The thing did allow him to return home. But he went home alone.

He never learned the meaning of the entity's transmitted messages; before the next cycle, he succumbed to tuberculosis. On the day he died—an hour before he breathed his last—a newscast indicated that astronomers had discovered something in outer space, moving toward Earth from the rim of the solar system, but by then, he was too far gone to understand.

At age seven, Dan Caefer took his first airplane trip, and it was a big one: New York City to London, to visit his grandparents, whom he had never met before. Of course, he was excited about meeting them and getting to see a new place like London, but more than anything, he was thrilled to be flying in a plane. Ever since he was really little, the sight of those huge birds taking to the air and the fantastic roar of their engines had fascinated him beyond words, and he had always said, "One day, I'm going to ride one of those." Now he was living the dream of his youth.

The sun had begun to set in the west, turning the sky marvelous shades of gold, red, and purple, but it was on the opposite side of the plane, and he could not get a good look past all the other people's heads. So he contented himself by watching the ocean and weirdly tinted clouds outside his own window. It was to his surprise that, far in the distance, he saw what he thought at first was another sunset. But then he realized there were lots of colors, all dancing and rippling, and he decided it must be some kind of rainbow.

Everyone else seemed to be looking at the sunset, eating dinner, or sleeping. No one noticed the colorful array of lights as they gradually slipped away behind the plane, and he decided he wasn't going to tell anyone, not even his parents. He had always heard there was gold at the end of every rainbow, so this would be his secret and his alone.

"One day," he said to himself, "I'm going to find that gold."

It was a promise to himself he knew he would always keep.

THE HAVENHOME

BY *WILLIAM MEIKLE*

*T*AKEN FROM THE PERSONAL *journal of Captain John Fraser, Captain of the* Havenhome, *a cargo vessel. Entry date 16th October 1605.*

My dearest Lizzie.

Today has been the worst day of my life. As I sit here, warm in my cabin, whiskey at hand, I can scarcely believe the deprivations suffered by the brave people of this far flung outpost. I should have stayed at home like you asked. You would have kept me warm. If only I'd done as you asked, then I might have been spared the terrible sights that met us at landfall.

We had no thought of winter when we left home port. Do you remember? It was a bright Scottish summer's day. You cried as we parted, and the sun made rainbows of your tears. I can still see you now, standing on the dock, waving us off. How I wish I could look at you, just one more time, one more time to warm my heart against the cold that has gripped us all.

After the auspices of its beginning, our voyage soon reminded us that the sea is not always benign. After four months at sea my crew expected some ease from the biting winds and cold autumnal spray, some shelter from the elements that had assailed them so assiduously. And some were expecting something more, having heard tell of the harbor tavern of our destination, and the warm doxies who waited there.

Cold comfort was all they found.

We arrived under a slate gray sky, having to tack hard against a strong offshore wind that faded and died as soon as we entered the safe haven of the natural harbor. I thought it passing strange that there was no one on the dockside to mark our arrival. We have been looked for these past two months, and the *Havenhome* is tall enough to be seen from many a mile. And yet no smoke rose from the colony, despite the chill in the air and the ever-present autumnal dampness. There was already a pall over my heart as we hove to.

"Mayhap there is a town meeting," the Pastor said as we stood at the prow.

"Aye, mayhap," I said. But my heart did not believe it. I knew already there was some dark power at large. Perhaps I do have a touch of the Highlander sight after all.

Jim Crawford was ashore before anyone else, running down the dock.

The first mate called after him.

"Do not tire the doxies out Master Crawford."

"I will have first choice," the deck hand shouted, laughing. "I'll leave you the ugly ones. But if you want any ale, you'd best be quick, for I have a terrible thirst."

We found him again when we disembarked and headed into town. He was first at one thing . . . he'd been right at that . . . he was first, but by no means last, to fall in a dead faint.

At our last visit some three years ago this was a thriving town of a hundred souls, living off the land that God gave them, and maintaining peaceful trading relations with the natives. There had even been talk of expansion, with land to the south earmarked for a church.

Now it will only be used as a cemetery, for they are dead . . . every last soul of them.

The fortifications have not been breached and there is no evidence of a fight. There were just the bodies of the dead, as if the Lord decided in that instant to take them to their heavenly rest. They lay, scattered on the ground like fallen leaves, faces gray, ashen and almost blue. They are cold to the touch, their eyes solid and milky, like glass marbles sunk in a ball of snow.

It was all the first mate and I could do to keep the men from fleeing.

Some did indeed fall to their knees in prayer and supplication.

"What could have caused this Cap'n?" the first mate asked.

"Mayhap t'was a freak storm," Coyle the cook said. "For surely we have seen the same thing happen to a man at the mast in the far north waters?"

"But these are not the north waters," the pastor replied. "This land is most clement, even in comparison to our own home. Men do not freeze in October. This is the devil's work, mark my words."

As for myself, I kept my peace then, but as I saw more of what lay on the streets I came to think they might both have been right.

I was in the court house, standing over the still, dead bodies of Josiah MacLeod and his family and trying not to weep when the pastor made his final report.

"We have searched the whole town, Captain. As far as we can tell, the entire population has been felled, for no one answered our calls, although our entreaties have been long and loud. God rest their souls."

The burials began.

The small ones are the worst. The sun has partially thawed their bodies, but when you lift them you feel the hard frozen core inside. It is all that you can do to keep from weeping as you lay them into the too-small holes.

After the burials were finally complete our pastor called for a service of remembrance, but I knew the mood of the crew better. I had the cook break open our cargo and prepare a feast while I myself ensured that the tavern was made ready. The men had made a fair pass at clearing up the stench and gore of the carnage that had been wrought there. I was able to hide the last stains of blood with the judicious application of straw and wood chippings. What I couldn't mask was the memory of the sightless eyes and the strewn limbs that had so recently laid scattered on the floor. I could only hope that a flagon of grog and the hearty company of my shipmates would dispel the chill that had fallen on my heart.

We set a great fire roaring in the hearth, cracked open what barrels we could find. We set to feasting and drinking with a gusto that only men far from home and long at sea will understand. Any guilt we might have felt at such merriment in a place where so much destruction had been wrought was quickly assuaged by the warmth of the fire and the sweet tang of the ale.

The evening began in fine fashion. The cook excelled even his own high standards. He managed to turn a few stone of potatoes, a leg of salted pork and some rough vegetables into a mouth watering feast for each of us. Ale flowed freely. For a while we were almost warm.

The Pastor recited "The Lay of Lady Jane," as bawdy a verse as any old sea-dog might muster. It was all the better coming from such an austere man of the cloth. Jim Crawford told a tall tale, of a man from Orkney who was twelve feet high with a two foot cock which he used to beat off foreign raiders. The room was filled with laughter.

"A tune from Stumpy Jack," came the call. When the eldest of the crewmen started on the squeeze box we could almost believe ourselves at home port once more. All went quiet as he started up, tune that we all knew well, for we had sung it many times afore, albeit with lighter hearts and warmer circumstances.

Once more we sail with a northerly gale
Through the ice and sleet and rain.
And them coconut fronds in them tropic lands
We soon shall see again.
Six hellish months we've passed away
Sailing the Greenland seas,
And now we're bound from the arctic ground,
Rolling down to old Maui.

Stumpy Jack was old, but his voice was as clear and true as a young man's. It rang through the rafters, promising of hot sun and even warmer women. We all joined in on the chorus:

Rolling down to old Maui, my boys,
Rolling down to old Maui.
We're southward bound from the arctic ground
Rolling home to old Maui.

Bald Tom found a tavern wench's skirts. There was much bawdy laughter as he moved among the tables pretending to be a doxie. If the talking and laughter was somewhat muted, and if some drank more than was good for them, we pretended not to notice. The

Ulsterman told of his exploits against the Turks in Vienna, Bald Tom, still wearing the wench's skirts, regaled us with tall tales of the Amsterdam brothels. Stumpy Jack sang the old whaler's songs before starting up that old sailor's favorite, "The Girl from Brest." We sang along at the top of our voices. The tavern rang loud, keeping the cold at bay, for awhile at least. For that short span, we made a common bond that life was good once more. It nearly was.

By the time things went bad most of the crew were too far into their cups to notice.

"Bald Tom went out to the privy some ten minutes ago. He has been gone too long," the first mate said to me.

"'Tis not unknown for him to linger over a shit," I replied.

"Aye sir," the first mate said, "But even for Tom this is too long. Especially when there is free ale and meat on the table."

He had it right. Bald Tom often loitered over his ablutions. He was teased mightily over it, but this was over-long, even for him. The pastor and I, being the two men least addled by the drink, went out into the night in search of him.

The cold was like a wall, hitting us square in our faces and taking our very breath.

"Let us leave him to his business," I said. "'Tis too cold to go looking for the steam from his doings."

In truth, it was not just the cold that had me trembling. I had the fear of the devil in me. The memory of the fire inside the tavern was fading fast.

But the pastor was made of far sterner stuff than I.

"Let us continue and look a little further. He may be in trouble," the pastor said. "And there is evil afoot tonight. I feel it in my bones."

"Then have at it man, but make it quick. Already the cold bites at my ankles. At the rate the men are drinking, there will be none left for our return."

He led the way round the corner of the tavern, tall and proud in his faith while I cowered, cowed, behind him like a whipped scoundrel. I am not sure if the pastor prayed, but I was surely calling on God's protection more than enough for both of our souls.

Bald Tom will be on the privy for the rest of eternity. We found him in the shed, squatting over the rough hole in the ground, skirts pulled up around his waist. He was no more a cold block of flesh;

frozen solid in mid-shit. Had the pastor not been there I believe I may have laughed . . . in jest at first, then later in hysteria.

"Lets us have him inside by the fire," the pastor said. "Mayhap he can yet be revived."

I nay-said him.

"Leave him be. He is deader than anything I have ever clapped eyes on. Deader even than Jim McLean of Banchory, and he had his head taken off by a corsair."

The pastor stood over the body to say the words that would speed Bald Tom to paradise, but I had known the man well. I'm certain that the resting place of his soul would be more than warm enough to thaw any part of him that was yet frozen after the journey.

The pastor was taking over-long with the formalities, while all I could think about was the fire in the hearth, and a flagon of spiced rum. I was about to turn away when it suddenly got colder . . . colder even than the time the sea had frozen around us off Trinity Bay in Newfoundland and we'd been locked in place for a month with naught but salted fish to sustain us. Ice formed in my beard. It crackled to the touch. The last half-inch of my moustache came away in one piece in my palm.

We looked at each other, the pastor and I. I hope my own eyes held less abject fear than I saw in his, but I cannot guarantee it.

"Have you finished telling the Lord of Bald Tom's piety?" I asked, speaking loudly, as if the very sound of my voice would keep the cold at bay.

"That I have, Captain," he replied. "But it is my own soul that concerns me at this moment."

"I have found that a flagon of spiced rum is good for most things that ail the soul," I replied.

"Then let us retire within, and you can show me," the pastor said. "For it is colder than a fisher-wife's teats out here."

Outside the shed something moved, a shuffling, stumbling. Then came a moan, as of a man in pain.

The pastor instinctively moved to help and stepped outside.

"No," I called. I put out a hand.

He was dead before I could help him. He froze, stiff as a board in the wink of an eye. One cold eye stared up at me in amazement before it too froze, all sight going as life left him. He fell, solid as a stone, part in, part out of the privy door.

The sound of shuffling got louder. The cold cut deep, reaching my bones. I am ashamed to say it, but I was mightily afeared, struck immobile with terror as whatever manner of thing was beyond the door crept closer. The noise stopped just outside the shed door. Something pulled the pastor out of the shed, his body scraping on the ground like a slab being slid from a tomb.

I bent, thinking to take his arms, to try to counter whatever had him. But one touch of his bare hand was enough for the cold to burn my palm to the bone. Whatever had the pastor tugged at him again. The body was dragged away out of my sight. But not out of hearing.

My ears were assailed with cracking and crunching . . . teeth grating on icy flesh and bone. I could not tell you what manner of creature made such foul sounds, for I could not bring myself to look.

The sounds continued for some time while the cold crept ever deeper through me until finally I could take it no longer . . . I squeezed past Bald Tom and made an attack on the shed's rear wall.

The noises of feeding stopped. Behind me the privy door creaked as something pushed inside.

I renewed my attack on the wall, kicking and punching like a man possessed. The wall fell before me like dry kindling. There was a single moment of icy cold, a breath on the back of my neck that I will remember for whatever life I have left, then I was away and heading for the tavern as fast as my legs would take me.

Once I made my escape from the privy I was too afeard to risk a look backward. If I had seen the pastor's fate I do believe I may have given up my soul to the Lord there and then. But all I could see in my mind was the roaring heat of the fire, a beacon calling me to safety. I was close enough to hear the crew singing:

There was a young lady from Brest,
Who had an enormous chest
You could place a whole city
On each of her titties
And hide a small hill in her vest.

I mouthed along with the words. Although I was afraid to speak them aloud, the very nature of them, reminding me of home and the fireplace around the inn on the harbor of a summer's evening, gave me what strength I needed to keep moving.

I had a bad moment when my feet slipped, and threatened to give way under me.

In my mind's eye I saw something reach for me, something foul and cold from the worst nightmare of my childhood. I felt its cold dead breath on my neck. I thought that my Maker had finally called for me.

I do believe I screamed, alone there in the dark. I may have lain there, unable to move if I hadn't at the very moment thought of you, my dearest Lizzie. It was the memory of you on the dockside that got me moving. I managed to scramble away and I burst like a fury into the tavern.

Some of the crew turned and, on seeing me, laughed. But there must have been a fell look in my eyes, for their laughter died on their lips. The room fell suddenly quiet.

"What has happened, Cap'n," the first mate called.

I had no time to answer. I turned and slammed the oak door behind me as soon as I was full inside, but even then I felt the cold seep through the wood to my hands.

"Stoke the fire," I called out.

No one moved. They were all stuck immobile by the shock of my sudden entrance.

I backed away from the door as a silver sheen of hoar frost ran across its surface.

"Where's the pastor? Where's Bald Tom?" the voices cried.

"Dead," I called out. "As you will be if you do not heed me. Stoke the fire! It is all that will save us now."

Young Isaac was having none of it. He was one of the ones who had helped clear out the tavern earlier; he'd seen at first hand the slaughter that had happened in this enclosed space.

"I'm not going to be taken like them others. If I'm to die, it will be out in the open," he called.

Before I could stop him he stepped forward and grabbed at the iron door handle . . . and was immediately frozen in place, icing-white like a grotesque cake decoration, mouth open in a mix of fear and surprise, his tongue lying like a cold gray stone in the floor of his mouth.

The men stood stock still, staring at what had become of the young deckhand.

"Stoke the bloody fire!" I called out once more. "Are you deaf as well as witless?"

The cold leeched through the door and started to reach for me. And still they didn't move.

"Have you forgotten those that we placed in the earth? Do you want to be like them? Stoke that bloody fire!"

Finally the first mate had the sense to respond.

"You heard the Cap'n. Stoke this fire, or I'll throw you on alongside the logs."

Some of the men at last set to piling the hearthside logs on the fire while the rest of us backed slowly away from the door.

The wood, and young Isaac, were by now covered in a good half-inch of silver-gray ice, glistening red in the reflected firelight.

"Cap'n," Jim Crawford said fearfully. "What is it?"

"Death," I whispered. "As sure as eggs is eggs, 'tis death for us all, if we cannot get warm."

I heard the first mate call out for more fuel, but I could not take my eyes from the encroaching edge of the ice.

The extent of it spread even as we watched, crawling along the walls as if laid down by some invisible painter, creeping across the floor toward our feet, tendrils reaching out, looking for prey.

As a man we stepped further backward, each of us trying to get closer to the fire which roared at our backs but seemed to give out little heat. In truth I have never felt such cold, not even in the far north where the white bears roam. It was as if my very blood thickened in my veins.

A strange lethargy began to take me. I took a step forward, toward the door, then another. In my head I heard you, my dear Lizzie, calling me in from the field, calling me home for supper.

"Captain!" the first mate cried. He pulled me back toward the fire, putting his own body between myself and the creeping ice.

"Best warm your hands," he said. "It's turned a bit on the nippy side."

I turned and faced the fire, feeling the heat tighten the skin across my cheeks. A layer of frost that had formed on my hands melted away. My blood began to move again so that I felt I might live, at least for a short time longer.

"Tell me Cap'n," Stumpy Jack said. "Is it Old Nick himself come to take us? I always heard tell that fire was more in his line of work."

"I can't tell you that, Jack," I replied. "But there's more than just Mother Nature working agin' us this night. Stoke the fire, man. Keep stoking the fire. It's all that stands between us and a cold grave."

I helped Stumpy Jack load more wood on the flames. The fire had grown so as to fill the grate. We had to stand back and throw the fuel on, but still the ice crept across the room toward us and we were forced to huddle ever closer together.

"It's getting right cozy," Jim Crawford said. "When I dreamed of cuddling up with a warm body in this tavern, it wasn't any of you I had in mind."

"I don't know about that," someone called back. "Give me a shilling and I'll do for you. I'll even take me wooden teeth out."

That bought a round of laughter, and raised our spirits. But not for long.

One by one the men fell silent, each lost in his own thoughts.

There was naught to be heard but the crackle of the logs as the fire ate through fuel as fast as we could throw it on the flames.

The spread of the ice slowed.

Finally it stopped, a mere six inches from our feet. It did not retreat, but neither did it encroach any further. I began to believe that we might yet survive the night.

"Is it over Cap'n?" the first mate asked.

"Mayhap. Just pray it does not get any colder," I said. "And we may yet see the morning."

And then it came, the thing I had been dreading, the thing that had taken the pastor.

From outside we could hear shuffling, and a peculiar grunting, like a pig after truffles.

The wind outside rose, from nowhere to a howling, shrieking gale. Heavy sleet lashed like musket-shot against the shutters. The ice crawled once more, began to creep ever faster toward our feet.

"If you have any good ideas Captain . . . ?" the first mate said.

"Truly, I can think of none, for what Christian man has ever endured such devilry?" I replied.

"Mayhap we should ask the Lord for some help?" the Mate said softly.

I asked myself what the pastor might do, were he still with us.

It took all of my strength, but I took myself further from the fire. I put my own body between the ice and my crewmen.

"Lads, we are in a dark place," I started. "I've led you into trouble aplenty afore now, and I've always brought you home safe. And so I will again. With a little help. The pastor has gone to join his Lord, but mayhap he'll turn back and lend us a hand if he hears us calling. Let us pray."

I led the men in the Paternoster. Their voices were strong and clear, but mine own faltered. I had been watching the ice.

Our appeals to our Maker made not a jot of difference. The ice thickened, inexorably, throughout the room. It still crept slowly forward, and had almost reached all the way to the toe of my shoes.

In the end it was the practical things that helped most . . . we rotated the men round so that all would have a spell in front of the fire, but even that proved of little worth as the supply of logs dwindled and the fire burned down.

"Break up the trestles and tables lads," the Mate shouted. "Everything that's not breathing goes on the fire."

We burned whatever we could find around us, from chairs and tables to the very leg of pork we had been eating earlier. The smell of cooking meat filled the tavern, but none of us were hungry.

We huddled together until you couldn't have squeezed a sheet of paper between us. In that way we kept ourselves alive.

But still the ice crept forward.

"Keep moving men," the first mate shouted. "Give everyone a sight of the fire."

The wind howled up a notch. The long night went on.

We shuffled in our tight huddle, looking forward only to our next spell in front of the fire, dreading our next pass in front of the door.

I came to believe there were voices in the wind, soft voices whispering hopes of peace and warmer climes if I would only close my eyes and allow myself to dream.

At other times I found myself talking to you Lizzie, saying all the things I plan to say on my return, if I am spared long enough to see that day.

At some point in that long night we forgot to shuffle, each of us lost in our own icy hell. After a while no one stoked the fire. The ice crept ever closer.

"Goodbye Jennie," I heard the first mate whisper, which was passing strange, as his wife was named Charlotte. That was the last I heard. I fell into an icy black hole that had no bottom.

An eternity later I woke, from a dream of sun and hot sand into a nightmare of icy death.

At first I thought myself back in Aberdeen in my own bed, wrapped and swaddled in a thick quilt against a winter's morning.

Then I moved.

A cold blue hand fell onto my face.

It was no bed-sheet I lay under . . . it was the dead, frozen bodies of my crew. They had done their last duty to me, keeping me alive through the night.

I crawled, on hands and knees like a whipped dog, pushing myself through the blue dead forest of my crew-mates' limbs, promising the Lord that I'd be his faithful servant if he'd only but grant me one final glimpse of warm sun on green pastures.

The Lord finally heard me. I dragged my body clear and stood in front of the dying embers of the fire, tears blinding me as I surveyed the frozen bodies of my crew.

There came a moan from within the pile.

"Cap'n," the first mate cried. "Are we in Hell?"

I reached into the pile and found his warm hand. He dragged himself out as I used what paltry strength I had left to help his escape.

"Not in Hell," I said as I lifted him to his feet. "But as close as mortal man should get."

More groans rose from the pile of frozen flesh.

Of thirty men who entered the tavern the night before, only six of us pulled ourselves from the tangled pile and out into the near-forgotten warmth of a morning sun.

"Fuck me," Stumpy Jack said, squinting in the sudden light. "I ain't been in a pickle near as bad as that since John the Baker's son insulted the Prince of Prussia's consort. I thought I was a goner for sure."

"We are all only here because of the Lord's mercy," the first mate said. "Have heart boys. We may yet see hearth and home."

"And Jennie?" I said.

The first mate smiled.

"Don't be telling the missus, Cap'n," he said. "Jennie is a widow in Liverpool . . . sort of a home from home, if you get my meaning?"

"Don't worry," Jim Crawford said. "We will ne'er get home again, so no one will ever know."

"Home again?" I said. "We may yet. But we must be strong if we are to survive another night such as the last one."

"As long as the sun shines, surely our strength will return," the first mate said.

Indeed, the simple pleasure of the warmth of sunshine on my face was already pushing the memory of the cold away. I no longer felt that I might expire at any minute.

We stood, blinking, watching the ice and snow melt away with un-natural rapidity until all that was left was a dampness on the ground and the silent dead bodies of our brave shipmates back in the tavern.

And that was when we six made our vow.

"There will be no more hiding in locked taverns," I said to them. "We have lost too many friends and we will lose no more. We will make our stand on the *Havenhome*. And this time we will be ready."

At first the six of us who survived that hellish night in the tavern felt joy at the mere fact we were yet alive, with so many of our fellowship having fallen. Afterward, the crew had a mind to up anchor and leave, never mind it would be near-nigh impossible for a crew of so few to get the vessel anywhere in open sea. In the end I shamed them into staying.

"I stay here," I shouted. "If you choose to go, you may leave me behind. Have you so far forgotten the fellowship that we shared that you can leave your friends where they lie? Would you deny them the comfort of the words of the Lord?"

None spoke.

"And what of when we six are home and safe? What will you tell their wives, their sweethearts? Would you be able to ever look them in the eye again? And when they ask in the taverns how it is that we six came home yet the others did not? Could you speak up and say that we ran like rats for the comfort of home while our shipmates lay dead in a tavern? I know that I could not. I will stay here, until we have eased the path to Paradise for our fallen."

"And I will stand with you Cap'n, as always. You have led us through many dangers. I have trust that you will not betray us now."

The first mate brought himself over to join me.

Together we stood there, while the others stared at us sullenly, weighing their thoughts of mutiny against their loyalty to me, their Captain.

In truth, I myself wanted little more than to flee back to your soft arms, but I held firm, although I half expected at any moment for a storm to brew up and freeze me, immobile, to the spot. The storm did not come, but the last remainder of my crew did, eventually coming sheepishly to join us.

"The Lord will reward you, in this life or the next," I said to each of them.

"Do not be too quick with your praise, Cap'n," the first mate said. "For mayhap they know as well as we do that four men, no matter how strong, could not even so much as get the boat out of this harbor, never mind across all the seas that separate us from home."

"Still, they have shown themselves brave enough to step down beside us. What each man holds in his heart lies between him and his maker, but their actions show them to be still true. For that, I give thanks."

"Then we will all give thanks together, to the Lord," the first mate said. "The pastor may not be here, but that does not mean we should neglect our debts. Let us pray."

The first mate led us in prayer, as solemn and faithful as if he himself was a pastor. Then Stumpy Jack started up the old songs. We sang "Wind and Sail, He Watches O'er Us," at the top of our voices.

I was the first to make my way back into that hellhole of the tavern, despite the heaviness that lay on my soul.

"Let us have at it lads," the Mate said behind me, leading the rest inside. "We cannot have our friends lying here in the dark when there is warm sunshine to be had outside."

And so we lifted and we carried, trying not to remember the times we had spent with those who were now no more than cold meat under our hands. I will spare you the details dearest Lizzie, but bringing the bodies of our fallen out of the tavern was a sore blow to our hearts. Some of us had a tear in our eye as we laid them in a row in front of the courthouse. But a far sorer blow was yet to come.

When we went to fetch the pastor and Bald Tom, neither of them was to be found.

I stood in the ruin of what was left of the privy.

I could find no sign that Bald Tom had ever been there, save for a single partially frozen shit on the ground.

Stumpy Jack wailed.

"The devil has taken them. And it will be us for it next."

He would have fled there and then if the first mate hadn't held him by the scruff of the neck.

"Have courage man," he said, loud enough for us all to hear. "Last night the Good Lord saved our sorry skins. He has a purpose for us all, even you, old Stumpy. All we have to do is trust him, and he will deliver us."

Those quiet words from the big man gave us all succor, but only until we dragged the bodies out to the cemetery.

None of us were prepared for the sight that met us.

This time old Stumpy did flee, screaming back to the boat as if all the demons of hell were after him.

The graves we had spent the last days digging all lay open, brown earth strewn every which way. The dead had not lain at rest, despite all the pastor's pleas and prayers. They had risen up, digging their way out of the cold earth.

There was no sign of any bodies, man, woman or child. Not a single one slept where we had put them.

"What shall we do Cap'n? Shall we take them back to the *Havenhome*?" the first mate asked, but I had no answer.

"Leave them here," Jim Crawford shouted. "Leave them here. For if those we have said the words over can yet rise, then surely there is no hope for any of us."

"I must think on it," I said. "And I cannot hold a thought in my head while these graves lie before me. Leave our dead be. I will repair to my cabin. Mayhap the Lord will send me guidance."

We followed Stumpy Jack back to the boat; more slowly, but with no less trepidation in our hearts.

By the time we got back onto the *Havenhome*, Stumpy Jack was already blind drunk and no use to man nor beast.

"We have to go back and bury our crewmates," the first mate said.

"Why bother? They will only be up and about again on the morrow," Stumpy Jack replied. He wept, a pitiful sight in such an old sea dog such as him.

"Jack has it right," Jim Crawford piped up. "Despite all our efforts, despite all the pastor's prayers, they've all come up again. And who is to know, mayhap the pastor and Bald Tom are with them even now."

Dave the Bosun's mate and Eye-Tie Frank stayed quiet. I saw they were already eyeing the grog. I allowed each man another half-cup.

"It's up to you Cap'n," the first mate said after swallowing a mouthful that would have floored a smaller man. "If you say we should go back and put them in the ground, then I'll make sure we all go as one."

May the Lord God forgive me; I left them there, lying out under the sun beside the empty graves.

"No," I replied. "Pull up the gangplank. We will spend this night on the *Havenhome*. I will sleep on it, and make a decision on the morrow."

But sleep was the furthest thing from my thoughts. I am ashamed to admit it, but I took to the grog, swilling it down as if the morrow did not matter, as if I had no responsibilities in the world. I know I promised you dearest, but my solemn vow was not enough to keep me from it. I can only say in my own mitigation that I was far from hearth and home, and sore afeared. And if it is any consolation to you sweetest, I have no memory of the act, and I suffered the most fearful of headaches on awakening.

It was the first mate who brought me out of my stupor.

At first I thought I had taken enough grog to blind me, but it was only that the sky outside had grown dark. Another night had fallen. There was a chill in the air.

"Cap'n. You need to see this," he said.

"Can't it wait?" I said, groaning as the result of my drinking gripped my head like a vise.

"Afraid not Cap'n. If I left you asleep, you might never wake again."

"That might be no bad thing," I moaned.

He slapped me in the face, hard. I was so astonished I almost fell on my arse. I probably would have done so had he not put out a hand to steady me.

"I'm rightful sorry Cap'n, but your men need you sober and in charge. We are in perilous waters, and hard times. That is a mixture that requires a Captain, not a drunken sot."

In all our time together he had never raised his voice to me before, let alone strike me.

I was of a mood to be affronted, but one look at the fear in his eyes melted all passion away.

"You have the right, sir," I said to him. "If you see me lift another flagon of grog you can throw me in the brig and toss the key over the side."

"Best save your vow of abstinence for a bit," he said with a grim smile. "You might need a brew after you've seen what waits out on the dock."

He led me up on deck.

Moonlight shone down, illuminating the dock.

A single figure stood there, staring up at us.

It was our first sighting of an aboriginal, one that froze the very breath in my throat. He wore a headpiece of feathers that rose in a crown above his head and fell in a long tail down his back. His clothing looked to be animal skin roughly sewn together. His feet were bare.

But that wasn't what drew the eye. I had heard tell that the natives of these shores were red, almost the color of blood, but this tall man was white as ivory, as cold as a stone. White eyes without a pupil stared up at us.

He raised his arms.

It snowed, out of that clear starry sky.

The first mate looked past the native, down into the colony.

"Dear Lord preserve us," he whispered.

I turned to follow his gaze.

The dead walked along the dock toward us, each of them staring with that white-eyed gaze. And there, at the front of the mob, stood a bulky man in a woman's skirts. Alongside him strode a tall grim faced preacher dressed in black.

Bald Tom and the pastor had come back to visit their old shipmates.

The first mate roused the remaining crew, all save Stumpy Jack who was so far gone in stupor that Gabriel's Horn itself is unlikely to have called him out of sleep.

Our first thought, nay, our only thought, was to raise anchor and head for open water, but we were denied even that chance. In less time than the blink of an eye a storm blew up, a wind so cold it would have frozen us to the deck if we hadn't had the foresight to wear our winter furs. Even at that, the cold bit at my nose so hard it felt like a nip from an excited dog.

"Up anchor," the first mate shouted, but too late.

The sea had frozen solid around us.

We were stuck hard in place. Old timbers creaked and moaned as the ice gripped tight.

"Will she hold?" I asked the Mate.

"She held together when the ice was three feet thick off New-foundland two years back," he said. "She'll hold now."

But I was starting to believe that it was colder yet than that day. I had to keep shifting from foot to foot; otherwise my soles would have frozen to the deck. By now snow fell so thick that I could no longer see the buildings of the colony beyond the dock.

"What purpose does it serve?" I said. I thought I had merely spoken to myself, but the Mate heard.

"The pastor used to say that everything, good or evil, was God's will, all part of a scheme of things, and that we would only ever understand when we were risen up on the Day of Judgment, and the veils would fall from our eyes."

"Then I wish the Day of Judgment would hurry upon us," I replied. "For I am sore perplexed, and have long since tired of this mummery."

"Be careful what you wish for Cap'n," the Mate said. "Be very careful what you wish for."

Jim Crawford came up beside us on deck, musket in his hand. It fell unused to the deck when he saw what faced us across on the dock. Stout fellow though he was, Jim Crawford fell to his knees, struck down in terror.

"We're done for," he squealed.

The first mate raised him to his feet.

"Not if we stand together as men," he said. "For truly that is the only way we will see home again. Cap'n . . . do I have your permission to break out the powder?"

"You have a plan?"

"More of an idea, but mayhap it will come to something."

"Then have at it man, have at it."

The Mate went below, while Crawford and I stood and watched the figures on the dockside.

They did not move. Their stares did not wander from where we stood. The snow got heavier yet, and still they did not stir.

"What do they want from us, Cap'n?" Crawford wailed beside me. "What do they want?"

In truth, I could not answer him, for fear had taken hold deep within me. It would not be shifted, no matter how many prayers I uttered up to the most high. My eyes were fixed on the pastor and Bald Tom, two men as far apart in temperament as you are ever likely to meet. Yet here they were, standing side by side, joined in a new hatred against their former shipmates that I was at a loss to understand.

The wind howled. The snow bit into my cheeks, but I was loath to move, loath to take my eyes from the host on the dock lest they creep up on me unawares.

The first mate came back onto deck, joined by Eye-Tie Frank. They carried between them a half-barrel full of thick pitch.

"I've mixed in the powder," the first mate said. "Remember yon corsair we met off the Azores?"

And indeed I did. In a flash I saw his plan.

"Will it burn against yon cold flesh?" I asked as I helped man-handle the barrel.

"I know nothing else that might," the Mate said.

He wrapped a linen cloth around the end of a broom-stick and dipped it in the pitch. He lit it from a small tinder box he kept in his waistcoat pocket.

"I trust no one but you with the flame," the Mate said, handing it to me.

I looked him in the eye, this man who had been my friend for the past twenty years.

"It's risky," I said. "I have mind of what happened to Slant-Eyed Jock."

"And I," the Mate said. "But I fear we have little choice."

He thrust his arm into the pitch. He came up with a handful of black ooze in his hand.

"Do it quick," he said. He thrust his hand toward me.

I lit the pitch. The Mate threw the lit mass away from him and it spluttered and spat as it sailed into the night. It hit Bald Tom on the chest, and ran down his torso, burning all the time.

The frozen man looked down, as if bemused. His whole face went up like a torch as the flame reached the powder that had been mixed in with the pitch.

Bald Tom fell to his knees, dropped forward. He tumbled off the dock and down to the frozen water below. He hit it hard, dropping through the ice with a sizzle and fountain of steam before he sank away out of sight, silent, like a stone.

Jim Crawford shouted in triumph, but the Mate hushed him sternly.

"I just killed a good man," he said grimly. "'Tis no cause for celebration."

"He were dead already," Crawford said.

"That don't make me feel any better about it," the Mate said grimly.

He stuck his hand in the pitch again, and came up with a second ball.

"You were lucky with the first," I said. "Mayhap it is best not to chance it again?"

"We both know we have no other choice, Cap'n. Light it up."

For a second time his arm seemed to grow a flame. The powder in the pitch spluttered before it left his hand. He threw it toward the dock, but it exploded and fizzled out well short, dropping away out of sight to the ice below.

"I can do better than that," Crawford said.

Before either of us could stop him he plunged his whole arm into the pitch, coming up with a far bigger ball than the Mate. He leaned forward and touched the flame to the oily mixture.

His arm immediately burst aflame, fire roaring up the side of his head, flesh crisping and melting. He screamed, just once, and fell away from us. The powder went up and the whole right hand side of Crawford's body burst, like a ripe fruit, a dead, smoking ruin before he hit the deck.

The Mate looked down at what was left of the man.

"Be careful," I said.

The Mate bent to get himself another handful, when Eye-Tie Frank stepped in front of him.

"Mayhap I have a better method," he said. He removed his cap, then his belt. He filled his cap with the pitch, and then tied it up with his belt. He was left with a two-foot length of belt with a ball of pitch on the end.

"Shame on you," he said to the Mate and me, his slight accent showing through. "Do you not do this yourselves at home to bring in the New Year?"

He lit the pitch, swung it around his head and sent it winging over the dock.

"That we do," the Mate said, unbuckling his own belt. "Although I am usually too far gone in my cups to remember it."

The fireball exploded just above the heads of the throng of the dead, sending burning flame over five of them.

The Mate sent one of his own after it. The air filled with black acrid smoke as flesh burned. The ranks of the dead did not move, even as their neighbors burned.

"All very well," the Mate said. "But we have a limited supply of belts and caps. And I'd rather my breeches didn't fall down . . . not in this weather."

Dave the Bosun's mate arrived on deck. We set him to finding twine and cloth, the better to make more fireballs.

For a while the air was full of flame and fury.

The snow got heavier still. Sometimes we could not even see the dock, but the smell of burning meat told us we still hit our targets.

We lost ourselves in a world of burning pitch and whirling snow, the only sound being the coughing, spluttering rattle of powder starting to fizzle, and the whoosh of flame as we hit our targets. The night went on without end.

I know not when the snow finally stopped, only that I looked up to see stars overhead and a full moon overhead.

"My eyes deceive me, Cap'n," the Mate said beside me. "For surely the moon was on the wane when we hove-to here."

"There is deception here, right enough," I replied, "But it is not your eyes. It comes from that one."

Out over the dockside, the white native with the feather chest still stood tall and un-burnt. Around him the ranks of the dead lay, finally at rest, a smoking chaos of limbs and torsos piled higgeldy-piggeldly in a hellish landscape strewn across the dock.

The native thumped at his chest. He made an expansive circle with his arms before thumping his chest again.

He did this twice before I realized his meaning.

This land is mine.

He pointed at Dave the Bosun's mate. The man jerked, as if jolted by lightning.

To our astonishment he threw himself off the boat, toward the pier.

It was a prodigious leap. I would not have placed a bet on him achieving it, but he seemed to have been given wings. He landed, a few feet in front of the white native.

The native thumped his chest again. He stroked Dave's face, gently, as if romancing a woman. Once more we had to watch a colleague freeze. His body went stiff, and a last plume of breath left him, floating high in the air. I could only hope it was his soul, fleeing to its place in Paradise, for the thought of a man being frozen but yet imprisoned, mute, in his own body, was almost too much to bear.

Finally Dave turned back toward us, blind white eyes staring out of a blue face. The native once more made the circle with his arms.

"He's showing us," the mate said. "He's showing us that all this is his . . . including us."

"It does not include me," Eye-Tie Frank said. He leapt off the ship, screaming his defiance. Whether he intended to reach the pier itself we shall never know. His leap was well short and he fell away below our sight, never to be heard from again.

The native stared at the two of us, his black-lipped mouth raised in a smile. He thumped his chest again. Somewhere, out in the wild reaches of the night, a wolf howled at the moon. It was answered, much closer, by a pack, a wild, ululating wail that seemed to pierce my very skull.

The first mate looked at me, and I at him.

"We have served together over twenty years, Cap'n. I have been proud to call you my friend."

"And I you," I replied. We both had a tear in our eye, there at the end.

"Goodbye Cap'n," he said, as the native on the dock pointed a long white finger, straight at him.

What happened next will stay with me for the remainder of

what is left of my life.

The first mate shook and juddered, in the same manner as Dave the Bosun's mate had done a few moments before. He gritted his teeth. He stuck both arms into the pitch, all the way up to his shoulders. Before I could move, he took the torch from me. He leapt from the boat, straight at the native.

"*Havenhome!*" he called, his voice ringing out loud and clear in the night. He landed just in front of the tall white figure, stepped forward, and grabbed it in a tight embrace. I have seen men's backs broken by that grip, but the native ne'er flinched. The Mate put all his strength into it, but the white figure was unbowed.

Then, at the last, as the skin in the Mate's face went blue, he yelled out once more, a formless word. He brought down the torch, and set light to his pitch covered arms.

I stood and watched, with tears running through a grim smile, as the pair of them burned. The feather crown went first, blazing all as one and sending flames up the creature's back. Where the first mate's pitch-covered arms touched its body they stuck, searing huge patches of flesh at a time.

Together the bodies fell on the dock. The Mate was surely dead by now, but the creature could not escape from his embrace.

Even then I thought the creature might break free, for the flames had begun to die down, yet clearly it still showed sign of what passed for life in that white frozen frame.

Finally, just as I was starting to despair, the powder in the pitch took.

A yellow flame shot ten yards into the sky. When it died down there was nothing left of either body that could be recognized . . . . just one single, fused mass of blackened flesh.

I am decided. This will be my last ever entry in this journal, made in the hope that what is related may help some other Christian souls from sharing the fate of my crewmates. In the meantime I can do little more than offer up prayers, for the first mate, and all the other brave men of the *Havenhome* who will ne'er return home.

This proud ship, my home these many years, has sailed its last, and I am no longer Captain of anything other than my own soul. In truth, I do not think I will ever be able to lead men again. If I make it to home port alive I will retire.

I will spend my time supping beer in the harbor and telling tall tales with the other old gentleman, content to keep my feet warm before the fires of hearth and home.

But that seems like a long way off, another lifetime where the sun shines hot and yellow on the fields, and my Lizzie stands at the door, smiling. I have some of the *Havenhome*'s tale yet to tell before I can begin my journey toward that most welcome of sights.

After the Mate had made his sacrifice I could do naught but stand there, staring at the smoking ruin of all that was left of my friends and shipmates. I paid particular attention to the charred mass where lay the Mate and the native, half expecting at any moment that a white figure would rise from the dockside to mock me once more.

Nothing moved except the stirring of acrid smoke on the breeze.

The wind died, like the last sigh of an old man on his death-bed. A cloud ran over the full moon. Slowly at first, then faster until water ran in runnels off the deck, the snow thawed.

And still I stood there, long into the night, long after the sun came up and the last of the frost was taken by the morning.

I felt empty, devoid of action, abandoned by hope. I was only brought out of my reverie by old Stumpy Jack, who emerged, blinking into the sunlight, looking near as dead as some of those lying on the dockside.

"Are we alive, Cap'n?" he said, "Or in Paradise?"

"Does this look like any Paradise you might expect?" I said.

He stood beside me for a long time, staring out over the smoking dock.

"Is it over?" he whispered.

"I know not whether it will ever be over," I replied. "But it is over for now."

It was Stumpy Jack who brought me inside, him who made me drink and eat, that I might stay alive when all of my brethren lay dead around us.

And even now, while I write this, the old man is showing more fortitude than I thought he possessed. He has brought the remains of the Mate and the native inside the ship.

"The rest of them Cap'n? What shall we do with the rest of them?"

There are bodies, mostly charred and unrecognizable, strewn all across the dock. The Mate's pitch and powder concoction did for them all in the end.

"By rights, these people deserve a Christian burial," I said.

"Nay Cap'n," Old Stumpy said. "Whatever part of them belonged to the Lord has already gone. And neither you nor I have the strength, or the heart, to waste in spending another night near this place."

I reluctantly had to agree with him.

We will scuttle the *Havenhome* here, on this dock. I will leave my journal in my chest, wrapped in oilskins. In that manner, if anyone should chance on the drowned boat, they may, if the Lord is with them, find this journal first, and stop before they unleash what Jack and I have left at the bottom of the hold.

We have gathered our provisions. We will leave tonight. The only other thing I take with me from my cabin is my Bible, in the hope it will give me solace in the nights to come. But I fear I will ne'er find hope again in the words of the Lord, for I know the pastor's white eyes will ever accuse me, even in the deepest depths of slumber. If the Lord did not see fit to save such a holy and devout man as the pastor, what hope is there for the likes of me, who has done so many things that require repentance?

Forgive me Lizzie, for I know now you will never read this. But if the Lord gives me strength, I intend to head down the coast, for warmer climes and friendly company. Mayhap I shall return yet to home port, and your soft arms.

You will fill my dreams until I am once more at your side. Be well my love. Be well for both of us.

—Your loving husband, John.

THE BEDLAMITE

BY *FERREL MOORE*

Day One

"**A**ND WHO IS THIS?" asked Captain Baker.

"This," answered Professor Essepi, "is Dr Phineas Lizotte."

"Welcome aboard the *U.S.S Vincent*, sir," the Captain said in a strained voice.

A persistent wind tossed shredded rags of clouds overhead, billowing them across the sky like a poor man's laundry. As the pale sun disappeared behind the clouds, the professor pulled his collar tighter.

While the two men looked each other over, Essepi studied their reactions. Dr Lizotte's bulging eyes peered at the Captain through silver rimmed spectacles balanced on a nose the width of a chart pencil. With a peculiarly long index finger, Lizotte adjusted their position as though he were studying a specimen through a microscope. The Captain stood proudly, with his feet braced apart and arm's folded across his broad chest.

"Where may I put my belongings?" asked Lizotte.

"Cherney," said Captain Baker to a sailor, "take the man's trunk and show him to his berth."

"Aye-aye, Captain," said Cherney.

"No one touches my belongings, Baker," hissed Lizotte.

"That would be *Captain Baker* to the likes of you," said Cherney.

Lizotte raised a hand as if to strike the man. "A dog like you will not tell–"

"That will do, doctor," said Essepi, his wry smile and sharp tone cutting Lizotte short.

Cherney apparently had missed the entire transaction; his gaze instead transfixed upon an odd-shaped ring on Lizotte's hand. It possessed a small spark of lightning when it flashed in the sun. Then, as if caught peeking at something he shouldn't, the sailor quickly turned away, his countenance shaped with an expression Essepi thought to be bordering on revulsion.

Stiff with rebuke, Lizotte brushed past the sailor. "Show me to my quarters."

As Lizotte moved away, other sailors stared at him as though he were a wild animal that had been brought on board.

"I'll tolerate no dallying," said the Captain to gawkers. "Mind your duties."

"Captain Baker," Essepi said, "please excuse the eccentricities of my assistant, Dr Lizotte. He is an academic. His bookish life has ruined both his eyes and caused his skin to look unhealthy due to lack of sun exposure."

"Is that so?" said the Captain.

"Yes, quite."

The Captain gazed at the packet of orders in his hand. "And you sir?"

"I am a trouble-shooter, for want of a better description."

"A trouble-shooter with a Presidential order giving him command to run roughshod of my ship for an unspecified mission," said Captain Baker sharply.

"Indeed," said Essepi. "It helps to have connections."

The Captain's eyes widened. "What is this?"

Three robed figures with thin, drawn faces, sunken dark eyes, and bald heads trod up the gangplank. Each bore an identical blood-red birthmark painted across his left cheek, as though caressed by the Devil's own hand.

"Priests from the isle of Crete," Essepi said.

The three hooded figures moved across the deck in unison. Pewter chains with crossed lightning bolts of iridescent black metal hung from their necks and shimmered like opal. Crewmen eyed them uneasily, while several crossed themselves and quickly looked away.

It was Essepi's fifth and last man that caused the most commotion, however. Two Union Army soldiers carried him on board slung from a pole by his ankles and wrists. A black cotton bag covered the prisoner's head, and a drawstring cinched around his neck. Hideous, muffled wails issued from the bag as though the man had been gagged.

With his associates finally boarded, Essepi excused himself to his cabin.

Day 2- Evening

Essepi sat across the table from Lizotte. Lizotte had earlier made a point of opening the storage room's door to secure their privacy. When satisfied, he ducked to re-enter the room. He climbed onto a bench, but averted his eyes from the flask and cup that sat on the table.

"You will have to tell the Captain something. He's getting nervous," said Lizotte, "and the men say that the bedlamite will bring them disaster."

"Bedlamite," mused Essepi. He rolled the word around and over his tongue as though it were a tender morsel. "Such a moniker is so much gentler than lunatic, don't you think, doctor?"

"The sailors think he brings bad luck, whatever he is called," said Lizotte.

Essepi laid aside his journal and removed his spectacles. Using a clean handkerchief, he scrubbed them clear of coal dust with a fastidiousness that a jeweler would have admired. He then placed them in a pocket-case and slid the case into his coat.

"Some of them are shoveling coal in the belly of this filthy ship," he said, draining a tin cup filled with whiskey. His tongue slid over his lower lip as though to savor the numbing sensation. "Others clean and oil cannon while their mates scrub the grime from the decking and the armor plating. The air is so filthy it's a wonder we can breathe at all," Essepi said. "When they are not cleaning, they are either patrolling empty stretches of ocean or being shot at by Confederate cannon. And they worry over bad luck? Their lives are miserable enough. I sincerely doubt that they would recognize bad luck if it dropped on them and crushed them."

He returned the cup to the bench and poured another half-finger. The liquor seemed to fascinate Essepi. His head shifted from this side to that as he spoke, sliding his shoulders as he did so like a cat preparing to pounce on a mouse.

As though in response, Lizotte yawned, revealing rows of amber colored sharp teeth that glowed like phosphorescent fungus in the dim light.

Glimpsing them, Essepi suppressed the desire to shudder.

Lizotte leaned forward and said in a soft, delighted voice, "You are obsessed with this bedlamite. He is your raison d'etre. But a great tumult closes in on us. We are at sea holding a metal pole while heat lightning crackles the night sky."

"You sound like a bloody prophet of doom," said Essepi. "These men can take care of themselves. I have instructed the Captain that the decks are to be patrolled both day and night. We have done what we can and that is enough. It means nothing to me anyway, unless we can save Secretary Marshall's son from his madness. I am counting on you. I do not wish to look like a misguided fool. He now hangs in manacles and chains in the brig chattering like a monkey. The Secretary of the Navy has gone mad. So damned what, he doesn't have much of a family left because of the war? What is it to me his only son acts like a primate and screams all night that the monsters are coming? Is that enough to drive a man over the edge? Considering that I am confidante to a lunatic with a bedlamite for a son, is it any wonder I bloody well drink?"

Essepi's nose filled with the greasy odor of stale wood.

"Yes," said Lizotte, "but when we have returned his son to his right mind, then Secretary Marshall will be compelled to give you whatever you demand. All of the gold that your family has given to fight slavery–"

"Slavery be damned. Let the slaves fight for themselves or keep picking cotton. We'll win this war and my dear father's business will take back our investment with usurious interest from the South or my family name is not Essepi."

"Your just rewards," said Lizotte with a sly wink.

"Until then," said Essepi as he raised the cup to finish it off.

"And what will you tell the Captain tomorrow?" asked Lizotte.

"Don't concern yourself," continued Essepi, "I'll think of something by then. "

A determined smile spread across Lizotte's face like a sliver of yellow moon, and he said, "It is the *why* of our journey that will shock Captain Baker."

"I don't care a whit if the very idea kills him," said Essepi. His head slid forward slightly. "As long as he takes us first to the location where this thing of yours will appear–"

"The Eye of Dagon."

Lizotte smiled.

"You are enjoying this," said Essepi.

The thrum of the steam engine filled the silence, and Essepi felt his mind suffuse with the amber state of indolence gifted to a drinker by good whiskey. His disconnected thoughts hovered about the image of Secretary Marshall's son chained to the brig's rough planks.

"Can you restore his mind?" he asked, dropping back against the wall.

"You doubt me, professor?" said Lizotte. "I guarantee that when we find the Eye of Dagon, I will fully restore Secretary Marshall's son to his former self. With the priests on board, they will chant day and night. This will make him ready for the moment when my craft can restore his sanity. I cannot repair his eyes, but yes, I can restore his mind," Lizotte added matter-of-factly.

A furtive, orange-yellow flame danced on the lantern's wick. In its light, shadows skulked along the walls. It sat between them on the table, and with each flicker of combustion it sent furtive shadows skulking around the room. Essepi allowed a skeptical smile to cross his face.

"Consider what I have already told you," continued Lizotte, "each time in the past the Eye appeared, the ships remained, just as now. Only the men were taken or driven mad. Remember the Sirens of the ancient Greek Mariners? There are many such legends from many traditions. But in the strange tales concerning the Deep Ones, we hear such narratives at their most terrifying. Remember, when the Eye rose but did not see the sign that it sought? Madness and death descended on anyone it looked upon. The Secretary's son perhaps saved his life by putting out his own eyes. He is the last man alive to have seen it."

"Stupid bastard," said Essepi.

"He is the only man I know of who seems to have survived an encounter with the Eye. But these events occur over and again in cycles going back as far as written history extends. I have been chasing this phenomenon for the greater portion of my life. It is said that the Eye of Dagon rises and claims its creatures each third cycle of the Red Moon. If the Eye rises and sees the sacrifice, then he shall pour out his words and the son of Lyssa and Dagon's hordes shall come forth to reclaim the seas with he who performed the sacrifice as his priest among men." Lizotte spoke as though reciting an ancient text.

"Meaning what?" asked Essepi.

"Listen to me, my friend," said Lizotte. "I have searched the darkest, wildest seacoasts of this earth to re-construct the history of such events. My work has made me a pariah in the eyes of my colleagues. I am shunned. I follow this labyrinthine path for my own satisfaction and since you are making it possible for me to see what no one else has ever seen and survived, I am in your service."

Essepi nodded, weary. He suspected Lizotte had an agenda of his own, but Essepi's whiskey flask was almost empty, and that transcendent catastrophe eclipsed any immediate concern with Lizotte's machinations.

Day 3

Essepi was up and on deck early. Peculiar dreams roused him from his slumber to a wine red sunrise.

"Good morning, Professor," said Captain Baker.

Essepi rubbed his eyes. He yawned, blinked slowly, and then glanced around as though making an inspection. There were sailors polishing brasswork and others burnishing the metal framings where the gun carriages rotated. The first mate shouted orders at those swabbing the deck. Essepi shook his head in disgust.

"Must they do this every morning?" he asked, sniffing the air.

Captain Baker said, "On board a ship, discipline is everything. Saltwater and coal dust, Professor, are like locusts that eat away everything on which they descend."

The morning sun rose slowly out of the ocean, an eruption of saffron brilliance at the edge of an ocean garden draped til then in violet blackness. The morning air was brisk, but whatever scents the sea air carried were lost in the sulfurous smell of burning coal and cleaning oil.

"Yes, well I can see the necessity of someone running around shouting to roust your crew awake."

The fuzziness had yet to clear from his brain after last night's drinking. He decided to wait until after lunch before his next swig.

"I expect them out of their beds and on their feet, then on deck with their hammocks lashed within ten minutes of the morning bugle," continued the Captain. "You find the schedule difficult? Within a week, you'll adjust."

"Never," swore Essepi.

"I must ask you," said the Captain, crossing his hands behind his, "do those priests of yours chant day and night? I have reports that they pray or chant or whatever they do without respite. At times, the men say that they are near wailing. Please have them restrain themselves, sir. They are causing unrest. Sailors are a superstitious lot."

Essepi wrinkled his brow and stroked his slight moustache, twisting the right tip between his fingers as though it were the end of an artist's paintbrush. He cleared his throat.

"Perhaps I shall," he said at last.

"And I thought they were held to a vow of silence," said the Captain.

"In their religion," replied Essepi, "chanting is not speaking. According to Dr Lizotte, they chant their litanies all day long for that very reason—to keep them from speaking."

"I see. Do these men ever eat? They have requested no food nor do they show their faces at mess."

"They are island men and unused to such close quarters. It is natural for them to keep to themselves," said Essepi. "They have their own food. It's a gruesome smelling braid of dried vegetables and herbs. They keep it coiled like a rope about their waist. But that and water are enough to sustain them. Now is that quite your last question on the topic?"

Exhaling in seeming exasperation, the Captain asked, "Tell me why they are here, Professor Essepi."

"That will come soon enough. You must remember that I am acting under the direct orders of the Secretary of the Navy, as are you yourself. Discretion is required."

"Then at least tell me, sir, why a blind madman is on my ship, manacled and chained in my brig? Even the cook crosses himself whenever that bedlamite is mentioned. The men dare not speak out to my first mate Mr Abilio or myself, but they expect disaster. They believe the man is cursed. For my own peace of mind, at least tell me why you brought him aboard my ship."

"Because," said Essepi, "he is *my* madman."

Sharp edges formed outlines on the Captain's face, and his eyes caught the glint of the rising sun. Essepi guessed that the man's tendons were tightening like piano wire pulled taut by the twist of a key, but there was nothing to be done for it yet.

Day 4

The next afternoon, Essepi met with Captain Baker in the Captain's quarters.

"Captain?" said Essepi in a low voice. "I am now ready to divulge the nature of our mission to you."

Baker's brow compressed into three thick folds of skin brushed with an oily dark sheen. His dark hair glistened in the lamplight as he rose from his chair.

"It's about damned time," he said.

"Seven ships have disappeared in three months," began Essepi, "and the Secretary of the Navy is a man of terrible temper in the best of circumstances. But seven ships with no reports of enemy presence—even the President himself is demanding an explanation."

"In these waters?" said Captain Baker, and he waved a hand toward the circle of glass behind his head.

Essepi shrugged. "We believe so."

"Gone without a trace?"

The ship creaked, like a horse testing the confines of its stall.

"No," answered Essepi.

"What do you mean?"

"I mean that each of the ships were found within a few weeks of their disappearance."

"And the crew?" said the Captain.

"Gone."

"Explain yourself, Professor."

"There's little to explain. The ships were floundering, untended by human hand."

"They were abandoned?" said the Captain.

"I'll take some of your whiskey before I answer that, if you please," said Essepi.

"I should have you manacled beside your lunatic."

"Then you would have much explaining to do at your court martial, Captain."

"I despise men like yourself," said the Captain. "You fight your wars from behind desks, while the rest of us battle from the front lines."

"Careful. It is understandable that you grate under the yoke of my authority, but you do not wish to figure prominently in my report."

Captain Baker grunted, then produced a flask from within a small chest and filled two cups.

"A toast," said Essepi.

"To the deep," replied the Captain and drained his cup in one swift inhalation.

"And to its secrets," added Essepi, and he did likewise.

"You were saying?" pressed the Captain.

Essepi wiped his mouth with the back of his hand.

"Right. Each of the ships was raked with what seemed to be claws."

The Captain raised an eyebrow.

"They were markings made by no creature known to natural science."

"Perhaps you should stay away from drink," the Captain said flippantly.

"Scoff if you will," said Essepi. "I've seen the gouges."

Baker waved a hand. "Go on."

"And on each of the ships we found markings carved into the railings. They're etched in some sort of glyphic language that we can't decipher."

"This becomes more fanciful with every word," laughed Captain Baker.

"They were similar to certain markings found on Egyptian tombs," said Essepi. "Only, there is something queer about them. No one is able to look at them for any length of time without developing a sense of vertigo. I've had entire sections of railing containing the symbols cut away and placed in protected storage until we can decipher their meaning."

What Essepi did not share with the Captain was that his workmen had gone mad while examining the symbols; but Lizotte alone seemed to be able to look at them with impunity.

"Claw markings and Egyptian symbols? That's quite a lot of rubbish you've brought aboard my ship, Professor Essepi. Simply tell me what we are looking for, now and I hope you have a good explanation. You may well command this mission, but I still command this ship and the lives of everyone on it are my responsibility."

Essepi reached across the table and poured another drink.

"All I can tell you," he said, "is that the bedlamite was the only survivor found on any of the ships. And the priests are perhaps our only chance to regain his sanity. If we succeed, we may learn what transpired when his vessel was attacked. *And*, he is the Secretary of the Navy's son. The Secretary would very much like the young man's brains to be unscrambled.

"There are rumors," continued Essepi, "of some new weapon being used. Some believe that sea monsters are at play. Dr Lizotte believes the latter is the explanation. It is our job to find the answers. I am hopeful that once we have found them, we can return the Secretary's son to sanity and put a stop to whomever or whatever spirited away the crew of the seven Union ships."

"I don't trust Lizotte," said the Captain.

Essepi emptied his glass.

"Dr Lizotte is my concern," he said.

Day 5

The late afternoon sky was the color of coal marks on an old shovel when Lizotte carried word to the Captain that Essepi requested his presence in the ship's brig. Although the Captain fumed to tell Lizotte that it was his ship and he would go where he chose when he desired, he instead called after the man's back, "Tell Professor Essepi that I will be along shortly."

Lizotte kept walking and did not respond.

The smell of the sea mingled with that of the stacks, and they were making good time. Yet, the first mate approached the Captain to inform him that the navigator reported that the compass was still malfunctioning. There was a hint of concern in his voice, and it was a concern that was spreading throughout the ship.

"It's not unheard of, Mr Abilio," said Baker, watching Lizotte disappear from sight.

Mr Abilio made no reply.

"The cause of these irregularities is unknown," Baker continued. "But see that the navigator makes a record of it."

What the Captain did not say, was that such irregularities had never before been heard of in these waters.

The first mate remained beside the Captain.

"Do you have something on your mind, Mr Abilio?"

"Last night, sir, a sailor on watch reported seeing Dr Lizotte drop something over the bow railing."

Baker did not turn to face him, but his face tightened.

"And what was the good doctor ridding himself of in such an unusual manner?"

"Seaman couldn't say, sir, but he told me that it looked something like a child's grave marker."

At that, Baker turned to face his first mate. "Bosh!"

"Yes, sir," confirmed Mr Abilio. "About that size. Shone like white marble. Not saying it was, but that's what it reminded the man of when he saw it. Whatever it was, Lizotte must have brought it aboard in that bloody trunk of his."

Baker considered this for a moment.

"Did the sailor approach Lizotte about this?"

"No sir. As you instructed, I've told the men that the professor and his people have the run of the ship. And if I may be frank, Captain, there's not a man on board who isn't shy of Dr Lizotte."

"Are you among those, Mr Abilio?"

"No sir."

"Remember this, Mr Abilio, men who drink choose bad enough companions, but men who drink and are privileged choose worse. Do you understand?"

"Yes, sir, Captain."

"Then I'll be attending to Professor Essepi."

As the door closed behind Captain Baker and his eyes adjusted to the dim light, he saw Essepi and the bedlamite. Were it not for the chains and thick iron bracelets securing the madman, the scene might have been that of a doctor ministering to a patient.

After a moment of fumbling with the bandages swathed around

the man's head, Essepi began to unwind the dark cloth. The professor's back blocked the Captain's view, but when he stepped away, Captain Baker jerked back in surprise. The lunatic's eyes were gruesome holes rimmed by crusted, enflamed scar tissue.

"Self-inflicted, we presume," said Essepi, using his coat sleeve to wipe away beads of perspiration from his forehead.

Before Baker could respond, the bedlamite revealed a mouth full of broken teeth and cried, "It's coming! It's coming!"

The man's wail was a pistol shot fired too close to Baker's ear. The Captain jerked his head back in shock. The prisoner's head fell forward, chin resting on his chest, and his body began to shudder.

"What is he saying?" asked the Captain. The words issued forth from his mouth in a hoarse whisper. "There's nothing for him to see, he's blind."

"The deep," croaked the blind man. "Rising from the deep."

Essepi shook his head. "In between incomprehensible ravings, he's been repeating the same thing over and again since the day that we found him."

Spittle formed at the corners of the prisoner's mouth. Essepi dabbed it away with a deft motion, like that of a parent cleaning a child.

"And you say this is Secretary Marshall's son?"

"Yes," said Essepi. "And as I told you, he is the only living survivor of whatever has been happening."

Essepi patted the bedlamite's head the way that he might a nervous dog's during a thunderstorm. The man's head began to loll, but his whole body continued to rock gently from side to side as though to lull himself to sleep.

"Mad as a hatter," said Essepi.

"This is all so difficult to believe."

"Quite," said Essepi without looking around.

"And you think these priests of yours can actually help this man?"

"So says Dr Lizotte," murmured Essepi.

God help us, thought Baker.

Later that afternoon, Essepi located Lizotte. The cadaverous doctor was dressed in black, and stood looking out at the ocean with his hands resting on the railing.

"Here you are," said Essepi.

Lizotte appeared not to notice him.

"The Captain asked me why each night you drop things into the ocean."

"It is an ancient custom," Lizotte said.

"Is that so? Funny you have never mentioned it to me before this moment."

"The Captain should not inquire after what does not concern him."

"I see," said Essepi. "Well, for the record, doctor, I will decide what concerns the Captain, not you. Now what is it that you have been doing?"

"It is part of the ritual to save the Secretary's son."

"I see. And the meaning of it?"

Lizotte pulled himself up to his full height.

"Did you know that in times gone by, professor, it was believed by some a race of gods lived beneath the seas? Did you know that those who followed them and became like them were believed to be immune from the ravages of disease and death? No? For an educated man, Professor Essepi, there is really a great deal that you do not know about the sea."

"The things you drop over the side each night?" prodded Essepi.

"Gifts. Offerings. Messages. Entreaties. In terrible times, it is well to be on the side of power."

That night, Essepi ensiled himself in his quarters and drank. He lay in a hammock that swayed with the ship's gentle rocking and thought of what the Captain had said to him earlier.

"The Captain says I fight from behind a desk," he spat. "Why not? Why bloody not? I should have stayed behind my desk. It was a damned sight safer there."

His vision blurred. Above the ship's noises he imagined that he heard the droning of the priests, chanting every waking moment of their lives in an attempt to turn away chaos and restore sanity. Stupid bastards, each and every one of them. Wasting their lives in the cause of their religion.

"What if your god is insane?" he shouted, and began to laugh so hard that he struggled to keep from tipping out of his hammock.

Day 6

The seas had grown rougher beneath a black mantle, and the air reeked of sulfur. A faint stygian mist suppurated from the water like an evil steam. Captain Baker and Mr Abilio leaned over the port railing to stare at the phenomena. Fear of the Captain's wrath kept the sailors at their posts, but by the time that Essepi and Lizotte had joined the Captain, the mumblings among the crew had become a persistent hum above the engines.

The fog smeared across the heavens like smoke from a smudge pot and quenched the stars one by one until it had erased them from the sky. The sea began to slowly bubble and boil.

"Lord Jesus, save us," said Mr Abilio.

Pale red moonlight shimmered across waters black as tar. Dark wisps twisted free from the sea and rose high into the night like spirits released from a watery tomb.

"We're into it now," said Captain Baker.

"Into what, Captain?" asked Mr Abilio.

"The Devil's own lair."

Fog embraced the ship, and soon those aboard the *USS Vincent* could see no farther than three feet clearly in any direction. Beyond that, it was like peering through gauze.

"This must be what we have come for," said Essepi. "What happens next?"

Lizotte leaned forward. "I have other business," he hissed.

"But it must be time now," Essepi said. "Time to save the Secretary's son."

"It is *my* time now," said Lizotte. "Thank you so much, professor, for making it possible. But we now part ways."

"What do you mean? What of the ritual?"

Lizotte grabbed Essepi by the hair, pulling him close. "Madmen are madmen," Lizotte whispered in Essepi's ear. "There is no cure. There never was. He will be a bedlamite 'til his last day."

A fireball ignited fifty yards from the ship. Flames roared across the surface of the water as though a gate to Hell had burst open. Men dropped flat against the ship's planking. Some rolled against the armor plating, clapping their palms over their ears as they slammed against the deck.

"Methane gas," yelled Essepi as he scrambled beneath a tarp. "Shut down the boilers."

At that moment Essepi's stomach lurched and he vomited. A foul miasma encircled the deck of the *USS Vincent*; men coughed and gagged.

"Do it," shouted the Captain.

"Douse the damned lanterns, too," added Essepi without showing himself. "And don't fire the guns."

"No guns?" said the first mate.

"Belay that order," said the Captain. "Explain yourself, professor!"

"A flash or a spark could ignite the gas," said Essepi as he climbed from beneath the tarp, coughing. "And I hate that bloody awful smell. It's some kind of sulfur gas that mixes with the flammable methane to give it that stench. The whole damned thing is bubbling up from the ocean itself."

Sailors and officers alike stood transfixed by the roiling waters around their suddenly too small ironclad vessel. They were adrift without navigation in an anarchous ocean of madness.

The air convulsed with a mighty roar like a maelstrom rising from the pit. The night was lit with grasping fingers of fire that reached up from the water to flash into fireballs like incandescent mushrooms, and men gasped as a fountain of water shot into the air like a shaft of ocean fury. Atop it crested something dark and oily black-bright, an orb.

When the water column smashed into the sea, the impact of the black orb was that of a cannonball dropped by God. Water sprayed outward in sheets and the air cracked.

In a panic, Essepi looked around for Lizotte, but his former associate had disappeared into the mist.

A febrile wind moved through the dark curtains of stench hanging in the air. It pushed across the waters like a predator hunting meat.

Mr Abilio pointed at the large black orb that rode the water and shone in the ruddy moonlight like polished anthracite.

"What do you suppose it is?" he asked.

"Satan himself," said the Captain.

Cherney put in, "Hell can't be far behind, sir."

"Hell has already arrived," said the Captain. "It feels like it's watching us."

Essepi slipped in his own vomit and hit the deck planking hard enough to jar his teeth. Lizotte had lied and Essepi had believed him. Now he lay there, needing another drink.

"Get up man," said the Captain. "You are pathetic."

The Captain was helping Essepi to his feet when screams from the direction of the bow pierced the fetid air. They were high and urgent and short-lived.

"Stay where you are," shouted Captain Baker. The fog pressed closer.

"What is happening, Professor?" said the Captain. "What is it that you've led us into?"

Before Essepi answered, another agonized scream cut through the darkness.

"What in God's name?" Essepi said.

Another scream followed, and then another, as though part of an agonized chorus.

Captain Baker and the professor stood transfixed. The vaporous mist had encased their movement as surely as if they were dolls held in place by cotton in a miniature display case.

The Captain looked at Essepi and it seemed that he was seeing him through a death shroud.

"Stay close to me," he told the professor.

The Captain opened the door and strode into the darkness. When he stopped before a mass of sailors tightly pressed together, Essepi almost crashed into his back.

"Stand aside," cried the Captain. "Stand back, I tell you."

Essepi pressed behind the Captain as though he were his shadow. The night was tumescent with cabalistic terrors and he feared separation more than injury.

"What is it?" he asked when he heard the Captain cry out.

Dark forms coalesced around them, their murmurations buzzing through the vapors like an evil hymn. The Captain reached back and seized Essepi's shoulder.

"Professor," he said, "professor is that you?"

"Yes, it is I."

Essepi's voice cracked like a splintering mast.

"What is happening?"

The Captain's hand raised and led Essepi's eyes up the armor plating to where three pairs of feet hung, blood dripping down from their toes, pooling on the deck. Still the Captain's finger levitated upward to the stained robes, up higher to where a metal spike protruded from the chest of each man, pinning them to the iron side of the ship. Sinister swirls of fomenting fog concealed their faces, but Essepi believed that their eyes would be wide open and staring straight ahead in horror.

"It's the priests," he said. "Someone has nailed them in place."

Mr Abilio shoved aside a seaman.

"I've been overhead, sir," he said to the Captain. "Dr Lizotte must have hung them over the edge and spiked them up one at a time."

"What are you saying?" demanded Essepi.

"What do you think he's saying?" said the Captain.

Looking down, Essepi saw the livid pool of blood extend a dark finger toward his boot as though to inculpate him. The broken lightning crosses of the priests lay shattered on the deck. When he raised his head, he saw that the three priests hung above him like meat on hooks.

Captain Baker snatched Essepi by his coat and slammed him against the wall. A pair of bloodied feet dangled on either side of him. "Where is Dr Lizotte?" he said.

"I don't know. I swear it. I had no idea. This is . . . this is madness. I thought I could control him but I can't."

"I asked where he was."

Enraged beyond words, Captain Baker repeated the arrogation and bounced Essepi's head off the iron sheet. The impact caused Essepi's mouth and eyes to fly open in shock and his consciousness wavered like a flickering flame.

"I tell you, man, I don't know. This is beyond me. Everything is beyond me."

"Give me your knife, Mr Abilio," said the Captain in a steady voice.

"Aye-aye, Captain."

Vague faces materialized in the mists that surrounded them,

and Essepi saw with deepening horror the utter disgust and fear that contorted their visages. The Captain held him high with one hand and with the other brought the point of Mr Abilio's knife to his chin.

"Let me do it," cried one of the ethereal faces.

"Gut him," screamed another.

"Nail him up like the priests," offered a faceless tormentor.

"For God's sake, no," howled Essepi. "I had nothing to do with this."

"You brought them on board," called a sailor. "You brought that monster on our ship. You have to pay."

"Quiet, all of you," commanded the Captain.

He brandished Mr Abilio's knife before Essepi's face.

"By the feet of God himself," he said, "I'll cut your throat from ear to ear if you don't tell me where he is."

The blade glimmered with a dull light.

"Captain," cried a man from behind.

"Silence, I said," the Captain roared.

"The water, sir—it's alive."

The Captain's fingers flew open, Essepi dropped to the deck, and Captain Baker spun.

The orb lit up and dazzled the night with colors no man had ever seen, and in its dark radiance the sea had indeed come alive with hideous undulating forms that moved inexorably through the diseased waters toward the ship like an unholy army of madness. The crew shrank back toward the three dead priests with a cry of utter terror.

"God's grace," cried one of the men. "Jesus and Mary be with us."

"Man the cannon," shouted the Captain. "Drive them back."

"Not the cannon," screamed Essepi. He had stepped to the Captain's side, his face wild and feral. "I'm on your side, believe me. I took control of your ship, but I'm giving it back. You are in command. But I told you, we cannot risk igniting the gas. Give me this one good act."

The Captain stared at Essepi. His right hand still clutched the knife so hard that his fingers throbbed. For a moment, he looked as though he would plunge it straight into Essepi's stomach. Then he faced the crew.

"The professor's right," he shouted. "No cannon to save us tonight and no pistols. Swords and knives only, men. Hack to pieces anything that tries to board this ship."

No one moved.

"If you do not move, I'll cut you down myself."

After a moment, the men moved toward the railings, drawing blades as they did so, their faces lit with fear of something worse than death. The dark waters around their ship churned with monstrous shapes that seemed part man and part fish.

"Behold the armies of Dagon," boomed a voice from above them.

The Captain backed away and looked up at the towering dark form of Lizotte who stood straight and imposing as a totem. One arm stretched high above his head and he held a staff as though he were commanding the night itself. Atop his head was fixed golden metalwork that flashed back the unholy colors of the orb.

"You've got to stop him," said Essepi.

"How?" asked Captain Baker.

"Kill him if you have to," said Essepi. "I authorize you to do it. Don't let him use the Secretary's son. Kill him, too, if you have to. He's lost his mind. What is life to him?"

Captain Baker looked at his knife.

"I don't need your authorizations. I am in command of my ship again."

With a grim face, he moved away through the fog to climb to the next level and come up behind Dr Lizotte.

"The Eye of Dagon has seen the sacrifice and approved," yelled Lizotte. "Through the mouth of the bedlamite, the god will speak."

The men gasped as Lizotte lowered his staff and jerked the madman forward, displaying him to the crowd. His eye sockets were deeper than night. Wild hair splayed from his head like Gorgon snakes. His ripped clothes hung on him like torn sails on a mast. He opened his mouth wide, and his cavernous voice bellowed through the night.

"Ph'nglui fhtagn," he yelled. "Iä Iä, Dagon . . . mglw'nafh Cthulhu R'leyh wgah-nagl. Fhtagn."

"Proclaim the oath of Dagon with me or die," called Lizotte.

In the waters behind them, the Eye of Dagon flared again with spectral, unspeakable brilliance.

"Iä iä," howled the bedlamite.

From the sea came a croaking chorus, and the sailors looked at the monstrosities that churned through the waters toward them, and then up at Lizotte's towering figure. The diadem fixed to Lizotte's head began to pulse and glow a panoply of clashing colors.

"Join us or die. Eternal life for those who take our oath. Eternal life! We will reign again and sweep mankind before us. We will rule the oceans from pole to pole."

The bedlamite opened his mouth again, and this time from it came a roaring like all the waters of the world converging in an obscene cacophony. Men covered their ears and dropped to their knees as blood poured from between their fingers.

The bedlamite cried as Captain Baker appeared at his back and, with one quick slice, slit wide the man's throat, causing blood to rush out from him like water from a pierced bladder. With a thrust of his foot, Baker sent the bleeding madman over the edge to slam face first into the deck at Professor Essepi's feet.

"What have you done?" cried Lizotte. "You are a fool. We cannot be stopped. You cannot stand against the power of a god."

"This is my ship," said Captain Baker, "and I decide who stands and who doesn't."

In a violent fury, Lizotte swung his staff at the Captain's head the exact moment Captain Baker plunged his knife into Lizotte's stomach, ripping upward. The staff cracked against Baker's head and, as Lizotte let go of it and pulled his hands to his stomach, the Captain toppled over the edge and crashed to the lower deck beside Essepi. His neck snapped on impact, and the man lay still. Blood and bile drained from his mouth and he coughed once, gurgled, and died.

Essepi bent to one knee and stared in disbelief at Baker's corpse, then stood, gazing at the upper deck where Lizotte thrashed. As he watched, Lizotte dropped, then pitched forward and slid over the edge. Essepi took a step back, stopping as he saw Lizotte's body hook on the spike protruding from the middle priest.

"The Captain is dead," cried one of the men.

The urgency in the man's voice caused Essepi to pull away. As he turned, his face hardened into a mask of rage, and then fell slack as he beheld slithering creatures pulling themselves over the railing. Essepi saw the prone, discarded figure of the bedlamite lying next to the Captain. He considered picking up the Captain's knife, and fighting with the sailors.

Instead, Essepi looked down at blood soaked body of the madman and said, "You and I are of a kind."

In the midst of the battle, he dropped to his knees and wept. The creatures tore and ripped at the sailors. Screams and battle cries mingled with yelps and keens as men and monsters alike slipped and fell in a mixture of blood and ooze.

As Essepi cradled the body of the dead lunatic, the sailors cut deep into gray-green slick torsos and the reptilian creatures bit and tore away at them.

Teeth and horned elbows ripped flesh and sinew away from their human prey, while Essepi cupped a hand under the bedlamite's skull to keep it from flopping up and down as they rocked. Hordes of creatures continued to clamber over the railings onto the squirming mass of bodies.

Tears streamed down Essepi's face. He whispered to the bedlamite, "Now I see what you have seen. Darkness may not be denied."

As the squealing, chaotic mass behind him swelled, Essepi finally set down the dead bedlamite and rose to his feet. He came around like an automaton and gazed at the carnage before him. His lower jaw dropped. The gory scene receded to the seared edge of his vision, eclipsed by the image of the Eye of Dagon rising above dark waters, lifted by a an undulation of alien colors.

Fish-men dragged the corpses of mutilated human and monstrosities alike over the ship's railing, disappearing into bloodstained waters. Essepi recoiled in horror when he realized that the Eye of Dagon was actually looking at him. The realization that the root cause of the bedlamite's insanity was *alive* shattered his mind into fractured fragments of consciousness. His vision filled with the utter alien nature of the Eye as he stepped toward the railing. The fish-men moved past him as though he were not there, and no human being remained alive to notice him.

The railing stopped him, though for a moment he teetered at its edge as though he would fall over, but he did not. The Eye of Dagon filled his vision and he felt his consciousness slip.

"Iä Iä, Cthulhu fhtagn," he cried out suddenly.

The Eye flashed brighter and suddenly Essepi thrust both thumbs into his eyes, shrieking in torment, repeating the action again and again. As he dropped to his knees, he began to tremble violently. Yet in his mind the Eye of Dagon dimmed and descended into the stained waters from which it had come. He felt rain begin to fall. It grew in force and intensity. Somehow, Essepi sensed the dissipating dark vapors that had risen from the sea, washing clean the deck of the *U.S.S. Vincent*.

Three days later, on an afternoon clear and clean with wisps of elusive white clouds brushstroked across a beryl backdrop, the crew of the Mohican class *U.S.S. Kearsage*, captained by Captain Charles W. Pickering, located the *U.S.S. Vincent* and its lone survivor. While attempting to guide the blood-crusted lunatic back to their skiff, the madman sunk his teeth into a sailor's hand and bit off his index finger. While the sailor screamed, the bedlamite flapped his arms in crazy windmills and ran straight for the ship's railing.

His body was never found, but Seaman First Class Bissoon swore til his dying day that when Professor Essepi's body hit the water, scaled tentacles reached up and pulled him under.

The Star of
Istanbul

BY *CHRIS AND LINDA L. DONAHUE*

Atlantic Ocean—1535

U RTHUUG'AAL DRAGGED HIS LIFELESS leg through the green slab streets of R'lyeh. He savored the Atlantic's colder, saltier water, preferring it over the bay waters of Devil's Reef.

Lord Cthulhu had summoned Urthuug'aal to the submerged city, its spires grander than the phosphorescent palaces of Y'ha-nthlei, where Urthuug'aal currently served. Pulsing, crimson veins covered Cthulhu's domed temple. Murky green, marbled steps, each cut to a unique height and angle, led up to the Master's tomb. Dragging his leg, Urthuug'aal began the arduous climb.

He knelt before the entrance and waited.

A glow drifted nearer. Kelp-like tendrils flowed down the attending Lurker's back, indicating great age. Lurkers, rare mutations among Deep Ones, possessed "the sight." They watched the world above for the sleeping Master. While dark, scaly Deep Ones were white only on their bellies, Lurkers were solid white and faintly luminescent. "Follow me," he said.

Though slumbering, Cthulhu's commands insinuated themselves into the thoughts of men whose minds were more evolved and open to the outer dimensions.

"Await my return." The Lurker floated away.

Urthuug'aal crouched before the Master's tomb, balancing awkwardly on his one good leg. Pulsing, mineral veins drew cosmic energy, sustaining the Great Lord while he slept. "Master?"

Cthulhu's voice, though cast mentally, nevertheless echoed inside the cavernous chamber. "Alt'ireen, Urthuug'aal." *Rise, Urthuug'aal.*

Grateful, Urthuug'aal stood, leaning slightly.

In human tongue, Cthulhu continued, "A rare window opens, a brief time to reshape destiny, to reclaim that which has been stolen."

The image of a crystal prism device flashed in Urthuug'aal's mind, bringing back a painful memory. Lost in unfamiliar waters, he'd come within a league of the device, close enough for it to drain the life from his leg, killing it.

"The Star-Prism?" Urthuug'aal whispered. "Forgive me for speaking, Great Lord, but why speak in man's tongue? And why *that* particular one?"

"Because you speak it, among others. Because you remember."

At only a century old, Urthuug'aal remembered being human. He was a hybrid, born of a human mother. As such he would always be impure among the Deep Ones.

"The time approaches," Cthulhu said, "when the Star-Prism will again recognize its true masters."

The crystalline device was an interface which plugged into one of many amplifying storage bases. When humans were barely more than animals, Cthulhu's servants had installed the device on this world to safeguard it from Elder Gods. As humans multiplied and evolved, they discovered the Star-Prism. Because the prism hadn't been programmed to recognize humans as "the enemy," it permitted their touch. Over time, as galaxies shifted, the interface lost contact with the home world and adopted Earth as "home." It reprogrammed itself to serve humans. Now it recognized Elder Gods *and* Old Ones as "the enemy."

"Fortunately," Cthulhu's voice boomed, "mortals, though their minds are incapable of understanding the device's complexities, know to discharge it at decade intervals."

Unplugging the crystal allowed the storage base to discharge. The creators made multiple bases, but humans had uncovered only two auxiliary bases. The primary base was here, built into Cthulhu's tomb.

The ten year process to discharge filtered the stored life-energy, then gradually fed it into the ground, making land fertile. If not discharged, a full base leaked unfiltered, pure life-energy—malignant, hostile alien energy—into the air, causing delusions and insanity among sentient beings.

"The time to discharge approaches," Cthulhu said. "Once the Star-Prism's interface is in transit, you will retrieve it."

Urthuug'aal felt suddenly dehydrated, though immersed in saltwater. The interface still functioned unplugged. Without a base, drained life-energy seeped directly into the atmosphere. Generally, the effects of short-term, small scale draining were unpleasant to lifeforms absorbing the unfiltered seepage—but the effects weren't as catastrophic as those in the vicinity of a leaking base. "Won't it kill me, Great Lord?"

"Not during the coming cosmic window."

More images flashed into Urthuug'aal's mind. He saw the Earth, its moon, and a distant, alien planet with moons form a perfect celestial alignment.

"Such a planetary alignment with the home world occurs perhaps once a century," Cthulhu said. "To occur without either sun interfering is rarer. To occur when the interface will be unplugged is exceedingly rare. Another such opportunity might never arise."

Despite the Master's explanation, the sheer agony of Urthuug'aal's one near-encounter stayed at the forefront of his fears.

"During this rare window," Cthulhu continued, "once unplugged, the interface's uplink will seek the home world. Between the alignment and lack of distorting solar energy, the link can make contact and update its programming which will reset the parameters to the original code."

Urthuug'aal's anxieties eased. Once reset, the Star-Prism would only drain Elder Gods. Any Old Ones, even a hybrid, could approach, even handle, the device.

Cthulhu's resonate tones rang ominously. "However, if a human plugs the interface into a base without affirming the reset parameters, the program defaults, once again, to human DNA values, reconfiguring the recognition matrix accordingly."

Meaning the device would continue to drain Old Ones. But in R'lyeh, the device could be calibrated to accept Old Ones as a natural part of this world. Then the device would be used as it was intended, for the Great Lord to protect this world from Elder Gods. If they could, the ancient enemy would eradicate all natural life here and rebuild the planet to an environment hostile to humanity and Old Ones alike.

"I understand, master." This mission was the most important task ever assigned him.

"Then you realize, if you fail, you'll suffer torments greater than any being in any galaxy has endured." Cthulhu fell back into slumber.

Outside the tomb, the pearly, luminous Lurker offered an amulet, a charged command disc. "With this, you may alter water molecules within sea or sky. Use it sparingly, as it may arouse the interface's defensive programming."

Southern Coast of Greece—1535

Aboard the galley, *Sultan's Scimitar*, Vizier Ihsan watched the sky. Inverted, purple clouds threatened an unnatural storm. In his bones, he knew something worse than a storm approached.

Admiral Khidr joined Ihsan at the sharp-beaked prow. He scowled at the weather. "We should've taken the *Gem of Osmanli*." A galleass—a heavier armed and more stable ship than a war galley. "But perhaps it's Allah's will we don't wreck upon the rocks."

"Speed is crucial," Ihsan said. It was safer hugging the coast in the smaller vessel anyway. "We're already late."

They were late before setting sail. To impress a visiting emir, Sultan Suleiman I had kept the Star of Istanbul a week past the Day of Exchange—which had coincided with the Day of Sacrifice. A sign that this exchange was particularly auspicious.

A sign that revealed why Allah had willed Ihsan to leave his mountain ten years ago and walk to the sultan's palace. The Venetian Doge had just returned the sacred stone to Suleiman the Magnificent. Sensing power inside the stone, Ihsan accepted his destiny and the post of astronomer vizier. For ten years, Ihsan studied the Star of Istanbul while it repelled evil, protecting the empire. For unknown reasons, the stone must change altars once every ten years.

Yet politics made fools of even the wisest men. "What is another week?" the sultan had argued. "The Venetian Doge will understand."

No explanation had swayed him. Perhaps had Suleiman read *Of Gods Beyond Olympus* by Apostolos, he would've understood. Or perhaps not. The ancient text mostly rambled. Apostolos, who'd discovered the stone and altars, had gone mad after deciphering the strange symbols encircling the first altar's base.

"Trust in Allah," Ihsan said. "He will see us through the storm and safely to our destination."

Admiral Khidr stroked his red beard, for which foreigners named him Barbarossa. "I know a sheltered inlet."

"We cannot delay," Ihsan said.

"So you often say," Khidr said impatiently. "Perhaps, vizier, we'd sail faster if you prayed harder."

Ihsan smiled patiently at Khidr, a recent convert. "Christians pray for what they want. We pray to understand and accept Allah's will."

"It's my will you go below. Sultan Suleiman will tack my hide on his wall if I let you blow overboard." Khidr laughed. "Then you'd really be a whirling dervish."

"You are confused. Only the Mevlevi whirl." The Mevlevi were renown intellectuals and aristocrats. So the mistake was more flattering than insulting. Ihsan added, "I should go below anyway." To check on their precious cargo.

From behind, Khidr muttered, "I know you're Bektashi—though you don't act it."

Ihsan's gait faltered. Admiral Khidr was right. Bektashi dervishes were exuberant and cheerful. During rites, they imbibed wine—unlike other orders—and women participated unveiled, equals of men.

Having looked into the sacred crystal's depths, having read of creatures inhabiting the ether between worlds, Ihsan knew what the storm hid. Such sobering knowledge robbed the joy of frivolous behavior.

Ihsan bowed. "It's more important, admiral, that you live up to your reputation than I appear a holy man by your standards." Khidr's prowess at sea had earned him the title *Kapudan Pasha*, Great Admiral, conferred upon him by Suleiman.

Between superstitious fear and reverence, the crew avoided the hold with the vault chamber containing the sacred stone.

Neither a candle nor lamp burned within the innermost chamber, yet a brilliant, bluish light shone from beneath the vault door.

Even as he turned the key, Ihsan felt unusual power emanating from the sacred stone.

Defying known laws of physics, the crystalline prism balanced vertically, almost hovering, its bottom point barely pressing into the red, velvet pillow. Without doubt, this unearthly element possessed mystical powers.

The stone called to Ihsan just as Allah had once called Ihsan to become a hermit and hone mystical skills. Ihsan sensed that within the sacred stone's crystalline depths there resided a message for humanity.

Gazing into the asteriated, hexagonal prism might reveal a sun, a dozen stars, or familiar constellations. Before leaving Istanbul, the sacred stone had revealed a greenish-white sun. After removing it from its altar, the sun burst into an amorphous, starry cloud.

A lifetime wasn't enough to unravel the stone's mystery. Being an old man, Ihsan knew he might not live to see the stone's return.

Perhaps the Doge would invite him to continue his study in Venezia. Because the sultan valued knowledge, Suleiman would understand. . ..

. . . If he recovered. Keeping the sacred stone too long had unleashed unspeakable evil upon the Osmanli people of the Ottoman Empire. The sultan suffered bouts of madness. Chaos thrived in Istanbul, spreading like a plague. Raving citizens wrought untold damage, rioting and looting, murdering and raping. The Mad Greek had warned such events occurred if the stone wasn't transferred according to the timetable—though he never explained why. Ihsan hypothesized the crystal underwent a transformation over time, like a lodestone changing polarity. Changing altars disrupted that transformation.

Once the Star of Istanbul rested in the Venetian altar, the stone's "polarity" should revert, returning peace and reason to the Osmanli people.

The stone pulsed. On his knees, Ihsan gazed into it, opening his mind to the cosmos, seeking contact with whatever sentient being resided within the crystal.

The stone was fiery hot, warming Ihsan's face like the desert sun at noontime. Only *after* the Day of Exchange had passed did the crystal, still ensconced on the alter, turn hot—another sign the sultan had ignored.

Inside the Star of Istanbul, Ihsan saw an alien landscape, an underwater city of green spires, its design seemingly wrought by fanatics. Throbbing, blood-red veins writhed across the city's largest dome.

Ihsan's heart thudded painfully, beating in rhythm with the vein's irregular pulse. The city's darksome design captivated him. He stared deeper, following twisting streets that interwove at impossible angles. The city was hideous, yet he couldn't look away.

Atop a plateau, a luminescent creature stared back with bulbous, unblinking eyes. A deep, gurgling voice, like a sluggish current, spoke in Ihsan's mind. *Surrender the Star-Prism and the Great Lord Cthulhu shall grant you life for as long as time is measured.*

The cold voice receded. The starry cloud replaced the city within the sacred stone's crystalline depths. The strange pulse gone, Ihsan crumpled to the floor. Struck by divine acumen, he realized the monsters he feared weren't coming from distant worlds, but from under the sea.

"Allah be merciful."

Lightning crackled. Thunderbolts rumbled. The galley lurched, tossing Ihsan into the chest containing his prized tomes and scrolls. For Ihsan, two storms raged, one outside and the other surging within his skull.

A deeper, more viscous rumbling, like magma oozing beneath a volcano, flowed into Ihsan's mind, each word searing hot. *Foolish mortal, we were here long before your feeble race walked upright.*

Beneath the Mediterranean

The saltier, more buoyant waters aided Urthuug'aal's dragging gait. His legion of Spawn and Deep Ones included those rarely born Gazers and Wailers.

A ship's keel parted the sea, sailing between the Ionian Islands and the Peloponnesian shore. Judging by its speed and the amount of water displaced, the ship suited their purposes. They followed the ship, waiting for it to anchor.

When the ship's crew lowered a longboat, Urthuug'aal led his legion upward. Urthuug'aal only broke the surface. Cool night air blew across his amphibious face. His webbed thumb traced the amulet's rim as he invoked the command Cthulhu had empowered within the disc's interior matrix. Their molecules made denser, clouds descended, becoming a thick fog.

In Latin, men cursed the change in weather. They sensed the fog's supernatural origin and sweated fear, an odor so strong, Urthuug'aal tasted it.

Urthuug'aal recognized the crosses on the humans' tunics. Maltese pirates navigated their longboat through the fog. Men holding lanterns crowded the primitively carved prow while others threaded oars to maneuver around protruding rocks.

A unit of Spawn slipped beneath the longboat, thwarting the pilot's efforts. They stranded it atop a rocky shoal.

The twenty-some pirates cursed louder when ordered into the water. A few shoved against the grounded boat while most readied primitive human weapons.

Urthuug'aal signaled the Wailers. Three gifted Deep Ones, their shapely limbs, extremely angular and twisted, scaled a weathered sea stack. Outside Cthulhu's tomb, Wailers sang the evening song of antediluvian madness, consoling the Master's often fitful sleep.

The beautifully mournful song gripped mortal hearts with abject terror, reducing brave men to quivering lumps.

"Heathen tricks," the pirate leader shouted. He climbed onto a barrel, swirling the ends of his fur-trimmed coat. "You cower like peasants! At what? Strange horns? You are Knights of Malta, chosen by God."

"'Tis sea devils," the men cried, clutching their ears and doubling over.

Their leader sneered. "'Tis some Greek slave performing for his Turkish master."

Though rare, the captain could be immune. Perhaps he dealt with madness because he was already insane. Either way, he would make a good study.

"Devils are inside our heads! Get them out!" one cried.

"My mind is being shredded!" another wailed.

"It's unbearable," one said before shooting himself.

Humans were weak. They killed each other and themselves. How they managed to climb the evolutionary chain defied logic. Once the Master rose from his tomb and subjugated humanity, they would find their proper place.

The pirate captain fired a primitive pistol, belching a cloud of smoke to project a small lead ball. His lucky shot nearly struck a Wailer.

Urthuug'aal signaled a hold, rather than risk a lucky shot actually hitting anyone. The humans would tire or go mad soon enough.

Terrified pirates fired wildly. Some splashed through the waist-deep water, seeking shore. In the fog, they mostly waded in the wrong direction. A few attempted to swim to the anchored galley. They mostly drowned themselves.

In the chaos, their leader bellowed, "Organize or you'll suffer worse than imaginary demons!"

His words had no effect. Their ammunition was running low and most had stopped firing anyway to pray.

"I want their leader alive for study," Urthuug'aal said telepathically before ordering the attack.

Like a rising atoll, the legion broke the surface, surrounding the stranded longboats. Deep Ones pulled under a dozen pirates. The Mediterranean quickly drowned their screams.

The legion left the longboat broken and overturned. Among the stranded pirates, only the leader survived—damaged, but alive. Still fifty-some pirates guarded the galley. Blinded by the fog, they mostly shouted in confusion, an effect of the Wailers' song when heard from a greater distance.

Urthuug'aal's legion surrounded the anchored galley. Digging claws into the wood, they climbed aboard. As soon as the Spawn and Deep Ones cleared the railing, the pirates screamed, releasing deep, pent-up terror the Wailers had brought nearer the surface. The legion leapt aboard, tossing pirates overboard.

One band of pirates, insanity gleaming in their eyes, rushed forward, swinging cutlasses. Though their blades bit into a few Deep Ones, they were ineffectual weapons, easily blocked. One good, raking blow quickly disemboweled humans. Soon, chunks of flesh and entrails made the deck slick with blood and tinged the air with a sweet metallic scent.

Finally, the Spawn dragged their captive aboard.

Urthuug'aal hobbled across the galley deck, his lifeless leg an even greater hindrance out of water. "Save us time and order their surrender."

"So you can kill them?" The pirate leader growled, though he lay on the deck where he'd been thrown.

"So they can sail and steer the ship."

A Spawn squeezed the bleeding wound at the Captain's shoulder, eliciting a wince.

He breathed hard, but nodded. "Obey your Captain! Submit . . . unless you've a mind to become fish food."

The crew surrendered. Urthuug'aal set the Gazers, Deep Ones with hypnotic powers, upon them. Mindless crews never mutinied.

Bearded Maltese blubbered for mercy. Gazers stared into the prisoners's eyes, stealing information, warping minds.

Spawn tied the pirate captain to a mast using Spawn-woven nets of fibers stronger than anything man-made. The Captain's hard gaze shone with determination and unshaken sanity. Rather than struggle uselessly against his bonds, he stood defiantly.

Surrounded by raw chunks of bloody meat, Urthuug'aal's stomach growled. He tore into a sizeable piece of thigh, savoring the fear-marinated flesh.

"You may possess useful knowledge and skills, pirate captain. Serve the Master and preserve your life. Serve the Master well and reap rewards far greater than you can imagine."

"The rewards I seek are found in the afterlife." The pirate spat at Urthuug'aal's webbed feet.

"Then you crave death?"

"No man craves it. To crave something means to actively seek it. And seeking death is suicide—a crime against God."

Urthuug'aal blinked. "Some of your men have recently committed such crimes."

"You'd driven them insane." The pirate swallowed hard. "They won't be held accountable."

"I've forgotten much of what it was to be a man," Urthuug'aal said. "Tell me, which God rewards pirates. What afterlife do you seek?"

The pirate scowled. "I am a Knight of Malta. Killing Turks is not piracy, but serving God."

"Our faiths are not so dissimilar."

"I strongly doubt that." Hatred tainted his voice.

"Serve Great Cthulhu, mortal, and deliver more death to the Turkish empire than you could in fifty ships. Or would you rather serve in their condition?" Urthuug'aal indicated the swaying, silent prisoners.

The pirate captain fell silent. The tangy scent of desperate fear cut through the savory salt and iron smell of fresh-spilt blood.

"Decide, mortal. The offer will not last." The window was narrow enough without wasting time bargaining for a human's aid.

The Captain nodded. "I've used slavers against other slavers. I've made pacts with Serbs to kill Turks and with corsairs to trap Tunisians. So long as my immortal soul is safe, I'd deal with the devil himself to bring ruin to Suleiman."

Humanity was weak, so very weak. Offer what they most desired and they were easily suborned.

Urthuug'aal ordered the man cut free. "What are you called?"

"Louis de Tourville, candidate Knight of Saint John."

"If you betray me, Louis, you'll know torments far worse than described by your Christian Hell." Urthuug'aal described the Star-Prism and those who possessed it. "Aid our Great Master by recovering the Star-Prism, which is rightfully ours, and madness will wreck the Turkish Empire."

Louis crossed himself. "By Saint John, I pledge to fight at your side to bring ruin to Suleiman and his slave-takers." He glanced at his crew. "What of my men? Will they recover their wits?"

"No."

"May their souls find peace in the Lord's compassion." He bowed his head, observing a moment of silence. Afterward, his demeanor was intense and focused. "From what you've said, the Star-Prism will be transported by Suleiman's admiral, the Christian traitor, Barbarossa. He'll take a warship, most likely his favorite galleass. There'll be an armed escort. Therefore, if I may suggest a strategy?"

Urthuug'aal nodded, certain he'd chosen well in preserving Louis.

The Ionian Sea

Janissaries watched for pirates. The head of Istanbul's *Sipahis*—feudal cavalry—*Agha* Mesut kept an eye on everything else. Yet after morning prayer, Ihsan spotted the drowning man. Perhaps because Ihsan knew the real danger came from under the sea, not upon it.

Janissaries rescued the unfortunate wretch. His clothing was that of a sea-going, Maltese knight—an infidel pirate. Scratches and gouges marred his arms. They didn't bleed, as the flesh around the wounds had swollen and puckered.

Admiral Khidr's shadow fell across the helpless Maltese who lay spitting up water. Khidr snarled at the man. "Toss him back. If his God wants him, He'll grant him the strength to swim to Malta."

The Maltese quivered, his face ashen, his eyes staring at nothing. Ihsan doubted the man could stand, much less fight. He must have floated for days.

"Have you no compassion?" Ihsan asked.

"For a pirate?" Khidr spat. "Divine Suleiman should have killed them all."

"Would not our sultan then be Suleiman the Merciless rather than the Magnificent?"

With a shrug, Khidr said, "Either he hangs or drowns. In the matter of pirates, my word is law."

Agha Mesut stepped forward. "*Kapudan pasha,*" he said, using formal address, "on *this* voyage, Vizier Ihsan represents the sultan. Divine Suleiman himself sent me to safeguard him. I interpret my duty as defending his person as well as his word."

Khidr squinted. "I heard the sultan was not receiving visitors. If he were seeing his officers, I wouldn't be here, wasting my time delivering baubles to Venetians."

Ihsan tensed. Few knew the sultan's true condition. Word that a ruler suffered madness often brought on another kind of madness among nobles, one that tore apart empires.

"I cannot say why you were denied an audience," Mesut said. "I know only that during a . . . wakeful moment, the sultan sent for me."

"Wakeful" was most likely a euphemism for lucid. If nothing else, Ihsan now understood why the head of Istanbul's cavalry was here.

With newly realized authority, Ihsan commanded, "I forbid any man to harm this prisoner while under my care."

Khidr growled at Mesut then Ihsan. "I should dump all three of you overboard."

Several Janissaries shot the admiral a warning glare. Due to the long standing relationship between the Bektashi and the Corps of Janissaries, Ihsan had their unquestioned support.

Khidr glared back then stormed off.

Normally, Ihsan wouldn't argue a pirate's well-deserved fate, especially not with a man whose brother was killed by pirates. But this pirate looked to possess firsthand knowledge of what awaited them.

His gaze darted erratically. Drooling, he ranted, "Sea devils! Fish-eyed monsters! Hiding in the fog!"

He leapt to his feet with unexpected strength. Screaming like a lunatic, he ran toward the rail.

Ihsan shouted, "Lash him to the mast—gently. And someone find bandages for his wounds."

Three Janissaries tied him securely to the mizzenmast.

Quietly, Mesut asked, "Are you certain, vizier, with all that's entrusted to you, that you wish to add this responsibility?"

"I have no choice." Once the Maltese ceased struggling, Ihsan asked him, "What happened? Tell me everything."

The Maltese stared with vacant madness. "When your end comes, remember that I warned you."

The Adriatic Sea

Drums only woke Ihsan from sleep. Something even deeper also awoke, that part of his mind he'd trained during those years in seclusion. He climbed topside. Searching for Admiral Khidr, Ishan dodged running Janissaries, armed with muskets and scimitars.

The *sipahi*, *Agha* Mesut, drew Ihsan aside. "It's dangerous, vizier."

"It's dangerous everywhere," Ihsan replied. "There is no hiding from what hunts us. If we survive, it will be Allah's will."

Mesut grunted. "Allah's will usually favors the wise over the foolish. So why does it seem we're aboard a ship of fools?"

"Because you are wise? Whereas I must face these demons," Ihsan said.

"Then we face them together," Mesut said.

Admiral Khidr gazed through a telescope. "More stinking Maltese pirates chasing a barge."

"I hope it's only pirates." Yet that awoken mystical awareness told Ihsan otherwise.

Khidr grimaced. "There'll be no talk of monsters, old man."

"May I?" Ihsan peered through the telescope.

A Maltese galley overtook a Turkish barge. Ihsan wished he could see the crew's faces. Yet all he could tell was that the oarsmen rowed in perfect, mindless rhythm.

Ihsan lowered the telescope. A queer sensation shivered through him; something evil was watching. If evil didn't already know, it soon would that the sacred stone was aboard the *Sultan's Scimitar*, not the merchant barge.

Ihsan leveled a hard gaze. "We should flee, admiral. *They've* noticed us."

"Who are they?" Mesut asked.

Khidr scowled. "*They* are pirates. Seeing as they've placed themselves conveniently in my way to harass a Turkish merchant, I'll not ignore them. It's my sworn duty to see them punished." Admiral Khidr turned away, ending the discussion. He signaled the nearest escort war galley.

All three escorts veered toward the pirate's galley. The Turkish barge changed course for the sultan's fleet.

"Leave the galleys to fight," Ihsan said, "while we flee to Venezia."

"The *Sultan's Scimitar* is a war galley—not a ferrying caique. We'll sail to Venezia, *after* I sink these pirates. Find someplace safe. I would dislike reporting your death to the sultan." Khidr waved, dismissing Ihsan. He snapped at Mesut, "If you're any sort of *sipahi*, you'll fight alongside the Janissaries."

The lead escort galley opened fire with a pair of small chaser cannon. A shot splintered a section of the pirate galley's railing. At once, the pirates turned.

No longer pursued, the merchant barge maneuvered alongside the *Sultan's Scimitar*.

A loud, splintering crack sounded to port. Yet the pirate galley hadn't fired a shot. The lead galley tilted up, exposing a gaping hole in its hull. Heartbeats later, the second galley's keel broke, splitting the vessel in half. The attacks could only have come from below . . ..

Yet Admiral Khidr swore, blaming unseen rocks.

His awakened awareness made Ihsan suddenly duck as a barrage of gunshot whistled overhead—though the attack hadn't come from the pirate ship. Amid surprised cries and curses, Ihsan turned toward the merchant barge. Dead-eyed Turkish sailors stood in a line, readying their muskets for another volley.

Moving behind the vacant-eyed sailors, Ihsan glimpsed one of *them*, sprouting tentacles from its mottled, smooth head. A cold numbness crept inside him.

A Janissary handed Mesut a gun, saying, "Can you shoot while standing or do you horsemen have to sit?"

Mesut grimaced. "I'm as fine a shot as any man here."

"Prove it, *sipahi*."

Following the Janissary, Mesut paused beside Ihsan, saying, "I won't be far, vizier."

"Go with Allah's blessing." Ihsan stared at the dead-eyed Turks crewing the merchant barge under the control of hideous monsters. The creatures controlled both ships. It was a trap.

The tentacled species resembled the sketch of Cthulhu, except they were wingless and man-sized. From descriptions, the frog-headed ones with ridged backs and slimy, corpse-gray hides were Deep Ones.

Cannon fire rattled the air. Ihsan barely heard the din. Yet his senses told him precisely when and where to take cover.

He prayed for salvation, guidance, and protection. Yet Allah gave no answer that even Ihsan's heightened, mystical senses perceived.

The Maltese galley dropped their sails and shipped their oars in a gesture of surrender. A pious man might take that as a sign from Allah, but Ihsan sensed icy betrayal in the air. Mindless men were unable to make decisions and unearthly monsters never surrendered.

Ihsan bolted toward the helmsman's station. Knowing worse awaited than death, he shouted, "Signal the galley! It's a trap!"

No one listened.

The last escort galley approached the pirates without firing. The escort's crew couldn't know that the merchant barge was not as innocent as it seemed. Just as they had no idea what really crewed both ships.

Janissaries aboard the *Sultan's Scimitar* fired swivel guns at the merchant crew. Bullets struck crazed crewmen who died without a cry. They welcomed death as an end of living torture.

As bullets struck demons, they shrieked in agony. Black ichor oozed from their wounds. Every dying shriek bored into Ihsan's mind, devouring another modicum of his sanity.

The pirate galley drifted on an unnatural patch of glassy-smooth sea where not a ripple moved. Yet elsewhere, froth crested the rolling waves.

"Sink them both!" Ihsan shouted. "The Turkish merchants are already lost!"

Over the musket fire and occasional cannon blast between the *Sultan's Scimitar* and the merchant barge, no one could hear Ihsan. Until an eerie calm descended upon the sea.

The sea turned to ice. As salt water didn't freeze, powerful evil was at work. The ranks of Janissaries prayed.

A cold mist coated the frozen surface. The sea erupted, throwing ice in all directions. A block of ice shattered the escort galley's prow. Another block damaged a mast and rigging. Steam rose between patches of rapidly melting ice as the once frozen sea churned and boiled. Waterspouts shot as high as a ship's mast. Columns of water struck the deck like a slaver's whip.

A giant wave lifted the last escort galley high, then smashed it downward. The bubbling sea boiled as well as drowned the men floundering in its choppy waves. One by one, they sank beneath the surface—their souls at last released.

Amid a sudden calm in the wind, a great swell cupped the *Sultan's Scimitar*. Water lapped the deck's edges. White foam, smelling of blood, spilled across. The oarsmen rowed, but the galley hung as if dry-docked.

The pirate galley rowed closer.

Finally, the unnatural swell lowered the *Sultan's Scimitar* between the pirate galley and the merchant barge.

Among the dead-eyed pirates stood one whose eyes burned with rational thought. A wolfish grin split his thick beard. He raised a sword, shouting, "Surrender and die easy, Turkish pigs. Or don't! I prefer you suffered."

His threat rallied the Janissaries, rousing them from their horrified stupor. They fired. When cannon and musket smoke dispersed, a dozen more pirates and monsters lay dead.

The sane-eyed Maltese, however, stood untouched. Either he was lucky or his devil's pact made him impervious to shot. The pirate laughed. "You were warned!"

Ihsan's heart beat in his throat. Deep Ones clawed the hull, crawling up it. They hopped onto the deck and searched with bulbous, unblinking black eyes.

Deep Ones crept nearer, bearing mouthfuls of teeth like sharks. One of them croaked, "Bring me the Star-Prism."

CHRIS AND LINDA L. DONAHUE

Janissaries backed away. Several collapsed, babbling. Only four men stood to fight—among them Mesut.

Ihsan ran for the hatch. "Merciful Allah, I pray it is not your will that your people perish to these alien monsters. Allow me, All-Powerful Allah, to act as your hand."

Just as Ishan reached the hatch, a nerve-scraping wail ripped through the air. Howling cries sent shivers of madness down Ihsan's spine. His bones vibrated, aching within. His mind teetered at the brink of insanity. *Wailers.*

He covered his ears, but couldn't shut out the demented song. To anchor his mind, Ihsan recited the thousand names of Allah. "Thou art the Merciful, thou art the Wise . . ."

Janissaries crumbled to the deck, moaning and sobbing. Crewmen abandoned their stations, leaving the ship to founder.

"Thou art the Triumphant, thou art the Generous . . ." His hands shaking, Ihsan found the key. Without breaking the soothing mantra, he unlocked the vault.

The sacred stone pulsed a brilliant cobalt blue.

Intense heat seared Ihsan's palms before he even touched it. From the chest where he kept his tomes, Ihsan removed the sleeve of *Hajji Bektash*, entrusted to him by his dervish order for good fortune. He wrapped the sleeve around the blistering hot stone, then hid it inside the folds of his waist sash. The heat drew the sweat from him in rivulets.

Where could he go? *Into the sea. Drown. Take the sacred stone.* At least the voice was his.

Ihsan laughed uncontrollably. The creatures came from below. There was no escaping.

A familiar, alien voice rumbled in Ihsan's mind. *Surrender the Star-Prism. Life eternal can be yours, mortal.*

"That is already promised me in the afterlife!" Ihsan bolted from the vault. These creatures could waste years searching the vast ocean. If Allah willed it, the sea floor would bury it forever.

The loss of so much sweat dehydrated him. Ihsan staggered topside, groping his way toward the railing. The world spun, making all directions seem the same. Trusting Allah, Ihsan plunged ahead.

A particularly deformed Deep One hopped toward Ihsan, dragging a leg. In a breath, the monster had crossed half the deck. It blocked Ihsan's escape and croaked, "Where is the Star-Prism? It belongs to Lord Cthulhu."

Ihsan spun around. Another creature, even more twisted, stood behind. Its reflective bulbous eyes quickly trapped Ihsan's gaze, rooting him to where he stood. Coarse, guttural alien words translated in his mind. *We come for the Star-Prism.*

Trapped, Ihsan knew he stared into a Gazer's eyes. He focused inwardly, finding the calm within the storm to renew his strength. He focused outward, forcing questions into the Gazer's mind. *What is the Star-Prism? What lives inside it? What can it show me of the cosmos?*

The creature laughed—but it answered.

Myriad images flooded Ihsan's mind, stars and orbiting planets. He saw their home world. The Mad Greek was right. His most garbled, rambling passages made sense now.

Though the Gazer's eye, Ihsan saw the Earth in space. He saw the planetary bodies in alignment and knew such an occurrence was exceedingly rare. This time, it had fallen upon the Day of Exchange.

"You cannot touch the crystal when it's on the altar, can you?" Ihsan shouted. "What do the constellations mean? Why do they change?" A moment later, he pressed his questions mentally.

More images flashed by. Ihsan's knees buckled. He collapsed, feeling himself wither as the life was sucked from him.

Someone shoved Ihsan, breaking contact with the Gazer.

Agha Mesut stepped into Ihsan's place, saying, "Go." He raised a dripping, ichor-oozing scimitar.

With a single swipe, the Gazer knocked the scimitar aside and sliced open Mesut's throat. Blood gushed for the instant it took Mesut to die.

Mesut possessed a strong soul. As it was passing from this world to the next, it released divine energy. Mesut's voice whispered, "It is Allah's will you survive."

Blessed strength flowed into Ihsan, replenishing him. He pressed a hand against the stone tucked securely in his sash then climbed over the railing.

Cannon shot ripped across the deck of the pirate galley. Dagger-sized splinters flew in all directions—killing more men and sea demons.

A lavish, Venetian fleet approached. Cannon thundered. Musket shot whistled through the air, renewing the battle. As Deep Ones and Cthulhu Spawn died, their last shrieks raked Ihsan's mind.

Ihsan flung himself overboard. Cold water enveloped him. His limbs and lungs seized up from shock. Trusting Allah, he didn't fight the sea. He was too weary anyway. Whether he sank or floated, he wasn't sure. But the last sight he recalled, before slipping into blissful blackness, was that of the Maltese galley capsizing.

The Venetian Doge's Palace
Ihsan woke, wrapped in silk bedclothes in an enormous chamber filled with gilt furnishings. He thought he'd gone to Paradise, but the aches in his body told him he still lived.

Then every memory—of Gazers, Wailers, Deep Ones and Spawn, of dead-eyed pirates and merchants, of cannon and musket fire, and of alien worlds, knowledge man wasn't ready to possess—rushed over him like a tidal wave. It swallowed him, dragging him down, leaving him in shock, as though he were again immersed in icy-cold water. The weight of this knowledge crushed him. He couldn't breathe. He was drowning in air.

Ihsan screamed, feeling a small release.

Suddenly, hands pressed him against the bed. A woman bathed his forehead with cool water. She was saying something and shaking her head. A Catholic priest hovered at the foot of the bed, babbling and counting rosary beads. A man in lavish, velvet clothing paced.

Why were they babbling incoherently? Surely the woman and man spoke Italian, a language Ihsan spoke fluently. And the priest must be praying in Latin, another language Ihsan understood. Yet their words were strangely unintelligible—alien even.

Ihsan felt for the crystal—but it was gone. His clothing had been exchanged for a silken nightshirt.

The pacing man was now by Ihsan's side, speaking slowly and repetitively. At last, the words bored through Ihsan's fear. "You had us worried, vizier. It's been five days since you were pulled from the sea."

Ihsan tried to speak, knew what he wanted to say, but words that weren't of his choosing struggled to rise instead. If he spoke, he knew he'd babble like a madman. So instead, he stared, pleading with his eyes.

"Once we realized your ship was overdue, the doge sent out a search party. The fleet captain informs us, he found your ship embroiled in battle. Regrettably, the *Sultan's Scimitar* was damaged beyond salvaging. Though many lives were lost, many were saved."

Ihsan thought of Mesut. *Many good lives were lost.*

"But rest easy," the Venetian man continued. "The Holy Rod—" their term for the Star of Istanbul— "is safe with the doge. In the great schemes of Heaven, that is all that matters, *sì*?"

Again Ihsan struggled to say, "It was Allah's will."

His mind slipped away from him. Instead of ornately carved bedposts, velvet curtains, and lavishly painted panoramas on the walls, Ihsan saw the alien city rising up from the sea. From every spire and domed building, hundreds of eyes watched humanity, waiting for another chance.

So this was what madness felt like.

Urthuug'aal sank to the bottom of the sea. The skin on his arm, where a bullet had dug into the flesh, was dying. If lucky, he would retain the partial use of his arm.

Having failed his Master, luck no longer mattered.

HIGH SEAS

BY *MICHAEL PENNCAVAGE*

"*I think the Deep Ones predominant colour was a greyish-green, though they had white bellies. They were mostly shiny and slippery, but the ridges of their backs were scaly. Their forms vaguely suggested the anthropoid, while their heads were the heads of fish, with prodigious bulging eyes that never closed. At the sides of their necks were palpitating gills, and their long paws were webbed. They hopped irregularly, sometimes on two legs and sometimes on four. I was somehow glad that they had no more than four limbs. Their croaking, baying voices, clearly used for articulate speech, held all the dark shades of expression which their staring faces lacked.*

While some changed more than others, some never did change quite enough . . . and was nearly human sometimes."

— "The Shadow Over Innsmouth"

TUG.

Pause.

Tug. Tug. *Tug.*

"I think I got one," Wade whispered, as if afraid the fish would hear him.

"You sure?" asked Leon from the other chair as he sipped a beer. His expression said he did not want to retrieve the gaff.

Wade's fishing pole bowed into a *U* in response.

Leon glanced up the tuna tower. "We got one!"

Simon looked down from the Captain's chair. He threw the engine in reverse. The boat's engines roared in response, slowly the vessel's momentum.

Wade flicked a switch on the reel and line began to unspool.

"Look at her go!" yelled Wade as he slid the base of the rod into the pole lock so it wouldn't be lost if the fish managed to pull the pole from his hands.

"Better get that harness on if you want a chance at catching that thing!" yelled Simon.

Leon helped Wade get strapped into the fishing chair.

"What do you think it is?" asked Wade. "Marlin?"

"Not likely," answered Simon. "We would have seen an *appearance* by now." He studied the pole for a moment, watching the inch-thick rod bend like licorice. "Shark."

"Great white?"

"You've seen *Jaws* too many times. Most likely a Mako. Maybe a Hammerhead."

Simon climbed down the ladder to the deck. From within one of the storage compartments he removed a diver's knife and sheath. He Velcroed it around Wade's calf.

"What's that for?"

"In case Bubba gets a little energetic and takes you and the chair for a little ride."

Wade swallowed hard and looked down at the deck. "The chair's bolted into the fiberglass!"

Simon lit up a cigar and looked out over the water. "And you have a quarter-ton of mean down there with no intention of getting caught. You can be certain that unless you cut yourself free, you'll be dragged along until either the line snaps or the hook rusts from its mouth."

"You've got to be kidding me!"

"Welcome to Deep Sea Fishing."

Wade grunted as he began to crank the reel.

Leon finished reeling in his line. "We've never hooked anything this large before. What do we do when he gets it up to the boat? Offer it a beer?"

"Depends on how much Wade tires it out," answered Simon. "Hopefully we'll be able to get a noose around the tail-fin. But if you land the fish while it's still frisky . . ." Simon opened the storage locker and reached inside. "We use this."

Wade looked at it curiously. It looked like a short fat cue stick. "What're you going to do with that? Ask if it wants to play nine-ball?"

"This is a bang stick." Simon answered as he pointed to one of the ends. "Place this end against the fish's head, press the red button, and *bang*! It's the equivalent of a shotgun blast."

"Isn't that a little extreme?"

"Extreme is the shark eating the boat."

"How are your arms holding up?" asked Simon.

"Shitty. How long has this been going on for?" asked Wade.

Leon glanced at his watch. "A little over an hour."

"Consider your self lucky. You could be at this all day."

"And what's to say I won't be?"

Simon looked at the reel. "The fish hasn't sounded in fifteen minutes. You probably won't have to let any more line out."

Wade grunted as he pressed his feet against the chair and heaved the pole like he was hoisting a bale of hay. Rivulets of sweat poured down his face. "You're saying I'm wearing it out?"

Simon looked out over the water as he put on a pair of chain mesh gloves. "At least enough for me to get him with the gaff and noose."

Leon looked at him incredulously. "You actually want to bring that thing on board?"

"Eventually. Might have to use the Bang Stick or drag it through the water backward to suffocate it first . . ."

A splash fifty feet off the port drew their attention. A large, gray mass was visible against the clear blue water.

Simon held the noose tightly as he positioned himself along the side. "Just bring it in nice and slow. Leon, go up to the controls. Push the throttle forward when I give you the signal." Simon watched as the fish edged closer to the boat. "Remember—nice and slow. No need for any of us to lose a limb."

"Man, that is one ugly fucking fish," remarked Wade as he leaned over the port side. The Mako was belly up, floating parallel to the boat. After bringing the fish up alongside the boat, Simon changed his mind and produced a baseball bat. Two well placed shots to the shark's head were, surprisingly, all it took to immobilize the fish.

Leon secured the noose around the tail fin while Simon unsheathed a filet knife that looked more like a machete. He sunk the blade deep into the fish's belly and sliced a long incision to its dorsal fin. The blue water suddenly became dark.

"OK," said Simon, wiping his balding forehead with his sleeve. "We give it five minutes to bleed out and then we get it on board. Any longer and we're gonna have every shark from here to Bermuda looking for a mid-day snack."

Wade watched as the cloud of blood slowly grew. Simon's incision had ruptured the Mako's stomach, expelling what the fish had eaten. Fish parts appeared briefly in the water before sinking beneath the crimson cloud. Then, amidst the chum, an object caught his attention.

Wade grabbed a net and scooped the object out before it drifted from reach.

It was a bottle. A plastic soda bottle. The label was gone, dissolved by the acids of the fish's stomach, but otherwise it was intact.

Leon took notice. "Damn. You would think with all of those bunkers in its belly it wouldn't still be *that* hungry."

Wade noticed that there was a piece of paper in the bottle. He uncapped the bottle, removed the paper, and read aloud.

To the person reading this. My name is Lester Hobkins, Captain of the High Seas. *My boat has been hijacked. I am being held against my will. This is not a joke. If, by the grace of god, this note is found, please contact the Coast Guard. This is not a joke.*

Wade looked at Leon and Simon in disbelief.

Simon lit up a cigarette. "That has got to be the craziest thing I have ever heard."

"What should we do?"

"Well, first thing we need to do is get Bubba out of the water. There's a Coast Guard Station on the way back to the marina. We'll stop in and give them the message. Let them figure out what to do with it."

Wade sat with Simon in the tower on the ride back.

They were still a few hours away from land when Wade spotted a cluster of boats tied side-by-side, bobbing gently in the waves. In the bay, where the water was more placid, it was a common practice for boat-owners to meet up and lash the vessels together, forming a large chain, usually to have parties on. However, for boats to be tethered this far out was much too dangerous. Wade raised his binoculars and began silently reading off the names that had been painted across the boats' sterns. *Kelly Jean, The Spinnaker* . . . Wade read the name of the last boat and almost dropped the spyglasses.

High Seas.

A man was sleeping in the aft of the *Kelly Jean*. Two boats over, a pair of women were sunning themselves on the bow of the *High Seas*.

Wade handed the binoculars to Simon. His lips became tight and compressed as he looked through them.

"What do you think?" asked Wade

"I don't know."

Leon looked up. "Hey, what's going on? Why'd we slow down?"

Simon handed the binoculars down and pointed. Leon had a look. "What the fuck?"

"It doesn't make any sense," said Simon

"Maybe we should get a little closer. Do a drive-by. See if everything looks all right," suggested Wade.

Leon climbed halfway up the tuna tower to get in on the conversation. "Hell yeah, we should. Did you see the two pieces of ass up on the bow!"

Simon re-lit his cigar and turned *The Privateer* toward the *High Seas*. Leon handed Wade the binoculars and climbed back down.

As they approached the vessel, Wade scanned the three boats with the binoculars. Not much else could be gathered. The three boats, each about forty feet in length, were bobbing uniformly in the waves. The man was still asleep on the *Kelly Jean*, the sun-hat jammed over his eyes. The two women on the *High Seas* seemed attractive from afar, and more so the closer the men got. One was a blonde, the other a brunette. Both sported healthy tans and wore bikinis that left little to the imagination.

Simon shifted the boat into idle and the rumble of the inboards lessened so he could talk. "Good afternoon, ladies," he yelled across the water. "How are you doing?"

"Okay," the blonde answered, smiling widely. She thumbed back to the fishing poles. A small bell was tied to each of the fishing poles. "Though we'd be doing much better if the fish were biting. We haven't gotten a jingle since lunchtime."

Simon cursed under his breath as he put the engines in reverse. The current had caused *The Privateer* to close the safety gap between the *High Seas*. They were drifting straight into the boat.

The women were quick to react. They grabbed *The Privateer's* railing and guided the boat up against theirs. Both boats had bumpers so the impact was reduced to a heavy *thump, thump.*

"Ahoy," said the blonde, tossing Wade a tether to prevent the boat from drifting away. He wrapped it around the *Privateer's* chock and the vessel settled in alongside the *High Seas.*

Simon made the introductions. "I'm Marcy," said the brunette. She motioned to the blonde. "She's Pam."

"Nice to meet you," said Wade as he made his way back from tethering his end of *The Privateer.*

"This your boat?" asked Simon.

"Nope. Just using it for a little fishing and tanning," she replied. "Ours is that one," she answered, pointing to *The Spinnaker.*

"*You* own it?" asked Simon incredulously.

"We both do," replied Marcy.

"Don't take this the wrong way, but you're the first women I've met that owned a boat that large," said Simon.

"And to think that the women's rights movement was only fifty years ago." Marcy answered mockingly.

They all shared a chuckle.

"Where is everyone else?" asked Wade. "It seems to be just you and *him*," he gestured over to man who was sleeping.

Marcy grinned. "Inside the *Kelly Jean* playing poker. I'm sure by now they're all passed out drunk, like Henry."

Simon's eyes narrowed as the sun moved out of hiding from behind a cloud. "How about the person who owns this boat?" he asked, gesturing to the *High Seas.* "Is he over there as well?"

Marcy stared at Simon for a moment before answering. "*Yes.* I'm sure Lester is drunk like the rest of them."

Simon looked at the *High Seas.* "He keeps it in good condition. Where is it slipped?"

"At the Coastal Marina," she answered.

"Really? Where is that . . ."

By the stern, Leon and Pam were engaged in a separate conversation. Leon stepped over to the *High Seas.*

"I'm getting a bottle of Bud. Either of you want anything?" Simon said.

Leon was practically drooling.

Pam smiled widely as she tossed back her hair. "We have a cooler full, if either of you want something to drink."

Simon and Wade watched the two of them make their way into *The Spinnaker's* cabin. Just before he ducked down, Leon turned to them. "Man, you should feel the air conditioning in here! Simon, you need to come over and take some notes!"

"We regularly stay overnight on the boat. It makes it more *pleasurable* if the air is cool," added Marcy.

Wade shuffled his feet. "So, any luck fishing?" he asked.

"No. Not since morning."

"What are you going for?" asked Simon.

"Just blues. Maybe tuna if we're lucky."

"What kind of the bait are you using?"

"Bunker. The blues go crazy for it."

Simon glanced off the stern. "Really? Where's your slick? You need a chum bucket if you want to keep the blues interested."

Marcy stared at Simon with the same annoyed glare as before. "That's disgusting. That might be what you *die-hard* fisherman do, but I can think of more civilized ways of fishing." She looked at the large cooler in the *Privateer.* "So, did you catch anything?"

"No. They all got away," Simon answered.

Wade noticed the frown on Simon's face. It was clear something was bothering him.

"Oh, that's too bad," replied Marcy, as she leaned over and swung herself onto their boat. "Especially with all of this tackle and equipment." Walking across the deck, she sat down on top of the cooler. Simon had purchased a custom cushion for the lid and Marcy stretched out across it. "This is *nice.* Much better than the hard deck of the other boat." As she arched her back to take in the sun her bikini stretched to the point Wade thought it was going to snap.

Wade looked over at *The Spinnaker*. "I wonder where Leon is?"

"I wouldn't worry about him. I think beer was the last thing on his mind," answered Marcy.

"You're not worried about your friend?" asked Simon.

"Oh, Pam can take care of herself down below," Marcy replied as she let a leg slip off the cooler. "What I'm curious is if you two are going to show me what's down below over here."

A strong breeze blew off the water, cooling the sweat that peppered Wade's brow. Wade watched as Henry's hat went airborne and landed in the water. Back on the boat Henry had not stirred. With the hat gone Wade was able to see his face.

And it wasn't what he was expecting.

The body had already begun to decompose and clumps of black, rotted flesh off his skull. His lips were shriveled and his eyes had long since rotted away.

Marcy rose from her perch and slowly made her way toward them. The smile was still on her face, but it now caused a shiver to pass between Wade's shoulder blades.

"What the fuck is going on?" he asked.

"Boys, don't let a dead body get in the way of us having a good time." Her smile grew wider and Wade noticed her teeth seemed to be unusually prominent. "And I *really* was hoping to have a good time with you both. At least as good as Pam is having with your friend."

Wade turned to look at *The Spinnaker*. Marcy used the opportunity to close the gap. Before he could react, she had wrapped her hands around his throat. Wade tried to break free, but Marcy, though several inches shorter and not nearly as heavy, maintained her grip as her fingers dug into his skin.

A pair of burly arms encircled Marcy as Simon placed her in a bear hug. "Calm down, missy." He lifted her up and away from Wade. "I can't have you killing my friend."

Marcy screamed and broke free of Simon's grip. She lashed out and slashed him across the face with her nails. Simon stumbled backward, his face awash in blood. He struck the side of the boat and fell overboard.

Wade ran over to the fishing pole racks. He grabbed the gaff and swung it as she lunged at him. The hook struck and went in just below her shoulder. Marcy screamed as blue ichor spurted from the wound. Wade used his momentum to push Marcy through the hatch that lead down into *The Privateer's* cabin. Wade quickly slammed the door and locked her inside.

He looked out over the water, but there was no trace of Simon.

His tan shorts were splattered with Marcy's blue blood. It emitted a foul odor as it began to dry in the midday sun. He listened for noises from the other boats but there was only silence. He removed the bang stick from the storage locker.

A wave rolled beneath the boat and Wade waited for the water the settle before he climbed over onto the *High Seas*. The cabin door was closed and he hesitated, wondering if anyone or *anything* was inside. He decided not to look, hoping Marcy and Pam were the only ones.

There was a large gap between the *High Seas* and *The Spinnaker* and Wade had to pull the tether line to bring the boats together. As he climbed over *The Spinnaker's* door opened and Pam stepped out.

Trails of blood flowed from her mouth and onto her exposed breasts. Wade glanced beyond the woman and into the cabin. The sunlight only managed to penetrate the first few feet but it was enough for him to see a blood-covered arm.

Pam glared at Wade with fury in her eyes. Off in the distance Marcy's incessant pounding could be heard as she tried to break free from her imprisonment. Pam opened her mouth and stiletto-like teeth flashed in the sun. "What do you think you're doing, little man?"

"Stay back," warned Wade, as he waved the bang stick at her.

Pam looked at the weapon amusingly. "Do you think your little pole can harm me?"

Wade held the stick hesitantly. He knew how to use to it, but did not know if it would be able to stop her.

"I made sure your friend's last minutes were happy ones." She edged closer. "You won't have that luxury."

"Who . . . what are you?" Wade asked. "What do you want?"

"What do I want?" Pam repeated. "I want to eat. Thankfully, men in boats are never in short supply."

"Why don't you go to the supermarket if you're so goddamn hungry?"

"It's not that easy. We must remain close to the water . . ."

Another wave passed beneath the boat and Wade stumbled backward to keep his footing. Pam lunged at him.

The boat continued to rock and Wade fought to regain his footing as he kept her back. The force of Pam colliding with him made Wade strike the side of the boat. As he began to tip backward he swung the bang stick at her. He pressed the button and released the charge as he tumbled from the boat.

Wade sank fast before he managed to right himself. He looked up through the water but did not see the woman looking out over the boat.

A tether was fastened to one of the boats. He looked down and saw that it was connected to a large diving cage twenty feet below him. Being so far out from land made the water much clearer and he could see what was in the cage.

People.

Dead people.

Lots of them.

Wades' lungs began to burn. He kicked up to the surface.

He surfaced behind one of the engines, fighting the urge to scream from what he'd seen. He spent a moment fighting his hysterics as he hung from the swimming platform. Finally, he gathered up enough courage to climb up and peer into the boat.

Pam was slumped against the inside of the hull. Blue blood covered the deck. The bang stick had severed her arm at the shoulder. She was staring straight at him and for a moment Wade thought she was still alive.

The swimming platform extended the width of the vessel, and to avoid stepping onto the gore-covered boat, he leaped from the *Spinnaker* to the *Kelly Jean*.

He made his way into the boat's cabin. Instead of a crowd of rowdy drunks, Wade was met by creaking wood as the vessel rocked slowly in the water. He hurried to the steering wheel, but the keys were not in the ignition. A short-wave radio was mounted to the dashboard but it had been smashed.

He realized the other boats were most likely in the same condition. He was going to have to go back to *The Privateer*. Simon kept the keys around his neck to prevent them from slipping into the water. But there was a spare set of keys.

In the cabin.

With Marcy.

Wade tried to swallow the golf ball that had formed in his throat.

Wade stepped over the gap between the *Kelly Jean* and the *Spinnaker. Maybe Wade had another bang stick in the storage locker.*

The door leading into *The Privateer's* cabin swung open and Marcy stepped out. Wade barely had enough time to shield himself before she grabbed hold and threw him against the inside of the hull. "You will suffer for what you did." She slashed him just above his eyes. Blood began to flow, blinding him slightly.

She dropped him onto the deck like a sack of potatoes and placed her foot on his chest. Wade couldn't push her off. "I'll enjoy dining on you over the coming days."

A dark tide began to pass over Wade as he became starved for oxygen. Marcy shifted her weight and Wade felt a rib pop.

And watched, to his surprise, as her head exploded into a bluish haze.

Bits of bluish gore and shards of bone peppered Wade. Marcy collapsed and blue ichor flowed out across the deck. Simon stood over her, a baseball bat clutched in his right hand. His shirt was stained red and his face was a mess.

"Never thought this would come in so handy," he said. "The other one got Leon?"

"Yeah. I used the stick on her."

"Blue blood. What the fuck is going on?"

"I don't know. Sure as hell not . . ." A loud shrill silenced Wade.

"What was that?" said Simon.

Another shrill sounded, followed by a third, each coming from a different direction. Wade looked out over the water. No other boats were in sight.

"I think you'd better get the boat started."

An out-of-place *splash* was heard at the far side of the *Kelly Jean.* A hand appeared from out of the water and gripped the boat's railing.

Simon leapt into *The Privateer* with Wade in tow. "Get the ropes!" Simon yelled, as he climbed up the tuna tower to the controls.

Another pair of hands appeared by *The Spinnaker's* swimming platform.

Wade removed the rope from the stern chock as Simon fired up

The Privateer's 800 horsepower engines.

As Wade hurried toward the bow he glanced over at the other boats. Six women had emerged from the water and were making their way across the other boats.

And more were surfacing.

The boat lurched forward as Simon gunned the engines. The bowline became taut. Simon pushed the throttle forward and then, sounding like a rifle blast, *The Privateer's* chock was torn from its fiberglass deck. Like a slug shot from a sling, the chock flew at the women, striking one of them, cutting her almost in half.

Simon managed to distance them before the others could reach *The Privateer*. Wade watched as dozens of the creatures began surfacing now, staring at them emotionlessly as the boat sped away, slicing through the waves.

A full investigation ensued.

Taking care to leave out all fantastical elements, Wade and Simon relayed their story to the Coast Guard. Marcy and Pam became part of a group of drug traffickers they had stumbled on. They took the officials back to the spot where the boats had been. The boats were still bobbing in the waves but there was no trace of any bodies. Not even Leon's.

An APB was put out for the owners.

No one was ever found.

Soon after Simon put the boat up for sale. A month later he moved to Montana. Wade put in for a transfer to Des Moines before autumn arrived.

Years passed. Memories faded. Wade married, had two daughters and a son. It was for Henry's sixth birthday that they decided to go camping along the Mississippi River.

It was on the final evening of the weeklong vacation that Helen and the children discovered, along the gravel banks, Wade's fishing pole along with five sets of footprints that led from the water and six that led back.

THOSE WHO
CAME TO DAGON

BY *JOHN SHIRLEY*

The Journal of Caleb Ward
June 21 (?) 1806

LESEUR, THE BOSUN OF a lost ship, declares me foolish to expend strength dashing off these lines, for all of us in the launch of the late *HMS Feveringale* feel the weakness of eleven days at sea without food and little more than a mouthful of fresh water for two days running. I hope that though we perish in the launch, my papers might be preserved and found with my body, if inclement weather does not consign it to the deeps. How I could wish for a rainstorm to bestow drinking water on us, if the storm did not blow overhard; one such gale, rendering but little rainwater, took our launch's only mast. O for fresh water! The equatorial heat is relentless, and I feel my throat chafe against itself, and burn with salt. Sometimes Tantalus has his way with us, when we scent the greenness of the West African coast, and espy a bit of palm or liana floating in the sea, but the current never carries us close enough to bring hope of a landfall.

The Reverend Mothe, though his voice sounds like a rusty pump, continues to spout of Providence, to be of good cheer, for God will not forget us. I have not succumbed to the temptation to ask him why God should remember us and not the scores of men (and the cook's wife) who died in the fire, or in the consequent sinking of the *Feveringale*. I have long been one of "The Lord's Stray Lambs": My regard for His creation was blackened by the knowledge of my inherited fate, even before we few survivors of the catastrophe were cast adrift, for as a young man I watched as my father died of a cancer; his going was slow and terrible. He had not seen forty summers. I know that my grandfather, and his father, died in the same way. The disease is in our blood and I fancy I feel it working its malignity upon me already. So it was that at close to the age my father was when he was stricken, I gave off clerking at the bank and took to poetry and the penning of Observations for the Weekly Journals reckoning that at least I might live out my greatest hopes for myself, for a few months . . . And then this! Cast adrift in an open boat! Yet it may be that this death by drowning or thirst is preferable to death by the slow inner consuming of cancer. It may be that this is a mercy after all. I could only wish I had died quickly on the *Feveringale*.

Any who chance to find this hasty journal will remark that the edges of the paper are scorched. I did manage to snatch a few necessaries from my trunk, even as the flames that engulfed the ship seared the trunk's right side—I burnt my fingers lightly doing so—and to one whose hope is to write for the *Boston Gazette*, quill, ink and paper are more necessary than the dueling pistol and compass I snatched up as an afterthought. (I do hope my handwriting is legible, there being more than enough swell and pitch and salty spray to make writing difficult. I fear my ink may dry out and sometimes I am tempted to drink it.) We had survived an encounter with privateers, Captain O'Brian having outrun them when they lost a mizzen, and we had triumphed over a breached gun-room which flooded because a drunken sailor forgot to close a port—we weathered these vicissitudes only to have the ship burn down around us for the misplacing of a candle! Dr Bessemen insists it was not he who left the candle too close to a case of spirits, but the fire commenced in his quarters. His loblolly boy, not having survived the fire, cannot protest his innocence. In truth, so far as we know, only those of us in the launch survive—dour old Bessemen, Gaddle the squint-eyed first mate, sallow, glowering Leseur (whose presence has always made me uneasy), the sailors Brackin and Milford, Sargeant Sparks of the Marines, and myself. We are all quite burnt and bearded now, looking like people any one of us would have avoided on the street in Boston—or perhaps London, for I am the only American, on a voyage that should have taken us to the Canary Islands, and though our nations are at peace, I have been more than once the object of a fully unjustified suspicion. Would I be so absurd as to sabotage a ship in which I myself am sailing?

There is a strange smell in the air, a foul reek carried on the rising breeze from the south: a dead whale nearby, perhaps. O and this is cruel, the ink is quite drying out. It does not mix well with seawater but I shall att

June 25, 1806

I was unable to finish my sentence, at the conclusion of the previous entry, for want of serviceable ink, but I recommence my journal aboard the ship which has picked us up, for here ink is plentiful, thanks to the generosity of Captain Hoek, the stout, bluff Dutchman who is the chief Argonaut of the *Burdened Pelican:* a brig of two masts, a ship neither big nor small. Only the peeling paint on the bow declares the ship's true name; her captain and crew call her "the dratted ol' *Pelican.*"

Three days I've been on this leaky old vessel, recovering strength, as the ship works its way north to Holland. Yet it makes scarcely any headway; "'tis all leeway," says the bushy-browed Captain—he speaks always around the ancient curved pipe clutched in his teeth, a pipe usually turned upside down and empty of tobacco. "The winds, the winds rush agin' us and agin' all natural blowin', for they should northerin' this time of year, do ye hear? But they blow southwest and we must tack, and beat and tack again and more, and scarcely any progress do we make. We must find an island to stop for water and meat, soon, if the wind do not change . . ." And so the time wears away, with little progress in our journey—but at least we are rescued! The other survivors of the *Feveringale*, perhaps surfeited with the sight of one another, have largely kept to themselves. I have a cabin to myself, once belonging to an officer now lost at sea. The officer was lost along with the ship's doctor and several other men during an "unnatural blow," as Hoek has it, not long before we were picked up. (They were pleased to have a new doctor, in our Bessemen, but when they discover his drunkenness and absence of real parts, they will be less sanguine.) Yet the first mate, Van Murnk, a heavy-cheeked man with hair so blond it is almost white and a face so sun-burned he sometimes resembles a Red Indian—a man, indeed, perpetually sodden with drink—claims that those who went missing, including "even Monsieur Galange . . . took it on their own to hie to the sea, and have not yet left us, mein herr, but follow in our wake." He would say no more and I had no wish to pursue his meaning and encourage the fallacies and fancies so common to sailors.

Van Murnk is not alone in his oddity; it must be said that it is, withal, a strange ship. The crew seem sullen and fearful except for discrete occasions when they are caught up in an inexplicable and outlandish glee, their eyes feverish, their mien giddy; they have a proclivity for gathering in groups far aft, whereupon they take up tittering and whispering . . .

Today is Sunday. Captain Hoek rigged church, this morning, and read from Proverbs, a certain desperation in his voice; but most of the crew remained well apart from the ceremony, staring with hollow eyes in the dull light of the overcast morning; with a cast of face both unreceptive and obscurely ashamed.

June 26, 1806

It called for some persuading—they were strangely uninclined—but I have taken a meal with Dr Bessemen, Rufe Gaddle, and Reverend Mothe. The Doctor and Gaddle seemed to share an unvoiced mutual understanding—something dire, judging by their expressions, and the dark glances they exchanged, their resonant silences. The pastor seems to be at odds with them over some matter he does not wish to evince in my presence.

"Have you not heard a sort of *droning* from below decks and aft?" I prompted, as we sat over our watered-down after dinner porto. "And other sounds I could not identify, a kind of squawking, a squeaking sound that almost seemed to form words? I went to investigate and found the way blocked by Leseur. He turned me back and refused to explain. The fellow was more forbidding than ever—the only one of us not to avail of the ship's razors since our rescue. A bit of beard is quite natural but he is as shaggy as an old bear. And the look in his eyes! Like a bear indeed—but a bear with a toothache!" Thus I tried to disarm them with levity, to ease the taut atmosphere and perhaps provoke confidences. But my attempts at humor at Leseur's expense were met with sullen stares from

Gaddle and the doctor—who was quite noddingly drunk—and a long sigh from the Reverend. At last the Reverend said, "Indeed I have heard the noises of which you speak." He gave the other two a vinegary look of accusation. "Perhaps someone else might share their knowledge of these . . . sounds."

"Why," said the doctor, after a pull at his porto, "they are but sea chantys. And you heard a cat, the ship's cat. How they do like to tease the poor brute."

Sea chantys! I most certainly had heard nothing of the sort. But I could draw them out no further, and after some grudging speculation about the weather and hope for a landfall, we adjourned.

I then went to the deck for some air, and met a man there I must describe. I find myself bemused by this most peculiar individual, a man the hue of coal who has only just emerged after several days in his cabin, and who now strides the deck as freely as any of the whites: one Louis Nukanga, an "associate in business" of the Captain.

Nukanga wears a fine suit of clothing, and his head is shaved bald. His only departure from European dress is the copper on his wrists, bracelets that one only sees when he lifts his arms to some task or gesture, and the sleeves fall back. I found myself staring at them as he approached the rail close by me and raised a spy glass to scan the western horizon, just at sunset. "The island, I feel its loom," he said (to himself, though I stood close beside him at the rail). "The island . . . I feel her . . ." So he muttered as he peered through the spyglass. He said something more in his own language—I know not what, precisely, but it had the sound of frustrated longing. It was then that I saw the bracelets, and made out the figures carved upon them. On the underside of the wide bracelet clasping his left wrist was a graven image of a creature I at first supposed some cephalopod of the deep, until I beheld its lower body that was almost like a man's; the other bracelet showed the image of a thing like a great scaled worm, with the face of a man, and tentacles bristling here and there—rude spirits of the African continent, I'm sure. The images seemed to spring out at me from the bracelets. I seemed to see both too easily, as if they drifted from their metal hosts and floated upon the air. Under each image was writing in a script I could not read; I have seen samples of ancient Sumerian, and while it was not Sumerian perhaps it was not so different. Strange, for that land was far north of the equatorial Africa from whence Nukanga sprang.

I pressed him for an account of his provenance. He hails from the jungles two days' march inland of the Gulf of Guinea, a place "not so far south of the Niger River," so he told me, where he had struck a deal with a Frenchman named Galange who was in partnership with Captain Hoek. A freed slave, educated by his Master in England, Nukanga had returned to a place called, "to freely translate, the Uneasy Mountain." Here was the home of his youth, but he found the entire village in bondage to M. Galange, who was searching for treasure, commanding a small but well-armed cadre of Dutch and French brigands to force labor upon the natives. At gunpoint, Nukanga's people dug shafts into the mountain, fruitlessly searching for rumored wealth. "The search was wont to kill my people," said Nukanga grinning, "So I showed Galange where he and Hoek could get what they desired, in exchange for a special arrangement for myself . . . Of course, I have promised them another treasure, in another place, on their return. If I did not, they would have cut my throat as I slept, so that I would not trouble them for my share . . . but Galange will do no more harm—he has gone from the ship . . . In a sense."

I registered his words but distantly; it was his grin that transfixed my attention. His teeth were covered in copper, and each one, I saw in the ruddy gleam of the setting sun, was inscribed with one of the unknown letters of the sort etched into his bracelet. What did his grin spell out?

"You try to read my teeth, eh?" he said, chuckling, lowering his spyglass. "These names you cannot read; their alphabet you are not likely to know. They are names you may yet wish to call out! You may wish to call them . . . and implore, yes implore for their mercy!" His eyes were glittering with a contained, cruel mirth as he spoke. "But you do not know how to cry out to them, to call for *mercy, mercy!*"

Stung by his contempt, which he hardly troubled to conceal, I felt constrained to reply, somehow. "I call on no deities, sir, neither yours nor those of my own land," I declared. "I am a man of the new era, a man who values Reason, and such men, the hope of the world, deny all superstitions—meaning no disrespect to your beliefs."

"Superstitions? If you meet a god, will you then believe?"

"Yes, if I recognize his godliness! But there are those who claim to bear gods within them—I have heard of such things, in the West

Indies, a practice called voudoun—and to meet this 'god' is to meet a man deluded!"

"I do not speak of such," he said, snorting dismissively, collapsing the spyglass with a sharp report of metal on metal. "I speak of . . . but soon enough, soon enough . . ." And with that he turned away, muttering in quite another language, and went below. So ended my interlocution with Mr Nukanga!

Only a few heartbeats later I was joined by the Captain, who had been drinking with Dr Bessemen. "Your Bessemen cannot hold his liquor—one bottle, or mebbe it was two, and he babbles without sense, and then falls to snore!" He clutched the rail and in his drunkenness seemed to sway in exact counterpoise to the swaying of the westering ship, his upright body like the inverted working of a pendulum. "My friend," he said, breathing a gust of spirits upon me, the unlit pipe wagging in a corner of his mouth, "what think ye of Nukanga?"

"He seems a strange mix of the learned and the superstitious! And he spoke obscurely of an island . . ."

"An island? Did he now?" He turned and peered into the gathering gloom, and sniffed the air. "I believe I can smell it. Land." He removed the pipe and called up to the lookout in the crow's nest. "Ho! You there! Do you see land to the west? An island?"

"I do not, Captain!" came the reply.

"Well watch close! We need the water, damn you!"

He then addressed me, while swaying in place and packing the pipe with tobacco he kept loose in a weskit pocket. "I do not trust Nukanga . . . he is a Jonah! Since he came on board the winds blow us always west, no matter how we beat and tack, tack and beat. Always west and even south! And our route is north and east!"

"For my part, I am glad the wind has taken you out of your way, for I'd have perished on the sea otherwise. But perhaps you are concerned to protect your cargo, Captain? We are driven into the sea-lanes of privateers by these winds . . ."

"My cargo?" He looked at me suspiciously. "What do ye know of that?"

"Nukanga says he helped you find a treasure, but he did not say what treasure . . ."

"Aye, if he said so much, it can't matter if ye know—and you seem an honest man. I would trust you, for I have need of someone to tell my mind. There are few enough—perhaps there is no one—I can trust . . . Come!"

He staggered away and I followed. We made our way below decks, the Captain swearing when he nearly fell going down the ladder. The Captain catching up a lantern along the way, we wended a narrow, malodorous corridor, descended two more ladders, each deck's passageway more noisome than the last, until we came to a locked room. Here a sailor leaning on the bulkhead nodded in sleep, musket clutched against him, keeping some sort of watch. "Idiot pig!" The Captain bellowed, snatching the musket and slapping the hapless fellow so that he stumbled sputtering away. "Ye sleep when I pay you to guard my cargo? Ach, I should hang you!"

Some time a-fumbling later, the Captain found his key and unlocked the heavy padlock and bade me come in. Within the low-ceilinged hold were a row of five goodly chests. "In the other hold, below, there is crude tin, copper, and other ores, but here is the real treasure! Now let your eyes feast, Mr Caleb Ward!"

He unlocked the nearest of the chests and flung its lid back. At first I thought it filled with rough rocks of quartz, but when he lifted the lantern over the chest I saw the blue glimmerings, as if from a multiplicity of eyes, shining back from the pure hearts of the gems. "Diamonds!" I cried.

"Quiet! Never so loud, ye hear?" he hissed. "Rough they are, but diamonds right enough. Five chests full! All mine, and Nukanga's— Galange has gone missing from the ship, I do not like to guess at how it happened. So he will not share the diamonds—so sad! And Nukanga offers four times as many in another place—but only when he is paid, he says, in Amsterdam! It was in Galange's mind, before we left the village, to make Nukanga tell of this other place—to use ropes and fire to make him tell. But I have no belly for torture, and who knows what friends the man might have, for he has cozened to some in civilized places! So I bear Nukanga, though he sneers and speaks in dark cupboards to the men, speaks things I don't know." He shook his head. "Things . . . I don't know."

He tried to light his pipe on the lantern, and repeatedly failed. In the end I held the lantern for him while he puffed the pipe alight—I was fearful of fire on the wooden ship, after what had happened to the *Feveringale*. Another kind of fire, a blue fire, glimmered in the chest of rough gems. The diamonds, I confess, made my heart pound. So many! And I was so poor! But I had been raised austerely and was unable to think of larceny, but for a fitful moment.

"Captain," I said, "I am indeed awed. You will be a rich man! But surely there are mysteries on this ship—there is murmuring, there is something like a chant, late at night, heard in the deep aft . . . Seeing this treasure, perhaps the mystery is solved. Could not the sounds I heard be a crew in conspiratorial colloquy? Could they not be thinking of making this treasure their own?"

"Eh?" He turned and looked at the door, then hastened to close the chest. "Ye think I would trust them? They don't know! They think it's all tin and copper ore. Ye have seen, and Nukanga, and none other! For this crew are not the men we took with us to the interior. Those men wait for us at the village of the Uneasy Mountain."

"What then, is the trouble with the crew, Captain? Is it my imagination?"

"As to that ye have heard—they do something aft, and below, in the orlop! O, aye, there is a sickness on this ship, a slow, infectious madness, like a man crying out in fever . . . while there is no fever! And something has taken our own doctor, and four of my best hands!"

"But with respect, Captain Hoek, are you not master of your ship? Surely you can penetrate this mystery by demanding an explanation; by entering the orlop where these rites are held, and seeing for yourself!"

"Had I courage . . . Something about the business affrighted me, so I sent the doctor, that night, as the storm rose . . . and where is he now? It was that very night he went missing, with them others! The crew say those five was swept o'er board. Myself, I think something . . . something *other*."

"What other, Captain?"

"Ach, my head hurts, I speak strange things when the drink begins to wear off. Have ye not noticed how many crew are hiding below, saying they are sick? How few remain to work the ship? I have almost no one left to turn to—and I say this: if you would find out what goes on below, you would find me grateful."

He would say no more. But I determined to do as he requested. I shall write a great story for the newspaper—I sense it coming!

I wrote out the previous entry two hours ago. It seems an age.

After I spoke to the Captain, I went on deck to stand brooding by the aft rail. A strong wind blew from the east, filling the sails, driving us west, ever west, at about seven knots. I had heard one of the hands say that it seemed if the Captain tried to tack, the wind shifted, to continue pushing the vessel west, as if actively, deliberately frustrating his efforts!

The wind in my face, I watched as the failing light seemed to soak into the glimmering white tips of waves, to re-emerge in the luminescence of the *Pelican*'s wake. Like diamonds!

I beheld something, then, disporting in the seam the ship cut in the sea. Dolphins? Seals? Sometimes I thought so, other times I thought they were more disturbing shapes; I thought I saw a buckle here, upon one, a strip of cloth trailing from another. There were at least three of them, sometimes I thought there were more. Whenever I supposed I had distinguished their shape, it would seem to change, skirled and washed in the dark sea, and I was again unsure of the creature's form. The thought came that they might be sharks, with bits of human victims trailing from their jaws . . .

Then a light opened on the stern of the ship, close to the waterline. It was as if a hatch—something I've never seen so low on a ship before—had been opened. Lamplight shone on the water and I looked eagerly to try to see what creatures followed in our wake, but as if aware of my scrutiny, they dropped back into shadow . . . I thought I saw something, before they went—a human face, staring up at me from the water. Perhaps a dead man, caught in some old fishing line . . .

I thought to tell the Captain—but then the chanting began, the sound coming from that same square of light, the anomalous hatch on the stern. I could not make out what was said. Sometimes I thought I heard, repeated amidst the gibberish, "*Dagon . . . thool-hew . . . dagon . . . thool-hew . . .*"

And the inchoate shapes in the wake of the ship seem to hiss and thrash in response. I heard a sibilant squeaking from them—like a dolphin trying to form words, and failing.

A chill spread out from the back of my head, to seep corrosively down my spine, seeming to drain all firmness from it, and I clutched the rail that I might remain standing.

"Come, this is foolishness!" I told myself. "Go now and see what is below and do not let your imagination play upon you! You wish a story to tell—here is one waiting to be found out!"

So I made myself go below, in search of the orlop . . . stopping momentarily at my cabin for that dueling pistol. I once more had to summon strength of will to continue my undertaking, for I had a sudden persuasive desire to lock the door of my cabin from within and sit on my hammock with that pistol in my hand, my eyes fixed on the door, the gun at ready . . .

No sir, I told myself. You will not hide from adventure. It is what you came to sea to find.

Thence I set out, making my way, lantern in hand, down two ladders and along the passage toward the stern—toward the orlop.

Just a few paces outside the door to the orlop I found my way blocked, once more, by Leseur, who seemed to huddle into the dim shadows of the narrow passage like a tunnel spider in its den. The light from my lantern seemed to shy from him; to quail just short of him. I was determined, this time, that he would not deter me—and a feverish curiosity was beginning to replace the fear that had crawled from that primeval cranny at the back of my brain, my inquisitiveness tugged by the droning chant from beyond the closed orlop door.

"Leseur—move aside, if you please!" I said, trying to keep the quavering in my hands from reaching my voice. "I have this night entered into Captain Hoek's service and he has sent me to make certain inquiries in the orlop."

When Leseur spoke, the sound seemed to come, muffled, from the base of his throat, and a sickly reek came with it, something more alien than a man's foul breath—and it was a smell I thought I recognized. I had caught it once before . . .

"*You may not pass unless Nukanga says aye.*"

"Move aside I say! I have a pistol, as you see—and I will make use of it!"

He turned and put a hand on the door—and there seemed a splaying in the spread of his fingers, as if each was melting into the next. I felt a shivering ring out from his contact with that door; it resonated through the damp timbers of the old ship, so that its seams worked in response, oozing with seawater; I was obscurely aware that water was pooling, very slowly, at my feet. Then the door opened; a glutinous yellow light silhouetted Nukanga from behind: a dark figure but for his teeth shining copper-red in the feebler light of the lantern I held. I leaned to peer around him, but could scarcely make out the room beyond; I glimpsed a great coil of rope, the outlines of a group of men seated on it, their backs to me, facing that anomalous hatch in the stern. The hatch, hastily built, had been of recent devising. And there was the smell of compressed seawater and decayed fish and living muck, that distinctive reek from the bottom-most trench of the sea. . .

I knew then where I had smelled it before—that day in the launch, just before we were sighted by the *Pelican*.

"So—you have come to us? I thought you would," said Nukanga. "Come a little closer and look, Caleb Ward . . ."

Leseur grudgingly pressed aside—there was just enough room to squeeze past him, an inexpressibly disgusting process, to slip into the orlop after Nukanga. I scrutinized the semicircle of crew. There were Brackin and Sparks and Gaddle and Milford and Van Murnk and two others, Hoek's crewmen, I had seen when I first came . . . and Bessemen.

But Bessemen was lying upon the deck, curled on his side, within the circle of rope on which the others sat, and he was not alone. He was clutched against a being not quite twice his bulk, a thing green-black and wetly slick; a creature with the proportions of a human woman but at its throat were gills, and in place of human eyes were round yellow orbs on the two sides of its oblate head; in place of hair on its head were tresses of slender fins; its mouth . . .

O it's hard to write it; for that means I must again invoke the image; I must once more see that lamprey mouth, that great round fibrous, membranous sucker clapped over Bessemen's eyes and forehead, sucking, and pulsing; taking and replacing . . . and Bessemen squirmed in the thing's grip, struggled to escape, his hands clawing, his bare feet scrabbling at the deck, finding no purchase, no escape. He was like a feeble child trying hopelessly to wrest free even as it was strangled by a brutish overpowering mother.

And Bessemen's nether parts, too, were entangled with the thing, were penetrated and penetrating, but of this I cannot bear to speak. I stared and choked and turned away, covering my eyes, even as the men seated on the coil of rope persisted in their chant, gurgling and squeaking syllables no human mouth was made to express, invocations interspersed with the litany, *Thool-hew eck dagon, thool-hew eck dagon!*

"Ho ho, my little friend," chortled Nukanga as I tried to claw my way from the orlop. "What is the matter? Hm? Do you suppose this man is the victim of a bestial predation?" He locked powerful hands on my shoulders and held me back with little apparent effort. "Not at all! He *begged* for this! He is but in the throes of transfiguration! And my friend—" He spun me about and looked me in the eye. "He will never die!"

The words struck to the aching quick of me. *He will never die!*

I wanted to run—but it was as if those words spiked me to the spot. "What?" I rasped. "What do you mean?"

"All men crave immortality—but immortality in this world comes with a price! But wait—what is this I see? For I am a magus of my people, and I see a man's fate written in his eyes . . ." He took the wrist of my left hand, and drew it close between us so that the lantern which I still held shone into my eyes. I blinked and tried to turn away. But with his other hand he took my chin in his big hand and turned my face to him. "Hold! I would look into your eyes . . . some gaze into a crystal ball to see a man's living fate but I would look into these soft orbs and see . . . your *death!* I see you lying on a hammock of a ship, and I see blood streaming from your mouth! You clutch at your chest and you groan but there is no doctor to attend you! You die the death of your father and his father and his father before him! A cancer eats at you and will take you before this year is worn away! Look—see for yourself!"

And then he struck my forehead with the heel of his hand, and it was as if the vision he had of my death was carried in the blow, from his hand into my flesh and bone and into my brain where it rippled mockingly before my mind's eye. I saw it clearly, more clearly than I see the paper on which I now scribble this account. I saw myself dying in a hammock, in a small, mold-splashed room; dying as my father had—all the signs of his death upon me. And I saw that it would be soon. And I knew the truth of this vision, as I would know the face of my own father, were I to behold him again. It was the truth of recognition. This was my death.

"But wait!" Nukanga said, as the image dissolved into his coppery grin, his exultant eyes. "That is your death *as a man!* And there is no escaping your death as a man! But if you were to become *other* than a man—then the curse of your destiny is lifted, and you will not die that death, *you will not die at all* . . . not if you become as those who come to Dagon!"

"No . . ." My heart shriveled within me as I began to comprehend.

"Choose! Only choose! Dagon has seen you, from the wake of the ship! Dagon has looked into you from the depths of the sea and Dagon desires you! You are choice, something quite choice to Dagon! Come to Dagon, and live forever . . . or die alone, spitting blood in that damp, forgotten ship's cabin . . . with no one to attend you, no one to pity you, no one to care!"

Then he let go of my shoulders and I staggered away, past Leseur, who was emitting a high pitched bark and a terrible stench—the sound, the smell, of his laughter.

June 27, 1806
It is morning and yet it is not morning.

Somewhere in this ashen mist, the sun has arisen. An etiolated light has diffused the mist. But it is scarcely like real day. We stalk the deck, looking to the West. Our eyes are burning and we can scarce see through the murk, but we sense the loom of the land; we smell stone and beach and fire and jungle.

"This is a volcano island," said Hoek, beside me on the quarterdeck, peering through the mist, wiping his eyes, peering again. "The kind that gives out smoke but never erupts. Just smoke and smoke and it churns with the fog and this soup we have, to choke in, ye hear? So little wind. Hardly a breath! Would I could turn away from this—but we have need water, we have need supplies . . ." He looked at me as if he wanted to ask what I had learned in my foray the night before. But I shook my head and turned away and he grunted as if in some personal confirmation.

I could not bear to think about it, let alone talk of it. Only with an inner struggle was I able to force myself to make this written account.

One phrase keeps returning to my mind, this morning . . .
He will never die!

No. I will not listen to that voice. I would rather die than lose my humanity.

I attempted to seek counsel from the Reverend Mothe. But the pastor will not heed me; he kneels, praying—coughing and sup-plicating—beside the mainmast. He will respond to no one. He prays with the desperate ardor of one who begins to doubt that he is heard.

I feel safer in my cabin, now, scribbling away, though the candle gutters as if it might go out—but it is even harder to breathe here, somehow. I will go on deck, and see if, perhaps, the wind has changed.

I have been on deck, and I wish I had not gone. The sky was a little clearer—the wind blows from the east again, and has broomed some of the ashen sky; the island broods nigh, dominated by a dark cone nestled in jungle so green it is almost black; streams that emerge from the hills about the volcano running dark down to the sea, like streaks of blood.

We are still almost a mile out from the rocky cove. And we are moving in, despite all the Captain can do.

For after the voice that came from the sea, the Captain wanted to move away from the island.

It was a feeble voice, a squeak and a hoarseness, but Hoek claimed he recognized it. "That is . . . that is Galange! One of those who was lost overboard! Ach—do ye hear it?"

"*In name of God, arête! Turn back, Hoek.*" Came the voice, a French tinge to it. "*Nom de Dieu! Do not surrender. Do not listen. All here is poisoned! Go back, j'implorer! In name of God . . . kill me! Fetch a musket and kill me!*"

I thought to see a man writhing in the dark waves, about a cable ahead of us, but then again not a man, for he had round yellow lidless eyes, and hands that were not hands. And then there was a great splashing about him, and the man gave a cry of despair as other hands, webbed and clawed—hands so dark-green they were almost black, like the jungle about the volcano—clutched at him from all sides, and dragged him under.

Then he was gone. But we seem to hear him still crying, *Fetch a musket and kill me!*

The Captain, his face gone whiter than his vessel's sails, turned and shouted orders at the affrighted crew. "You there, wheel her about! We will tack, and turn about! We will lower a boat and pull the ship if we must . . . but we will not go to that island!"

So the few crewmen still willing to respond tried to turn about—and we had not gotten but a few strakes turned before there was a splashing and crackling from the rudder, and the Captain made haste to the stern. I followed him and looked over the rail . . . and saw that the rudder had snapped away. Or perhaps I should say, it *had been* snapped away. Something had torn it off. The ship was now drifting rudderless. And the wind was shifting, as if of its own accord . . . and driving us in toward the island.

Hoek went about the ship, trying to steer the ship by adjusting the sails—but nothing availed us. There was another force pushing us in: swimmers, many swimmers, not quite seen in the murk and dark water; we saw the splashing of their legs, their finny limbs, as they put shoulders to the hull of the ship and directed it into the dark stone arms of the cove.

"Do you fear this consummation?" Nukanga asked me, as he joined me at the bow of the ship . . . as the island loomed near. "Do not fear it. You do not wish to die young, alone, coughing blood like your father. Surrender to the god whom my people once knew—who many worshipped, in many places, and knew by many names! Once we were a seafaring people, who lived on the shores. But seeking to end the surrender of our children to the dark gods of the sea, the village elders took us inland to the Uneasy Mountain. Yet even in the shadow of the mountain were rivers, and upwellings from the stone. And here Dagon called to us, and said, *Where you go, I follow!* And so it will be with you, Caleb Ward—with Captain Hoek, and with this ship. Why do you think I brought them here? Do you suppose we were ever truly bound for Amsterdam? No, my friend. I have no interest in diamonds. My mother, my sisters, my only brother—all died in Galange's mines before I arrived! I swore revenge! And to kill Galange and his men was not enough! Galange has already gone to serve Dagon!"

As he went on, I was aware of a struggle behind us—Captain Hoek and a few others shouting, ordering muskets to be used, weapons to be fired, and then someone sobbing that the muskets would not fire for the ash in the air; I heard the slipping wet sound of slick limbs and flippers on the deck as something crawled onto the ship from the sea; I smelled that unholy reek; heard the sounds of struggle, and claws on wood; I heard Reverend Mothe shrieking as he was dragged to the side . . . A sudden cessation of the shrieking, with the sound of two large objects splashing into the waves . . .

I did not turn to look. I simply gazed at the great black cone of the volcano and listened to Nukanga:

"But you—you shall have an honored place at Dagon's side!" declared Nukanga eagerly. "Hai! You amuse the god! And it is your only hope . . . *of life!* Choose, Caleb Ward . . . Choose! For those who do not submit to the transfiguration . . . will become food! And Dagon, and his minions, they eat slowly, my friend—so slowly! They take many months to consume a man . . . months of sleepless agony! Choose, Caleb Ward! Transfiguration and immortality—or the slow awful revenge of the people of the Uneasy Mountain! *Choose!*"

June 28 (?) 1806
Can scarcely write. Not sure how long ship aground. Others all taken. Scream in night. Some make other sounds. Soon, myself.

Difficult to write. She changed me. Change almost complete. Words come hard. Forgetting old language. H'Beth K'hrauh-sug-uth! New words—yet very old. They come instead. Cthulhu Yog S'hruth Dagon!

Fingers changing. Hard to hold quill. The webbing between fingers; the new claws. My eyes do not focus well, out of water. The sea calls. Must answer.

The horror that is myself, new self—beyond expression. Cannot tell. Cannot say it.

Will seal journal in box with wax. Place this account in boat, set to drift. Perhaps warn others. Tell them: If choice given, choose well. Not as I chose. Choose carefully.

Choose death.

CLOWN FISH

BY *MATTHEW BAUGH*

THERE WAS A WOMAN standing on the water, or so it seemed. As the *Lady Anne* drew near it became clear that she was actually perched in the crow's nest of a sunken vessel. She didn't try to signal, she just watched with a strange intensity as the ship approached.

That worried the *Lady Anne's* crew. They were as tough a lot of seadogs as could be found, but pirates are superstitious. The strange sight had planted thoughts of witchery in more than one mind.

As they drew nearer, it became clear that the woman was young and pretty. Her thick hair hung wild about her shoulders and her skin was sun-darkened to a rich olive. She wore the tatters of what had once been a fine dress.

"Drop anchor!" Captain Redfern bellowed. "Take soundings. If her mizzen top's showing it may be she tore her belly open on a shoal. We'll not do the same."

The girl watched as the ship came to rest. She seemed only mildly curious as she pulled her ragged skirt to her thighs to dangle her feet in the water.

"Blimey!" a seaman named Quinlan said. "She's as shameless as a red savage, isn't she Hawk?"

The youth called Hawk didn't reply. The girl's attitude gave him an uncomfortable feeling. She didn't seem excited at the prospect of rescue. Neither was she frightened at the prospect of what a ship full of men might do to her. He wondered if the time she had spent on her peculiar perch might have driven her mad.

At sixteen, Hawk was one of the youngest crewmen on the *Lady Anne*. He had shown enough courage and physical prowess to earn the respect of most of the crew. Despite that, they never let him forget his origins. His people were the *Lenappe*, sometimes called the Delaware. His name among them was *Mèxkalaniat Pèmihëlak*. Moravian missionaries had translated this as 'Jeremiah Flying Hawk' when they baptized him. Among the pirate brethren he was simply 'Hawk', which suited him.

"Harry Dawkins!" Redfern cried. "Ready a longboat! We'll bring the girl aboard and get a good look at yon wreck while we're at it. I've a mind to gaze inside her hold."

"Aye Cap'n!" the big man answered. "Though 'tis not the ship's hold that I long to prise open."

That brought rough laughter from the men. Black Harry Dawkins was second only to the Captain. The crew admired his courage as much as they dreaded his temper. He was utterly fearless, though he lacked the good sense to be a proper ship's mate. Still, in the crude democracy of the buccaneers, such niceties as clear judgment often mattered little.

At the ocean floor something stirred. It had been sleeping for several weeks. As it grew older its periods of slumber would lengthen to millennia. For now the thing was young, at least by the standards of the race that had spawned it. Its hunger for nourishment outweighed its need for rest.

It could sense the prey approaching. The small creatures were not yet close enough to grasp. Very soon though, it would be time to feed.

The boat crew consisted of Redfern, Dawkins, Hawk and three seamen named Rafferty, Quinn, and Morgan. They pulled through the water a little awkwardly, hampered by their attempts to catch a glimpse of female flesh over their shoulders.

As they drew close the girl slipped the tattered dress over her head. Her golden form slid into the water, disappearing from sight.

"After her, blast your eyes!" cried Black Harry. He made no move to pursue the girl himself. Though recklessly brave, Harry Dawkins was no swimmer.

"Belay that!" the Captain shouted. His command came too late to stop Hawk. The youth had cleared the oars with a great leap.

The water was well-lit by the late afternoon sun. Hawk caught a clear view of the girl as she hung motionless for an instant. Her hair floated out in an unearthly halo. He thought he had never seen anything so lovely. She turned and flashed away from him.

Hawk gave chase with all he had. He was a powerful swimmer and could hold his breath longer than anyone on the *Lady Anne*. The girl looked back, her eyes wide yet unafraid. She turned down toward the keel of the wreck. She had nearly reached it when Hawk's iron fingers caught her ankle. She kicked hard. Hawk held on with both hands and dragged her toward the surface.

His lungs were nearly bursting when his head broke water. The girl hardly seemed winded. She braced her other foot against his chest to push free. Her kick brought her into the shadow of the longboat. Black Harry's big hand caught her wild tresses. The girl gave an inarticulate cry and struggled. Harry laughed at her as he hauled her in.

"She's a fine prize!" Harry grinned as he helped Hawk aboard. "I owe ye a reward Redskin."

The light was starting to fade as they continued to the crow's nest. Redfern swore softly when they looked inside the small perch. The bottom was strewn with strings of pearls, bright jewels, and golden coins from a dozen different nations. There was also a black book with gilt edged pages.

"Some nest our little bird's got here, ain't it?" Black Harry murmured.

They loaded the cache and headed back. Harry Dawkins spoke the thoughts that were on all their minds.

"If this wench has been pulling up pretty baubles for herself, then that hulk must be packed with treasure. This may be as rich as the old days when Spanish ships carried the gold of the heathens back from the Americas."

"I've never heard of such a treasure ship in our time," Redfern countered. "'Specially not one crossing from Europe. I wonder what vessel she be."

"She's the *Annunciata*, Cap'n," Hawk said.

"And how do ye know that?"

"'Tis painted on her prow," the youth answered. "I saw it when I was swimming after the girl."

"Where did a heathen like you learn his letters?" Black Harry asked.

"I sailed with Captain Clegg for two years," Hawk replied. "He taught me."

"Clegg? Why would that devil teach you anything?"

"He told me that he could not go home without having taught as least one of my people how to read scripture."

Harry threw back his head and laughed. A moment later the others joined him.

"That Clegg was a right madman, God rest him!" Captain Redfern said.

Hawk was silent. Captain Clegg had been one of the few Englishmen he had ever respected. Elias Redfern was another. Most of the crew were Americans, which was a different matter for him. He had counted many of that people as friends. With war between England and her upstart colonies imminent, they seemed his natural allies.

It had been the British who fought so savagely against his people during Pontiac's Rebellion. With the help of some smallpox-infected blankets, they had wiped out his band. Hawk had only been a child then. He had sworn revenge on the English. He had joined the pirate brotherhood to prey on them.

Of course, being a pirate led him to plunder the ships of many nations. The girl's vessel had a Spanish name. He wondered again how it had come to its fate.

The prey was very close now and the thing's tentacles twitched with anticipation. It knew the surface creatures well, for its dreams had often touched their simple minds. They were not at home in this ocean. They huddled in great numbers in their floating wooden vessels. Once the vessel was breached they would be unable to fight or flee.

The surface creatures were stationary for the moment. Only a little longer and they would come close. The thing waited. Like all of its ancient kind, it knew the value of patience.

Every eye was on the girl as they brought her on board. Redfern had made one of the rowers give up his shirt to clothe her. The men's eyes strained to pierce the fabric. While Hawk was well aware of her body, it was her eyes that held his attention. They were the bright color of summergreen trees. He would have found them pretty if he had seen even a glimmer of humanity in them.

Black Harry Dawkins was up the ladder a moment after the girl. He brandished a long dagger.

"Back dogs!" he growled. "This one's all mine."

"Are you giving orders on my ship, Black Harry?" Redfern asked in a low voice.

"Nay, Cap'n," the big man replied, "but I do lay claim to her at the forfeit of half of my share in the treasure. 'Tis my right by our articles."

He caught the girl's hair and pulled her into a rough kiss. As he did Hawk felt a terrible void in his stomach. It was as if the ship had sailed over the world's edge and hung there, poised to fall. He thrust the bigger man away from the girl with both hands.

"Hell's bells!" Black Harry snarled. "Are ye makin' challenge against me, ye red whelp?"

A sheen of sweat broke out on Hawk's body. Black Harry was as good in a fight as any two men on the ship. To challenge him was to die. Still, the nameless dread he felt outweighed even his fear of death.

"Speak up dog!" Harry demanded. "Do ye want her enough to die for her?"

"I don't want her at all," Hawk replied. He tried to keep his voice calm. "I just can't allow no hurt to come to her."

"Hah!" Black Harry grinned. "I never would have thought to find such chivalry in a painted savage. Ye've signed on to the wrong crew if ye want to see such as her handled gently."

Harry brandished his knife.

"Belay that!" Redfern cried, stepping between the two men. "There's more here than parceling out one little wench. We must needs learn if she be worth any sort of ransom. That was the remains of a lady's dress she were wearing, after all."

"A nut-brown wench like this?" Harry jeered. "She's some servant girl, I wager. No doubt she plundered the dress from the wreck, the same as she did the baubles."

"Maybe," the Captain said. "But I think we'll find out 'afore I throw her to you wolves. In any case, I want her to tell us where the rest of the treasure be."

Black Harry nodded sullenly. He was the bully of the ship, but even he respected Redfern's judgment.

"Fine by me," he glared around. "Until we decide, I want no man to touch her!"

"Bring the lass to my cabin," Redfern commanded. "She'll be safe enough there, ye have my word." He turned to Hawk. "Since ye be so keen on protecting her, you're with me."

It was past midnight when the girl finally said something. Hawk had been speaking gently to her, as he might to a wild animal. They'd given her food, only to have it ignored. That bothered him; she was more slender than was fashionable but looked healthy enough. What had she been eating on her mast-top island?

Redfern hadn't spoken much. He had been watching from his hammock, taking an occasional pull of rum. He had finally drifted off to sleep.

"What is your name?" Hawk asked for the hundredth time.

"Columbina," the girl said. Her voice surprised him. It was soft and pleasant where it should have been parched.

She met his gaze now. There was still a vacancy in those eyes. It was the look of someone whose soul had gone wandering.

"My name is Hawk," he said.

She laughed. It had a distant sound to it.

"Hawk and dove, hawk and dove," she chanted in a singsong rhythm.

"Where are ye from?" he asked.

"Columbina is a clown."

The words troubled him. They sounded like folly but he thought that she was trying to convey something with them.

"How long ago did your ship go down?"

"She dances on the stage," the girl sang. "*Arlecchino* dances with her, in and out and in between with the sparkles all around."

"Sparkles?" he seized on the word. "Are ye trying to tell me about the treasure, Columbina? If ye do, the Captain will keep ye safe."

"Always safe," she crooned. "*He* watches over me."

The answer brought back the nameless dread Hawk had felt before.

"Columbina, who is *he*?"

"Hawk and dove," she murmured. Unexpectedly she flung her arms around his neck. Her soft lips pressed his cheek. Before he could react she backed away. She curled up on the deck pulling arms and legs in tightly. He touched her back and felt it move with the easy rhythm of her breathing. She was already asleep.

"Not much of value in them words, eh lad?"

Captain Redfern was sitting up, watching him with amusement.

"Cap'n?"

"I thought it better to let ye do the talking. Ye've a prettier face than old Elias Redfern." He nodded at the girl. "She be madder than Clegg."

"Did ye hear everything?"

"Aye lad, and I know the meaning of a little of what she said. Columbina be a dago name and it means 'dove.' I reckon she were impressed by the contrast in her name and yours."

"What about that other name, *Arlecchino*?"

"I don't know, though it also has a dago sound to it." Redfern stroked his beard thoughtfully. "Just the ravings of an addled girl, I reckon. Mayhap she'll tell us something sane in the morning."

"What about the book?"

"Ye mean that Bible she had?" Redfern asked. "I hadn't thought to look."

The book was no Bible, that was certain. It was written in a language neither man could read. The title was the outlandish sounding *Cthäat Aquadingen*.

"I reckon it to be Latin," Redfern decided. "I think me that '*aqua*' be the word for 'water.'"

Hawk flipped through the pages, looking for anything he could recognize. Though the book had been damaged, sections were still legible. He made a noise of surprise as he came to a picture of a creature rising from the depths. It looked like some unnatural melding of cuttlefish, bat, and man.

"What is it?"

"The Kraken, I wager," Redfern answered. "It be a sea monster what pulls ships down to their graves, or so they say in the north countries."

"Is it real?"

"I've not met any man who has seen one with his own eyes. 'Tis a story I've heard the world round, though. Even the heathen natives of the South Seas speak of him. They call him Ku-tool-hu or some such name."

Hawk looked at the book again. A shiver ran down his spine.

"An evil book," he muttered.

The Captain sat up to watch the girl while Hawk tried to sleep. It was difficult, for he was tormented by dreams. In them, he and the girl were dancing on a dark stage surrounded by diamond flashes of light. When she reached for him, her arms seemed boneless and incredibly strong. The lights vanished as she pulled him to her. He felt a touch on his cheek, like soft lips. The touch spread until his face was engulfed and he couldn't breathe. Her skin had turned rubbery. The feel of it repulsed him. He fought with all of his strength but couldn't free himself.

He awoke in a sweat to see the Captain drowsing in his chair. Columbina had moved in the night. The warm length of her body was stretched against Hawk's back. She looked as innocent as a kitten.

He moved to a chair and didn't sleep again that night.

"Well?" Black Harry demanded. The crew was gathered in the early morning light as Redfern and Hawk brought the girl on deck.

"Her mind be lost," the Captain answered.

"'Tis not her mind I'm interested in." Harry said. With a grin he caught the girl's slender wrist.

"She has a devil in her!" Hawk's voice was quiet. Something in it made the big man pause.

"That be foolish talk," he snarled. "Can ye prove what ye say?"

Hawk was at a loss. He could tell them of his half-remembered dream. Would even this superstitious lot give any credence to that? If they did, they'd likely call him a Jonah and cast him adrift with her. He knew in his bones that he was right. He just didn't know any way to express it.

"Speak ye dog!" Black Harry demanded. "What devil are ye talking about? Has he a name?"

"*Arlecchino*," Hawk replied.

Harry frowned. He'd been a ruined gentleman before joining the brotherhood. Hearing that name seemed to stir a memory in him.

"That be the Italian name for Harlequin. Some say he represents the Devil, but he's no more than a painted character in comedy plays." He frowned thoughtfully. "Where did ye hear that name?"

"The girl."

"What else did she say?"

"Naught but foolishness," Redfern answered. "She did call herself Columbina."

Black Harry laughed out loud.

"Columbina be the name of the lady's maid in the same plays," he said. "She and Harlequin be lovers. There's no deviltry here, just a daft girl dreaming of the theater."

The dread that had filled Hawk had never fully left, now it returned with greater force. He was certain Black Harry's actions were pushing them toward a terrible end.

"By your leave Cap'n," the big man said. "The lass is mine."

Redfern nodded assent.

"I challenge," said Hawk.

"Are ye mad?" Quinlan cried. "He'll make chum out of ye!"

"Belay that talk!" Redfern roared. "I'll let no man-jack who sails under me back away from a challenge once given. What say ye, Harry Dawkins?"

"The lad's got more sand in his craw than I thought," Dawkins answered with a grin. "I'll fight him."

"What weapons?" the Captain asked.

"I don't want to take unfair advantage of the savage," Black Harry replied. "Hatchet and dagger."

Hawk nodded. He preferred a good cutlass to the traditional weapons of his people, but it would be bad form to complain about the choice.

The crew cleared a space on the deck as the two men armed themselves. Harry Dawkins flexed his powerful arms with a grin.

His massive chest was covered with a mat of black hair. He stood more than a hand's breadth taller than Hawk, looking twice as massive. Though Hawk was as strong as any crewman his own size, he couldn't hope to match Harry.

Dawkins came at him suddenly with a powerful slash of his small axe. Hawk ducked away rather than trying to parry. Speed was his only advantage in this fight. He didn't plan to risk a clinch. He danced back from a series of blows without making an attack of his own.

Black Harry was a canny fighter. He feinted with his hatchet to mask a dagger thrust. Hawk's reflexes saved him from a killing blow at the cost of a red wound across his chest. With a grin, Harry moved to press his advantage.

Hawk stumbled away from the big man's steady assault. In a desperate move, he brought his hatchet whistling down toward Harry's head. Black Harry pulled back to avoid the stroke. He knew that Hawk's wild attack would leave him open. One quick stab would end the fight.

But Black Harry's head hadn't been the youth's real target. As he sprawled forward he continued his slash, burying the weapon's blade in the big pirate's foot. With a scream, Harry fell to one knee.

The big man was tough. He held out the dagger to keep Hawk back while he pulled the hatchet free. The weapon didn't want to come loose. Harry cried out as metal grated against bone. The weapon came free with a rush of blood.

Hawk used his foot to flick Dawkins' discarded axe away. The man slashed at him clumsily. He slipped past it; his dagger cut across the hairy wrist.

Ignoring the pain, Harry switched the knife to his good hand. He used the rail to pull himself to a standing position.

"Ye've crippled me, ye heathen!" he said through clenched teeth. "Come finish me if ye can."

"Enough!" Redfern bellowed. "You're beaten, Harry Dawkins. Leave it at that."

"I'll die before I live as a cripple," Black Harry snarled, "and I'd rather die this way than another. Come on savage!"

Hawk didn't see any way clear of killing his crewmate. With a wild cry he leaped. Harry had been waiting for that. His dagger darted at the youth's throat. Hawk ducked and the blade cut across his forehead. He scrambled back, blood flowing into his eyes.

Black Harry lurched forward, dagger extended. Hawk managed to catch his wrist. The two struggled for a moment, Harry's superior strength forcing the blade toward the smaller man's throat.

Suddenly there was the sound of a splash.

"The girl's gone over!" someone cried.

"After her!" Redfern bellowed. Several more splashes followed as men hit the sea.

Hawk took advantage of the distraction to stomp on his opponent's injured foot. As Harry cried out, the youth heaved with all his might. The big man was slammed to the deck.

Hawk took a step back, wiping the blood from his eyes. Though Harry was weakened by his bleeding foot, his eyes were defiant as he struggled to rise.

"Enough!" Redfern barked. "We've got more important matters than the two of ye! Hawk, get to a boat. Quinlan, Morgan, take Dawkins below and tend his wounds!"

The water stirred above. The thing felt a familiar presence. Its bait was returning. Very soon now the prey would follow. Very soon would come the feast.

They found the shirt the girl had worn floating near the ship. She had disappeared from sight.

"She dove there, Cap'n," one of the men said. He pointed to a spot many yards ahead. "If she came back up, I ain't seen her."

They reached the spot and Hawk went down with three other divers. As they descended, he caught sight of the girl's pale form. It sped away with the grace of a porpoise. He chased the phantom deeper into the gloom. Abruptly it changed direction and vanished. As Hawk glanced around he saw something else. He had descended to the shoal which glittered all around him. He reached out to touch a gleaming object. His hand came back with a lady's necklace, diamonds sparkled in the faint light.

Hawk kicked upward. A moment later he broke surface near the boat.

"Did ye see her lad?" Redfern called.

"She's there Cap'n," he answered. "I nearly caught her but she's fast as an eel."

"She must be able to breathe water like one as well," Redfern mused. "She's not broke surface since we've been here. There must be a cave down there with air trapped in it."

"I haven't seen such," Hawk said, "but I found this."

He tossed the necklace into the boat.

"Bless me, but that's a sight," Redfern murmured. "Be there more?"

"Much more Cap'n! The ship must have torn her belly open and poured out treasure in her wake."

"Hear that buckos?" the Captain called. "Forget the lass. This is treasure enough to buy every strumpet in King's Town!"

Redfern sent word to bring up the *Lady Anne*. The boats stayed out as platforms for the divers. Nearly every able-bodied man worked at bringing up the glittering wealth. There seemed an unlimited supply of baubles, far more than the *Annunciata* should have been carrying. As they worked, Hawk felt the familiar dread growing in him again.

It was mid-afternoon under a bright sky. Hawk was struggling to pry a silver candelabra from the seabed. Suddenly something long and dark slipped past him. How long he couldn't tell, for its lower end disappeared into the shadowed depths. It moved with the boneless grace of an eel. Before he could react, the thing looped around one of the swimmers. The helpless man was pulled into the darkness.

Hawk's eyes widened in terror as he remembered stories of *Màx-axkuk*, the giant water serpent of his people. He saw the thing rise again. It wasn't alone, there were many of them. A dozen or more serpentine shapes reached for the men. With a start he realized that they weren't serpents. They were tentacles attached to some unseen beast far beneath. His heart pounded as he remembered the picture in the book.

Whenever a flabby arm caught a man it pulled him down with terrible speed. As one tentacle vanished, two more rose to take its place. They seemed to be attracted to movement. Hawk realized that clinging to the ocean floor was the only thing that had saved him. That couldn't last long. His lungs were burning with the need to breathe.

He drew his dagger and turned loose. A kick against the shoal sent him speeding upward, legs kicking. He broke surface a dozen feet from a longboat. As he swam toward it, one of the tentacles rose above the vessel. It smashed down, splintering the sturdy craft like kindling. Half a dozen men were cast into the sea where more arms waited for them.

Hawk had turned to swim for the *Lady Anne* when something thick and cold looped around his body. He barely had time to take a breath before he was dragged down. He stabbed at the tentacle with all of his might. The dagger point slid uselessly off of the rubbery flesh. The light around him dimmed. The pressure in his ears became unbearable as he was drawn deeper.

Another loop coiled around his body and squeezed with appalling force. Hawk lost his grip on the dagger as air bubbled from his lips. He knew that he was going to die. He closed his eyes and prayed that it would be quick.

Something else touched him then. Slender arms wound around his waist, warm flesh pressed against his body. The pressure eased. The gripping tentacle slipped away. He felt himself begin to rise.

Hawk opened his eyes and saw the girl's face close to his. Her eyes were lifted to the surface. Her hair floated up in a dark cloud.

Around them the deadly tentacles were still claiming victims. Occasionally one would move after them, only to drift away as soon as it touched the girl. After an unbearable time, they emerged into sunlight. He gasped in draughts of air.

He opened his eyes to see the wreckage of boats on the water. There were no men in sight. He turned to see the *Lady Anne* floating at anchor. There was something vast and dark in the water beneath her. It rose and tentacles emerged to tear at the sides of the ship.

It was almost unbearable to look at the monstrous form. There was a wrongness about it, as if it did not fit in this world. It seemed to twist reality by its mere presence. Hawk's mind ached with the effort of trying to grasp it. Dimly, he heard his own voice screaming.

The meal had been a good one. A few of the small creatures had slipped away but that was unimportant. There would always be more and they were easy to trap.

The thing hooked its claws into the belly of the *Lady Anne* and ripped it open. Her cargo spilled out to join the shining wealth that littered the shoal. The damaged ship sank into the deeper waters. She settled on the sea bed near a dozen other hulks.

The thing settled amid the wooden bones of its victims. Soon it would need to feed again. For now it was sated. Now was the time to sleep.

Hawk woke to the sight of a sunset. The sound of lapping waves was all that he could hear. It took him a moment to orient himself. He was sitting in the crow's nest where they had first seen Columbina. There was no sign of the girl, nor of his ship.

He scanned the sea and saw a long, low shape moving toward him. It was one of the ship's boats. As it drew closer, he could see Captain Redfern and eight crewmen. Somehow they had evaded the doom that had claimed the *Lady Anne*.

"'Tis good to see ye lad," the Captain said as they helped Hawk on board. "I'd not thought any other could have survived."

"Columbina saved me," he answered. "I don't know why."

"Columbina," Redfern repeated. "What was she?"

"Maybe once she was just a girl on a ship," Hawk answered. "I think that thing keeps her alive to lure men in."

Redfern shook his head wearily.

"It were the same monster as in that cursed book. The Kraken, come to life. I wonder if the lass called it forth somehow."

"I don't know."

"Did ye see what became of her?"

Hawk pretended not to hear the question.

"Best we be away from this place Cap'n," he said.

He stared back as they rowed. He knew where the girl must be. If he could look into the depths he would see her. Columbina was dancing on her dark stage, surrounded by diamond glitters as she wove gracefully in and out of the arms of her *Arlecchino*.

ICE

BY *HEATHER HATCH*

===

JOHNSON LOOKED OUT AT the glistening white expanse, glad for the barrier between him and the snow covered ice. He noted the research ship's position and speed in the log book—along with the calm emptiness of the Antarctic wasteland—and turned to Ivers, the man at the radar.

"Still no sign of Dr Fenton?" Johnson asked.

"Nope. Nothing from Saunders—how much longer are we waiting out here?"

Johnson shrugged. "Captain says another day."

Ivers frowned, but shot Johnson a curious look. "That'll be Walsh's doing, won't it?" Rumor had it that the doctor's pretty young assistant had convinced Captain Hennessy to stay a little longer in hopes that he would contact *Perseverance*. The crew didn't expect to see the scientist again, and didn't terribly mind. Helicopter crews made passes every three hours along the shoreline ice, seeking any sign of Fenton's party. Five passes brought no news. The radio returned nothing but static.

"Could be." Johnson didn't actually know—he was the third mate, but still too new to the crew to have quite gained enough of the Captain's confidence to be included in these decisions.

"You don't think we'll find him, do you?" Ivers said.

"No."

If anyone asked Johnson what had happened, he would have

said that it was the ice. It resented human intrusion as though it were a living thing. This was not the more familiar tamed territory of the Northwest Passage where he had spent most of his adult life making runs with the great icebreakers, clearing paths for lesser ships to wind their way through the Canadian north. This landscape hated with an intensity that drove off all living things. No human would contract to stay longer than a year. Even the native wildlife migrated away to a few spots of warmer water during the long days of winter darkness. Along the border of the Amery Ice Shelf where *Perseverance* currently lay, the ice marshaled its forces, growing into the ocean with constant input from inland ice sheets and glaciers. This small patch of coastline birthed some of the largest icebergs known to man.

Ostensibly, Dr Fenton's team was investigating this phenomenon, but having seen the equipment they'd brought and noting (more significantly) what they hadn't, Johnson wondered. Miss Jillian Walsh was as close-lipped as ever about the experiments. She ghosted through the onboard lab, hardly sharing a word with anyone. This was generally how the crew preferred things—as little contact with the researchers that employed them as possible. The distance she usually kept, even from the Captain, only accentuated the unnatural aura that shrouded the expedition. None of them had any business being out there in the first place, let alone staying any extra time. Johnson was sure they would be longer than a day, waiting. They would stay until the men's fear of the ice and their desire to return to the warm embrace of civilization outweighed their interest in the extra cash. Two more days, he judged.

The second mate, O'Connor, entered the bridge. Johnson nodded to him.

"Nothing new to report. The next 'copter goes out in an hour. We might have a little weather brewing, but it's not much for this time of year."

"We'll see," O'Connor replied. "Winter squalls down here can blow out of nothing. I'll keep an eye on it."

Johnson passed over his watch, and headed below. It was almost possible to forget the oppressiveness of the darkness and ice in the ship's brightly lit interior. Music streamed up from the galley—old Andy was blasting out the tunes as he prepared the crew's next meal. Snippets of Stan Rogers drifted through the halls, along with the smell of boiling meat and vegetables.

Johnson passed the next hour curled up on a couch in the officer's rec-room with a Tom Clancy paperback before heading up to the wardroom for dinner. Captain Hennessey was already there, with Saunders, the flight crew chief.

"Still no news," the chief was saying, "it's a wasteland out there."

The Captain nodded. "We might cut back then—passes every five or six hours instead of every three. That should help conserve fuel."

Both men smiled to the newcomer as he took his seat, helping himself to the spread.

"That'd only make for one or two more attempts," Johnson commented, "unless we're staying longer?"

"I'm not sure yet," Hennessey replied. "The money's good, but we're due a storm. Calm like we've been seeing is just unheard of in an Antarctic winter."

"I keep forgetting you're a northman, Johnson," Saunders added. "You seen a proper storm down here yet?"

"I've seen enough. This place is wild—dangerous."

"You'll get used to it." The Captain popped open a bottle of port, and poured them each a glass. "I've been with this ship seven years now. I wouldn't say Antarctica's shown me all her secrets, but I think I know her temper well enough."

Perseverence mostly made summer runs ferrying scientists to and from the various research outposts and projects that aimed to domesticate this last frozen frontier.

"It's not so bad," Saunders added. "This is a good ship—it'll grow on you." Johnson knew that the chief was likewise familiar with the Antarctic runs, and had worked with Hennessy on previous tours.

"Yeah sure," Johnson grinned, "like a tumor."

"Ha!" The chief laughed. "Maybe. I'll tell you what is weird though—Walsh and Dr Fenton. Those two are a strange breed."

"Well funded, though," Hennessey added thoughtfully. "Fenton is a newcomer to the scientific community, so I hear. He has rich and powerful supporters who shelled out to reinforce the hull's ice strengthening for this trip. They've been good money."

"Yeah, too bad we can't seem to return the favor, eh?" Saunders shook his head. "But I guess we'll keep trying."

Johnson nodded and sipped his port, keeping his thoughts to himself.

A few hours and several sea stories later, he stumbled aft toward his cabin through the heart of the ship, slightly tipsy from the after-dinner drinks. He returned the nods of the men on shift as he passed, struggling to put names to faces. They weren't his watch, and he saw them rarely. Johnson wondered what they made of the current situation. Most likely they shared the opinions he'd overheard—*they'd take the money, for now.* Unlike most of the officers, the men were a mix of nationalities. He'd had to demonstrate a rudimentary command of Spanish in order to secure his position, but he often overheard fragments of conversations in other unknown tongues and dialects.

He caught one of those fragments as he passed by the research labs, the alcohol softening the syllables even more than the low voice that whispered them.

"... *aln fthya h'yii leng bthy'a mwf'gtme* ..."

The snippets echoed ominously in his mind, but Johnson pushed aside his apprehension. The labs were off-limits to the crew, and it was his job to make sure they weren't causing any trouble. Losing their research party was bad enough—this was not the time for pranks, or even outright sabotage, no matter what was thought of the project, their situation, or Miss Walsh.

The hatchway was open, the hatch itself secured safely against the bulkhead. Darkness filled the corridor beyond, but further strains of eerie whispers betrayed the intruder's presence. The entrances to three of four labs remained closed but the second hatch starboard was similarly held open. Had the prankster intended to ensure a quick escape route, Johnson wondered, or simply been afraid of closing himself off in this forbidden space? He wished he were a little more sober, and was glad he'd declined the Captain's offer of a final nightcap.

As he approached the lab, he also wished he'd thought to switch on the overheads. Light from behind him stretched tentatively into the gloom, revealing shadows in the darkness. It seemed for a moment as though the malevolent Antarctic twilight had invaded *Perseverance.* Johnson frowned.

"... *gi'ldc ia cwflm'ne! Ia cwflm'shi! Ia cwflm sngh'ne'shi!*"

The low pitched voice rose to a crescendo as he stepped into the frame of the hatchway, reaching to the side to fumble for the light switch. The scene before him gave him pause.

There was no intruder here, only Walsh herself. She stood in the dark before her strange instruments, staring into a screen or monitor that reflected an unearthly green luminescence on her pale skin and white lab coat. A strand of black hair, free from her tight braid, coiled carelessly along her cheek and cast its own strange shadows. She fell quiet, leaning forward expectantly into the weird light.

Johnson stepped back. He stumbled and caught himself on the hatch, pushing it back into the wall with a bang. Startled, Walsh straightened and turned quickly in his direction.

"Sorry," he muttered, backing away, "thought I heard someone . . ."

She responded only with a curt nod before returning to her vigil. Johnson wasted no time escaping, seeking better lighted corridors and the security of his own quarters.

The third mate's quarters were only roomy relative to the accommodations provided for the crew. *Perseverance* was a large vessel, but carried a lot of equipment. The men were housed four to a room with some extra space for lockers and a shared desk. Johnson's room had a single bed in half the space, with a larger wardrobe, desk, and a small shelf where he could secure other personal items. He'd posted a picture of his wife there, standing in front of their new property outside Cavendish. She was smiling, holding her wind-buffeted hair out of her face and shading her eyes from the sun.

Johnson smiled himself, thinking of Angie, and the sun. This room was his refuge, a place where he could dismiss disquieting thoughts and forget about Jillian Walsh's strange language, the ice, and the darkness. Cut off from the rest of the ship, he felt more connected to the outside world. It was silly, even superstitious, but he didn't like to think of home or Angie outside of this sanctum. He didn't want the ice to taint those things he held most sacred.

With the extra money from this trip, they should have more than enough to finish paying the loan they'd taken to cover the renovations on the old farmhouse—the whole reason he'd agreed to take this job. He'd only had a few weeks home before he'd left for the south, and wasn't due back until early August. That would give him a few months before he took up his seasonal position with one of the great northern icebreakers. Probably the *Laurentian Queen*, if Jake Sohmer hadn't retired as Captain. That was a cheering thought too—he liked Jake. He'd spend the fall with family and the winter with old friends in a more familiar cold, where the ice and snow seemed less hostile and with no strange researchers to muck up the ship's schedule. His mind set somewhat at ease, Johnson readied himself for sleep.

He dreamed of ice. He stood on the familiar deck of the *Queen*, bundled in his red cold-weather suit, watching it break up before him. White chunks drifted around the vessel's heavy bow, trailing along her sides, pushed out of the way into her wake. The winds howled, an unnatural high-pitched shrieking. The sound was the first sign that something was wrong.

The ship was still. The ice receded without its usual groaning and crunching. There was none of the teeth-jarring rattling and shaking that was part of life onboard an icebreaker as the bow ploughed over the frozen waste ahead. This ice was breaking up on its own, fleeing the vessel's crushing power. Looking back toward the stern, he could see that they had cleared more than just a narrow channel. The ocean behind *Laurentian Queen* swarmed with activity—thousands of chunks of frozen white bobbing toward the horizon and freedom under the uncaring gaze of southern stars.

He'd come outside with no radio, no way to call up to the tower and tell them to stop. He waved his hands toward the bridge, hoping to flag someone's attention. Didn't the instruments show what was happening? They had to stop, to turn back. They couldn't let this happen. Looking out into the water, he could see the ice was not alone. There were things in the water, some in the ice itself, marring its pristine whiteness. Were they seals, or sea lions, disturbed by the patterns of the ice? *No.* They were too black and they didn't move like any fish or animal he'd ever seen. Some were rather large . . . Shouldn't the sonar pick them up? What were they?

They were breaking out of the ice. It wasn't the wind shrieking, it was them, the things in the water, crying at their release. Could they hear it in the tower, or did the wind carry the sound away too quickly?

He couldn't see them now, just the ice fleeing before the ship's advance. Had he imagined them? Could he still hear the shrieking? He listened harder. Was that the wind? Or the grinding of the hull against the ice?

He awoke with the mad howling still in his ears, and it took a moment to identify the sound. There was no wind in here, no shrieking monsters, no scraping of metal on ice. The ship's alarm blared from the speaker above his bed, calling all hands to their stations. A quick glance at the clock showed that it was two hours before his watch. Johnson slipped quickly into his gear and headed to the bridge, trying to shake the memory of the dream from his mind despite the piercing cries of alarm that echoed through the ship.

Perseverance pitched and rolled heavily as he scrambled up the gangways. The predicted storm must have blown up, then. As he came to the upper levels he could hear the wind, the real wind, screeching as it raked across the hull. The freezing Antarctic seas pounding the ship's sides roared in chorus, and he could only imagine the size of the waves that leapt across her deck. As he ascended to the bridge, he saw the towering plumes of water.

The Captain was on deck, as was a ragged looking O'Connor.

"The storm came up an hour ago," Captain Hennessey briefed him quickly. "Just when the last patrol was due back."

"Did they make it in?"

Connor shook his head. "No. We barely picked them up on radar before they got blown out. If they're lucky they had a chance to land and sit this sucker out."

"What's our status?"

"The radar is out, GPS isn't far behind, and we've got half a dozen other systems threatening to fail." Hennessey frowned, looking grim. "Adams is down sorting out the engines, but we need to get the equipment secured on deck." Adams, the first mate, had some engineering certifications and his experience would be put to best use below. It was still O'Connor's watch, but such technicalities became meaningless in an emergency. Johnson was fresher, if a little unsettled from his dream.

"I'll do it," he offered.

"Good man." Hennessey pursed his lips and nodded his approval. "Be careful."

Johnson decided to take men from his watch—men he knew he could rely on. They listened as he explained their tasks, raising his voice to be heard above the fury of the storm. Guzman, a younger crew member from Argentina or Chile, would take point for Andersen, the watch's engineer. Two other Argentineans, Garza and Ortega, would be along for extra manpower and weight. There was no point bringing radios—there would be nothing to hear but wind and water. Hand signals would have to do. Their task was to recover the GPS antennas. All understood the danger and the importance: with no way to take their bearings, *Perseverance* could easily become as lost as Fenton's team. One rapid double check of the safety lines and gear and the team was prepped to face the storm.

It was deafening. Within seconds they were drenched in frigid water. Their suits were well insulated, but the cold was still shocking and the waves and blowing snow raked at any weak spots, threatening exposure to the elements. Lightning flashed, but the wind tore away the sound with the same sudden violence that slammed Johnson into the bulwark and rolled the ship dangerously to port. Andersen and Ortega were likewise swept from their feet, held only by their safety lines.

Johnson gasped in icy air, despite his re-breathing mask, just as the ocean surged across the deck once more. His lungs protested against the cold and the pressure, but he pulled himself along the bulwark with the others. It was madness to think they could survive out here for any length of time. It was madness to think the ship could survive and not be smashed against the ice shelf. He could sense it in the distance, its waves of menace stronger than the raging wind and water. The thought filled him with determination—he could not contemplate giving in so easily to whatever malignancy reigned out here. He blundered into Ortega, who looked back seeking guidance. Johnson waved him onward. It was ten meters to the closest tower of three. They would salvage one, the minimum necessary, and head back to relative safety.

He was exhausted by the time he'd reached their goal. Andersen was already wrestling with the antenna casing. Manipulating anything wearing the thick protective gloves of the exposure suits was difficult enough without the uncooperative weather. The others, Johnson included, gathered round as close as they could to provide some shelter from the elements. The headlamps attached to their suits provided only basic illuminations for the task. Someone, maybe

Garza, signaled an incoming wave. They clung to each other, locking arms as water mixed with chunks of floating ice gushing across the deck and knocked them backward into the tower. *Perseverance* had turned to ride the waves, but the unpredictable nature of the storm thwarted this strategy.

Once the deck cleared, they could see that the tower had snapped at the base; it was hanging only by a mess of wires. Andersen gave two thumbs up, and cut the remaining lines with a pair of heavy shears he drew from his tool backpack. Johnson helped him lash the antenna array—a section of twisted metal and plastic nearly a meter long—to Guzman's back. There was no question of someone simply carrying it. Everyone needed their hands free to navigate their way safely.

The team turned back toward the hatch, Johnson now in the lead. It was not visible through the swirling whiteness at this distance, and he felt his way forward using the guide rope. He stumbled onward, trying to keep his balance as the ship rode waves fifteen meters high. The sound of his heart throbbing in his ears drowned out even the screeching winds. He tried to dwell on success, on their imminent victory over the ice and this chaos he felt it had somehow birthed.

They had to be close when he heard it—a deafening crack, louder than his pumping blood, than the winds and thunder. At first he thought it was the ship, that the hull had somehow split, but it was not the sound of metal. It came from the left—from the south. Where else? It came from the ice. Johnson braced himself against this newest attack.

He heard it before it came into view—the rushing roar of an ocean gathering all its strength into one great wave, larger even than the titanic walls of water that currently warred around the ship. *Perseverance* slowly came about, into this newest threat. Too slowly. Her diesel engines strained at the effort. Johnson clung fiercely to a deck stanchion, looping the safety rope around it twice before the sea threw its might against him.

Then he awoke, sure that he had dreamed again though he could remember nothing specific. Visions of green lights dancing in the sky filled his head, dark whispered voices echoing across the expanse of white, and a vast, cavernous blackness . . . His body was wracked with pain. The storm had ended. Was he still on the ship? Yes. Johnson stood shakily, leaning heavily on the stanchion. His right leg protested violently and he nearly passed out. Had he done this before? He was no longer lashed in place. Where were the others? The wave, or the ice, must have crushed his leg. He was lucky to have survived, though he was sore and likely bruised all over. His exposure suit offered six hours of protection from the elements. He was cold now, but nothing was frozen. The stars provided little light, and the battery in his headlamp was dead. The deck seemed empty save for pools of freezing water and chunks of ice strewn about by the wave. Johnson looked out across the water.

The ice shelf loomed perilously close, blotting out the sky barely ten meters away. Its edge projected a hundred meters into the air and hundreds more into the depth of the ocean. Two points off the starboard bow he could see the mouth of a great chasm stretching into the heart of the ice. Smaller fissures emanated from it, isolating irregular blocks of frozen sea water that threatened to work their way back into the ocean. An eerie wind whistled through the cracks.

He couldn't hear the engines. He was still groggy, and it was difficult to think clearly through the pain of his leg, but the wind's strange voice highlighted the silence of *Perseverance*. Maybe she was adrift, or worse, grounded on the ice. How long had it been? he wondered. Some of the ship's windows still glowed with light, no doubt powered by a backup generator. Setting his jaw, Johnson pulled himself along the side of the vessel toward the nearest hatchway. Apart from the wind, he could hear waves lapping against the hull, pushing the ship closer to the ice shelf. Not grounded yet; a minor miracle this close to the ledge.

Several agonizing minutes later, he fumbled open the hatch through which his team had exited. The rest were surely lost, the scientists, the 'copter crew, and who knew how many others. Johnson initially found the emergency lights glaring in contrast to the gloom to which his eyes had become accustomed. He heard the wind moaning an atonal song through the halls, and for the moment nothing else.

"Hello?" he called.

Silence answered. The ship rolled slightly, pushing him off balance into the wall. He leaned his bulk on the broken leg. Fresh waves of pain flashed through his mind.

This time, he woke to a bright light shining in his eyes. He blinked it away. His injured leg felt better, but he couldn't move it.

"You're awake."

A woman's voice. Walsh, leaning over him with a flashlight. It was cold enough that he could see the fog of condensation in the light's beam. She wasn't wearing an exposure suit. His head was uncovered, but the cold seemed a distant phenomenon.

Johnson sat up, carefully; his vision swam. He didn't feel the weight of his exposure suit. He was folded halfway between the floor and the wall, gravity pulling him down into the corner.

"I splinted your leg and gave you a shot of morphine," Walsh said. "There's no need to make this any more painful." Her tone was clipped. She straightened and stepped backward, steadying herself with one hand against the tilted wall. She didn't seem to have changed since he saw her last, bending into that strange green light. He could almost see it now, shining in her dark eyes. Her expression was unreadable.

"What's going on?" The emergency lights still shone, but they were dimmer. He could not longer feel *Perseverance* rolling with the waves.

"It's over."

"What is?" They were in the equipment locker, not far from where he'd fallen. The drugs—he was sure it must be the drugs—gave the cold air an oppressive quality, as though it were trying to smother him. The wind carried an offensive smell, like bad breath.

"Everything," she said. "Can you stand?"

Johnson pulled himself up, again using the wall for support. The morphine muddled his senses, and he knew the leg hurt even though it didn't bother him. Things swam in the darkness at the edges of his vision. Walsh passed him a set of crutches, then turned and started picking her way through obstructions he couldn't quite make out in the dim lighting.

He followed after a moment, limping carefully. It was easy to keep track of Walsh as she pushed ahead, light reflecting off her white lab coat. Items secured during the storm were strewn around the deck—tribute to the strength of the giant wave. His limited mobility and the odd angle at which *Perseverance* perched made it difficult to maneuver and he fell farther behind. Most of the hatches off the main passage were sealed. He stopped to listen when passing the engine room, but no sound escaped through the steel door. Bracing himself carefully, he turned the heavy wheel, pulling it up toward him. It didn't occur until afterward that the hatches may have been sealed to keep out water.

There was water in the engine room, but it was not deep enough to reach the top of the gangway. It lapped at the catwalk where Johnson paused to take in the scene. The engine was partially submerged, dead. There were bodies here as well, floating face down. Some were suited-up, but all were bloated and unrecognizable. He counted six. The entire engineering crew. No, there was Andersen, he had been lost overboard. Something rippled the water below the surface. He backed away, letting the door drop closed. It was nothing, he told himself, a trick of the light, plus the drugs and pain.

Walsh had disappeared, but the route she'd been following led to the bridge. Johnson didn't check any more rooms. The ship was dead, her hull breached, and they were grounded. Surviving crewmen would have taken a raft, if any were left. There was a Russian outpost in the bay, Progress Station, and if they'd made it through the storm and the giant wave, they might have reached shelter.

Angie. He had to get out. She'd have been watching the weather, seen the storm brew up. She'd worry, but the ice hadn't got him yet. His quarters were below, somewhere. He would save her from the ice, or at least her picture. But he couldn't make a trek to Progress Station on his own. He'd find Walsh, and they'd head there together. There were inland stations on Amery as well, but even if his leg wasn't broken he doubted they'd be able to reach safety that way. The ice would use its secrets against them.

Johnson stumbled to the bridge. He'd jarred his injured leg enough on the uneven footing that he could feel it throbbing. The angle of the ship was such that he had to pull himself up though the hatchway, passing his crutches through first. Walsh was there, shivering against the gyroscope casing, staring through the glass. Hennessy's body lay draped across the navigation station with a pool of blood freezing on the computer terminal under his head. Ivers lay slumped against the bulkhead, a blank, dead gaze following Walsh's to the view through the window.

Perseverance lay with her bow facing the largest of the cracks in the ice shelf, like an offering splayed before some strange frozen altar. Open channels to either side teemed with life, the creatures from his dream escaping out into the world. Snow, or some other particles, blew out of the darkness, probing the vessel's wounds and permeating the cold air with an insidious organic stench. The crack revealed its mysteries to its witnesses—more dark shapes frozen in the ice, outlined by fractures that groaned under their own weight. Directly above them, the largest of these jutted out into the Antarctic air. In the wind and twilight, an indistinct colossus constrained in the ice flexed and wriggled distorted black limbs so that it, too, might drop to freedom in the frigid ocean waters.

Walsh seemed enraptured by the scene though she must have heard him approach. Johnson could not stand to look, turning his eyes to the researcher instead. He pictured her standing bent over a terminal, whispering in some strange language, enveloped in the haunting green glow that still shadowed her eyes.

"Did you do this?" He needed to understand, to know there was something here he could comprehend.

She turned, a slight downturn of her lips the only change in her expression.

"No more than you, or any other fool on this planet." Walsh paused, giving Johnson a moment to struggle with his incomprehension, then she looked back to their looming doom. "We had theories, but, no." She shook her head at the window. "It had become truly inevitable . . ."

Was she lying? What had she been doing, then? He thought of Angie, exposed to this ice and the evil it had harbored for untold ages. Could she be safe in Cavendish or any other haven? He remembered the thing in the engine room—no hallucination after all.

"What do they want . . . these creatures?"

Another thundering cracking noise punctuated her silence. Something slammed against the hull, nearly tumbling him again. Stabbing pain pierced his morphine stupor. Johnson looked to the rift. The monster's frenzied struggles increased as the ice around it weakened. Starlight reflected off some hard black surface, a claw, beak, or some other chitinous appendage waving freely, lashing out at the ice and air. It wailed loudly, its cries shedding more ice from the cocoons of its allies. The sound pierced him more deeply than the pain in his leg, and he stumbled into the hatchway as his instinct to flee overwhelmed him.

Walsh was right—it, everything, was over. No raft could save them, nor could any sunny thought spare the world this madness. *It* cried again. It cried hate and revenge, destruction and chaos. It cried for its terrible freedom, voices from the water chorusing their own dissonant shrieks. The ice surrendered with a final booming report, raining an avalanche of crystal shards onto the ship and smashing through the weakened glass of the bridge windows. Walsh fell, covering her head as her body was riddled with projectiles.

Johnson had barely a moment to look up as the Amery shelf disgorged its sinister miscreation, still half ensconced in its ice block, screaming triumph as it fell toward *Perseverance*. A ropey gray-green arm, ridged and tipped with a grasping black pincer, smashed into the bridge. He flinched, was flung backward, and only briefly felt the impact of the giant monstrosity as it crashed into the ship, shattering the hull and remnants of its prison as it escaped into the world.

THE WRECK OF
THE GHOST

BY *TIM CURRAN*

No perceptible face or front did it have; no conceivable token of either sensation or instinct; but undulated there on the billows an unearthly, formless, chance-like apparition of life.
—Herman Melville

OF WHALES, THERE WERE precious few. We were north of Umnak Island with a latitude of 56° 15'N and a longitude of 169° 26'W, bearing north-northwest. In the past thirty-six hours, our luck had been practically nonexistent. We had sighted but a single pod of small Grays that weren't worth dropping the boats for or sinking iron into. And there had been one massive Fin Whale that dove out of sight long before we were in range. At high summer in the Bering Sea, you could expect large numbers of Grays making for their feeding areas up north, but our luck had brought us nary a one. We had 1200 barrels in the hold, only three hundred of which were full of whale oil.

Not a Humpback or a Greenland Right to be seen.

Not alive, that was.

And that was perhaps the most disturbing thing. For these grounds were rich and, other than those mentioned, in the past eight hours we had encountered only two Greenland Rights and both were dead. Great floating carcasses like the hulls of overturned brigs, flocks of birds pecking away at them. Dead whales were no rarity in these waters. Often they were harpooned and lanced by whalesmen, making their runs and dying miles away, never to be retrieved. But these bore no marks of the harpoon nor lance, instead they were viciously mutilated as by some predator. Great slabs of blubber had been cleaved free, their flanks set with linear incisions and sawtoothed lacerations that cut right to the bone beneath. The second whale corpse had been stripped from rostrum to blowhole, its skull gleaming in the sun, its flukes ripped clean. Both were fresh, far as we could tell, great beasts slaughtered by a force unknown and inexplicable. Besides the usual slick of oil around the carcasses, we saw a great quantity of a pale coagulated slime floating about that looked very much like the spermaceti squeezed from the case of a sperm whale . . . though much more viscid. It carried a sharp, foul odor about it that sickened several crewmen. I likened it to the stench of a tannery . . . chemicals and rotting hides.

This was not the work of sharks nor killer whales, for neither had the equipment nor bite to produce such prodigious wounds.It was a strange business and not I or the other mates or even Captain Inglebritzen, that stern old Dutchman, could make sense of it.

But our business was not the postmortem of dead cetaceans, but the killing of whales.

The Dutchman, as our Captain was wont to be called, summoned myself and the mates up onto the quarterdeck at seven bells. Silver-haired and mutton-chopped, he stared out over the restless sea.

"What say you?" he asked Clegg, the first mate.

"We stay our course," Clegg said. "North-northwest. These grounds are rich. Our luck will turn."

"And you, my man? What sayeth you, Mr Hollywell?" the Dutchman said to me.

"Aye, sir, I concur with Mr Clegg."

Greer, the third mate, agreed as well.

Clegg said, "We have the word of the *Buxton,* sir, and that's fine by me."

Yesterday morning we had encountered the *Buxton,* a Yankee whaler out of Nantucket making her homeward run, barrels full. They had seen great numbers of Greenland Rights, so thick, said the chief mate, that "one could all but tip-toe over their backs."

"Make it so, then," the Dutchman said. He cast a wary eye upon me. "And the log, sir?"

A couple of hands and I had already ascertained our speed with line and sandglass. "We're making twelve knots, sir."

"Keep her so."

I joined my harpooner, Shwayneeg, up at the forecastle rail, feeling the spray of water in my face. Shwayneeg was a Carib Indian like all our harpooners, a man of very few words. But I could see right away, as he cast his tattooed face in my direction, that he had something to say.

"Out with it," I said to him.

"We see two dead whale, torn and ripped by a great mouth." He shrugged. "Soon, we see more. Then three dead whale and four. A trail, eh? Leading us somewhere."

"To the grounds," I said. "The grounds."

"Aye. But grounds of *what* me ask you?"

I didn't bother questioning Shwayneeg on this point, for very often much of what he said was nonsensical to white ears and if he did not wish to elaborate, no force on earth could make him do so. I stood there at the rail, the sharp bow of the *Ghost* slicing open the belly of the sea in a wash of white foam. The sky was clear and the wind crisp. A finger of smoke wafted from the try-works stack behind the foremast where blubber was rendered. The decks were white from salt spray and the constant scrubbing to keep them clean of blood and oil.

The *Ghost* was a three-master, square-rigged on the fore and main, fore-and-aft rigged on the mizzenmast. A finer bark had never sailed. She had a crew of thirty-five including harpooners, hands, mates, and shipkeepers, four fine whaleboats hanging from davits at her bulwarks ready to be lowered and give chase at a moment's notice. Her bow was high and sharp enough to cut a throat, her belly deep with whaleoil casks. She handled the seas well and her master, the Dutchman, was an old hand at our business.

As I stood there, feeling her under me and knowing her as well as my own body, I looked astern and saw the path of foam she left in her wake. It twisted and surged atop the hilly landscape of the waves, finally dissolving in the crests of great rollers. Closing my eyes against the spray, I could hear the hissing of the foam and the distant thunder of the sea breaking before our bow. The wind roared aloft in the masts, spars creaking and chain-sheets grinding. It was the sound of motion and progress and pursuit.

At eight bells I mustered the watch and put two new hands on the forecastle and sent three men from steerage scrambling up the ratlines to the mastheads as standers. From the moment a whaling ship left port standers were up in the masts. We switched them every two hours. I was dearly hoping three new sets of eyes would bring us news of those elusive spouts we hunted.

I left Shwayneeg at the bow and made my way to the waist of the ship, sighting Clegg there at the main hatch. He was alone. His harpooner, Oddrog, another Carib, was absent. Usually, a mate's harpooner is constantly with him. They are inseparable. But something was brewing with our boys this day and I knew what it was. Clegg stood there, watching the heavy seas boiling about us, the ship rolling from port to starboard and back again. He was studying the sea with his spyglass, giving with his legs to maintain his balance with the pitching of the decks. Without taking his eye from the glass, he said anon to me:

"Well, Holly, I see your man is chasing his own ghost like mine."

"It's the whale carcasses, sir. Shwayneeg is spooked over the business."

"As is Oddrog," he said. "I dare not even mention them around him for fear that he'll fall to the deck, cut himself red, and begin to sing his death-song. What do you make of it?"

I listened to creaking and groaning timbers overhead. "Thing is, sir, I don't know. We should be thick amidst our whales; nothing but dead ones. It doesn't wash."

"Aye. Oddrog is of the impression we are sailing straight into some whale's graveyard of all things."

It was nonsense . . . but I could not repress a chill at the idea of it. I listened to the breeze rushing amongst the rigging overhead, the canvas blown full with a breath of wind. These sights and sounds had always filled me with an exhilaration and, by night, a calmness and sense of purpose. But today, they were lonely and forlorn sounds. I wanted nothing better than to dismiss the vagaries of our harpooners, but I couldn't. For I was beginning to feel something myself. Something stirring in the pit of my being, something cold and grim opening in me like the petals of a mortuary flower. I could not dismiss it. I could liken it to nothing but the sense that disaster was looming, something unknown but immense and even palpable with its grim weight.

"And you?" said I.

Clegg collapsed the draw-tubes of his telescope. "I wish to God I knew."

As he made his way to the quarterdeck and the Dutchman, I wondered if the whole crew wasn't feeling it. For hadn't they all been on edge these past few days? Somber, surly, nervous? Yes, arguments were common, camaraderie nearly nonexistent. The mates and I had broken up several altercations and the Dutchman, despite himself, had to punish more than one man.

And why was that? Because of something they sensed or merely the hard life they led?

Ours was not an easy life, granted. It was monotonous for days on end and often quite unprofitable, particularly for the hands that received but a sliver of the total lay. Life on a whaler meant long years at sea, fatigue, frustration, even danger. And when it ended, there was never any promise of profit. The work was of the most grueling and unpleasant variety. Once a whale was towed back to the ship, a cutting stage would be hung over its body. And it was from this that the Captain and mates would flense the blubber from the whale's carcass in great five-foot sections using spades, flensing knives, and blubber pikes. Hooks were attached to these sections and they were hoisted aboard by the crew and sectioned. And then the real work began for the hands. On decks slick with blood and oil, they would work with cutting tools, slicing blubber while the ship pitched to and fro, a stench enveloping them that could not be washed off, but had to be worn away through days or weeks. With mincing knives, the blubber was cut, down in the blubber room and pitched into great kettles in the try-works that bubbled in the brick furnaces there. The boiling oil was baled into copper tanks and drawn off into casks that were stored down in the hold.

The men were never idle. They were in constant motion with danger to all sides. Some were crushed on deck beneath slabs of blubber that might weigh an easy ton; some were gored by cutting blades; others fell into the churning shark-infested waters; and still others were scalded by boiling whaleoil. And even when the last cask was filled and stowed, the men were put to work cleaning and scrubbing, the stink of smoked blubber clinging to them in a nauseating pall.

It was said that merchant vessels and men-of-war could smell a whaler coming and I had no doubt of it. I myself had noticed for days after returning to port that every time I sweated, I could smell the blubber and oil and blood. And I could only imagine the stink emanating from them that processed our kills.

No, ours was no easy life, not for mate nor hand. But the hands had it worse and I never doubted it. They lived in a world of rotting fish and rancid whale oil, blood and grease and urine, shoulder-to-shoulder with the unwashed, reeking bodies of their shipmates crowded down in steerage or the forecastle. They lived the hardships of voyages lasting some three and four years and at the conclusion of which, the pay was often poor or nonexistent. They had their reasons to be unhappy, I knew.

But I wondered if that's what was bothering them, if it wasn't perhaps something more. Some impending sense of doom and tragedy that they could feel and was stitching each and every one of them up into their own shrouds. Because, I swear, I was beginning to feel it myself.

A few hours later, after a dinner of sea bread, salt beef, and cracker hash, I stepped on deck at four bells to take charge of the starboard watch. The seas, I soon saw, were not running as high, which I saw as a good, hopeful sign. Our head was still pointing north-northwest and Mr Clegg was on the poop with the Dutchman, apparently involved in some heated discussion which was absolutely none of my business. What the skipper and the chief mate discuss is of no consequence to the second. Men were scraping rust and peeling paint. The breeze was fresh, but not bitterly so for the Bering at summer. The seas breaking before our stem were uniformly gray and frothy. The sun was out, gleaming off brassworks and skylights. I felt uniformly cheerful after my brief nap and a bite.

But it was not destined to last.

Up on the foremast, one of the standers began to shout: "Oi! There's something up ahead! I see three of 'em . . . carcasses maybe!"

Everyone started calling questions at him there on the masthead, but our hearts had already sunk. If it had been a spout he sighted, the time-honored call of "THERE SHE BLOWS!" would have been cried out.

"What do you got, lad?" the Dutchman called up.

Aloft, the stander kept his eye to his spyglass. "Can't be sure!" he yelled down to us. "Three shapes . . . dead, maybe, I see no spout! But . . . but there's movement out there, by Christ!"

The Captain did not look happy. "Where away?"

"Three points off the weather-bow!" called the stander.

Mr Clegg was at the wheel by then, spinning the spokes, bringing our head around accordingly.

The stander shouted down that the mysterious shapes were maybe a mile and a half, perhaps two from us. The Dutchman told him to keep his eye on them and to sing out when our head was true. Usually, aboard any whaler, this is an exciting time. But with no spouts espied, we were a glum and guarded lot, expecting the worst and knowing, somehow, that we would not be disappointed. The entire crew was on deck now, each man hoping against hope that a spout would be descried, for that meant more full barrels of whaleoil and a richer lay for all. I stood up in the bow, waiting for those shapes to appear and almost dreading the moment when they would. The wind filled our canvas and our bow sliced through the onward rushing waves. The ship rose and fell, timbers groaning and rigging creaking as we glided forward.

Soon enough, the foremast stander called out, "Dead ahead! Just off the port bow!"

Standing by my side, Shwayneeg, whose eyesight was utterly amazing, tapped me on the shoulder. "There! Them shapes show themselves!"

I saw them now. Two great whale carcasses drifting on the rolling sea, their mountainous bulks lifted to the crests of huge waves and then sunk down into the troughs between with a slow, easy motion which belied their immense weight. Both were Greenland Rights, massive females, glistening black and barnacled as their rounded backs broke the water. I estimated they both had fifty feet on them and a likewise amount of tonnage. There was enough blubber on whales that size to fill hundreds of barrels.

Or would have been had they not been mutilated.

For even at our distance, I could see that the poor creatures were not only dead, but horribly mauled. The carcasses looked as if they'd been hit by cannon shot, just ripped and mangled and nearly exploded in places. Great chunks of blubber had been torn free, the water awash with oil and blood and what looked to be loops of entrails. I could see drifting mats of that pale, viscid slime. Both were off our leeward side. The closest was nearly torn in half; the other was gutted down to the skeleton on one side, while the other side appeared unscathed. They both rolled with a grisly, slopping motion and the stink of their blood and meat was overpowering.

"Another ahead!" cried the stander. "Something . . . there's something after it!"

"Now we see," Shwayneeg said to me. "Now we see."

"Hands!" called out the Dutchman. "Lay the main-yard aback! Let go the main-braces!"

Clegg, manning the wheel, luffed and soon the weather-leeches lay flat and the ship was no longer moving, just rolling with a gentle see-sawing motion like the sea itself as the weather main-braces were let go.

The Dutchman was up at the bow, eye to his spyglass. "By God, what in the hell is that horror?"

We could see that third whale now, another Right, to our windward. I judged by the size—sixty-feet, I guessed—that it was a big female. A simply gigantic animal. Like the others, I could not imagine something that could attack such a creature. But something was. Even through my glass I could not be entirely sure. I saw . . . I saw something ghostly-white and undulant breaking the surf, tearing at the whale with great slicing motions. With each strike the whale shook, jerked like a piece of bread being struck by a fish in a pond. But this was no fish and I honestly could not say what it was, only that its motion and rolling form filled me with an avid repulsion. Each time the beast hit the carcass, the whale jerked and huge plumes of bloody spray shot up into the air.

"Mates! Harpooners! Crews! Stand by your boats and prepare to lower!" the Dutchman shouted out.

"We're . . . we're going after that thing, sir?" I said.

"Damn right we are, lad! We'll have this beast! This sea-monster and whale-killer! We'll sink iron into it and stuff it for a figurehead, this damn horror which eats away our livelihood!"

The idea of going after that nightmare seemed ridiculous to me and I knew the same was felt by the entire crew and you could see it in their pale faces. But the Captain had given an order and we had to obey. And as afraid as we all were to face that thing in open whaleboats, we were all curious to get a look at it. To see such a thing in the flesh, that great behemoth and slaughterer of whales. The

Dutchman told us not to just bring our usual weapons—harpoons and lances—but to arm ourselves well. And so we did. The men took axes and gaffs and pikes and the Dutchman gave each mate in command of a boat a fine Sharps .52 caliber carbine.

Clegg, Greer, and I mustered our crews to our respective boats. We climbed into our oilskins. Weapons were loaded and line tubs fixed. The cranes swung our boats out over the sea. The entire crew was watching us, steely, tense. Six men including mate and harpooner were assigned to each boat. The rest of the crew, known as shipkeepers, stayed on board the *Ghost* while we hunted our prey. Only the foremast stander was still up in his nest, the mizzen and main standers had come down to watch the proceedings. Never, ever had there been a more tense moment aboard any whaler in my life.

The Dutchmen sucked in a lungful of air and called out, "Lower away! Lower away, my fine lads! Out ye go to give the devil his due! Lower away, I say!"

The whaleboats were lowered into the sea and we scrambled over the sides of the *Ghost* and jumped aboard our respective craft. After casting loose, I put my crew to the oars—Posun, DeKamp, White, and Shornby—and manned the rudder, while Shwayneeg stood in the prow, waiting for his chance to throw iron. He was singing some ancient dirge under his breath as he always did when a kill was in the offing, though today with much more vehemence than usual. His dark eyes smoldered in his bronze, tattooed face and he was no longer with us. The blood of his people ran hot and ancient in his veins as he sang and tied off the whale line from the tubs to the iron straps of his primary and secondary harpoons.

Our whaleboats were thirty-footers with six-foot beams. They were razor-sharp at stern and prow and cut through the rolling seas quickly. We came around the bow of the *Ghost*, Greer's boat making way behind us and I saw Clegg's boat to port leading us on.

"Spread out!" Clegg called to us, his boat riding atop a breaking gray wave. "Spread out and scatter! We'll come to the beast from three directions! Mind now!"

"You heard the First!" I shouted at my boys. "Now, pull and pull and pull! That's it, lads! Pull for God and country! Pull for your mothers and wifes and sons born and unborn! Pull, by Christ! Bring us to that ugly whale-killing monster so that we can put the iron into him and give him a taste! Pull, I say! Pull and pull and pull, damn you all!"

This was the most exciting part of the business; just ask any man who has stood his boots on the deck of a whaler while she pitches and yaws, throws the greenhorns to and fro and the mates stand solid as posts. This was the moment that ordinarily cancels out the weeks of boredom as you row at your quarry and bring him in range and the harpooner lets fly his iron. Then it's the sleigh ride and when the whale tires, the mate delivers the killing blow with his hand lance. "Chimney afire!" call the hands as the *leviathan* spouts a fountain of blood and the real work begins. Ordinarily, I say. But this was no ordinary quarry and every man in the boats knew it. We were going up against the unknown and we felt it deep in our marrow. There was always tension and always fear, but the fear we knew at that moment was a much older fear, electric and primal and godless.

The dead whale was easily sighted now. Even the roll of the waves could not take that huge black form away from our eyes. Like the other carcasses, this one rolled and slopped and cast its death-smell into the air . . . blood and blubber and entrails. But this smell was overpowered by a much stronger stench. That same caustic, revolting odor of the tannery, the slaughterhouse, and the charnel. That odor had nothing to do with a dead leviathan, but something quite alive. This was the smell of the thing itself: its life-force, nauseating and malignant, stewing like surgeon's waste in buckets.

"Dear God," said one of the hands. "That stink!"

Yes, it was enough to ream out your nose and turn your brain to mush. A more unnatural, polluted smell could not be imagined.

Thirty yards from the whale I could see her in great detail. A Greenland Right without a doubt. I could see her stacked nostrils and twin blowholes, the rounded glossy back and the ivory pend-uncle patch near her tail which told of her great age. Like the others, she had been savagely mutilated. Her shanks were nearly divorced of blubber, great gashes cut into her that were deep enough to lose a man in. Huge chunks of meat had been ripped free by some circular mouth that must have been easily ten feet in diameter. The sea was roiling with blood and oil, wormy pink loops of viscera drifted just beneath the surface. Macerated hunks of flesh and organ bobbed like the floats of jellyfish.

And slime.

That same greasy pale slime moved in waxy rivers and sluiced against our keel. Great gelatinous ribbons of it hung from oars like the phlegmy spawn of fish, steaming and rancid.

I had never, ever once felt pity for the leviathan. She was raw material to me. Something to be transformed into casks of oil that would themselves become coin in my pocket. But there, my stomach in my throat and a hatred burning in my brain, I pitied her. I honestly pitied that poor creature. I saw her beauty for the first time, recognized it for what it was, and knew I would never sink my lance into her braincase ever again. For there *was* beauty in the leviathan. Streamlined, symmetrical beauty in what I had once thought to be but a swimming tub of blubber to be harvested by harpoon and hook. The stroke of her flukes was poetry and the breeching of her spout was God's own song. And it was blasphemy to slay such a grand creature. With that in mind, my hatred became hot coals upon dry tinder, filling the whole of my being with rising flames. I hated the thing which had brutally killed this old girl and I lusted over its death.

"Pull! Pull! Pull!" I shrieked above the roaring seas and the complaints of my oarsmen. "Bring us to her! Bring us to her! Quick now, you bastards! Row steady and strong! Aye, the closer and the closer!"

And the closer we got and the more of that gore and slime we cut through, the stronger the stink grew and the more we saw of the dead whale. It rose up like an island before us, a massive mound of bobbing flesh that was nearly as long as the *Ghost* herself, the rounded back rising up to almost the height of the ship's bulwarks. She had been eviscerated, opened up like something from a dissection room, what was inside scattered in all directions. Great sections were scathed with slash marks, but untouched other than that. Still others were laid right down to muscle and base anatomy. I could see part of her bowed skull and the pitted holes drilled into the bone by teeth I could not conceive of. Through her flanks I saw the splintered rungs of her ribs and from her back rose the jutting blood-stained staves of her spinal vertebrae. She looked, in places, like a ship laid bare to keel and frame.

It was an atrocity.

As hypocritical as that may sound from a man who killed whales for a living, I say that now: it was an atrocity.

The smell of that unknown beast was so strong, Shornby retched over the side and several others gasped and choked. It was like breathing in the gagging methane stink of swamp vapors. The beast was nowhere to be seen, yet we all knew it was damn close. Shwayneeg stood up in the prow with his harpoon, his iron, scanning the whale's carcass and the fouled sea all about it. I could hear the men in the other boats swearing and complaining, the fear so thick on them it sweated from their pores.

Then the sea around the carcass roiled in a maelstrom of whitewater and that huge cetacean cadaver began to move and bob like it was coming to life. The stench was suddenly much stronger and my eyes watered, tears running down my wind-burned face.

"Him coming now," Shwayneeg said, utterly divorced from human terror as only one of his race could be. "Him coming."

Water whirlpooled and gushed around the carcass as if from some great turbulence or suction below. And then ... then a single white tentacle rose up from behind the other side of the whale. It was white as corpse-flesh, set with irregular bumps and knobs and thick around as a hogshead. I cannot adequately judge its length, only that it could have easily wound itself around a fifty-ton whale and that what it was attached to was still submerged. It rose up and up, dripping and swaying in the air like a cobra rising from a basket. Its underside was set with puckering ovals much like mouths which were fixed with circular fans of teeth that were easily the length of marlin spikes. They weren't teeth but claws, I reckoned, but they looked the part just as those puckering ovals they came from looked like mouths.

I heard someone in one of the other boats cry out.

In my boat, DeKamp said, "Oi ... that's a great monster squid, it is! A bloody great ship-eater! The kraken!"

Shwayneeg made a grunting sound. "Him no squid. Him no nothing man ever saw before. Him something old, old, old. Old as the sea. Him should not be no more. Him should be long dead, him should–"

And that was as far as he got, for that great gigantic tentacle coiled itself and struck out with a wild, blinding fury. It whipped out like a cat o' nine tails with a wet snapping sound and those teeth or claws on its underside hit the whale and gouged out a trench of blubber and meat that became a clotted spray of gore that rained over the boats. It hit us in a cold, meaty mist. A chunk of blubber struck Posun and laid him flat, knocking the oar from his hands.

We were covered in slime and blood and atomized whale meat. It was on my oilskins and in my face. And as I brushed it away from my eyes with a shudder of disgust, the creature rose.

It rose up from behind the whale, dwarfing it.

I heard men scream. I may have screamed myself.

It was a great undulating, fleshy mass of jelly, mounded and humped and ribbed obscenely. The entire mass was gray-white and pulsating, veined with purple networks of throbbing arteries. It was writhing and fluid, something that was many things and nothing in particular. Twitching growths rose from its body, looping coils of tentacles and . . . eyes. Mammoth emerald-green eyes that were stupid with blind hatred, but perversely intelligent. There had to be six or seven that I could see.

"Row!" I heard Clegg call out. "Row the hell away!"

I wanted to give the same order, but I was frozen with horror. I heard a gunshot and saw a bullet drill into that pulsing mass, and then another. It shocked me out of my paralysis. I remembered the gun in my own hands and brought it up, aiming quickly and firing. My bullet punched a hole in one of those emerald eyes and it irised shut with a bile of watery green tears.

The beast let out a thunderous roar, continuing to rise.

Its tremendous ill-shapen body set with thousands of slithering tentacles, I saw it had not one mouth, but *three*. Three mouths oozing a pale slime. They were not side-to-side mouths like those of ordinary animals, but huge and oval and puckered like the mouths of old men. Any of them could have swallowed a whaleboat and its occupants in one bite. They shriveled down to the size of beer kegs and then opened back up to their full measure which must have been three or four fathoms in diameter. They did this again and again as if they were breathing. Inside those hideous blowholes were enormous yellow teeth like broadswords, unsheathed, sliding from the gums. And not just a single set, but three and four sets which moved independent of one another, chewing and thrashing up and down, side-to-side.

As we watched, a set of those teeth jutted from its mouth and took a great bite from the whale, tearing free a slab of blubber that must have weighed a ton. The jaws retreated with it and the blowhole mouth puckered closed.

It was at this time that I saw something utterly appalling. There was a great cylindrical mass encased in a sac of membranous flesh floating near the whale. It was her calf. She'd been pregnant. And what was particularly gruesome was that there was movement within the birth sac; the fetus was still alive or nearly. But then several of those white tentacles wound it up and dragged it under and it was gone.

At this point, the beast sank back into the sea with a weird squealing/mewling sound. The water blew up in a great spray, hissing and frothing, and a shock wave ran through the sea, striking our whaleboat and nearly turning her turtle.

We were shocked, horrified, driven insane perhaps by what we had seen, what we had witnessed. I shouted no order, for my men knew what had to be done. They manned the oars and I worked the rudder bringing us back in line with the *Ghost*. She was there, rising and falling in the heavy seas. I could see men at the rails. I knew they shouted out to us, but there was nothing they could do. My men worked the oars and I saw Clegg's boat to our leeward side making for the ship. And it was then that I saw something that took the breath from me: the hull of Greer's overturned boat and not a soul in the water near it.

We all saw it and seeing it, Shwayneeg began to slash himself with his knife, singing the low sepulchral tones of his death-song.

We made it nearly half-way to the ship when the waters began to roil around us. Something butted into our keel, nearly turning us over. Clegg's boat was in equal distress. Something hit it and pitched two men into the water. And then around us, that white slime filled the sea and the waters boiled and frothed and I saw a series of white humps break the surface. The beast was not done with us.

One of my men screamed.

Shwayneeg jumped to his feet, a shrill wailing coming from his mouth. He grabbed his harpoon and I my killing lance.

"That's him! That's him!" I cried as if this was some ordinary Sperm or Gray Whale. "Give it to him! Give it to him!"

A perfect balance of muscle, determination, and bravery, Shwayneeg tossed his iron and buried it in one of the humps. He threw his other harpoon and sank it, too. Oddrog, Clegg's harpooner, had done likewise. The sea exploded around us and the creature ran. It darted away, dragging us with it, foaming waves breaking before our prow and nearly swamping us. It ran, towing both boats behind it, and then simply stopped, the sea surging and pitching. Peering over the gunwale, I caught sight of those eyes just below the surface staring up at me with a deranged, alien glee. I let out a cry and rammed my lance into one and the creature jerked, our whaleboat rising up five or six feet out of the water and then crashing down, everyone thrown into her bottom.

I heard Clegg call out as his whaleboat was tossed into the air, men flung in all directions. The boat came down, hull up, and the men swam wildly for it. One of them was yanked beneath the surface and another was gripped below the waist by something and dragged off in a frothing spray at least a hundred feet before being pulled under. We rowed in the hull's direction. But it was no good. The beast kept bumping us, turning our head this way and that. I caught one last glimpse of Clegg, Oddrog, and two hands clinging to the hull and shouting out. Then a brace of white, slimy tentacles erupted from the sea and closed over them like a clenching fist. They went down and did not come back up.

We tried to row to the *Ghost*, but the sea boiled like a pot from the motions of the beast. Waves broke against us and fleshy appendages slapped against our keel. One of those tentacles rose up off our starboard side and White struck it with his oar. When that had no effect, he grabbed his axe and cleaved the thing nearly in two, a gushing mass of slime oozing from the wound . . . then it lashed out, encircled him, and yanked him under. And with such constricting pressure that blood flew from his mouth.

Back on the *Ghost*, the Dutchman must have been aware of our plight for the ship was in motion, sails filled and bow cutting. She was sailing top speed in our direction. At least, that's what I thought. But at that speed they would never have stopped in time for us. No, our Captain had another idea. The sea around us was filled with the rising mounds of that gelatinous horror and the *Ghost* made right for one of them, ramming it, her keel cutting a trench right through it. The ship jerked with the impact, listing badly to port, then righting herself at the last moment and ghosting to a stop, hove to.

The beast was gone.

We had a chance and we knew it.

Shwayneeg took to the oars with the others, making for the ship. But we never made it. For the ocean around the *Ghost* was on fire. At least, that's how it looked. A great white phosphorescence erupted around her with bubbles and froth and plumes of steam. And out of the stagnant depths, the beast rose up like some slimy fetal nightmare expelled from a womb. I saw its heaving, nebulous form rising, pulsing and throbbing, the color of white fat and set with barnacles and fungal marine growths. From it grew eel-like ropes and pale coiling tentacles, things like the stinging tendrils of sea anemones and the whips of jellyfish, flanks pitted like coral and honeycombed like the flesh of bryozoans. An absolute monster. Hideous in all respects. Bloated and serpentine, a thing of slobbering blowhole mouths and wide gelid sea-green eyes, slimy and offensive and somehow primeval. It was composed of everything that haunted the sunken ravines and other things you could not imagine. As if life, all life, had sprouted from this chimeric, multiform monstrosity, a seething garden of organic profusion.

And this, then, is how it took the *Ghost* before our eyes:

It rose up and up in a tide of pustulant gray-white flesh, vibrating and creeping and slithering, coming right over the bulwarks as men screamed and ran to and fro. Writhing, steaming coils of the beast spilled over the decks and gargantuan tentacles and fleshy ropes hundreds of feet in length corkscrewed up the fore, main, and mizzenmasts like jungle serpents. It exuded a flood of that pale slime that overflowed the decks and drowned men in its snotty depths. The ship listed badly to port with that incredible weight, creaking and groaning. Spars and yards snapped like sticks, shrouds and rigging collapsing and decks buckling and still more of that colossal, creeping horror came aboard. Those translucent green eyes swept the decks with a raw, primeval hunger. Tentacles and tendrils and clasping crab claws swept men into those slobbering, mewling mouths.

I think all of us on the whaleboat screamed until tears came from our eyes.

But there was nothing to do but turn away or study the horror in detail. I saw as much of the beast as I would ever want to. It had a twisting, bloated worm-like body set with tentacles and spines and claspers and dozens of crawling convoluting appendages. Its flesh was not only extremely white as of corpses, but almost transparent in places so that you could view the workings of the arcane anatomy within. It was protoplasmic, yet chambered and rigid; a mollusk, a crustacean, a monstrous worm. From its sides, rawboned and segmented legs like those of a locust sprouted to assist in pulling its weight aboard. It was, essentially, everything and nothing. Every horror and slimy monstrosity dreamed up by every sailor in his most feverish nightmares since men first plied the sea.

It broke up the *Ghost* like a toy ship thrown together out of sticks and odds and ends. Booms fell and stays snapped. The mizzenmast collapsed completely and then down came the main and foremast with their shrouds and canvas and lines. Her port bulwarks were staved in and the sea filled her holds. About that time, the beast yanked her right over to her chains, so that her port bulwarks touched the waterline and I saw those tentacles sweep the decks clean like brooms sweeping debris into a dustbin: deckhouses, spars and masts, hatchways and lifeboats were shattered into wreckage and swept overboard. And then the decks completely fell in and the ship was literally broken in half and the sea rushed in. There was a rushing, roaring sound, an eruption of bubbles and effervescing foam and the *Ghost* went to her sunken grave in the grips of that monster. There was nothing left to mark her passing but a great whirlpooling vortex and floating debris cast in all directions.

I saw men try to swim away from her only to be yanked down or crushed or ripped asunder by the beast. Two sailors swam madly for a floating yard and a mammoth set of spiked jaws rose up from beneath them and snapped shut like a beartrap, taking them down with a gurgling hiss.

And that is all there is to say on the matter.

There were no survivors and our ship was gone and we were cast far out in the Bering Sea. Our only chance was to row back the way we came, to make for the Aleutians. But after what we had just been through, no one dared move. We sat there in the boat, stock-still, sculpted things, figureheads incapable of motion. The whaleboat drifted, the sea bobbing with the remains of the *Ghost*. It was not until after sundown that we dared move. And it was then that Shwayneeg finally spoke.

He said, "It is said that in the beginning, them ones came from the sky and seeded this world with life. They created the beast to serve of them. And the name of the beast is a forbidden one. No man shall know of it. But we know of him for the beast, he is here. We have seen him."

That's all he said and all he needed to say. Just a myth-cycle of his people as my own people have their own creation myths. Except, perhaps, there was a germ of truth hidden away in that age-old story that was probably handed down father to son orally since the dawn of time.

No matter, we took silently to the oars and the sound, the motion brought the beast. It took Posun and DeKamp first. Then Shornby. Those tentacles slithered into the whaleboat and plucked them away. And then later, it got Shwayneeg. It was pitch black, but I heard him cry out. I heard the rubbery sound of that tentacle as it wound him up, heard it constrict him, his bones shattering like crockery. I felt his hot blood break against my face. That was how my only true friend met his end. Afterward, I lay stunned and shocked and mindless in the bottom of the boat, waiting for my turn, waiting for the tentacle that would smash me to a pulp and drag me down to that puckering oval mouth.

But it never came. I remember the long chill night, the sun coming out, but little else. I was feverish and delusional. My only clear memory is the sound of oars and men's voices, hands taking hold of me and how I fought when they touched me. I was rescued by a boat crew of the *Katherine H.*, a whaling brig out of San Francisco. When I was lucid, I told them my story, but they judged me mad and locked me away for the rest of the journey so the hands would not hear my story.

Yes, they thought me mad as you no doubt do now, too.

No matter. Only understand that when you ask me why it is I will never go to sea again that I have my reasons. And they are, I think, good ones. For there is something that haunts the dark graveyard depths, something from an age beyond time when an unknown race descended from the sky and brought all life into being on this desolate, barren world. And one of the primal things they created from the cold clay is still out there, deathless and ravening, still haunting the depthless stygian canyons and abyssal plains that are a cemetery of skeletal, sunken ships littered with the bones of drowned men. And so I will never go to sea again. I will not be the prey of something that should have died black eons before. For the name of the beast is forbidden and no man shall know it. Ancient and evil, nameless and unnamable, it exists only to suck the sweet marrow from the world.

THE STARS, IN THEIR DREAMING

BY *GERARD HOUARNER*

VERY MORNING WAS LIKE his first at sea, Isham waking to humid, salt tang air, creaking wood, the bell ringing the hour and the watch, the sea lapping at a ship's hull. At least the hammock was long gone. And the food and uniform were better. He'd been one of the few from the enlisted ranks to earn an appointment that afforded quarters and bunk, and the commission had opened doors after he'd left the United States naval service.

He'd gone to sea searching for what it had taken from him. He'd joined the Navy to master the sea with shot and sword, line and sail, and make it give back what he missed like a heart, both eyes and a tongue. He'd seen war at Vera Cruz, and worlds he'd never knew existed in Europe and Japan. He'd worked hard, as much to forget as to conquer.

But he never forgot, nor mastered the sea. And it never gave him what he wanted.

"The sea doesn't give back its dead," his mother had warned. But he'd seen the lie behind her words in bloated corpses floating on the water, battered bodies washed ashore. The sea did return the dead. Just not the one he needed.

Isham sat up in his bunk, rubbed his nose and eyes. The smell from the new deck had gotten worse after picking up the cargo. At least the moans and cries had quieted since the schooner left the Kongo and the continent's interior with the shackled victims of pillage Captain Drummond required.

The smell wouldn't leave him, no matter how much snuff he inhaled, or how long he rubbed and blew and even stopped up his nose. It was worse than anything from a fish market, open sewer or field of battle. It was a living stench, thick with suffering, a choking cloud of despair inhabiting his body, possessing his senses, taking him as far from Ruth's memory as a typhoon wind could take a ship from its true course.

But it was not memory he was searching for.

Isham rose, grateful the sea was at peace with the ship. Soon the bells for his watch would ring. He preferred the night and early morning, getting the ship ready for the Captain. There were always possibilities just before the dawn, in the darkest of night.

Like what might happen if the sun never rose. Would the dead rise from their graves? Would Ruth return to his arms, delivered by his father sailing his boat back to shore? Would his mother finally come down from her Innsmouth window, looking for her men to come home?

So early in the day, the heat had yet to raise the stench of chattel into an invisible, clinging mist that would feel as if it was pulling him down through the lower decks into the water.

The sun had yet to lay bare and naked the wounds of a new day.

Hard tack and molasses. It was enough for him as he dressed, his brisk movements stirring dreams and shadows.

Isham grunted. Buttoned his coat, pressing his fingers hard against metal to anchor himself in the waking world.

The dreams, they wouldn't leave him, but followed from sleep to waking, lurking in the cabin's gloom on the borders of Isham's vision, dancing with shadows born from lantern light as they had since Captain Drummond signed him on, with the Hamite, mumbling his cursed readings from a book filled with Arabic script like a demented priest sending up prayers to a dead god, by his side as a witness.

The dreams were beyond his understanding. At least the foreign wonders he'd experienced in his travels to Asia and Africa had been earthly in their design and origin. Though sometimes he'd screamed and other times felt as if he'd died, the hallucinations and delusions born from absinthe, laudanum and the many other chemistries to which he'd succumbed in his search for solace had dragged him through fears he could trace to his own human soul.

But in the dreams that came to him on *The Marie*, he discovered a sepulchral peace, deeper than anything he'd found in the opium pipe, where no fear or joy could touch him. Visions of slowly moving shapes, gliding, turning, rising like smoke eels and storm cloud whales in the depths of a murky, viscous sea, haunted him. He reached for these creatures, as if to caress them. But they were insubstantial, and like a fisherman without line or bait, he could only watch as they went by. Their wake did pass through Isham, though, touching his mind, his brain, the bones, organs and tissues of his body, manipulating them all by merely containing him for an instant in their swift, unknowing passage. He always felt as if he was changing in the dreams, but into what, he could never tell.

Ruth had always kept him company in his sleep ever since the sea took her, but she had yet to appear in these dreams. But even without the ache of her empty presence, he found no peace in his rest.

Sleeping on Captain Drummond's ship was like descending into a grave, then slipping through that portal between worlds to fall through a vast and silent emptiness to surrender, finally, to the embrace of an unyielding darkness, still and waiting, as if something beneath a great weight of time and distance might stir, and move, and perceive.

And through mere perception, change the fabric of the world.

It was when he was mostly in the waking world that Isham missed Ruth's company, even as a ghostly memory. But the briny aftertaste of the sea after the dreaming hinted at a path through forgetfulness that might take him to his Ruth. That hint of salt made Isham tend to the dreams, stare into the cabin's shadows where they huddled. In the waking world, memories of his ship dreams and of Ruth mingled, and drove him to wish he could sink lower into sleep's depths to find the place to which Ruth might have drifted when she vanished from all human concerns.

He might even discover his father in those dreams, so long lost he hardly remembered him, and drag them both up and out into the waking world, into the sun and onto land, making the sea at last give up its dead.

But he'd happily leave his father behind, and even throw his mother down from her tower to join her husband, if the sea would barter for Ruth.

Madness.

Yes.

But sweet madness, if it brought him closer to his Ruth.

He should never have signed on with Captain Drummond. He should have jumped ship with the sailors making for the African shore rather than spend another night on the ship.

He had rights. The means of escape. He was still sane, of sound mind and body.

Isham's hand hovered over the guard of his sword.

No. He didn't care that the Hamite's witnessing would never stand up in court. Nor was he concerned that the ship had been transformed into a slaver as soon as they reached African waters. He wasn't looking for reasons to break his commitments or even excuse his presence should an American or British warship catch them with their illegal cargo.

He'd known *The Marie* would carry him to his destiny when he'd heard the rumors surrounding the ship and the kind of crew being recruited. Captain Drummond's sad history of his own wife, lost delivering the daughter who then died hours after her birth as if unable to bear the grief of her loss, the guilt of her murderous nativity, had also caught his attention. Unlike Isham and the sea, Captain Drummond had not had the comfort of a nemesis in Nature to distract him from his grief, an enemy to strive against, an objective to conquer. He'd buried the ones he loved, not lost them, and had been left with nothing else but to seek out a purpose to suit and salve his maimed soul.

When Isham first heard of Captain Drummond and *The Marie*, he hadn't been able to tell for true if the name belonged to Drummond's wife or daughter, or if it had some other significance, perhaps to the ship's previous owners. Details about registry and ownership conflicted, with some knotting ties between Drummond and the infamous Lamar and his schooner, *The Wanderer*, or the Wilcox family in Providence and Arkham. And talk of the Captain invariably drifted to liaisons with cults, false prophets, even fearful uprisings, from consultations with Laveau to darker prophecies anchored in the bottomless depths of remote seas spoken in foreign tongues invoking the end of days.

Everyone had a story, from the lowliest mate to the Harbor Master who'd needed a bribe to let *The Marie* slip out to sea in the middle of the night. Isham had been warned.

The warnings had served as a bait. Truth didn't matter. The Hamite, the Captain's strange passion, whatever its source and goal, the dreams, even the stench and the mismatched quilt of a crew were all part of a great and steady wind that filled his own sails with hope.

The Captain understood loss. The maddening ache drove him as hard as it did Isham. They might have been brothers—there was salt enough in the tears they shared, the blood they'd spilled, and in the ocean that held the secrets of their salvation.

He'd had a feeling Drummond would take him far from the fields he knew, where at last he might find his Ruth.

The bell rang the hour and the watch.

Isham stood before his cabin door.

From below, a scream broke the calm of midnight water. The surgeon had at last started up his practice—no, the scream was short; the boatswain was at it again.

He called out to God, but He did not answer.

He called out to Ruth, but it was the sea that answered for her.

He stepped out on to the deck just like it was his first time on the water, his prayers spoken and ignored, ready to follow in the paths of those he'd lost.

The old mate was still awake and in the rigging, staring into the cloudless sky. The moon had already set, and the stars were out in a blazing encampment. Usually, the mate kept quiet, hiding his hands as he stared at the horizon or at the spaces between the stars, as if waiting for the treasure ship of his secret pleasures to appear. He never slept, but always seemed lost in his own dreams even in the most savage of storms. He might have had much in common with the Captain, or even Isham, but he never spoke of what haunted him. His age and quiet demeanor didn't stop him from working hard, or fulfilling his appetites with what fell to hand until he found the ship for which he waited.

Isham knew the type from his childhood and early years at sea.

"It's still up there," the old man said. The ocean nearly swallowed up his words, as it did the starlight.

Isham looked up without meaning to, forgetting his officer's bearing. The star had appeared after they rounded the Cape, doubling the blow of the unexpected turn their trip had taken. When signing on, they'd all been told they were picking up cargo bound for Cuba. Most understood they were getting involved in the trade. But after filling the pens, the Captain had taken them down the coast for South Africa, where they were told illegal mining operations needed labor. Now the story the Hamite weaved was of Zanzibar and the Sultanate's incredible offer for their cargo, though they'd left the African coast behind them and experienced crew whispered no such offer was possible with slaves plentiful from overland routes.

The mystery of their destination was wearing at the bedrock of trust in Captain Drummond and his promise of top wages. But it was the star that was making them all feel cold and quiet.

The star had remained fixed in the sky ever since it first appeared, dim, red, nameless. At first the men had laughed at the notion of an object that wouldn't follow the constellations and the moon and all the rest making their journey across the sky. The Captain and the Hamite offered no reassurances. And then, with each passing night, the star had grown brighter, larger, like a fiery cannon ball discharged from the other side of the world hurtling down on them.

Or like a beacon, drawing them closer to a strange and distant shore where all demands and questions would crash against the sharp and secret rocks of their fulfillment.

"Yes," Isham acknowledged, sighting the star without effort and confirming its presence as if noting the anomaly for the ship's log.

"Hasn't moved."

"No."

The old mate had nothing more to say. He might have been another furled sail bound tightly to the yard.

Isham was glad for the reprieve.

The chaplain was up early, though there hadn't been a service for the crew since the ship had put out to sea. No one wanted one. The Captain, he'd been told once, had signed a chaplain for the sake of any souls that might be found among the cargo. More than once, he'd been told it was the chaplain who'd helped back the trip, for the sake of his own discussions on sin with the Lord.

He climbed out of the hold, heaved himself on to the deck like a crippled walrus. Dipped his hands in a tub of the wash water. Went forward, following his habit of blessing the way ahead and informing God of *The Marie*'s progress, in case God had forgotten to notice.

The boatswain followed almost immediately. His duty of inspecting the rigging took him past Isham. He stopped for a moment, turned to Isham, and whispered, "They have names, sir. The chattel, they have names."

He giggled, which turned his hard-edged, furrowed face of bone and scar, speckled by blood, into an open, festering sore.

"Clean yourself up," Isham barked. The boatswain jumped and acknowledged the order, but Isham couldn't tell if there'd been a smirk thrown in for good measure. They'd already had an exchange about the boatswain's habits in the pens. Isham had been concerned about lost cargo eating into the profit, but Captain Drummond had ordered him not to bother the few men who found entertainment below.

"There's three hundred down there," the Captain had said. "A hundred will do, I think. The trip will take a good number, I'm afraid, but even with that there's enough to go around for everyone's needs."

Isham, torn between two questions, asked the one most relevant to finding his Ruth: "A hundred will do for what, sir?"

"Captain's business," Drummond had replied, closing the book on any further inquiries.

So the chaplain and the boatswain, and a few others, made their way down to the new deck, and every week or two, another body had to be brought up and tossed overboard. The surgeon watched. Isham didn't know what he was waiting for.

The practices below-deck seemed to make the star weigh less heavily on the crew members who preferred not to spend the night in the yard arms watching the sky. And perhaps, for the survivors, one less meant more room and comfort for the passage.

Isham couldn't tell. He never went to the pens. He feared the stench alone might kill him.

There were shapes in the clouds casting shadows on the sugar-loaf sea.

The chop was fiercest when the ship fell out of sunlight, into the jaws of the shadow shapes. Twice a squall had blown in from nowhere and spun the ship around, sending all hands into the rigging to save the sails. They were odd clouds, portents of their fate. Most of the crew looked away, ruminating among themselves about the weather's fickleness.

Isham recognized shapes in their billowing from his childhood. They were like old friends.

When Ruth was very young, Isham would take her out to ride their horses through the marshes around Innsmouth, and into the hills to find a view of the sea and the clouds. These were the happiest days of their lives, with hours of freedom from his mother's grieving over her drowned husband and Ruth's rapacious father, always lurking by the docks for an opportunity to take advantage of misfortune. Isham had been hired by Ruth's father to be her tutor, as a way for him to buy his way into the favor of Isham's mother. The money was needed, and Isham had quickly discovered the light Ruth brought to his fog-bound spirit. Her father thought so little of Ruth, he never thought of her as anything but the woman he wanted her to become. He gave no thought to Isham at all.

In the hills, they'd find a field and lay on their backs while the horses grazed on dandelions and sweet grass. He had her recite the *Iliad* and the *Odyssey*, passages from the Bible and the rules of etiquette for the young lady she would soon become. They even worked with numbers and explored history, though her father was more interested in her developing into the kind of safe and marketable commodity he could sell to the young and well-connected captains putting into port.

Isham carried her books when they walked in town, though he had no use for books. He was a man of action. A conqueror.

The cloud shapes they identified took them to far off lands where gods and goddesses looked down on mortals, where armies clashed and castles fell, and where beasts enacted all the laws of the natural world. The clouds took them far over the sea, beyond their bodies and their years.

They both learned lessons. For Isham, they were pleasurable. For Ruth, apparently, she learned too quickly the limitations that were to define her life. She would have no choices in who she gave her heart to, no freedom to make her own way through the world.

She learned her time with Isham was as much an iron bilbo as her duty to her father.

She could have brought shame to Isham, to her own father, by revealing all that she'd seen, heard, done, in her young life.

Instead, she gave herself to the sea. And it took her.

And never returned her body.

Isham stared at the clouds as *The Marie* rocked and bucked like a wild horse in the sudden rough water. He gave out orders and made the ship secure, but never took his eyes from the clouds, where he could see Ruth's face looking down on him, smiling, her eyes deep, dark hollows promising forgiveness, inviting him closer, granting permission at long last for all that he ever wished from her.

The clouds, they were old friends. They would never betray him.

When the sea had calmed once more and the sun was setting, the Hamite led the Captain out, because his eyes were sewn shut and he could no longer see, and tied him to the wheel as if he were Jason steering the ship past the Sirens.

The crew murmured, stopped work, shouted in protest. A few wept.

Their guiding star appeared in the evening sky, piercing the thin cloud cover. Isham felt its presence before he sighted it.

The sound of splashing turned a few heads to the water, where a shark broke the surface, embraced by a squid. The struggling pair vanished beneath the waves.

Isham brushed the Hamite aside and grabbed the Captain's forearm. "Sir?" he said, all his questions bundled in the syllable.

"The currents and winds shift," Captain Drummond said, facing forward, never bothering to turn to the sound of Isham's voice. "The dead stars lie. The world is changing. But I'll steer us through the chaos. I know where our journey must end."

Isham didn't dare repeat the Captain's words to the crew. Instead, he barked orders, and the men scrambled to obey, choosing the routine safety of command over madness.

"Think they'll mutiny?" the surgeon asked, appearing suddenly by Isham's side, absently working on a piece of scrimshaw with a small, thick, sharp blade. "I never worked a pirate vessel, before."

"Get to your station," Isham said. "You might be needed before the night's over."

"I have no doubt of that." The surgeon smiled, bowed his head, and made his way below. To the pens.

The scrimshaw he dropped on the deck hurt Isham's eyes when he glanced at it.

Another star appeared in the sky beside their red companion, this one blue and glittering like a diamond. Together, the stars drew them on, and filled their sails with dreams.

The days passed quickly after the Captain took the wheel. For Isham, it seemed only an hour passed between sunrise and sunset.

The crew bustled to preserve their sole shield against a sea whose mystery had suddenly deepened. Isham checked their position, but the chronometer had failed, and the almanac lied. Or perhaps the stars and moon proved unreliable.

There was no turning back.

For the first time in all his years at sea, dread claimed Isham's spirit. He'd tried to conquer the sea and make it surrender what it had taken, but had never felt so defeated as when he saw Captain Drummond steering the ship blind, the Hamite standing beside him reading from the Arabic text.

Then he thought of Ruth, and his heart leapt and his stomach bubbled just like the first time he'd seen her in her father's house. There was his hope, his own vision by which to navigate.

"I'm on my way, Ruth," he whispered to the stars.

The cries and howls from the pens troubled Isham's sleep more than the dreams, but it was the chanting the chattel had taken up that kept him from getting any rest at all.

"What is it that they say?" he asked the Hamite when he came on to his watch. "Is it some kind of native plea for help?"

"These people sing of life, birth, the glory of harvest, the sadness of death," the Hamite said, his voice hoarse and cracked. "Their cry now has nothing to do with the lives they left, only with what waits to embrace them."

"And what is that? What kind of master are we selling them to?"

"One who can grant us all freedom and eternal life, and the power to fulfill our every desire."

"Is that what your book tells you?"

"Not the book," the Hamite said, tapping his ear. "It is the voice I listen to that holds all our promises."

Isham walked away. He hardly noticed the stench from the pens anymore.

Another immoveable star appeared, ten degrees closer to the horizon than the other two.

It seemed to Isham that the moon itself was fading, along with the stars he knew.

It also seemed that there were less men on board, and that the surgeon, chaplain and boatswain were spending all their time below.

The cargo no longer had a voice.

"Captain?" Isham said, standing behind Drummond. The Hamite lay collapsed at the Captain's feet, blood seeping from his open mouth. Isham had already taken his book and thrown it overboard.

"R'lyeh follows the stars, so you must to follow them, too," the Captain said. "Sail until they align and you will find–"

"Sir, I can't navigate in these waters."

"The stars, in their dreaming, will guide us to the dreamer. See what the living stars show you. Why do you think I closed my eyes?" The Captain laughed.

Isham felt chills go up his spine at the sound. Several of the crew looked to him as if for reassurance, then turned quickly away.

Captain Drummond pulled out a pocket watch and held the instrument up. The hands were frozen, though the mechanism still ticked, just like Isham's own timepiece. "Mathematics, astronomy, time, they're all useless here, now, a hundred million years ago or another hundred million years in the future." He heaved the watch overboard.

Isham heard a second, louder splash, as if a crew member had jumped ship going after the watch.

"Sir, a hundred million years doesn't make sense, the Bible says—"

"My friend, there are many bibles."

Isham remembered why he'd approached the Captain. "Sir, the stores are spoiling. Something's growing in the brine, the pork is worm-ridden, even the hard tack's crumbling. Half the men are on sick call from the water. We need to put in for supplies."

"Something below us waits."

Isham thought of Ruth. His nerves steadied. "Does it want us?"

"It doesn't want anything. We're the ones that desire."

"Ruth," Isham whispered, startling himself. Tears burned his eyes.

"Not too much longer, now," Captain Drummond said. "Very soon."

Isham found the old mate tangled in and hanging from the fancy lines. His trousers had come off, revealing a bloody gash between his legs. His eyes were gone.

Isham cut the lines himself and let the body fall in dark water.

The rest of the crew had grown listless. Even the voice of command failed to stir them. A few were bandaged, or wore their stitched wounds proudly like Polynesian tattoos. They'd come up from the pens, where Isham knew the surgeon was holding court.

He heard them talking below about dreaming, changing, becoming. The surgeon promised so much.

Isham fought the temptation to ask him about Ruth, to see if the surgeon might find his love in the apparently malleable flesh of sailors and bring her back to him.

But he was afraid she'd come back to him with bulging eyes or the odd webbing the surgeon favored between his subjects' fingers, and consoled himself with the promise of what was yet to come.

The Captain anchored *The Marie* off of Ponape Island, and Isham took a boat in for supplies. Three of the four men who came with him vanished. Only the boatswain accompanied him back with the barrels of fresh water and fruit they'd collected.

Isham had the boatswain turn over the clay shards they'd found marked with pictures of towers and other things too difficult for the eye to study. He smashed the shards with a block on the deck and almost broke through the deck boarding in his fury.

The sky filled with bright stars that never moved, until it seemed as if the ship was stranded in a cave from whose ceiling creatures hung and stared, their eyes glittering and remote, studying the water and waiting for what lay below to rise.

Cold fire danced in the upper rigging at night, and shapes swooped against the night sky, their dark gliding forms outlined against the peering stars.

Sailors writhed on the deck, even the ones who still had limbs.

Isham stayed forward, shouting Ruth's name into the darkness.

He refused to sleep, afraid he might never wake.

"Captain?" Isham said.

The boatswain and surgeon, along with a few crew members carrying swords and firearms, were watching a line of shackled men, women and children come up from the pens and quietly throw themselves into the sea.

"What if you could enslave an angel, or a devil?" Captain Drummond said. "What if you could dredge up a sleeping giant and put it in chains, and let its power make your world whole?"

"How?"

"Tempt it. Lure it. Like a fish, with worm meat."

The slaves never looked up or at each other. They were already dead, and made almost no sound when they jumped into the ocean, except for the rattling of their bondage.

The chaplain stood off to the side, weeping. "Their souls are saved," he repeated, rocking from side to side.

Isham went to stand beside him, so that his chanting of Ruth's name might mingle with the chaplain's prayers and both receive a blessing.

He caught the slaves after they'd come back, their chains gone, cutting down the Captain and throwing the surgeon, chaplain and boatswain overboard.

They could have waited. *The Marie* was listing to port, taking on water.

The women, their faces scarred as a defense against being taken, and the children were hauling off the remains of the crew too maimed or weak to fight them off.

One of the intact sailors found strength to climb into the rigging and shriek.

Isham drew his sword and stood in the way of the band carrying Captain Drummond. He noticed their hands and feet had taken on webbing, and their eyes glistened by the alien starlight with the flash of extra, transparent lids. To his surprise, they were alive.

"What master do you serve?" he asked them.

They answered him in their own tongue, but he heard, as if he was dreaming, another set of words: "We serve our dreams."

"But you're not free," Isham replied.

"Neither are you," came the answer. "But we do not belong to you. Someday we will return to our homeland. But not before we visit yours."

They dragged the Captain past him. A child stopped and took his sword. Two women followed carrying a limbless sailor's torso. He lived, though his empty eyes opened on to the harrowed landscape within him.

Isham noticed the stench of *The Marie*'s cargo was gone, at last. He had nothing left to fear.

A woman approached him. At first, he saw only black skin and scars on her cheek. Her ribs and bones showed and her breasts sagged from privation.

But by starlight, she changed, as if shedding false skin to reveal her true self.

Isham cried out.

She held out her arms.

"I'm sorry . . .." Isham said, falling to his knees.

She whispered to him, and his dreams told him she offered only comfort, not recrimination.

"Ruth," he called out.

She took him by the hand into the sea.

The next morning, Isham woke from a dream into a day like no other he'd ever lived.

DEPTH OF DARKNESS

BY *WILLIAM JONES*

"Order and reason, beauty and benevolence, are characteristics and conceptions which we find solely associated with the mind of man."
—Karl Pearson, *The Grammar of Science*

IT WAS REPULSIVE—NOT AT all what Jason Webb had expected. An iciness formed in his gut as he entered the main lab, gazing at the gigantic shard hauled from the depths of the Atlantic.

The enormous stone rested in the center of a modern metal cavern that spanned nearly half the length of the ship's main deck. Nestled along the lab's dull gray walls were monitors, benches, sinks, freezers and an array of instrumentation.

"This is astounding," Carolyn Cox said, trailing Jason. She was a marine archeologist and leader of the second science team aboard the research vessel *Eris*. She stepped through the hatchway, and with a push of her rangy frame, snapped the bulkhead door closed.

"And this is only the first specimen," she continued. Carolyn was clad in khaki shorts, deck shoes, and a Danforth Institute tee-shirt, her sandy-blond hair pulled into a knot behind her head.

"I think it's ugly," Jason said.

"You would."

Jason pulled a cart burdened with monitoring equipment from its stowage space and pushed it toward the harness platform. The semi-rectangular slab stood nearly twelve feet high in the mounting harness, almost reaching the ceiling. It glistened as though still wet, and an unending series of inscriptions covered its surface. The ragged edges revealed that it was part of something larger.

Carolyn clanked up the platform, halting before the slab. She ran a palm along its surface. "It feels and looks like polished obsidian, but that isn't possible. It must be some form of metamorphic rock." She shifted around the artifact. "I see what appears to be crystal inside it. And these inscriptions—" she traced the arabesque patterns with a finger— "they are extremely intricate and possess a fine texturing in the grooves. A bit like sgraffito."

"It's the writing that gets me," Jason said. "I can't seem to focus on those symbols. It's like they are wiggling or something." He unrolled several cables with suction cups attached to their ends.

"You don't have your sea legs yet," Carolyn said.

"The legs are fine. It's the eyes that have the trouble." Jason climbed the platform and pushed the suction cups onto the black, glassy surface. The result looked like an electronic squid had attacked the artifact.

"I wish they had let us examine it before it was cleaned," Carolyn said sharply. "It might have been possible to use hydration dating if we could develop a profile. Being in the ocean would present difficulties, but . . ."

"The primary team didn't clean it," Eric Lerner announced at the base of the stairway that descended from the upper lab. "Dr Gregson took samples for dating purposes. Otherwise, the artifact is in the condition we found it."

"That can't be," Carolyn said, shuffling past Jason. "The surface shows no erosion or even underwater growth of any kind."

"Its present state is the same as when we found it on the ocean floor. A mystery Dr Gregson is working on," Lerner said.

Lerner was the Danforth Institute liaison and expedition manager. From the start, Jason had disliked him. They were from different worlds. Or, maybe Jason just didn't belong in Lerner's world. Working class kids didn't go to universities to become researchers. Paying for his education had been an unending battle, but it had been a dream worth fighting for—or so he'd thought. Still, it all came easily to Lerner. A choice of schools, followed by a pick of jobs. Yet, to Jason, it seemed Lerner hadn't found pleasure in any of it. He seldom smiled, and seemed incapable of laughing.

Early on, Jason had dubbed Lerner "the plastic man," because he always looked the same. Even after three weeks at sea, the wiry man appeared every day in a sports coat, slacks, and loafers.

Lerner set his gaze on Carolyn. "I want your team–"

"You mean the two of us?" Jason interjected.

"I want your team," Lerner continued, slowly, ignoring Jason, "to focus on the inscriptions and provide answers about the low frequency electromagnetic radiation emissions."

"Working on the V-L-F-E-M-R," Jason said. He loved spitting alphabet at Lerner. He flipped switches on the data recorder, jabbing keys.

Carolyn turned toward the artifact. "My team? Bryan was the last, our geologist, and you reassigned him."

"Resources are limited out here," Lerner said flatly. "Adapt."

A heavy sigh escaped her. "Some of the markings resemble cuneiform—very different from the other inscriptions, and they are crude constructions. My guess is that they are probably graffiti added at a later date. As for the rest, if it's a language and not artistic patterns, it is something completely new."

"I'd imagine so," Lerner said, stepping forward, gazing at the object that once rested over three thousand feet below the Atlantic Ocean. His lips compressed into a tight smile.

He turned to Carolyn, and said matter-of-factly, "The prelim dating places the artifact at three billion years."

Jason preferred working in the science labs on the platform deck. Sure, the rooms were compact, and crowded with equipment, but they were private. That was something he'd come to miss. That and a steady floor.

The *Eris* handled the ocean well. But it wasn't like the solid pavement of Brooklyn where he'd grown up. In Wiliamsburg, he'd spent summers watching the ships move across the Upper Bay, entering and leaving the naval yard. He'd never imagined he would end up working as a computer scientist for a private research institute on board a ship. Jason liked small boats and swimming. Any fondness he had for the deep ocean was quickly washing away. Each time he hit land, he vowed never to return.

"Do you ever get tired of just sitting on the bench and watching the game?" he asked.

"You mean always getting second priority?" Carolyn said. She was seated at an electron microscope, gazing into twin eyepieces.

"Yeah," he said, spinning the swivel chair toward her. "That and the way everyone acts. Once we located the site, a cloud of secrecy fell over everything. And now everyone on Gregson's team ignores us, including Bryan."

Carolyn adjusted the microscope, twisting several dials before throwing her hands in the air. "This thing needs calibrating. I can't get a clear image of the sample." Leaning back, she faced Jason. "You know the institute's research is mostly compartmentalized. When you're in close quarters, all of the rules and procedures are amplified. Besides, Lerner is always hanging around. So no one wants be reprimanded for breach of protocol."

"Or maybe it's the gun toting guards he's placed everywhere."

Carolyn shook her head. "We're in international waters. That artifact makes the *Eris* a nice target for pirates."

"Pirates are the least of my worries," Jason said, laughing. "I guess I always expect it to be different out *here*. We're on an ocean, not in some sprawling city, and everyone seems far too serious."

"This isn't a vacation, Jason. The work we're doing is important—and serious."

He inclined his head. "*Important*? Are we doing something important? I don't know about you, but most of the time I feel left in the dark. Look at the data I collected from the artifact. It's worthless. I get bits of EM radiation, but the signals keep dropping out." He pointed to a series of lines scrolling across a monitor. Several peaked and oscillated, then formed straight traces. "I could see maybe one sensor failing, but not all of them acting intermittently."

"Could be the saltwater," Carolyn said. "It corrodes equipment quickly."

"Don't think so. Everything is sealed in rubber. Besides, the few measurements I did get are useless. The amplitudes are too low. I placed sensors directly on the artifact, and still the signals are too attenuated to get a quality measurement. It's not the equipment failing."

Carolyn's eyes fixed on him. For a moment, it seemed as if there were a warning in them. "You're saying that it would be impossible for a surface vessel to *hear* the artifact's pulses?"

"At the depth we found it, yes. But Lerner claims it was the pulse that helped the last expedition locate the site. Someone's holding back information. I can't do *serious* work without facts."

For several moments Carolyn perched on her chair in silence. The *whoosh* of the ventilation system filled the room. Finally, she said, "Either it was detected like Lerner says, or someone had a treasure map to what appears to be an object that existed on this planet before humans did."

"You buy that three billion year date?" Jason said.

Carolyn turned and snugged the electron microscope eyepiece to her head. "The stone might be that old. However, the inscriptions could have been placed there last week. One doesn't prove the other. We need to examine it again."

A cold knot formed in Jason's stomach when he returned to the main lab. The air felt oppressive and heavy.

He skidded across the decking, trying to remain upright. During the night, a storm had moved in, bringing with it large swells that rocked the *Eris*.

"Looks like you skipped breakfast too," he said to Carolyn. She steadied herself against the artifact's harness frame.

"It's not the weather," she replied. "I wanted to get several rubbings of the surface, and Gregson has the lab scheduled for most of the day." As she spoke, she moved a cake of rubbing wax over paper taped to the stone's surface. Jason recognized the strange pattern forming in the wax's green residue.

Without fully knowing why, he suddenly uttered, "That won't work." The words, or rather the thought, came unbidden. He spouted it offhandedly, as if it were some bit of knowledge he'd stowed away years ago and it had suddenly broken loose. Doing so sent chills scurrying across his flesh.

"I'm also taking photographs," Carolyn said. "I use the rubbings because they capture the texture."

As he approached, the revulsion he'd felt previously returned, intensifying. It wasn't from the ship's motion; it was a growing trepidation he sensed when near the artifact.

"I don't mean that." Jason now stood next to her, hanging onto the framing. Thoughts with the feel of memories lurked at the edge of his mind, slippery and dark. "There's something more here," he said hesitantly. "Can you feel it?" His words were driven by ideas alien to him. "It's like the markings extend into other senses. Maybe into other dimensions."

Carolyn stopped sliding the wax across the paper and faced Jason.

"Don't give me that look," he said. "Let's go with the theory that the markings on this thing are nearly three billion years old . . ."

"So today you're not a skeptic?"

"That's around the time when life first appeared on Earth," he continued, trying to keep pace with his thoughts. "If that's true, then whatever made it wasn't human. Why would they be limited to our five senses?"

A wave crashed against the *Eris*, momentarily painting the starboard portholes white. The ship's engines groaned, laboring against the storm.

"That's a big assumption premised on a big assumption," Carolyn said.

The fore bulkhead door swung open. Water splashed through the threshold, followed by a guard draped in a yellow slicker. The bulky man sealed the door and stamped his boots on the floor. The sound seemed hollow against the roar of the surrounding storm.

"Lerner wants the lab guarded at all times," Carolyn said softly. "Maybe you were right. Some of us seem to be in the dark."

"I think there's more to it," Jason said. "Lerner knows something we don't. But I don't think he understands what this stone really is."

Diaphanous thoughts whirled through Jason's mind, occasionally solidifying, other times drifting away. He took a long, slow breath in an attempt to focus.

From behind, he heard the guard shrug off the slicker.

"Our equipment doesn't work on the stone because only part of it is in our dimension," Jason said. He struggled to slow the stream of knowledge flowing through his mind, mingling it with his own when possible. "And what we take for inscriptions are just some sort of . . . side effect. A perception problem. In our dimension they look like markings. But they're not."

Carolyn dropped the cake of wax into a bucket hanging on the frame. It swayed with the ship. "How do you know all of this?" she said, her face tightened in confusion.

"I don't. I think I'm getting it from the artifact—flashes, ideas."

"You can read it?" Her voice had an edge.

"Not 'read' in the sense we think of," he said. "Maybe I've *tuned* into it or something like we do with the ship's wireless network. I don't know. It could be some people are more sensitive to it. There isn't a concept that fits. All I know is that my mind is catching glimpses of something too big to understand. And it feels wrong."

Suddenly, as though struck by lightning, a stream of unrelenting images surged through Jason's mind. His head filled with fire; thoughts burned as they passed through his consciousness. *Things*, creatures inhuman, horrors beyond his comprehension solidified in his thoughts. Gigantic beings with barrel-like shapes and snaking appendages and dread eyes coalesced.

For an eternal moment scenes unfurled, ideas corrupted by a monstrous foulness. Then, as abruptly as it had started, it stopped.

The heavy *thrum* of the engines pulled Jason from his dazed state. His eyes focused on Carolyn. She lay curled on the platform, arms wrapped around her knees, shaking.

He crawled to her. She whispered words, alien sounding.

"Carolyn," he murmured. "Push it away."

The whispering faded, leaving only her lips to give shape to the inhuman language. Jason pressed a hand against her forehead. "Come back," he said gently. "Come back."

With a start her eyes shot wide. Quickly she scrambled to her feet, dropping against the framing. Jason followed, wrapping his arms around her.

"It's just me," he said.

When she'd stopped trembling, he let her slip from his embrace. For a long moment she gazed into the distance, eyes glazed.

"Carolyn?"

Her pupils widened. "Did you . . . *feel* that?" she asked. "Those *thoughts*."

Jason nodded. "I think we just read the artifact. Or at least part of it."

"No-no . . . that can't be," Carolyn stuttered. She glanced at the giant stone. "It would make those creatures the progenitors of life on this planet. Everything would be stained with their malignance. That's not possible."

A retching came from the far side of the lab. Jason followed the sound, already knowing what to expect. His head ached, and terror tightened in his chest.

The guard continued to purge his stomach until the sound became a sickening hack.

"We need to leave," Jason said, nudging Carolyn down the platform steps. "Get to the bridge."

Even though he didn't fully understand it, parts of what he'd sensed started to take shape. Life on the planet wasn't a happenstance of nature. It had been brought here.

The guard climbed to his feet, eyes dark, black half circles painted beneath them. Raw hatred twisted his face.

"Move!" Jason yelled, dragging Carolyn to the starboard door.

The guard bolted forward, making a sound that was part scream and part hiss.

Carolyn yanked the handle. Wind and water blew through the portal. Beyond, bruised clouds moiled in the sky, and gigantic waves pushed the *Eris* across the surface.

Gripping the frame, Carolyn pulled herself onto the slippery deck. As Jason stepped forward, the guard tackled him. The momentum carried both men through the opening.

The two tumbled against the railing. Cold water lapped at the deck, splashing high. A hacking cough sounded in the rushing wind as the man clawed at Jason with steely fingers like talons.

Jason swung. His fist glanced off the man's jaw. The guard tore at Jason's chest and throat, a frenzy of motion.

Carolyn appeared behind the guard, tugging at his water-soaked shirt. She jerked back, a .45 pistol high in her hand. Screaming, she slammed the weapon against his skull. The man tumbled to the deck.

Bracing against the railing, Carolyn stared through Jason. Her once gentle, delicate eyes now seemed to be forged from rage. A curtain of water folded over her, yet her pale hands held tight to both gun and railing.

"Let's get to the bridge," Jason yelled above the booming waves. Slowly he tugged the pistol from her grip. With his other hand, he grabbed her arm. The two ambled forward, climbing to the third deck.

The bridge ran nearly the width of the ship, ending at both sides with open-air observation wings. Square, sloping windows framed the front and sides, with wipers pushing away water—more spouted over the bow in glistening sheets, dousing the view after each swipe. Anchored below the forward windows was a panel filled with displays, gauges, controls and telephones.

Two doorways flanked the rear of the bridge, one on each side: the radio room and the chart room. A cushioned bench pressed against the back, with windows above, giving a view of the main lab and an enormous crane. A stairwell divided the aft windows.

Water pooled at their feet as they stood in the empty bridge.

"Don't tell me everyone jumped ship," Jason said. He shuffled along the helm, grabbing handsets one after another. Each was dead. Carolyn remained behind, swaying with the *Eris*.

"Are you with me?" he said. Returning to her, he placed his hands on her shoulders.

"If you mean, *am I going to kill you?*" she said. "No." Pulling free, she settled on the bench. "But *you'd* better keep the gun either way." She stared distantly at the floor. "For a second," she said softly, "I *did* want to kill him."

"That wasn't you," Jason said, remembering the terror and hatred that had filled his mind. He hefted the semi-automatic pistol. It felt unfamiliar and reassuring.

The ship pitched as it cut through hollows and swells. On the horizon, heavy water formed ridges with white caps joining a distant, dark sky.

"The artifact stirred something in us," Carolyn said, still rocking with the ship's motion. "I'm not sure that man was still human."

"He was," Jason said. "I think the artifact hit everyone on board—a broadcast or something. Who knows what's going on now. It's like it downloaded some information, or activated a sleeping program."

Lights flashed on the ship's helm. An amber line circled on the radar console, revealing scattered dots. Jason had no idea what it meant.

"We have to find the Captain," he said. "The ship seems to be on some kind of auto-pilot, but I don't think it's smart enough to navigate a storm."

He moved to the stairwell, stopping. "Stay here. I'm just checking the wardroom."

Carolyn nodded.

The area seemed lavish compared to other sections of the ship. Wood paneled walls surrounded a rectangular conference table, bar, couch and television. Aft stood a metal hatch, leading to the second deck and the upper lab. To the right was the Captain's quarters. A muffled voice sounded from the stateroom.

Jason sneaked across the carpeted floor. He pressed his ear against the door, holding his breath. Two muted voices came from within.

Steadying himself, Jason kicked. The frame splintered, and the door slammed open.

Captain Hall sat in a cloth-covered chair. Eric Lerner slumped on a bed, handcuffed to the frame. His form lolled back and forth as though in a drunken stupor.

"You knock on doors around here," Captain Hall said sluggishly. He raised a revolver. "Anything else can get you shot."

Lerner laughed, a raspy bark. "They have awakened us from our dream," he said, his words thick and slow. "Our gods call to us. They call to *you*."

Hall lowered the revolver. "Do you know what he's going on about?" A nearly dead bottle of scotch was anchored in a holder on a low table next to the Captain.

"That's for me," Captain Hall said, following Jason's eyes. Gesturing at Lerner with the revolver, he added, "I gave that loon a shot of sodium amytal from the med-locker, for all the good it's done."

"We've fooled ourselves," Lerner continued. "Civilization, advancement, progress. Humanity believes in those dreams. Dreams bred into us . . . we are slaves to the Elder Ones."

"Can you make sense of it?" Hall asked.

Jason shook his head. "Not really. But I think he knows more about what's going on than anyone else."

Jason's heart hammered in his chest. He pressed the pistol against his leg, fingers damp. "I'm sure we could figure it out if we get to port," he added hopefully.

"No crew left," Hall said, dropping the gun to his lap. He grabbed the bottle by the neck and emptied it in one gulp. "There's no GPS," he coughed. "No radio. Don't know where we are."

"We move from place to place—progress!" Lerner stammered. "In the end we die with nothing . . . for nothing! Our gods made life disposable."

A low rumble echoed throughout the *Eris*. The vibration carried through the floor.

"Someone's at the crane," Hall said. "That won't do."

Hall grabbed the revolver and shot Lerner. The man's head snapped back. The report shook the cabin. Reflexively, Jason raised the pistol.

Without a word, Hall shot himself.

Gore splattered along the walls; dark lines of blood raced to the floor.

Jason stumbled backward, a numbing blackness swaddling his mind, obscuring the world. In a void, he drifted, replaying memories that were not his—that were not human. An infinite abyss convulsed before him, squirming and twisting, uniting into a vile scene reaching back to an unfathomable time, where alien creatures created and destroyed life, using and discarding it with cold indifference.

He felt a distant tug, a touch. The world returned with a roar.

"Come on!" Carolyn yelled.

A hard hammering sounded at the aft hatch. From the ship's bowels came the low groan of metal rending.

"They're tearing everything apart," Carolyn said frantically.

The ship dipped to port as though something had grabbed and heaved it. Jason crashed against the wall. Carolyn landed next to him. With a lurch the ship righted itself. The growling engines choked and died. Yellow emergency lights flicked on.

"We have to get off this ship," Jason said.

"Give me the gun." Carolyn eyed him coldly. Her soaked clothes clung to her frame; thick strands of hair spilled over her shoulders.

"No." Jason's finger tightened on the trigger. The muscles in his abdomen constricted as he moved toward the bridge.

The lever on the aft hatch rattled.

Then Jason followed Carolyn's eyes to the Captain's quarters.

"I didn't do that," he said. "But if we stay here, we'll end up like them."

A squealing came from the hatch as though someone were prying at it with a crowbar. Carolyn ignored the sound, cocking her head upward.

"You were right," she said hoarsely. "I should've said something before. Lerner knew about this *thing* long before we'd found it. He'd been searching for years. The institute had records about a lost city. I . . . I just never believed it. There are too many tales of Atlantis and sunken cities. I figured it was just another legend."

The hatch crashed open, and a loathsome, slouching shape dashed through, eyes wild, face contorted in a vicious mask.

Jason fired three shots in rapid succession. At least one hit the mark, sending the man reeling backward. He hit the floor with a heavy thump, convulsing, spitting blood.

An acid rage burned through Jason's body, pumped by a jackhammer heart. From a shadowy place inside, a primitive craving urged him to hunt down the others. *To kill each of them.*

Carolyn stepped forward. "We can't let that stone be found."

He sucked in deep lungfuls of air as a pressure built up inside his chest. Rage welled. Suddenly he bent over, vomiting in heaving gasps, a fist squeezing his stomach until nothing was left, until the seething anger vanished.

There was a darkness in humanity, Jason now understood. A darkness unfathomable. It was ancient, and alien, and ran so deep . . . so deep that there was a hope it would be forgotten. He let the pistol slip from his hand.

"The *Eris* won't survive this storm," he said, rising. "But maybe we can."

Quickly, they stumbled up the stairs to the bridge. Lights on the helm flashed and buzzers sounded. The ship rolled back and forth, caught in the grip of the storm.

When Jason stepped onto the bridge wing, wind and rain pelted him. Water churned below.

From a stowage locker, he retrieved a nylon bag. He loosened the drawstrings, and with a heave, he cast it into the air. The ripcord in his hand jerked, and the inflatable raft began to expand as it dropped to the ocean.

He clasped Carolyn's hand. Together they jumped from the *Eris*.

ABOUT THE CONTRIBUTORS

MATTHEW BAUGH lives in the greater Chicago area with his wife, Mary and two cats. He is a great fan of pirate movies old and new (except for the one by Roman Polanski). Unfortunately seasickness makes him unsuitable for the pirate's life so he writes stories and serves as the pastor of a church.

TIM CURRAN lives in Michigan and is the author of the novels *Hive* and *Dead Sea* from Elder Signs Press. ESP will also be publishing the next two volumes of the *Hive* trilogy. His short stories have appeared in such magazines as *City Slab*, *Dark Wisdom*, and *Inhuman*, as well as anthologies such as *Horrors Beyond*, *Shivers IV*, and *Hardboiled Cthulhu*.

LINDA DONAHUE is an air-force brat who grew up traveling. She has degrees in computer science, Russian studies, and a Masters in earth science education, along with a commercial instrument pilot's certification and a SCUBA certification. When not writing, she teaches tai chi and belly dance. Linda's short stories and novellas can currently be found at Yard Dog Press and soon from Fantasist Enterprises Press and Carnifex Press.

CHRIS DONAHUE, husband of Linda, is an electrical engineer currently with Dallas Water Utilities. He is a former Navy reservist and life-long military history buff. He has stories in *Flush Fiction, Houston, We've Got Bubbas* and *Loving the Undead*.

ALAN DEAN FOSTER'S sometimes humorous, occasionally poignant, but always entertaining short fiction has appeared in all the major SF magazines as well as in original anthologies and several "Best of the Year" compendiums. Six collections of his short form work have been published. Foster's work to date includes excursions into hard science-fiction, fantasy, horror, detective, western, historical, and contemporary fiction, and produced the novel versions of many films, including such well-known productions as *Star Wars*, the first three *Alien* films, and *Alien Nation*. Other works include scripts for talking records, radio, computer games, and the story for the first *Star Trek* movie.

STEVEN GILBERTS began displaying his work at science fiction and fantasy conventions in 1995. In 2003 he made the leap into the publishing field starting with *Space and Time* magazine. Now, living in a small Dunwich-esque southern Indiana town with his devoted wife Becky and an assortment of furry critters that run the household, Steve produces work for publications such as *Space and Time* magazine, *Dark Wisdom* magazine, and *Cemetery Dance.*

HEATHER HATCH is currently working on her third pirate-related graduate level degree, and thus her story here has nothing whatsoever to do with pirates. She is nevertheless highly qualified in swashbuckling and plundering as well as the more docile pursuits of history and archaeology.

C.J. HENDERSON is an Origins Award-winning author and the creator of the Jack Hagee private detective series, and the Teddy London occult detective series. He is also the author of the *Encyclopedia of Science Fiction Movies* as well as scores of short stories, comics and non-fiction articles. www.cjhenderson.com.

WILLIAM JONES is a writer and editor who works in the fiction and hobby industries. His works spans mystery, horror, SF, historical, and fantasy. Some of his works include *The Strange Cases of Rudolph Pearson* and *Frontier Cthulhu*, and a few of the anthologies he appears in are *Blood and Devotion*, and *Thou Shalt Not*. William is the editor of *Dark Wisdom* magazine, and he teaches English at a university in Michigan. www.williamjoneswriter.com.

GERARD HOUARNER was married at a New Orleans Voodoo Temple and works at a psychiatric institution. His latest novel, *Road From Hell*, as well as the anthology/collection *Dead Cat's Traveling Circus of Wonders and Miracle Medicine Show*, are available from your favorite bookseller or www.necropublications.com. Latest news: www.cith.org/gerard or www.myspace.com/gerardhouarner

MICHAEL McBRIDE is the author of the *Chronicles of the Apocalypse* and *God's End* trilogies, *The Infected, Blood Wish*, and *Zero;* plus the forthcoming *Legion of Wrath* and *Spectral Crossings*. His short fiction has appeared in *Cemetery Dance, Dark Discoveries, Dark Wisdom*, and various anthologies. He dwells at www.mcbridehorror.com.

PAUL MELNICZEK is the author of *Restless Shades, Frightful October, and A Halloween Harvest,* and has sold work to over 100 markets.

WILLIAM MEIKLE is a Scottish author, with six novels published in the States and three more coming in 2007/8, and over 150 short story credits, all in the independent fantasy and horror press. His work has appeared in the UK, Ireland, USA, Canada, Greece, Saudi Arabia and India.

FERREL MOORE owns a technical service company based in the Detroit area. His interests include martial arts and monster hunting. Currently he is the caretaker of a beautiful white Turkish Angora cat that he hopes some day soon his son will reclaim.

MICHAEL PENNCAVAGE is a finance manager for an internationally recognized company during the day. In the off hours he has been an Associate Editor for *Space and Time Magazine* as well as the editor of the fiction anthology, *Tales From a Darker State*. Fiction of his can be found in approximately 50 magazines and anthologies from 3 different countries such as *Alfred Hitchcock Mystery Magazine* in the U.S., *Here and Now* in England, and *Crime Factory* in Australia. One of his stories "The Converts" was currently being filmed as a movie for release this fall.

STEPHEN MARK RAINEY is author of the novels *Balak*, *The Lebo Coven*, *Dark Shadows: Dreams of the Dark* (with Elizabeth Massie), *The Nightmare Frontier*, and *Blue Devil Island*; three short story collections; and over 90 published works of short fiction. For ten years, he edited *Deathrealm* magazine and has edited the anthologies *Deathrealms, Song of Cthulhu*, and *Evermore* (with James Robert Smith). Mark lives in Greensboro, NC, with his wife Peggy. Visit him on the Web at http://www.stephenmarkrainey.com.

DARRELL SCHWEITZER is the author of *The Mask of the Sorceror* and 2 other novels, about 270 stories, and much else. Recently he edited *The Secret History of Vampires* (with Martin Greenberg) for DAW. He is a former editor of *Weird Tales*. He is a 4-time World Fantasy Award finalist.

JOHN SHIRE is a writer, photographer and book designer trapped in an entirely different career. His work has appeared in numerous magazines over the last decade and he runs The Library of the Sphinx and Invocations Press. None of this, however, will save him when the time comes.

JOHN SHIRLEY is a screenwriter and the author of many books including *Demons, Crawlers, Wetbones, Black Butterflies, In Darkness Waiting, Cellars*, and *Warlord* featuring John Constantine, Hellblazer. His Web site is www.darkecho.com/JohnShirley.

STEWART STERNBERG is a writer, educator who still sleeps with the lights on, and believes there are things scratching at the windows that are best ignored. He lives with his wife and three dogs, teaching alternative education in a rural school district. Interests include gaming, politics and American History. He also serves as a deacon at the *Church of the Starry Wisdom*, reformed.

CHARLES P. ZAGLANIS was able to claw his way to the Associate Editor position at *Dark Wisdom* Magazine through Machiavellian machinations and pure dumb luck. Pointed in Lovecraft's direction at a tender age by an Iron Maiden cover, Charles published RPG material with Chaosium and then moved on to fiction. His skewed vision of reality can be read in his short stories and anthologies.

Visit him at: http://deep1hybrid.blogspot.com/.

LEE CLARK ZUMPE joined Tampa Bay Newspapers as proofreader and staff writer shortly after earning a B.A. in English at the University of South Florida. His nights are consumed with the invocation of ancient nightmares, dutifully bound in fiction and poetry. His work has appeared in *Weird Tales, Dark Wisdom, Horrors Beyond, Corpse Blossoms* and *Arkham Tales*. Visit www.freewebs.com/leeclarkzumpe.

EXPLORE TERRIFYING LANDSCAPES OF SCIENCE UNBOUND

AVAILABLE FALL 2007
EDITOR: WILLIAM JONES
COVER BY DAVE CARSON
336 PAGES

LIMITED, SIGNED NUMBERED
HARDCOVER :$45.00
ISBN: 0-9779876-2-0
TRADE PAPERBACK: $15.95
ISBN:0-9779876-3-9

canny contraptions, weird devices, technologies beyond the control of humanity abound in the uni-
se. Sometimes there are things that resist discovery. When science pushes the boundaries of under-
ding, terrible things push back. Often knowledge comes at a great cost. 21 unsettling tales of dark
ion are gathered in this volume, exploring the horrors beyond our reality.

Featuring Lovecraftian horror, dark fiction and science fiction by William C. Dietz, Richard A. Lu-
f, A. A. Attanasio, Jay Caselberg, Robert Weinberg, John Shirley, Stephen Mark Rainey, Paul S. Kemp,
ne O'Neill, David Niall Wilson, Lucien Soulban, C.J. Henderson, Paul Melniczek, Greg Beatty, Ekat-
na Sedia, Michail Velichansky, Tim Curran, Ron Shiflet, Alexis Glynn Latner, John Sunseri, and Wil-
n Jones.

WWW.ELDERSIGNSPRESS.COM

LDER SIGNS PRESS, INC.   P.O. BOX 389   LAKE ORION, MI   48361-0389   USA
248-628-9711   WWW.ELDERSIGNSPRESS.COM   INFO@ELDERSIGNSPRESS.COM

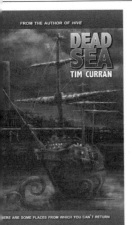